# A MEASURE OF
# MADNESS

Also available from Alyson Books
by Gordon Merrick

The Lord Won't Mind
One for the Gods
Forth Into Light
Now Let's Talk About Music
An Idol for Others
The Good Life (written with Charles G. Hulse)
The Quirk
Perfect Freedom

# A MEASURE OF MADNESS

# GORDON MERRICK

alyson books
los angeles | new york

MANUFACTURED IN THE UNITED STATES OF AMERICA.

THIS TRADE PAPERBACK IS PUBLISHED BY ALYSON PUBLICATIONS,
P.O. BOX 4371, LOS ANGELES, CA 90078-4371.
DISTRIBUTION IN THE UNITED KINGDOM BY
TURNAROUND PUBLISHER SERVICES LTD.,
UNIT 3, OLYMPIA TRADING ESTATE, COBURG ROAD, WOOD GREEN,
LONDON N22 6TZ ENGLAND.

FIRST PUBLISHED BY WARNER BOOKS: 1986
FIRST ALYSON BOOKS EDITION: DECEMBER 2001

01 02 03 04 05 a 10 9 8 7 6 5 4 3 2 1

ISBN 1-55583-507-4
(PREVIOUSLY PUBLISHED WITH ISBN 0-446-30240-6 BY WARNER BOOKS.)

COVER PHOTOGRAPHY BY ROBERTO ROMA.

For Charlie—
An anniversary celebration

**H**e had noticed the big ornamental brass numerals on the way down the hill from his modest hotel near Constitution Square. They struck a note of urban chic, the sort of thing that would pass unnoticed in front of an expensive bar in the East Sixties at home but was conspicuous here in this shabby commercial environment. The elegance of the numerals drew him after a lonely week of sight-seeing in the strangely flavorless city, neither Eastern nor Western, neither rich nor poor. One of the oldest centers of world civilization seemed to have no character or personality, no past and no discernible future, more like Detroit as he remembered it from his childhood than the now of 1975. It was just a noisy, dingy, dusty backwater town called Athens.

Half a dozen steps led down from the street to a sort of basement area where the elegant numerals, a 2 and an 8,

1

flanked a highly polished wooden door. The public was encouraged by an American Express credit card sticker on a glass pane set into the door, but there was no indication of what was on offer for his signature. He descended the short flight of steps and entered. Pausing, he reminded himself of the American Express sticker—it was enough to curb an impulse to beat a hasty retreat.

He was standing on a railed landing overlooking a cozy London club. A welcome fire blazed in an open hearth. The paneled walls were hung with prints. Polished wooden tables and ladder-back chairs were set about on the brick floor, and a handful of people sat in front of drinks. He heard familiar jaunty music; Fred Astaire was putting on his top hat. For the first time since he'd been in Greece, he wondered if he was dressed properly—wash cotton pants and a tweed jacket but no tie. He shrugged and went on past a table spread with copies of *Time* and *Newsweek* and the *Herald-Tribune* to a few more steps that brought him down to floor level in front of a mahogany bar. A dazzle of bottles and glasses were ranked behind it. He ordered a local brandy and soda from the bartender, who served him without interrupting his conversation with a knot of customers at the other end of the bar.

"I say, that'll be for me, Niko." It was an order that was obviously meant to be overheard. From the way the bartender glanced at him, he gathered that somebody had picked up his tab.

In another moment he found himself shaking hands with a tall man who muttered something inaudible. "You're buying me a drink? Thanks a lot," he said. "My name's Philip Renfield. Phil will do. I didn't catch yours."

"Johnny Marston. You Yanks are wonderful. You really try to remember names."

"I don't have all that many to remember at the moment.

You're the first person I've talked to for a week. You a Brit?''

"Rath—er. You don't look like a chap who'd be alone for long.''

Phil smiled and took a swallow of his drink, covertly looking over his new acquaintance. They were about the same height and if there was any difference in age, it couldn't be much. Johnny Marston was well under forty. They were dressed with similiar informality, except that Johnny was wearing a tie. Phil had had time to see that all the other men in the place wore suits and ties, like businessmen. The women were smart and citified, more so than most of the women in the streets. English was the only language he'd heard spoken. "What *is* this place?'' he asked, fingering his open collar.

"Here? I daresay you could call it a club except that nobody knows what you have to do to become a member. It caters to the young professional community. I don't know why I come. I'm a painter—or a con man, depending on how you look at it. What I like is that the drinks are twice as big as anywhere else in Athens. You can't come in without getting a bit pissed. A sensible arrangement.''

Phil chuckled. He liked the guy. He liked the casual assurance with which Johnny had come over to pick him up. Totally at home with himself. He was very intelligent looking, with oddly out-of-balance features—a strong, bony nose, adequate chin, piercing eyes, an unexpectedly sensitive but humorous mouth. He was ugly but confident of his sex appeal. Phil felt it in the way he handled himself, moving in beside him without being invited, studying him openly over the top of the glass. "I guess I *will* be pissed on another of these,'' Phil admitted. He rattled the ice in his almost empty glass. "The next one's on me.''

"Fair enough. Have you been in Athens long?''

"Just a week. I'm beginning to think that's enough. It's not what I expected."

Johnny shrugged. "It's changed rather in the last two thousand years. Have you taken a look at the boys?"

Phil felt the question in his groin but tried not to look flustered. "As a matter of fact, I have." He wasn't surprised that Johnny had raised the subject so casually. He gave the impression that he knew all about everything. His air of cool superiority challenged Phil to overcome any embarrassment. "They're not what I expected, either. What became of the Greek gods?"

"Dear me. Haven't you heard? They were expelled by the Muslim Turks and settled in Southern California. A sad loss." Phil laughed and Johnny switched to Greek as the bartender collected their empty glasses. "A double in this one, my Niko. I have high hopes for the night. Don't you wish you could get your hands on him?"

"You're a terrible man, Johnny." Niko turned his back to them while he poured the drinks.

Phil smiled to himself, feeling a bit sneaky for understanding Greek. He couldn't tell Johnny now without spoiling his game. When the fresh drink was put in front of him, he nodded to Johnny over the top of it before taking a swallow that would have choked him if he hadn't been prepared for it. A double double. "You seem awfully at home here. Do you live here?"

"In Athens? Not if I can help it. I can't say I live anywhere, but Crete would suit me very nicely. Have you been there?"

"No, but I've thought of going. Maybe I will."

"Isn't March an odd month for a holiday in Greece? You don't look somehow as if you were here on business."

"No. A vacation." He wasn't about to explain his decision to get out of New York for a month or two. He didn't want to make himself look ridiculous or, worse, pathetic. He was here to forget. The cliché almost made him yawn but it was true. "Is the weather in Crete the same as here?"

"Warmer. I had a dip in the sea before I left yesterday."

"How do you get there?"

"There's a plane. I prefer the ferry even though it sinks quite frequently. I like boats."

"So do I. People always talk about cruising the Greek isles. Have you ever done that?"

"Yes indeed. Millionaires with yachts are my natural prey. Once they allow me aboard they don't know how to get rid of me. There's something about the Aegean that makes you want to go on and on."

"I did a cruise with friends along the South of France a year or so ago. I'd've gone on and on if they'd let me. Unfortunately, we weren't millionaires. We had to go back to work."

"You Yanks call it the work ethic, don't you? Hideous." Johnny glanced at him sharply for a moment. "You know how to sail?"

"More or less. That's the only time I've done any deep-sea sailing, but I picked it up easily enough. It was terrific."

"We should steal a boat and sail away together. On and on. How old are you? Late twenties? Thirty?"

"Thirty-three."

"That much? I'm only a couple of years older. I say, why don't you come to Crete with me?"

"You're going back?"

"Of course. Tomorrow afternoon. It's an easy overnight journey on the boat."

"Maybe I will." Their eyes met briefly. Phil felt a pleasant little tug of contact between them, perhaps the dawning of friendship, something more rare than sexual -attraction. If he hadn't understood the brief exchange in Greek, he wouldn't have guessed that a seduction was under way. Johnny was playing it cool.

They chatted relaxedly, mostly about Greece. Johnny had an Englishman's reticence; he volunteered little information about his life and asked no prying questions about Phil's occupation or personal involvements. As Phil grew familiar with the play of humor across his strong, homely features and ceased to be wary of the touch of his spare body as he shifted about in front of the bar, he decided that sex wouldn't be a sweat with Johnny. For half his life, or at least for the last fifteen years, he had been trying unsuccessfully to figure out why he was a homosexual. He prided himself on his logical brain and had found that most of life's problems followed discernible patterns of cause and effect that led to reasonable explanations and solutions. Homosexuality defied logic. He couldn't understand where it came from. When he had realized that his wanting guys wasn't just a passing phase, he'd thought there must be some physiological explanation for it, some mix-up of genes or imbalance of hormones, and used to study himself at length in the mirror, looking for feminine characteristics that would support this theory. He saw only a rather conventionally good-looking, wholly masculine male with a straight nose and a firm mouth that to him wasn't particularly sexy. He tried to imagine his straight black hair hanging to his shoulders and knew that he would look simply like a guy with long hair.

Once he'd accepted the facts of his nature, reason told him that when he fell in love, assuming that it would be with somebody who shared his inclinations, it would be the same as anybody else falling in love, with the same demands and the same rewards. Like marriage, only between two people of the same sex. It apparently wasn't as simple as that, as the last couple of years had painfully demonstrated. Fortunately, aside from feeling the possibility of friendship more keenly than he usually did with chance encounters in bars, he didn't think there was any chance of falling for Johnny in a big way. He wasn't even sure he was ready to go along with whatever plans he had in mind.

Phil had started on his third drink and was feeling the second in a cheerful sort of way. "I see what you mean about the drinks here," he said.

"Bang on, what? I say, do you have any plans for the evening?"

"No. I told you, I haven't spoken to a soul since I've been here."

"Extraordinary. A handsome chappie like you wandering the streets of Athens unmolested. It gives one a new outlook on human nature. I have to meet a bloke in the Plaka, but that won't take long. We could have a spot of dinner after."

"What's the Plaka? Is that what you said?"

"Dear me. What kind of a tourist are you? The Plaka's the old town under the Acropolis. Not very old, mind you. Not ancient old. Just a century or two. Everything down here on the level was built day before yesterday. The Plaka is where the mischief is."

"Nobody told me. I could've used a little mischief the last few days."

"It's never too late. We'll find some mischief together."

They finished their drinks. Alcohol accelerated camaraderie. Phil felt as if they were becoming real friends in a way he hadn't felt friends with anybody for a long time. It made him realize how lonely he'd been, not just for the last week but for a year or more, ever since his efforts to break with Alex had started to devour him, devouring his life, swallowing him up. He had only barely saved himself; he was still intent on his salvation. He put a grateful hand on his new friend's shoulder. It felt lean and solid to the touch. "Take me to the mischief," he said. Dropping to the floor from the stool, he took a second to find his balance, and then the drinks seemed to settle in him soberly.

Night had fallen while they were inside. The neighborhood was brightly lighted and in the dark the shops had an almost stylish glitter. There was a cold wind blowing. The day had been chilly but a bright sun had warmed it. It was winter now. Phil hunched his jacket closer around him and thought of George. George was never far from his thoughts, especially when he was with a guy on a cold night and sex was in the air. He hadn't seen George for ten years and everything about him was still vivid in his memory, the look and smell of him, the touch of his hands. His body still went warm and slack with desire. Damn George.

"You don't mind a bit of a walk?" Johnny asked.

"Not at all." They continued down the sloping street and skirted Constitution Square, where the grand hotels created the brief illusion that this was a real metropolis. They continued on through narrow shabby streets, the shops closed and dark. After a few blocks they began to climb. The streets became winding lanes. Trees hung over walls, silhouetted against a star-filled sky. It was a pastoral scene, totally removed from the noisy bustle of the Athens he had begun to know.

"I had no idea that there was anything like this here," Phil said, breathing heavily from the climb. "It's nice."

They passed a brightly lighted square crowded with tables and people boisterously eating and drinking. Music swirled out over them, fast, with a heavy beat underlaid by an Eastern wail. Johnny led the way along another curving street, turned right, turned left until Phil had lost all sense of direction, and brought him out on a much wider street, straight, with bright lights and many signs, all announcing bars. Music issued from every door. There were quite a lot of people strolling about, many of them obviously tourists. Young men stood beside the doors, calling out to passersby. Johnny waved and nodded to them all as if he knew them.

"Mischief," he said.

"I see what you mean," Phil said. He'd been warned that young Greeks would expect to be paid, which had been enough to keep him away from them. He didn't like the idea of buying people for his pleasure.

They came to a crossroad that turned out to be a steep flight of steps bisecting the street they'd been following, rising to the left, descending into the fathomless night on the right. Phil could see lights far below them. Johnny pointed up to the left. "That's the base of the Acropolis," he explained.

"Is that where we are? I've been up there a couple of times but I didn't notice any houses around."

"The Plaka's tucked in at the back where you don't see it. Here we are."

They had crossed the steps and turned in through a door before Phil had seen what the place was called. It appeared to be a restaurant with a small bar at one end. There were a few people sitting at tables, nobody at the bar. Johnny went to it and rapped his knuckles on it. A man in a white jacket emerged through a door behind it.

"Is Pano here?" Johnny asked.

"Pano," the barman called over his shoulder. "The Englishman." A short heavyset young man with a tough-looking, unprepossessing face appeared. He came out through a hatch from behind the bar and shook hands with

Johnny. Their greeting was more businesslike than cordial. Johnny touched Phil's arm.

"This is my friend Philip Renfield," he said, demonstrating that an Englishman was capable of remembering a name. "He's an American."

Pano shook hands. "We'll have drinks," he said in English. Without asking what they wanted, the barman served ouzo. They poured water over the single ice cube and drifted toward an isolated table. Phil hoped he wasn't intruding, but Johnny seemed to expect him to stay with them. They sat at the table and engaged in pointless conversation for a moment about Americans and the United States and the glories of Athens. Phil admired the way Johnny handled the situation. He was polite but aloof, making no attempt to disguise his sense of his own superiority. He was obviously in charge.

"There's no need to take up your time," Johnny interrupted in Greek with cool civility. "I just wanted to find out if there's been any progress."

"Everything is in order. I think you will know something definite in a week. Our friend in Crete will tell you." The Greek glanced at Phil. "Your friend knows about it?"

"Not yet, but he may be with us. I think he might be useful. When I know something definite, I'll decide."

Phil tried not to listen as the conversation moved on to details of time and place that made no sense to him. Knowing Greek was getting to be a major embarrassment. It was one of his more unlikely accomplishments. It had started with his taking ancient Greek at school after George had turned his life upside down and set him off in all sorts of new directions. The classic Greek view of homosexuality as expressed in much of the literature had hooked his curiosity. He'd taken to the language with astonishing ease, even though everybody had warned him that it was a bitch. Later, when he'd discovered a Greek family running a grocery store in his neighborhood in New York, he'd made friends with them. The son had spent all one winter enthusiastically teaching him modern Greek—in bed.

He heard Pano say something about a boat, and in spite of himself his attention was held. "It mustn't be Greek," Pano concluded.

"Naturally. I've got that arranged. Tell your friends I'll expect some money when they've made up their minds."

"Of course. You were well paid the last time."

More followed that Phil resolutely let pass while he swallowed his drink. Johnny's Greek was more fluent than his, but the accent was belligerently English. Phil's Greek family had always told him that he had a good ear for the way it sounded. If he was going to see more of Johnny—and maybe become useful to him—his linguistic secret was bound to come out. The best he could do was to postpone the revelation so that Johnny might forget exactly what had been said in his hearing. After all, he hadn't learned anything very sensational. Johnny was hoping to be paid for doing something with a boat. The boat couldn't be Greek. That was the only detail that suggested it might be some sort of clandestine operation. Smuggling? He remembered Johnny's sudden interest when sailing was mentioned. Did Johnny think he could be useful handling a boat? After ten years of an unadventurous and sedentary life, Phil wouldn't object to a change of pace. He had nothing to do for the next few weeks. There was something vaguely piratical about Johnny, coolly devil-may-care and insouciant. He liked it.

Phil finished his drink while Johnny was disposing of the Greek as if he'd received him in his own house. "I don't have to take more of your time," he said. "We've settled all the details. I'll let you know if I have any last-minute difficulties, but I don't expect any. I probably won't see you again until afterwards.''

Pano rose and shook hands and disappeared behind the bar. Johnny looked at Phil and shrugged. "Sorry to keep you waiting. Shall we go?''

"Sure. We're not having dinner with him?'' It was a deliberate deception to demonstrate that he hadn't understood the conversation, and he wondered why he bothered. His speaking Greek wasn't worth making such a thing about.

Johnny looked at him with a sly smile. "Dear me, no. I don't want to bother with him. I'm ready to concentrate on you now.''

Phil smiled. "A pleasant novelty. I think I'm beginning to like Athens.''

Within minutes, they had lost themselves again in the maze of village streets. Phil found himself wondering if he would be able to find his way back to Pano's place. He couldn't imagine why he would want to but didn't think it would be difficult. There couldn't be many stepped streets like the one they had crossed, even in the Plaka. Standing with the base of the Acropolis to the left, the bar-restaurant was just a few doors on the other side to the right. Apparently there had been enough of a hint of mystery in Johnny's visit to set his imagination working, although he didn't quite know what it was working on. He published textbooks, not thrillers. Johnny put a hand on his shoulder as he turned him in toward an inconspicuous door. Glad to get out of the cold, Phil entered a small, rustic, low-ceilinged room filled with tables, all of which appeared to be occupied. The restaurant was doing a thriving business, but the atmosphere was agreeably subdued. Sweet metallic music dropped limpidly into the hum of conversation. At a glance, the modestly dressed clientele looked like average middle-class Athenians. Johnny nodded him toward an archway. Phil went through into another small, crowded room. One wall was formed of glass doors, closed against the cold, that gave onto a lighted courtyard filled with potted plants. There was an empty table against the glass. They went to it, Johnny guiding Phil with a hand on his arm. By the time they'd seated themselves, several passing waiters had greeted them.

"This is nice," Phil said, spotting the source of the music. An old man with an angelic smile was sitting at a table against the wall plucking a zither with agile fingers. The sounds were haunting but curiously cheerful.

"You're a man of taste and refinement," Johnny said with an approving smile. "I was afraid you might be expecting something along the lines of the Hilton."

"The Hilton doesn't sound very Greek. Actually, Greek friends in New York have taken me to a place like this. They say the food there isn't as good as real Greek food." He'd made his point about knowing Greeks; his knowing Greek might come as less of a surprise.

"It's real here. Maybe the best in Greece. Unfortunately, that's not saying a hell of a lot. You're a New Yorker?"

"By choice, not birth. Like most New Yorkers. There wasn't really much choice. That's where my work is."

"Work again. I wonder what it could be. If you were English, I'd've guessed by now. We give ourselves away in little ways. You Yanks are mysteries. I won't rest till I've solved you."

Phil laughed. "Why don't I tell you?"

"No. I pride myself on my intuition. It's rather important to me at times. A bloke who lives by his wits must keep them tuned. I guessed right about chaps, didn't I?"

Phil glanced about quickly. "Yes," he said, smiling into intelligent eyes. It was a worn face, agreeably weathered and dependable. Its attraction was difficult to define. He didn't go in much for casual sex, but now he was looking forward to going to bed with him, if that was still Johnny's intention. Thank God Johnny wasn't a pretty boy. His violent infatuations with a face or a body embarrassed him. Making love with Johnny would be a peaceful affirmation of friendly affection. So far, it seemed to him the best that homosexuality could offer him. He felt wonderfully free of Alex. "It's pretty easy to spot a poof," he said, still smiling. "That's what you call them, isn't it?"

"That's what we can call ourselves if we choose to. I shouldn't recommend it to the general public. I might take offense. And you're not in the least easy to spot. It took a flash of divine inspiration, aided by wishful thinking. I daresay it boils down to your being much too handsome to be anything else. Virile beauty is wasted on females."

"Mine isn't." They burst out laughing. A waiter approached and greeted Johnny by name. They exchanged pleasantries.

"Will you have the red wine as usual?" the waiter asked in Greek.

"I'll ask my friend." He looked at Phil as he switched back to English. "I think all Greek white wine tastes resinated, even when they swear it isn't. Is red all right with you?"

"Sure. I agree with you about the white. I thought there was something the matter with me."

"There can't be anything the matter with you if you agree with me." He confirmed the wine order to the waiter and rose, putting a hand out to Phil's shoulder. "Come on. Let's see what there is to eat."

"See? Where?" Phil asked, getting to his feet.

"In the kitchen where the food comes from. You *have*

been frequenting the Hilton. In Greece we deal with basics.''

Johnny kept his hand on his shoulder and guided him around tables to the other room. The kitchen was part of it, filling the end of it, wide open and separated from the tables only by a counter. A man in a long white apron welcomed Johnny by name and began to lift the lids of the big pots that were lined up on an iron range. Johnny peered into them. ''I always take a little of everything,'' he explained. ''It's like an enormous meal of hors d'oeuvres. What would you say to that? Of course, if you fancy any one thing in particular, you can always have more of it.''

''Sounds fine.'' Johnny made their order in Greek and guided him back to the table, where a bottle of wine was waiting. They helped themselves and sipped it while they looked each over with amusement and approval. ''I'm glad you picked me up,'' Phil said. ''This is turning into a good evening. Have you settled on what I do yet?''

''It's coming. You have daring and imagination. That's more suitable for a con man than an ordinary businessman. Have you to do with telly? The cinema perhaps. You could be an agent for very successful writers or performers. How's that?''

Phil chuckled. ''Do I seem so theatrical? I'm pleasantly surprised. I guess you're getting warm, sort of. I run the textbook division of a big publishing house.''

''Textbooks. Blow me, if you'll pardon the expression. Shouldn't you have a pipe and horn-rimmed glasses?''

''Give me time. Actually, it isn't quite what it sounds. The house was very heavily into textbooks once upon a time. They ended up with a few standards that barely paid the postage. They let me give it a whirl while they decided whether to pack it in entirely. I've always thought textbooks should be interesting, even entertaining when possible. It's been a huge success, I mutter modestly.''

"Daring and imagination. Just as I said. I'll give myself goodish marks for that.''

"Have you ever done any illustrating? I'm always looking for artists with bright ideas.''

"Are we launched on a lifetime association? Maybe you'll make an honest man of me. And I may turn you into a crook. A fair exchange.''

The waiter reappeared and in a moment the table was covered with small dishes. The array included crisp fried squid, stuffed eggplant, stuffed vine leaves in a pale yellow sauce, some sort of meat-and-onion stew served in a small earthenware pot, a bean dish in which Phil recognized fresh dill.

"It's all for both of us?" he asked. "It should keep us alive till tomorrow.''

"Share and share alike. Matey.''

They ate and drank and ordered another bottle of wine. Phil found the food extraordinarily good, simple fare cooked with a refinement he hadn't encountered in Greek food before. Johnny's flirtatiousness remained aloofly ironic.

"How're things here now politically?" he asked after they'd made substantial inroads on the food.

"Since the reign of terror? The pure light of democracy shines once more on the land.''

"Were you here during the Colonels?''

"Yes indeed. Off and on. After all, they've been gone for less than a year.''

"How long were they in power?''

"Well now. I shouldn't think that would be difficult to work out. This is 1975, isn't it? I never remember. They came in in 'sixty-seven and were thrown out last year. Seven years, if my sums haven't failed me.''

"Was it very bad?"

"The regime? Only if you were politically active. Everybody else hardly noticed."

"It was outright dictatorship, wasn't it?"

"It wasn't Hitler. The police are inclined to be brutal under the best of circumstances. The Greeks expect it."

Phil had noticed that beneath the detached, ironic manner, Johnny had an extraordinary capacity for watchful concentration. He felt it now. Everything in Johnny seemed to gather into a controlled, steely determination to observe, as if he were noting every nuance of word and gesture. "I should think that's all the more reason why power shouldn't fall into the hands of the military."

"Quite so. The astonishing thing is that it wasn't worse. I decided from the beginning that the minute I felt the boot of the oppressor I'd do something about it—presumably leave. I never did. Mind you, everybody I knew who had reason to feel threatened did go. There was no underground resistance worth mentioning. I mean armed resistance. That might've come if it had lasted."

"I've never lived through anything like that. It's probably just as well, I don't know how I'd behave."

"Heroically, I expect. Like me."

They teased each other with their smiles and Phil could feel Johnny's attention slacken and dissipate. He was increasingly fascinated by the Englishman. He was up to something. Of course, there had been the bits of private conversation he'd overheard, but there was more to it than that. He'd felt it from the start and continued to feel it in the selective way Johnny focused his interest on him. It wasn't just wanting to get him into bed. Johnny wanted something more of him. He intended to stick around until he found out what it was. He suspected that he would want it too, no matter how unexpected. He wasn't sure that his remark about turning him into a crook was meant entirely as a joke. Johnny communicated a wide experience of real life. He could talk familiarly about armed resistance and living under a dictatorship, whereas the most intense experiences in Phil's life had had to do with trying to make sense of his sex life. Alex had finally worn him out. Phil wanted to do himself over like a derelict house—a complete remodeling.

They disposed of the remaining food and sat back with satisfied smiles and lifted their glasses to each other. "Good," Phil said, his eyes lingering on Johnny's nondescript attractions. His abundant sandy hair was appealingly frizzy around the edges in a peculiarly English way. He had high English coloring and his skin was clear. His mouth was a contradiction; the aloof, amused superiority that lifted its corners was daunting, yet he'd caught glimpses of sweetness and affection in it when he'd spoken to the men who had greeted him, the waiters and bartenders. The fact that his chin wasn't aggressive made him feel that it wouldn't be difficult to get under Johnny's guard.

"There's not much in the way of fruit at this time of year," Johnny said. "Would you like pudding—cake or tart or some such nonsense?"

"Good lord no. I couldn't eat another bite. It was marvelous."

Johnny looked almost boyishly pleased. "I *am* glad you liked it. We'll have coffee." He emptied the last of the wine into their glasses and asked for the bill when the coffee came. Phil tried to pay it and Johnny reluctantly agreed to split it. It was only a few dollars. They drained their glasses and stood. Johnny paused when they were once more in the street.

"What now?" he asked. "A pub crawl, perhaps some mischief? Or would you like to come home with me? I daresay I should include dropping you back at your hotel as one of the possibilities, but I'd rather not consider it.''

"I've seen enough of that hotel room.'' They were holding each other's arms, drawing each other closer. "Take me home with you.''

Johnny gave his arm a little squeeze. "A man of taste and refinement. I must've done something right this week. I don't usually get what I want so easily.'' The ironic little smile played around his lips. "Do you feel up to another walk?''

"Sure, but it's *cold*.'' Phil pulled his jacket more snuggling over his chest. "Let me buy us a taxi.''

"Righty-oh. No sooner said than done.'' A car blinked its lights and pulled in beside them. Johnny gave the address and they climbed in. To Phil's flustered astonishment, Johnny moved in over him and put his arms around him and kissed him. Recovering himself, Phil surrendered to the seductive pleasure of Johnny's mouth. Johnny's lips were firm and passionate. Phil liked the way Johnny's hands moved on him. Strong, hairless hands. He'd noticed them. Johnny was just what he wanted—a man sure of himself, knowing what he wanted, not susceptible to emotional hysteria, mature and well-balanced. They'd probably be arrested, but that wouldn't bother Johnny. In his no-nonsense way, he'd decided that it was time for them to make love. It made Phil feel wonderfully safe and free.

Johnny drew back and slid a hand down Phil's front until he found his erection. He gripped it and stroked it lightly. "Lovely. I've been waiting to take you home all evening. I use the word *home* in a purely symbolic sense. As I told you, I can't rightly be said to live anywhere. My friends always seem to have space to spare for me. Most convenient.'' He spoke without interrupting his caresses. "Why bother with rent and furniture and all the other things that complicate life? I once spent almost a year in the mountains of Crete without its costing a farthing. I was passed from village to village and entertained royally for weeks at a time. I offered to pay of course, but the Cretans still think it an honor to offer hospitality to foreigners. My friends were scandalized. They thought I was taking food out of the mouths of the poor. The villagers didn't think of themselves as poor when I was with them. It all depends on the point of view, the angle you look at things, don't you think?''

Phil felt Johnny's watchfulness and his tentative efforts, physical and intellectual, to stake some claim to him. He found it puzzling and exciting, as Johnny's hand moved on him more and more deliciously. Phil made a murmuring sound of pleasure. ''Don't make me come,'' he said barely above a whisper.

''Could I?''

''Lord, yes. Any minute.''

Johnny laughed softly. ''You're a darling. We don't want that.'' He squeezed Phil's cock and removed his hand as he sat back.

Phil reached for the hand and held it on the seat beside him. ''What were you saying about angles? Do you mean there's no absolute right or wrong in anything?''

''Do you think there is?''

''I've always thought so, not that it's done me much good. Wrong often has a way of coming out on top.''

''Maybe you've been reading too many textbooks. You're coming to Crete with me, aren't you?''

''Yes.'' Phil was amazed that he didn't pause for an answer.

''Good. Then I'll try to make you like it, regardless of right or wrong.''

Aware that they'd left Constitution Square behind them,

Phil was beginning to get a rough idea where they were. Lycabettos Hill was up ahead of them somewhere, and they were going through a mixed area of new and old apartment houses set on straight tree-lined streets. They were back in the featureless, rectilinear modern town. He was vaguely disappointed in Johnny for not living somewhere more interesting. They turned several corners without encountering anything that recaptured the charm of the Plaka and came to a halt beside a tree. Across the sidewalk, a lighted glass-and-grillwork door like others on both sides of it in the block marked the entrance to a dingy apartment house. A panel of buttons and nameplates was beside it.

Phil slid forward to check the meter. "I've got it," he said. He paid while Johnny got out and crossed the sidewalk and made the familiar motions of getting out a key and unlocking a door. A tall lean stranger who moved efficiently, without fuss or fumbling, Phil thought, as he waited for the driver to count out change. A new lover. A happy surprise.

Johnny was waiting for him, holding the door open and letting it swing shut behind him. An old-fashioned cage elevator was at the end of a dimly lighted corridor. They lurched and clattered up past open landings, closely confined in the narrow space, their eyes questioning each other with the caution that usually preceded the consummation of an untested attraction, when there was still time for second thoughts. Phil had none. Johnny seemed to grow and fill out as he acquired the reality of a man who wanted Phil and was going to have him. Johnny gave the impression of fully occupying his place in the world, a man demanding his rights as a man and accepting his responsibilities as a man, with none of the soft, ambiguous shady areas Phil was accustomed to among the inhabitants of the gay world at home. His homely face was increasingly attractive as Phil grew familiar with it.

They jolted to a halt at the fifth floor and Johnny extricated them from the cage with a hand on the nape of Phil's neck. He led them up steep narrow stairs and held another door open and they stepped out into a garden. It took Phil a second to remember that they must be on the roof. A small one-story house was in front of them. A penthouse? A walkway formed of vines trained up trellises led to the door. Johnny threw an arm around him and their feet crunched on gravel as they moved toward it in the dark. Johnny opened it and reached inside and switched on lights.

Phil entered a modest living room furnished with shabby comfort but no attempt at style. There were a few upholstered armchairs and a sofa that had seen better days. Books were piled everywhere, on a desk, on tables, on the floor. His eyes picked up details before being dazzled by glory. A big picture window at the end of the room framed the floodlighted Parthenon. It looked almost close enough to touch. Phil took a deep breath as Johnny moved in behind him.

"My God, Johnny," he exclaimed. "You're a magician."

"I'm not always pleased with the lodgings my friends choose for me, but this has its points."

"I'm finally in Athens. It's even warm. I didn't think anybody here had central heating."

"There's none here. It gets blistering hot during the day. It's just beginning to cool off." He gave Phil's jacket a tug and he let it go. Johnny dropped his and pulled off his tie and unbuttoned his collar. Phil was pleased to see that no tufts of hair sprouted from it. "I could manage some more wine. What about you?"

"I never say no when I'm enjoying myself."

"A sensible rule." Johnny disappeared through a door at

the side of the room. Phil dropped onto the edge of the sofa and sat looking at the incredible view. He was amazed that only a few hours ago he'd been ready to leave. He loved it here. He kicked off his loafers and peeled off his socks and wiggled his toes comfortably. Being with Johnny made him feel comfortable. He was looking forward to seeing the big cock he'd felt against him in the taxi. He thought of George. As usual. He'd been formed sexually by George during the three years that life had been dominated by his first lover, and a weakness for big cocks was part of it. Not that his passion for Alex had been diminished by a rather modest one.

Johnny returned with an open bottle and two glasses. He filled them and gave one to Phil with a cheerful gleam in his eye. "Have you started to get undressed already?" he asked.

Phil lifted his feet in front of him. "I hope you don't mind my being barefoot in your living room."

"My depravity knows no limits. I'm absolutely wild about bare feet in the living room. But why stop there?".

"I was waiting for encouragement." They looked at each other and laughed. The ironic little twist of Johnny's lips was gone. He looked as if he was enjoying himself, the gleam in his eye straightforwardly lustful. Phil's cock responded vigorously to Johnny's strong, intelligent appeal. He took a thirst-quenching swallow of wine and set down the glass as he rose. He glanced down at his slacks. "I do believe I've got a hard on. Is that depraved enough for you?"

"I'd feel very depraved if you didn't." Johnny backed up to a table and used it for support while he removed his rough peasant boots. By the time he had dropped them, Phil was standing naked in front of him. He saw Johnny's expression lose its detachment as his eyes lit up with pleasure. Johnny reached for his own trousers and released his erection. Phil's scalp tightened. Not quite George's equal—nobody's every was—but a force that instantly won his surrender. Phil stepped forward, eluding the hands that reached for him and dropped down and made love to Johnny's cock with his mouth.

Johnny pushed himself to his feet, holding Phil's head, and remained motionless for a moment as if acknowledging Phil's submission. His fingers strayed through Phil's hair and his cock stiffened before he slowly withdrew it. He leaned over and gripped Phil's biceps and drew him to his feet. They fell into step together, Johnny guiding them across the room, a hand stroking Phil's shoulders, sliding down his back, lingering on his buttocks until muscles quivered with anticipation. The two men seemed closely attuned to each other by instinct, adapting to each other easily and naturally. It didn't usually happen like this when sex still remained to be tested.

Johnny snapped on the light in a small room, patted Phil's behind, and led him toward the single bed against the wall. Phil went to it and pulled the covers back and stretched out on his side. He was proud of his body and loved being able to share it unequivocally with a guy who wanted it. It had been good from birth, and as a kid he'd worked diligently to make the most of it. It was everything that a well-formed, highly trained body could be, without being heavily muscular. His cock couldn't compete with Johnny's, but it wasn't bad.

He heard the whisper of fabric as Johnny took his clothes off. He heard him moving around the room and shifted slightly so that he could see him. He was naked at last, a lean, wiry figure carelessly put together, his fair skin ruddy where it had been exposed to the sun, all of his strength concentrated in the big cock that lifted in front of him with thrilling purposefulness. Phil's heart accelerated. He liked the casually confident way Johnny was preparing to take him as if he had known all along what Phil wanted.

Phil watched him approach, his cock so tautly rigid that it looked as if it had a will of its own leading Johnny to its goal. Phil relaxed, offering himself, and his racing heart steadied and subsided. Johnny dropped a towel beside him and climbed up and straddled him. He ran a hand between Phil's buttocks, applying a lubricant. He lifted Phil's hips, placing him where he wanted him. He handled Phil with matter-of-fact command. Anybody with a cock like Johnny's was bound to feel self-assured. Phil abandoned himself to Johnny's direction.

Johnny guided his cock into him with skillful ease. There was a moment of pain and then they were past it as Johnny slid deeper into him, filling him sublimely. Phil cried out a triumphant welcome.

"Oh, God, it's good," he gasped.

"Everything *does* seem to go together rather nicely. If I'm not careful, this could easily become a habit."

Phil choked on laughter as Johnny began to move in him. "God, yes. Don't fight it, Johnny. Take me."

Johnny did so, taking his time to learn their bodies' needs, inventive but controlled, extending the range of communication until they achieved complete mutual satisfaction. When their bodies were at peace, they washed together under a shower that looked as if it had been added as an afterthought. It drained into a hole in the middle of the bathroom floor.

"That was good," Phil said as Johnny soaped him with caressing hands.

"My word. I might go so far as to call it memorable, but then I'm not used to making love to gods. You Yanks have reinvented the body beautiful, complete with alabaster limbs. I sometimes think I'd like to be a sculptor, but I'd go raving mad trying to equal the beauties of nature." He turned Phil and traced the contours of his buttocks with his fingertips. "I don't believed even Donatello could've managed your bum, and he did some choice ones."

"Your cock and my bum—they're definitely meant for each other."

"You're quite extraordinary. You offer your physical perfection with such princely generosity. If I'd known what I was getting, I'd've never dared hope for it. Pearls before swine."

"That sounds awfully defeatist. What's the point of being perfect if nobody tries to get me?"

Johnny turned Phil back to face him. They smiled contentedly at each other through the feeble stream of water. "Quite so. I imagine even gods like to feel wanted. I was doing you a favor, mate."

"Thank you, Johnny. If you want to do me another, you can rinse me off."

"I daresay we're quite clean enough." He scooped water into his hands and splashed it over Phil while he traced his pectoral muscles and the formation of his pelvis. "All that stunning pelvic definition, as we used to say in art school. Michelangelo made a specialty of it, but I've never seen anything quite like it before in a real live chap. You're a statue, mate."

The tantalizing hands were stirring Phil's cock to life again. For the moment, it was deceptively bigger than Johnny's. "I hope I'm not like a statue in bed."

"I can't rightly say that you are. OK. We can dry you now and then I'll tuck you in for the night." He turned the water off.

"Where're we going to sleep?"

"There's only the one chaste little bed. I'll take the sofa."

"Don't be silly. I'm not going to take your bed."

"Of course you are. I don't let myself get used to beds, although I'd love a nice big one to roll around in with you."

"There's always the floor. I want to hear more about Crete. What about that wine? Shouldn't we finish it?"

Johnny put on a skimpy blue-and-white-striped cotton dressing gown, and they collected the bottle and glasses and returned to the bedroom. Phil stretched out on the bed with the sheet modestly covering him. Johnny pulled it down around his hips, barely covering his cock. "You don't drape statues. I'll tell you about Crete and feast my eyes on your considerable charms." He sat on the edge of the bed and they sipped their wine. "Do you have any textbooks about Knossos?"

"There's quite a lot about Minoan civilization in our book about preclassical Greece. That's why I was thinking of going there."

"It's near the main port, Heraklion. We're going to a little port called Chania at the western end. Crete is quite big, as Greek islands go."

"Do you have a place for me or do I go to a hotel?"

"I usually stay with a family that keeps a room for me. We'll find something for you. How would you fancy living on a boat?"

"You'll make a sailor of me yet." Phil hoped for additional clues to the plans Johnny had discussed at the bar and to his part in them. "What sort of boat?"

"She's a beauty—a forty-foot sloop, very comfortable. Two can handle her easily, but she's made for heavy seas."

"She belongs to a friend?" Phil asked, expecting Johnny to take advantage of the opportunity to reveal some adventurous money-making scheme in which his sailing skills, such as they were, would be useful.

"Quite so," Johnny said dismissively. "I take care of her sometimes when he's not here."

"When you say living on her, you mean we might go for a cruise?" Phil persisted.

Johnny shrugged and refilled their glasses. "Later maybe, if you don't run away. March can be unsettled. I'm all for the seafaring life, but the Aegean doesn't always behave like a gentleman. We might have to leave *Mistral* tied up, but that needn't prevent you from living on board if you fancy free lodging."

Obviously, Johnny wasn't ready to share any secrets. Remembering that in the bar he had spoken of the boat as a possiblility rather than a certainty, Phil asked, "She's there now?"

"Yes, indeed. The owner won't be back for two or three months."

Phil was intrigued; deviousness didn't suit Johnny's assured, superior manner but information about the boat seemed to alter slightly at his whim. "Who's the owner? I wouldn't've thought a Greek would call a boat *Mistral.*"

"That's a good guess. Bernie's an American. We'll see. If the weather's fine, I may join you on the boat. Do you have any fixed dates at all?"

"Not really. I haven't had a real vacation for years. I told them I might be gone more than a month. I'm recovering from a broken heart."

They smiled at each other, Johnny with the little ironic lift of his lips. "The only cure for that is an army of insatiable lovers. On second thought, I'll leave you alone on the boat even if it breaks *my* heart. The quay is crawling with handsome youths."

"That's asking for another broken heart. I'll stick with

you, Johnny. You know how to make me feel good. I'm ridiculous when I fall in love. It's always with the wrong guys. Heartless beauties. Never again."

"I say, that won't do. Never trust a chap whose head rules his heart. Not the right sort at all. You should be grateful you can fall in love. I've been trying to all my life." He looked briefly startled by his words and then emptied the bottle into their glasses. He held his glass close to his lips while his eyes moved slowly over Phil's reclining body. He slowly lowered his glass as his eyes grew more absorbed and he reached out and his hand lightly followed where his eyes had been, along Phil's shoulders, over his chest, under his pectoral muscles, following the "pelvic definition." He seemed to shake himself out of a trance. "I don't imagine any tolerably sane adult can fall in love with a body, but I could come awfully close with you." His hand moved on and dropped onto the sheet where it covered Phil's cock. Phil grunted with satisfaction, feeling the surge in his loins. His cock stretched out on his belly, free of the sheet's modesty.

"That's always been my problem—falling in love with bodies," he said. "Or pretty faces. I'm an embarrassment to my friends."

"Love's fool decked out in a beautiful body. What a combination." Johnny stroked the rigid cock that was generously offered him. "I'll wager Manoli has you before many moons have passed."

"Who's Manoli?"

"Our current pinup boy. He's wreaking havoc with the foreign colony, poor drolls. His body is very nearly as perfect as yours. The thought of you together makes me swoon with erotic fancies."

Phil edged lower and slipped a hand under Johnny's flimsy robe and squeezed his big cock. "I doubt if Manoli can compete with that. Tell me more about the seafaring life. I'm trying to imagine what it would be like to have a boat. I'd want to do something with it, go somewhere. Don't you have any plans?''

''I try not to make plans. Life is simpler without them.'' Johnny drained his glass and dropped over Phil, putting his cock in his mouth. Phil's thoughts of the conversation in the bar were suspended as Johnny reasserted his imaginative mastery of his body.

Phil went to sleep in the narrow bed, taking stock of his altered circumstances. He was no longer alone and at loose ends in a foreign country. He had a friend. The next few weeks had acquired some sort of shape and purpose. The slight mystery that surrounded Johnny might lead to almost anything. For the first time, he was glad he'd come and was looking forward to tomorrow. He was going to sail off across the Aegean; he was going to Crete. A legendary world awaited him.

T he activity on the dock had a cataclysmic air, as if only seconds remained to avert some unimaginable catastrophe. Men shouted from ship to shore, metal clashed as rectangular tins were stacked for loading, crates flew through the air. According to Phil's watch, twenty minutes remained before the scheduled sailing. He stood well back from the end of the gangplank, hoping not to be trampled to death by the onrushing horde. Hawk-eyed women laden with bundles and cardboard suitcases tied together with string hurled themselves into the fray as all of Greece seemed to be trying to get on board.

It was difficult keeping any eye out for Johnny while protecting himself from bodily harm.

He'd already decided that if Johnny didn't turn up he'd go to Crete anyway. His belongings were packed in the suitcase at his feet. He at least knew the name of somebody there: the irresistible Manoli. Up until this point, he'd followed Johnny's instructions. He'd checked out of his hotel and gone to the 28 Bar at noon. He'd had a couple of cold beers while he waited, and when he was still waiting at one, as Johnny had warned him might happen, he'd taken the underground train from Omonia Square to Piraeus.

"Just say, *Pou inay toe vaporee ya Heraklion,*" Johnny said, and Phil was glad to be able to tell him that he'd picked up enough Greek to manage.

"I told you I knew some Greeks in New York," he explained. "One of them rather more than slightly, if truth be known."

He'd found the boat and bought his ticket and had some lunch at a taverna across the quay where he could be sure that the boat wouldn't leave without him. He thought of all the times he'd waited for Alex. His lover's remorse was always as annoying as the waiting and his excuses were insultingly predictable: he'd met a beatiful guy and hadn't had the strength to turn him down. Since Phil had accepted infidelity as part of falling in love with Alex, he had nobody to blame but himself.

He stood now in the midst of the tumult of departure, congratulating himself for not caring much whether Johnny appeared or not. He enjoyed being with him and he gave Phil the feeling that he could make life exciting, but the night with him had been one of the happy hazards of travel. You couldn't expect continuity on the road; you took things as they came and moved on. There was something a bit fishy about Johnny. Maybe he should be glad not to know more about him. He didn't like hanging around alone, waiting. He had always had a prudish horror of cruising the streets, and he was afraid he might look as if he were loitering with indecent intent. He was aware of young men eyeing him, and he resolutely refrained from looking at them.

He craned his neck, peering over heads to make it clear that he was here for a purpose, and caught a glimpse of Johnny headed toward the boat. His spirits rose. He was smiling as he stooped to retrieve his bag. He straightened and stretched again to peer over milling heads. Suddenly his feet felt as if they were embedded in cement. He'd been hit in the stomach. He couldn't move.

As reason returned, he told himself that he was dreaming. It was impossible. It couldn't be George. George was thousands of miles away. He'd caught a glimpse of a handsome youth who looked to be in his twenties, whereas George was thirty-five by now, probably beginning to look middle-aged. He gave his head a slight shake and shifted his feet to make sure he was mobile once more. He lifted himself on tiptoe and spotted Johnny again, separated from him by a hundred shouting people. The guy he was talking to was turned from him now. The set of the man's shoulders and the back of his head were definitely reminiscent of George, but his hair was different, black and straight. The thought of meeting somebody who even reminded him of George sent a wave of panic through him, and he decided hastily that he was trapped in the crowd. Johnny wouldn't worry about not finding him. He might think Phil had got lost or changed his mind, but he'd stick to his own plans. He lived in Crete and was going home, regardless of Phil. They would find each other on the boat.

Phil let himself be drawn into the vortex that was swirling around the end of the gangplank. He stumbled out of the crowd onto the ship's covered deck and found a quiet place at the rail where he could watch the passengers streaming aboard. He dropped his bag and wiped sweat out of his eyes with the back of his arm and waited for Johnny, bracing himself to face the stranger who for one blinding, glorious, appalling instant had been George. The greatest shock had been to realize that after ten years the prospect of seeing George could still knock him for a loop. At irregular intervals over the years, they'd been on the telephone sounding each other out about seeing each other again. Phil had always ended by saying no. Only two years ago George had called and pleaded with him to come back to him. He was in some sort of boy trouble and needed him. Phil wasn't interested in George's troubles. He was having enough of his own with Alex and thought that George deserved his. His stony rejection of George's pleas still haunted him. What would they say to each other if they met? It could happen any day, any minute. For it to happen in Greece would be an impossible conincidence, but you never knew.

The new arrivals continued to scream at each other around him. They appeared to be in agitated motion even when they were standing still. Johnny was finally ejected from the top of the gangplank like a cork from a bottle. Phil called and waved. Johnny sauntered over to him, aloof and unruffled.

"Quite a scrum," he remarked dryly. He gave Phil's shoulder a pat. "I knew I'd find you on board. Good lad. I was delayed. Do forgive. You booked first class?"

"Yes. You said—"

"Quite so. So long as one of us did, there'll be no

difficulty. We'd better go straightaway to the steward to make sure we get a cabin.''

Phil picked up his bag and followed him along the deck. He saw that Johnny was carrying only a small battered leather briefcase. "You're not with anybody?" he asked, his heart skipping a beat.

"With anybody? How do you mean?"

"When I was trying to get to you through the crowd, I thought I saw you with a guy.''

"Ah, yes. A handsome chap? That must've been the egregious Manoli. He came up on the freight caïque. He thought I might be on this boat. He had a message for me. He'll be back in a day or two.''

Phil drew a breath of relief. Whether or not Manoli looked like George, he had time to prepare himself for the possibility. The steward greeted Johnny familiarly by name, and they arranged for a cabin. In the bar, Johnny was again greeted by name by the jocular bartender. They ordered beer and Johnny asked him if he'd had any trouble finding the boat.

"It couldn't've been easier. Actually, what I laughingly call my Greek is coming back to me. Hearing you speak it has unlocked my tongue. In a few days I'll be able to discourse eloquently about the weather.'' Phil's conscience was eased. Johnny had been warned that anything he said in front of him might be understood.

Johnny smiled. "You're looking smashing today. Greece is beginning to agree with you. I told Manoli I was bringing somebody with me who'd stir up our sleepy little community.''

"I take it Manoli is for the gents.''

"Nothing nearly so simple. Manoli is for anything he fancies. It's the gents who're for him. They're turning him into a whore, but I daresay a few ladies competing for him could do it just as easily. He hasn't found out yet the full range of choice at his disposal. Manoli's a simple island lad. He'll find it much easier to understand an American millionaire or an English milord installing him as his favorite than if a lady proposed it. I mean, as far as the Greeks are concerned, women just don't do that sort of thing. They're all at home minding the babies.''

"It sounds as if Manoli is in for trouble."

"I wonder. Perhaps he'll turn whoring to good use. There's so little here for a chap like him—good-looking, bright, uneducated, ambitious. He sees the world go by— the American millionaire on his gleaming yacht, the English milord doddering off into the hills on a donkey— we're all the same to him, me the English milord, you the American millionaire, all of us offering a way out if he happens to strike our fancy. I know of cases where it's happened. One is having a career in the theater in the States and being very well kept on the side. Another is living a life of ease and luxury in Mayfair. Manoli is trying to learn how to make it happen to him. Whoring is the obvious answer.''

"You're an amoral pig, Johnny. Why don't they stay here and live a life they understand?''

"Because it no longer exists, mate. I've seen Crete transformed in fifteen years from a pastoral paradise to a tourist trap. Manoli and his ilk are caught in it. You'll see. You can tell me what you make of him after you've been to bed with him.''

"Have you got that all arranged?''

"It was arranged in heaven, as surely as the sun rises and sets. It would be amusing if he fell in love with you. I'd rather enjoy seeing him begging for attention, but it's too much to hope for. He's not the type.''

"You'd be amazed at the types that've fallen in love with me," Phil said with playful bravado.

"Not in the least. You must've been a marvel as a boy. You still look like a boy at moments, so it's easy to tell. Your body's a work of art. I've no complaints."

"Neither have I. I haven't thanked you properly for last night, starting with your picking me up. I've been excited about this trip all day. I'd've never done it without you. Bless you."

Engines began to rumble beneath them. Johnny glanced at his watch and smiled at him with affection untinged by irony. "We're mates, eh, chum?"

"Right, Johnny." There was a renewed outburst of shouting, fore and aft. Whistles blew. Bells clanged. There was a great thumping against the side of the hull. Phil supposed that something was being done with the gangplank. Their glasses began a little jig on the bar.

"We can have another beer while we're getting out and then I'll show you the Aegean," Johnny said.

The boat went through the mild convulsions of departure. It stopped and started while whistles blew and bells clanged. The engines idled and pounded. They were free finally, moving slowly through the crowded port. Phil saw a parade of miscellaneous shipping pass the curtained windows of the bar.

"When do we get there?" he asked.

"Eighteen or twenty hours from now. Midmorning, I should think. I expect we'll be home by noon. Did you tell the Athens hotel where you were going?"

"No. I just told them to hold everything and that I'd let them know. Isn't that what you suggested?" Johnny had made his rather odd point that morning about not leaving a forwarding address. By walking out of the hotel, Phil had severed all ties with what he thought of as his life. He was completely in Johnny's hands. After a few initial misgivings, it felt fine to disappear for a while.

They finished their beer and Johnny led them around the bar to doors that gave onto the forward deck. They stepped out into a crystalline world of blazing sun, crisp pure air and sparkling sea. They were just clearing the mouth of the harbor. The sea ahead of them was dotted with islands. Off to the right was a smoking heap of industrial installations on an island in close to the mainland. Johnny identified it as Salamis.

"As in the battle?" Phil asked.

"Quite so. If the Athenians hadn't beaten the Persians several thousand years ago, we'd all probably be weaving carpets. It doesn't bear thinking about."

They stood at the rail while Johnny indicated other points of interest. That was the Peloponnese. They couldn't see it but Corinth was over there. The classic world had been a cozy place. Crete had been at its farthest limits, a different civilization, lost for centuries after the mysterious catastrophe that had obliterated it.

On the open deck below them, passengers were settling down for the voyage. They lay about amid piles of their belongings—bundles, baskets, trussed chickens. The women looked as if their final hour had struck. They sat with their legs stuck out in front of them under voluminous skirts, swaying with agony, crossing themselves, their eyes rolling. A collective moan rose from them. They all held little cardboard buckets in front of their faces although Phil didn't see any of them vomiting.

"The sight of water does that to them," Johnny commented. "For a hardy seafaring folk, they're very sensitive."

The wind was chilly; when they found some shelter from it close to the bar door, they sat on uncomfortable little plastic chairs and basked in the bright sun. The roll of the ship, the metronome rise and fall of the bow grew more pronounced as they got out into open sea, and had a soporific effect. They eventually decided on a nap and went below to their cabin. It was a dingy cubicle with room for two bunks, one above the other, and little more. It was hot and airless; the porthole was rusted into place.

"There might be drawbacks to living on the boat," Johnny said. "I think I'll put you in Kyria Vassiliki's place and then we'll see. You'll want a few days to find your way around."

"How long do you expect me to stay?"

"At least a month, if I have my way with you. Now that I know you'll be there, I'm definitely going to think about that cruise. We could have a jolly good time together."

"I'm sure of it, but I'm not used to travel." He wondered when Johnny would tell him what the cruise was all about. Maybe never. Maybe he could accomplish some secret mission without Phil being aware of it. "Not having any definite plans is peculiar. I have to change my whole way of thinking."

"Not a bad thing to do from time to time. Going off without leaving an address is a step in the right direction. When you travel, you should let everything you do be determined by where you are. Otherwise you remain a tourist."

Getting out of their uncomfortable clothes became a balancing act; they teetered about and bumped into each other in the confined space. A sudden lurch pitched them onto the lower bunk, laughing together.

"This requires a more scientific approach," Johnny said. "Here. You stand up and hang on to the upper bunk. So. I'll take care of the rest. This may lead to a certain degree of physical intimacy. I hope you don't mind."

"Try me." By the time Phil was naked, he had a hard on and it was in Johnny's mouth.

Phil gripped the frame of the bunk and let himself sway to the movement of the ship. "Everything I'm doing is determined by where I am," he said.

Johnny laughed and lifted his head and looked up at him, his hands roaming over him. "The environment isn't favorable to serious fucking, but this is very pleasant. You make me wonder about beauty. How subjective it is? Do I want you because you have a beautiful body, or do I think it's beautiful because I want it?"

"I'm a philosophical conundrum, but I like what you're doing with my cock."

"So do I. It's one of the nicest cocks I've ever met."

"Let me know if you have need of my immediate services."

"I'll wait my turn. Take a nice long time to come. It's like sucking off an acrobat in the middle of his trapeze act."

Phil elaborated on the fancy by hanging on the bar with his legs straight out and doing chin-ups, teasing Johnny with an athletic display. He thought of the things he and George used to do when they worked out in the gym they had rigged up one summer in a barn at the dairy.

The ship steadied as the sun set and they pursued their southward course. They had a few drinks and a terrible meal—something described as "rozbif" and limp spaghetti—but a bottle of wine helped get it down. They went out on deck where it had grown noticeably warmer and sat for a while under a sky glittering with stars. Clusters of lights here and there on the horizon marked more islands.

"I'll forgive the cuisine. This is all right," Phil said. "I guess this is the longest time I've even spent on a regular passenger boat. I like it."

"At least you know you're going somewhere. Anything to stay out of planes."

"We're old-fashioned, Johnny. When did you first come to Greece?"

"A long time ago. I imagine it's getting on toward twenty years. Sixteen or seventeen. I haven't been here all that time, of course. On and off. Whenever I sell a few pictures. It's the right place for a con man. All Greeks are con men. Opportunities arise. If money drops in my lap, I stay a little longer. Mind you, I don't steal it. I'm quite an honest con man. If I'm given money to do something, I do it. The only people I really con are the police. That's what they're there for."

"What are you talking about, Johnny?" Phil asked, wondering for the first time whether he should watch his step with his enigmatic Englishman. "Give me an example. You're talking about illegal things?"

"Everything is illegal somewhere or other. When the Colonels were playing at dictatorship, it was illegal to keep a gun. You were supposed to turn them in to the police. In the islands it was flying in the face of natural law. Everybody's always had guns. Naturally, smuggling became a lively trade."

"You've smuggled guns?"

"On a very small scale. A dozen rifles make a very awkward package. Of course, you can take them apart up to a point. Being a foreigner is an advantage. To begin with, Greeks trust foreigners more than their own compatriots. And then the police prefer to leave foreigners alone unless they absolutely insist on getting arrested. It's the same with drugs."

"Drugs too?"

"The same sort of messenger-boy service. A certain amount comes into Heraklion from Turkey. It's said to be a relatively free-and-easy port. The trick is to find somebody who can move it to its destination in Athens without getting into trouble, or running off with it. This isn't your big well-organized gangster operation. There's still room for a gentleman amateur. A night on this glamorous ocean liner permits me to devote a few more months to my art.''

Phil was impressed in spite of himself, feeling the little thrill of adventure that he had the night before, by Johnny's cool familiarity with the "real" seamy side of life, where real consequences were more serious than the frivolous substitution of one lover for another. He supposed he understood enough now about Johnny's conversation in the Plaka bar; a boat would obviously come in handy if you were fooling around with contraband. He couldn't imagine getting involved in it himself. There was something sloppy about Johnny's thinking, typical of more and more people he knew who didn't think it mattered what you did if you could get away with it. The standards he'd been brought up to think of as essential to a decent life were all going down the drain.

"I suppose I'll sound prudish," he said, "but I don't like breaking the law. It's not just because it's the law, but you're bound to get mixed up with people I'd rather not have anything to do with.''

"All of life is choice," Johnny announced in the dark. "If you don't accept that, you're anti-life. You can't have everything so you have to choose what comes first. For me, it's independence. What about you?''

"I'm not sure I know. If you work—I mean at a regular job—you don't have all that many choices.''

"Quite. You become anti-life. Travel should do wonders for you, even if it's only to Crete. You may throw over your job and enlist in our army of lost souls. I imagine stranger things have happened but I can't think of any offhand. You strike me as a tough nut to crack."

"I do?"

"I think so. You may be an incurable romantic at heart but you have it firmly under control. Perhaps too firmly."

"Isn't that the choice you're talking about?"

"So it would appear, yet life is a slippery business, especially in a place like Crete where nothing is quite the same as what you've learned to expect elsewhere."

Phil thought he understood what he meant as soon as they debarked in Heraklion the next morning. He had the impression that he'd stepped off the face of the earth. Aside from the hours at sea getting to it, there was nothing in particular he could pick out as creating this sense of remote isolation. A square flanked by cafes could have been in Athens, but something about it placed it uniquely here, self-contained, a world apart. A few men struck an exotic note in baggy pants stuffed into the tops of their high boots and shaggy capes, but most of the people were dressed in conventional European clothes. Rugged hills fading into blue in the background suggested a continental scale that couldn't be contained on an island. Everything looked slightly out of line, dislocated in space. Perhaps the dislocation was in himself. Having reached his destination, he became more sharply aware that nobody knew where he was.

They boarded a crowded bus and were grateful to find two empty seats. Waiting for departure, Phil gazed vacantly at the static scene in which he was embedded. He noticed a young man with a conspicuous mustache, walking along outside the bus, peering up through the windows. When he came abreast of Phil, he stopped and his eyes seemed to settle on something or somebody near him. Phil glanced at Johnny, who was paying no attention. He glanced back at the man with the mustache, who had apparently come to a decision and was walking briskly forward toward the door. He climbed aboard and found a vacant seat near the driver.

In another few minutes, the motor started and they were off. They rode for an hour or more along a winding road beside the sea. It was a timeless, deserted landscape with little evidence of the tourist development Johnny had referred to. They caught occasional glimpses of well-tended estates behind walls, but for the most part it was open farmland and olive groves. Phil's sense of isolation and alienation persisted.

The bus stopped finally in a busy modern-looking town of substantial two- and three-story buildings where most of the passengers got out. The man with the mustache was still sitting near the driver. They drove on through the town for a few more minutes and came to a halt at the edge of a wide quay bordering the still, spacious harbor. The driver left no doubt that they had reached the end of the line by leaping up from his seat and dropping out of the bus to the ground himself. Phil and Johnny shuffled out with the few remaining passengers, including the man with the mustache.

They had barely set foot on the big paving stones of the quay when Johnny was enveloped in a languid welcoming embrace. "You are back, my Johnny," a big blowsy-looking man said, hugging him absentmindedly to his stomach. His small, delicate features were crowded into the middle of a broad, fleshy face. The overall effect was beneficent. "You weren't gone long."

"I brought a friend back." Johnny didn't look at him, so Phil didn't feel obliged to acknowledge the oblique introduction and pretended not to be listening. "I saw Pano," Johnny added.

"Yes. He is well?" the big man asked.

Phil remembered that the young guy in the Plaka bar

had been called Pano. "I guess so, my Andoni," Johnny said. "Everything seemed fine."

"I see your boat is here. I have money for you."

Andoni's vague, affectionate crooning voice seemed to confirm the connections Phil was tentatively making. The boat. Money. Popular topics of conversation here, as well as in the Plaka. The boat, money—and drugs? Johnny and Andoni made an unlikely pair of drug smugglers. The older man was wearing cotton slacks and a plain cheap sports shirt, the collar pressed flat around his neck like a piece of cardboard. He wore socks with his lumpy sandals. Phil let his eyes wander on to explore the unfamiliar surroundings, waiting for Johnny to give their arrival some focus. He felt as if he were being drawn deeper into a remote, impenetrable riddle. He wondered suddenly if he would ever be able to find his way back to the known, finite world. Everywhere he looked invisible barriers seemed to enclose him in an almost palpable remoteness. He felt strangely uneasy yet exhilarated, as he unconsciously looked for an exit.

On the seaward side, the port was enclosed by long moles that left a narrow opening marked by a light tower. Beyond, the empty sea stretched to an inconceivable horizon, out of scale like everything else here, a vast ocean that didn't appear on any map. Phil could see that the port installations continued in a dogleg off to his right; he caught glimpses of masts through gaps in the buildings that bordered the quay, cafes, a little round church standing by itself, a ramshackle two-story building that proclaimed itself a hotel. The cafes were repeated on all three sides of the port, a vast array of tables and chairs set out for a spectral horde. Phil had never seen a place look so deserted. They were overlooked by a scattering of severe, rather decrepit-looking houses that rose in tiers on a low steep hill.

Phil turned back to Johnny as he slowly disengaged himself from Andoni's lethargic but determined embrace. "Meet me at the usual place," Johnny added guardedly as he directed Phil away from the sea with a touch and a glance and the tilt of his head. "Shall we find roofs for our heads?" he suggested.

"I wouldn't mind shedding some of these clothes," Phil agreed. "It's summer here." It was the kind of day he'd been waiting for—everything outlined sharply in clear golden light, the sun blazing in a cloudless sky, a lively breeze whisking up crisp white wavelets beyond the mole. Several fruit trees were in bloom on the hill, spreading delicate arms over tumbled walls and outcroppings of rock. Phil decided he liked feeling totally cut off from the world; the silence was unlike anything he'd ever known, offering him sole possession of the place. He glanced at Johnny, who met his eye with his sly, ironic smile.

"This is about all of it," he said. "Do you like it?"

"I guess so. I don't really feel I'm anywhere yet. Why aren't there any people?"

"It's not even eleven yet. They'll be along. We'll get our sleeping arrangements sorted out and then we can settle down in front of a comforting brew."

"Aren't we going to see the boat?"

"The boat? Ah, yes, the boat. Later. I have to get the key. It's locked up."

"How do you lock up a boat?"

"The cabin's locked. We could go stand on the deck and gaze up at the mast if you like."

"You can splash water in my face. It'll be just like going for a sail." Phil was pleased to get a laugh out of Johnny. He didn't want the boat to become an issue or a mystery. He liked the easy, straightforward friendship that was developing between them, and the easy, straightforward sex that went with it. For once, he couldn't see any risk of complications arising from a natural human contact. It seemed to him that ever since George he'd spent all his time trying to extricate himself from unwanted attachments or misdirected passions. It was either that or shutting himself away with his textbooks and monkishly dedicating himself to rising sales. All that was behind him for the time being; he would be safe and satisfied with Johnny so long as he relaxed and took things as they came without indulging his tendency to make judgments. A little drug smuggling never did anybody any harm. He was ready for anything Johnny might propose.

They were headed for a more substantial-looking hotel than the one next to the little church. They skirted cafe tables, passed the hotel and turned into a side street away from the port. Behind the hotel, the street turned and narrowed and began to steep climb up the side of the hill. The buildings adapted to the slope, tumbling irregularly into whatever crannies offered a foothold.

After a short climb, Johnny stopped in front of a weathered door. "This is where I've been staying," he explained. He opened the door and stuck his head in. "Kyria Katerini," he called. There was an answering shout from within. Johnny pushed the door open wider. "Come along. You might as well see where my room is so you won't need help to find me. Is it rash of me to assume that you might *want* to find me? We'll soon see." He smiled playfully as he ushered Phil in. A sagging staircase rose before them. Subterranean caves seemed to burrow into the hillside behind it. Johnny led the way up. A wiry little woman in black appeared at the head of the stairs above them.

"You are back, my Johnny," she said with crisp affection.

"Yes. A short trip. I brought a friend." The woman grasped Phil's hand in a frim grip as he reached her level. "I'll show him my room and then take him to Kyria Vassiliki's. I hope he can stay there."

"Why not? She has nobody."

"Good. Has anybody asked for me?"

"Not this time. I put some letters on your table." Johnny was home; Phil could see it in the way his body seemed to relax into his surroundings and in the way he and his landlady looked at each other. He began to feel as if the place really existed.

"Let's go up," Johnny said to him in Greek. Could they stop pretending that he didn't speak the language?

"Shall I leave my bag here?" he asked. Johnny nodded and he dropped it before they climbed another flight of stairs. They came out into a big room that seemed to take up the whole top story of the house.

Long windows to the floor gave out onto a balcony with a view of the port over haphazard tile roofs. There was a bed against the wall at the far end and a few other bits of furniture, but they were lost in high-ceilinged, well-swept space. Only a long kitchen table strewn with painting materials near the windows was an assertion of Johnny's occupancy. An easel holding a blank canvas stood near it. Canvases on stretchers were stacked on the floor against the wall, their backs turned. Johnny dropped his little case on the table and gazed at a couple of letters lying on its surface before poking them suspiciously with a finger. He turned to Phil with a quizzical smile.

"Home, sweet home, what? You don't find all this luxury a shade ostentatious?"

"Not if it suits you. I hope to find something simpler for myself."

"Let's get on with it."

"I'm not allowed to see your work?"

"Later, if you like. You know where I am now."

They went down through the house and out into the narrow street to resume their climb. After a few minutes, Johnny stopped in front of another door and this time banged a knocker. "If she'll give you a good price, I think it's about the best you'll find here," he said as they waited.

The door was opened by an ample, amiable-looking woman who greeted Johnny with the cordiality that Phil noticed was the common reaction to him. He was apparently well liked. They climbed more stairs, caught glimpses of other people in rooms they passed and ended up once more on the top floor. This one was divided into several rooms leading into each other, railroad style. Like Johnny's place, the front room had long windows giving onto a balcony overlooking the port. Unlike Johnny's, there was a great deal of furniture, mostly beds. There were so many beds that Phil had trouble identifying the rooms' different functions, but he spotted a two-burner stove and a sink in one, a toilet in another.

He listened to Johnny and Kyria Vassiliki chatting companionably about him—where he was from, how long he was staying, how many members of his family were with him—with brief excursions into local gossip. When Kyria Vassiliki asked why one man would want to keep all the rooms for himself, Phil threw caution to the winds and joined in.

"I don't think I'd want to share a place like this," he told Johnny. "It's too open. There wouldn't be any privacy."

"Try to explain privacy to a Greek. Beds are beds. She'll probably be happy if you're willing to pay for three or four of them."

Settling for fifteen dollars a week brought negotiations to a happy end. Phil asked for a key to the street door and was assured that it was never locked. When the woman left them, they exchanged a smile, Johnny's wryly reproachful. "What gave me the notion you didn't speak Greek?"

"I don't think I actually said so. I said it was coming back."

"I don't think it went away very far. Fortunately my life is an open book. I hope you found my private conversations interesting."

"I tried not to listen. I know you have some business with that guy in the Plaka. I know your friend Andoni has some money for you. That's about all."

"It doesn't sound very interesting, does it? Maybe you'll find it less dull as we go along. I think you will, actually."

"I wouldn't be surprised. I might as well settle in and wait." He opened his bag on the floor. There was a decrepit armoire in the front room where his new landlady had left them. He disposed of his jacket and sweater and turned back to Johnny. "Watching me unpack wouldn't be very interesting either. How about a beer?"

"Let's go. Do you think you'll be all right here?"

"If I'm going to get my money's worth, I'll have to spend the next month in bed. Actually, it's perfect. I'll be famous for my pajama parties." He pulled off his shoes and socks and found a pair of sandals in his bag. "There. Bless you for getting me out of Athens. This is all right."

A few minutes' walk down the steep street brought them back to the port. There were more people moving around the wide quays. The sun was high and it was hot enough for the breeze to be welcome when they left the protection of the buildings. Johnny appeared to have selected the little humped church as their destination. As they approached it, he veered off into one of the generous displays of cafe tables. They settled in the sun on straight chairs with woven straw seats. A waiter ambled over with the cordial greeting that Johnny commanded from all the locals. As they ordered beer, Phil saw the man with the mustache skirting the tables, heading toward the sea. He passed within a few yards of them but didn't look at them and kept on going. Phil glanced at Johnny to see if any sign of recognition passed between them. Johnny was chatting casually with the waiter and ignored the passerby. In another moment Phil forgot his brief curiosity in the pleasure of downing a long swallow of cold beer.

"God, what've we been waiting for?" he exclaimed gratefully. "Ever been to New York in March, Johnny? Rain. Sleet. An icy wind whistling off the park?"

"London can be fun too."

A middle-aged woman dressed as if for a visit to a suburban shopping center at home—tweed skirt, sweater and pearls—lingered near their table, shuffling through a slim packet of letters. She selected one and sank into a chair beside them to open it. "Morning, men," she said in a brisk American voice, with a brief glance at them.

"Good morning, Anne," Johnny said with dry formality. "Aren't you pleased to see me back?"

"What?" The woman looked momentarily confused and then put her letter down. "Of course. Good heavens, Johnny. You're back. It's about time. That letter gave me a turn. I was afraid my daughter might be coming to see me. It's all right. She's not. Did you just get in?"

"Yes. I brought Phil. Philip Renfield. Anne Mason."

Phil's hand was given a firm shake across the table. He responded warmly, finding her attractive in an unexpected way. She had a square, straightforward face, as sensible as her clothes, and her eyes held the promise of hearty humor. Her graying hair was as smartly groomed as if she'd just come from the hairdresser. She gave Phil an approving nod. "You don't look hysterical, thank God. All hell broke out while you were gone, Johnny. Have you heard? Manoli's gone."

"I saw him in Piraeus yesterday."

"Oh, good. I hope he has sense enough to stay away."

"I shouldn't think so. He'll be back in a day or two."

"I give up. The buggery boys are going to end by killing each other. I thought they were going to the other night. I don't know why Manoli gives in to them."

"There are a number of things in heaven and earth that it's best for you *not* to know, Anne."

"I don't doubt it, but that isn't one of them. Manoli's a nice simple Greek boy. He's no match for the buggery boys. I wouldn't mind if they cared about him, either one or both of them. They're taking a depraved delight in torturing him. They're quite sickening. Oh hello, Don. I was just talking about you."

The last was addressed to a big overblown youngish man with thinning curly hair and a round cherubic face who pulled out a chair and settled comfortably into it before Anne had finished speaking.

"Blackening my character as usual, Annie?" Don asked with an ingratiating giggle.

"You manage very nicely on your own," Anne snapped crisply. Phil admired her undisguised hostility. Without knowing the people or issues involved, he suspected that moral indignation was a rare and valuable quality in a place like this.

The newcomer directed his unabashed smile at Phil; it had a sort of vacuous charm. "I hope you won't let her put you off me. You're absolutely stunning. Don't tell me you belong to Johnny.''

"We're one big, happy family, Don," Johnny said indifferently. "His name's Phil Renfield. Yours is Don Abbot. From here on you're on your own.''

Phil shook another hand, this one soft and slow to withdraw. He shifted uncomfortably in his chair. He hated any sex play in mixed company, and didn't want to seem to ally himself with Don on the heels of Anne's attack. He retrieved his hand without ruffling Don's cherubic composure. The latter beamed.

"We'll have a party to welcome this stunning creature. Seven o'clock. Tell everybody.''

A girl moved in behind Johnny and draped her arms around his shoulders and pressed a cheek against his. Her face settled into an expression of deep repose, radiantly innocent.

"Hullo, old bean," he said, patting her arms.

"You've been gone for days," the girl sighed. She looked at Phil around Johnny's head. "I'm Sally. You're new. Did Johnny bring you? Are you going to stay?''

"Johnny has me firmly installed.''

"You must be nice if Johnny brought you." She hugged Johnny and came around to settle in a chair beside him. She looked very young, with firmly modeled cheekbones, a mass of straight brown hair falling around her face and a sweet smile with big square white teeth. "Is Manoli back?" she asked Don.

"He'll be back. There's a party tonight for Phil.''

"A number-one party? Will there be whiskey?''

"There has to be whiskey for Phil.''

"That'll be nice. There's Cynthia. Cynthia," she called in a clear little-girl voice. "Don's giving a party tonight. Whiskey.''

"Good, darling. You'll like that." A tall girl with a mass of auburn hair piled haphazardly on top of her head dropped into a chair beside her. She appeared to have a voluptuous body under a marvelously eccentric garment of brightly printed cotton composed of many flounces and ruffles that reached to the ground. Sally's slacks and man's shirt took on a severe military look by contrast. A couple? Phil wondered as the two girls seemed to settle down against each other as if they belonged together. Cynthia gazed across at him with placid curiosity. "Hello," she said.

"He's Phil," Sally explained. "Manoli's coming back."

"Are you a friend of Manoli?" Cynthia asked.

"No. I mean, I haven't met him."

"I'm sure you will. He has to be here for Mardi Gras. We have an arrangement." She pulled a big canvas carry-all up onto her lap and began to poke through its contents. Sally leaned over it with her, pulling out bits of fabric for comment. Cynthia tugged at the end of a garland of paper flowers and displayed it briefly. They murmured together, as solemn as children playing at being grown-ups. The party continued to grow—a quite good-looking young man who didn't strike Phil as sexually interesting, a slim, clever-looking couple of about forty. Names were spoken, but Phil missed them in the casual confusion of chairs being moved, baskets of shopping put down, orders given to the waiter. He noticed that Johnny somehow provided a fixed center for the group, as if everybody wanted to touch base with him, even though Don was making a bid for attention with expansive invitations to his party.

"Another of your dismal booze-ups, dear?" a light, waspish voice demanded rudely. Phil turned as a slight figure dropped into a chair beside Anne. He had a brief impression of extreme youth—hair in schoolboy bangs on

his forehead, a trim figure in a shapeless seersucker suit—
but a second glance told him that youth was an illusion.
The slight figure was wizened, the bangs teased down
from a balding crown.

"Dismal? You mean we can count on your being there,
dear?" Don asked, matching sting for sting.

"Don't you two get started on each other again," Anne
interjected. "I've just been telling Johnny about the other
night."

"You weren't much help, you dreadful woman." The
young-old man pouted in a practiced way, as if it were
recognized as one of his charms. "You said I was a
corrupting influence."

"So you are. Isn't that what you've always wanted to
be?"

He looked pleased with this estimate of himself. "That
*is* the effect I seem to have on people. But really, darling.
*Manoli.* I've corrupted some of the most brilliant men of
our time. Leave Manoli to obscure Canadian merchants.
It's the best he can hope for."

"Who's a better judge of that than the toast of the
prewar Paris underworld?" Don beamed at the burst of
laughter that greeted this exchange. Beneath the bantering
tone, Phil detected the venom. It gave him a little chill, a
premonition fed by Anne's indignant outburst. He was
glad to be an observer with no stake in whatever games
were being played.

There were several new arrivals and a few departures.
He didn't try to keep them all straight, assuming that he
would learn who they were with time and if he cared
enough to find out. He gathered from chance remarks that
there were working writers and painters among them. He
quickly placed the youthfully aging "prewar toast" as a
minor celebrity whose name he'd known for years. An

American, John Robert Finlay had been something of a cult figure in the avant-garde of the thirties based in Paris. He had been the lover of Cocteau, or perhaps it was Gide. Phil had tried to read his incomprehensible scribblings and had seen his strange fragmentary drawings without being impressed, but his influence on the cultural climate of the era had been undeniable, if limited. His name figured in all the textbooks that dealt with the period. When Phil heard somebody call ''John Robert'' across the table, he sat up with interest. The use of both names was a distinctive trademark; people always referred to *John Robert* Finlay, never to John or Robert alone.

Encountering this relic of a vanished age intensified his sense of isolation in time and place; he was caught in a time warp. Finlay had an odd gnome's face with bulging hyperthyroid eyes and a slight cast, but beneath the distortions of age Phil could see a sprite with an elfin, androgynous physical magnetism. He had the assured manner of one who was accustomed to being courted and deferred to.

Phil could feel a close-knit, self-contained community taking shape around him. The foreign colony was what the place was all about; the local population existed as a working frame. Johnny was a stabilizing force, the glue that held them together. For once, the heterosexuals were a subdued minority. Interesting.

The waiter kept them supplied with beer and wine. A festive mood spread around the table, but Phil didn't have the impression that this was a special occasion. With the sun blazing overhead and the sea sparkling at their feet, it seemed appropriate to celebrate for no particular reason. His spirits rose with mindless euphoria, embracing all the company. He hadn't felt so good in years. The big platters on the table held fried potatoes and spicy bits of octopus in oil, and everyone picked at the food while they drank.

Conversations were passed around the table and were shattered by jokes. They all laughed a great deal.

Phil became aware that Johnny had gone, but he was soon back before Phil had time to wonder if he'd been abandoned. Others began to gather up shopping bags and bundles and head off around the port with parting references to the party that evening. Eventually, Phil and Johnny were left with Bryan and Angela Shackleton, a married couple and therefore presumably belonging to the minority, but at least in Bryan's case, Phil had his doubts: Bryan's cordiality bordered on flirtatiousness. Phil found them both attractive, lively and intelligent and physically alluring. Bryan had a lanky, loose-limbed body that looked much younger than his mature, expressive face. Phil had long ago given up expecting to have any sexual response to a member of the opposite sex, but he felt at ease with Angela and liked the immediate, uncomplicated friendly feeling that sprang up between them.

Bryan hitched his chair closer to Phil and put a hand on his shoulder while they all decided they didn't want any lunch. Phil liked the hand on him. It was a simple expression of an urge to make physical contact, without anything furtive or suggestive about it. He met Angela's eyes and they smiled at each other with understanding and burst out laughing.

"You men. You're not the only ones who have ideas," she said. Bryan gave Phil's shoulder a final pat as they gathered up their shopping and stood. They were a well-matched couple, both tall and slim and gracefully built. As Phil turned to watch them go, he saw the man with the mustache sitting at a nearby table twirling worry beads around his fingers.

"Do you have any idea why a guy seems to be following you?" he asked Johnny.

Johnny tilted his head toward the nearby table. "Over there? You noticed him? Very alert of you. Do you really think he's following us?"

"Well, he seems to like hanging around us. He's been with us since the bus."

"He's being awfully obvious about it, isn't he? You might say he wants us to notice him. Shall we take a walk and see what happens?"

"Sure." They both signaled the waiter. "You're a man of mystery, Johnny. Does this sort of thing happen to you often?"

"What kind of a life do you think I lead? I've never been followed in my life. I don't know why we should assume he's interested in me. Maybe the mob's sent somebody from New York to rub you out."

"That's a possibility. I hadn't thought of that. The only trouble is that I don't know anybody in the mob."

"That's easy to say, but I'll give you the benefit of the doubt. Maybe he took one look at you and decided to follow you to the ends of the earth. You have that effect on people. Look at the Aussies. They both wanted to take you home with them."

"I like them. I take it they allow each other a bit of leeway."

"Not at all. They share everything, including Bryan's boyfriends."

"It's like that, is it? I felt something—sort of direct in her, almost masculine. I wasn't sure it was sexual."

"You might call her sexually aggressive, in the nicest sort of way. Giving pleasure turns her on, and her mouth is a marvel, if you know what I mean."

"Near enough. It's quite a foreign colony you have here."

"I want to hear what you think of them all." They were

interrupted by the waiter, who wandered up to them making notations with a pencil on a small pad. He announced a result. Phil and Johnny each put a few dollars' worth of drachmas on the table.

"Are you sure that's all I owe?" Phil asked as they stood.

"That's your share. Don't start paying for the rest of us. We'll ruin you." They walked toward the edge of the quay, passing close to the man with the mustache. They skirted the little church and continued toward the outer mole.

"What about Anne?" Phil asked. "What's she doing here? She doesn't seem to fit."

"She's a very good painter, surprisingly enough. She likes the girls but doesn't do much about it. She feels protective about Manoli. She has standards, like you."

"I liked the way she slapped Don down, not that I have the slightest idea what *that's* all about. I feel too good at the moment to care much about standards. Everybody's perfect."

"That's the way. Suspend thought. Relax. I'd hardly recognize the rather wary chap I picked up day before yesterday. You're beginning to get a tan. By tomorrow, you're going to look eighteen and I'll probably fall in love with you. Perhaps I will right now."

"Now would be a good time. I'm ready for anything." They laughed and jostled each other playfully as they reached the last of the cafes. The hidden arm of the harbor opened out to their right. It offered wide and extensive shelter, with substantial quays on both the sea and land side. A small coastal freighter was tied up near the entrance, unloading sand.

"Aren't you going to check to see if we're being followed?" Phil asked as they headed out along the quay opposite the seawall.

"I have. He's back there but taking his time, just wandering along as if he didn't have anything in particular on his mind. He probably knows there's nowhere we can go except around the port and out again, unless we jump on a boat and sail away. I doubt if he'd care if we did. I'm beginning to have some vague idea why he's there."

"I'd probably find it more interesting if I knew what you know."

"Don't worry. I've been planning to tell you. We'll find somewhere to sit down."

They were passing serviceable-looking fishing boats tied up stern-in along the quay that was shut off from the town by nondescript sheds and a couple of forlorn shops. Nobody apparently had attempted to develop this area of the port in any attractive or commerical way. It looked like a parking lot for boats. Here and there among the fishing boats, little unpretentious pleasure craft, motor and sail, were moored. He kept an eye out for a boat that might be Johnny's—it must be here somewhere—and wondered what he had to tell him, hoping that it wouldn't be anything that would spoil being here. So far, he liked it.

They had gone quite far along the quay before he saw a boat that he considered worthy of being called a yacht. He judged it to be almost forty feet long, sloop rigged, with a gleaming black hull and white superstructure and a lot of chrome fittings that glittered in the sun. He didn't know enough about boats to know whether two could handle her, but she looked reassuringly sturdy and safe. His pace slowed and his eyes lingered with delight on the boat's sleek lines and traveled up the tall mast. He was aware of Johnny looking too.

"You like her?" he asked.

"She's a beauty. That's my idea of a boat."

"Let's go aboard."

"This is it?"

"That's it."

"You're a lucky bastard, Johnny."

"You're lucky for knowing me."

They stood where the stern lines had been made fast to the quay and looked down at the comfortable expanse of teak deck. The boat's defiant name, *Mistral,* was spelled out in brass letters on the fantail with the port of origin, Cannes, beneath it. Naming a boat after a treacherous wind seemed to him like tempting fate, but maybe that wasn't a bad idea occasionally. "How long is she?" he asked.

"Thirty-six or -seven feet."

"Is that too big for two people to handle?"

"Except for getting the sails up and down, one can handle her easily." Johnny crouched and tugged at one of the stern lines to bring the boat in closer. "Jump when she's close enough. Ready?"

"Another foot or two. OK." Phil dropped to the deck across a yard of water. He moved forward so as not to be in Johnny's way and kicked off his sandals, which he'd been taught was correct nautical manners. Johnny came leaping after him and the boat surged forward to the ends of the lines. They inspected the wheel, mounted amidship under a glassed-in hood to protect it from the weather, and Johnny pointed out the instrument panel behind it with gauges for the motor. He put a hand on an elaborate piece of hardware that was screwed into the deck holding the cable sidestays.

"For releasing the stays when we're tacking," he explained. "There's another there on the starboard deck in easy reach of the helmsman. They look complicated but it couldn't be simpler. You just throw this arm and pull it back to take up slack. There're winches at the foot of the mast for hoisting the main and the jib. Those winches back there are for trimming them. After you've been out for fifteen minutes, you'll be able to run the whole show without taking more than a few steps from here.''

Phil eased himself up into the high swiveled seat that was attached to the deck behind the wheel. ''OK. Let's go.'' They looked at each other and laughed happily at the prospect. ''Seriously, Johnny. What's the catch? Do I have to smuggle dope if I want to go for a sail?''

''I might come up with something more interesting that that.'' He unlocked the hatch and pushed it open to reveal a companionway leading down to the cabin. ''All the comforts of home. Come have a look.''

Phil paused with his foot on the top step and looked back along the deserted quay. ''What happened to our tail?''

''He was there until we came on board. Perhaps he's seen all he wanted to see.''

''What was that?''

''The boat? I'm only guessing, but it could be that.''

''If you say so. I want to see the boat myself. Show me.''

They stopped at the foot of the companionway and Johnny pulled back a sliding panel to open a compact gallery. Opposite was an equally compact ''head'' that combined a toilet and shower in curious juxtaposition. The saloon beyond was bright with rough-textured fabric. Two banquettes that obviously doubled as bunks faced each other against the bulkheads with a table between them. There were books in shelves and a rack of charts. Everything was carefully fitted and shipshape. Curtains stirred in the breeze from the open portholes. It was hot but not stuffy. Phil dropped onto one of the banquettes.

''Better and better. I'll buy her.''

"There're two more bunks forward. A bit cramped but she sleeps four in a pinch. Do you think we could manage another beer?"

"Anything that'll loosen your tongue. I want to know your secret. I know you have one."

"Yes, quite an important one, but not from you anymore." He turned back to the galley and brought out a frosty bottle and two glasses. He put them on the table and sat opposite Phil. When the beer was poured, Johnny smiled mischievously across the table. "Very well then. Are you ready to strike a blow for freedom?"

"Good heavens. Is that what we're going to do?"

"If we wish. I don't know all the details, but I can tell you the rough outlines of the plot. There's a bloke on a prison island who wants to get off. They won't tell me his name, but it seems he's a good guy who was working with the bad guys, in this case the Colonels, for subversive purposes. He was a biggish wig with the junta but played an important part in getting rid of them. The people who know about him, the intelligence boys, mostly our lot, the Brits and the Yanks, didn't want to blow his cover. They thought he might be useful again, so he was treated like his colleagues—rounded up and put away to await trial. The people I know want me to pick him up in the boat and deliver him to friends who'll take it from there." Johnny sat back with a noncommittal smile.

Phil's head was in a whirl. For a moment he thought Johnny might be pulling his leg, but an instant's reflection told him that it was the sort of thing he would expect of Johnny—adventurous, devil-may-care, involving high-level politics and serious issues, much more interesting than dope. It also sounded like fun. "You mean, this guy has been sitting in a prison for a year just to prove he's in favor of a military dictatorship?"

"Yes, but it's probably not what you imagine. He's living on an island as comfortably as he chooses to make himself. The Greeks have used the remote islands as prisons for centuries. It's cheap and practical. Nobody can go anywhere because no commercial shipping is allowed. They don't have to waste money building prisons. You can build yourself a seaside villa if you feel like it. The prisoners have to check in a couple of times a day but otherwise they're on their own."

"And you think you can sail in and carry him off?"

"His friends do. They'll presumably choose a safe pickup point, a deserted cove. Something of that sort. They'll give me instructions when the time comes." He pulled a chart out of the rack behind him and spread it out on the table. "Here we are. The Peloponnesos. Kythera. This little blob here." He ran his finger over the chart, smoothing it from mainland Greece down over the conspicuous island of Kythera to a speck of land with no name that lay on a southern course toward Crete. "It's not big enough to be included on the chart, but it's got a name like Scrofulous. Something like that. A good day's sail from here." They leaned across the table with their heads together for the geography lesson. Chania at the western end of Crete looked unexpectedly close to the long, dangling fingers of the mainland. "They're planning to take delivery of the body at Kythera. From there, a fast power cruiser can be out of Greek waters in no time. So long as nothing goes wrong at Syphilis or wherever, it should be a pleasant four- or five-day sail. Does it appeal to you?"

"I'll say. When do we go?"

Johnny looked at him and chuckled. He lifted a hand to Phil's face and his eyes were thoughtful behind his smile. "You make it more exciting than I'd expected it to be.

You'll have to be patient for another week or two. They want to be sure the weather's settled first of all.''

"Where do you fit into it, Johnny? How did you get involved?''

"Pure conincidence. I apparently know some of the man's friends, whoever he might be. My contacts call him Stavros, so I imagine that's not his name. I happen to fill their particular bill. They wanted a small foreign yacht. They say the authorities don't pay much attention to foreigners sailing around the island. A Greek would be in rather serious trouble if he were suspected of trying to make contact with a political prisoner. I could manage alone, I should think, but I'd rather not. I had to find you. That's why I pricked up my ears when you talked about sailing the other night. You're much too good to be true. Just to prove I'm quite unhinged by you, I'll even give you half of what they give me.''

"How much is that?''

"A thousand—dollars, that is—has been mentioned. That makes it a cut-rate charter but it's a worthy cause.''

"Is there any danger involved? I don't see the point of the tail.''

"I don't either, really. There's the danger that Stavros will be prevented from leaving, but that's his worry, not ours. If they stop him after he's with us, I daresay we could have a few uncomfortable hours until we were rescued by people who know who he really is. We might even be expelled from the country for appearance's sake, but we'd be let right back in again. As far as I can see, the tail must be one of Stavros's people making an extra check. Maybe they want to see for themselves that the boat's right for the job. Who else could be interested in me? As cloak-and-dagger operations go, I'm afraid this one won't rate very high for chills and thrills.''

It sounded thrilling enough to Phil. Expelled from the country? How many people did he know who'd helped a political leader escape from prison? If not dangerous it was at least original. He was lifted on a fresh wave of euphoria. "Forget about the money. I won't take any for something I'm dying to do. It would be like being paid for going to bed with you. You can't put a price on pure pleasure."

"My word. What honeyed lips." He gripped Phil's neck while his other hand unbuttoned his shirt and stroked his chest. "Is now a good time for pure pleasure?"

"I feel so marvelous already that it's almost frightening to imagine feeling any better. Let's see what happens."

They enjoyed themselves enormously. Sex could be simple fun; his chest had often heaved with passion during the act, rarely with laughter. He thought how sensible Johnny had been to establish their independence of each other right from the start. There was something claustrophobic about the place itself. He would have to be passionately attached to Johnny not to feel hemmed in at times. Separate beds, quite a few of them, suited his current mood.

"I wish I'd met you long ago, Johnny," he said after they'd tidied themselves up in the head and were lolling on the banquettes, towels carelessly thrown over themselves, having another beer. "I told you I'd come here to forget. I already have, just in the last two days." He told him about Alex and discovered that instead of embarking on a complex tale of dedicated passion, he was confessing to a wrongheaded infatuation with a spoiled, vain, faithless young man whose beautiful face was his only genuine attraction. It was remarkable that the face remained unblemished by the viciousness and depravity that were his essential characteristics. It had taken Phil over five years to admit to himself how deeply flawed he was, five years of pulling him out of other people's beds, five years of tears and pleas and promises, five years of humiliation. Alex was a mental and spiritual sadist and needed a victim, which repeatedly brought him back to Phil. Phil was powerless against him. Their craving for each other's bodies was the only thing they shared equally. They had made love while the party where they met was still going on, in their host's bed where they were allowed to spend the night. By morning Phil was in love and his torment had begun. He sounded absurd to himself as he told Johnny about it and was almost too embarrassed to go on, thinking about the last time he'd seen his maddening lover. Not quite a year ago. Phil had caught him at home one Sunday evening after several frustrating days of missed appointments and unanswered telephone calls. At least he never had to wonder what Alex was up to; Alex was always embarked on a new adventure.

"At last, sweetie," Alex said in greeting. He fell onto the sofa of his disheveled little living room. He lived in a nest of expensive discarded clothes. Suits and slacks and opulent silk shirts were draped over chairs. "Why did it take you so long to rescue me from the evil child who abducted me? You wouldn't believe it. Only eighteen and an absolute abyss of vice. He wouldn't let me go."

"Did you lose my telephone number?"

"I was naughty." Alex looked up at Phil from great luminous, innocent eyes, and his robe fell open. He was wearing his cock stretcher.

"For God's sake, take that thing off," Phil protested. It was an unsightly and somehow ludicrous contraption that Phil had never been able to look at directly.

"We must do what we can to correct the little deficiencies of nature," Alex said complacently. "We're not all hung like you, sad to say. Being with you is a constant reminder."

"Being with me!" Phil was suddenly raging. The last few

days, although they had done nothing to alter the deadly pattern of their life together, had this time strained his patience to what he felt, hoped, might be the breaking point. Maybe the moment he'd longed for had finally come, the moment when they could say good-bye without a pang of regret. "If we were together, maybe we'd make sense about something more important than who has the bigger cock."

"Now, sweetie, don't get started on that again. We're much too clever to get trapped in the gay marriage scene. Frilly aprons wouldn't suit either to us." Under cover of a corner of his robe, he detached his ridiculous apparatus. He was naked when he flung back the folds of silk. He had a partial erection. "We still turn each other on. How many queens can say that after five years? I'll bet you're getting a hard on. Show me."

Alex was right, but Phil was determined not to give in to him. Still seething with rage, he looked down at the charming body, slight and boyish and hairless, and had thoughts about how carelessly it was shared. "Listen, I've just about had it," he said, struggling to keep his voice steady. " Do you have any idea what that means?"

"Really, darling. Not again. You can't leave me *every* week. Come here, big boy. Come here, my big lover." He lay back and leaned his head against the cushions. He knew how to use his body with devastating effect. Even though Phil could anticipate every move, Alex eased himself closer, while adopting a pose of wanton provocation. Phil found this act less difficult to resist than when Alex chose to be soft and helpless.

He straightened and took a grip on himself. "Don't let's play games," he said harshly. "I suppose you've been having fun for the last three days, but I haven't. What's the point of saying we love each other if we run off with any pretty kid who comes along?'' He saw Alex's cock lengthen and begin to lift, and his voice quieted in spite of himself. ''Dammit, we have a wonderful time together—*when* we're together. How long are you going to fight it? Why don't you get out of this dump and let us live somewhere we can *be* together.''

Alex looked up with a beguiling smile and lifted his chin, presenting Phil with the glorious creation that was his face—the sweep of his brow and the great guileless eyes, the perfect tilt of his nose, the exquisite modeling of his lips and the long thrilling line of his neck. ''Oh darling, won't it be heaven someday? When we're old and nobody else wants us, we'll still have each other. I've been thinking about you. It would've been so exciting to see you with Artie. He'd have gone mad for your big thing. Just like me. If only you weren't so uptight, we could have wild times together. I know you'd love it if you let yourself go. Come here.''

Alex flung his arms out and gathered Phil closer and went for his big thing. Phil, both disarmed and repelled, let him open his pants. Alex had a knack for making him feel heroically endowed, and he couldn't repress a twinge of shame for being so susceptible to Alex's attentions. He saw his erection spring up to Alex's enthralled face and thought of himself and George when they had first come together—two splendid, ostensibly wholesome young athletes, champions, models of schoolboy excellence, both with the flaw that led them to each other rather than to the girls who would have been their destiny in the usual course of events. There had seemed to be something gloriously outrageous in their hunger for each other's bodies, as if they had discovered a pure essence of desire outside nature. Where was the glory now, standing in an untidy living room, indulging an exhibitionistic taste for showing off his cock? Why next? Would he finally give in to Alex's invitations to wild times? The word *love* should never have been pronounced between them. It was a desecration. He had to free himself from the spell of mindless beauty.

"Stop it," he ordered roughly. He wrenched himself away and got himself back into his clothes. "You've forgotten the difference between making love and getting your kicks with anybody that strikes your fancy."

"Oh sweetie. Now you're cross with me. Please don't be." Alex pulled his robe around himself and played his soft, helpless card. As always, Phil felt himself melting. "It's always so thrilling to be with you again after we've been apart a little while. We're still young, after a fashion. We mustn't let being in love turn us into little dried-up old gnomes. You've always agreed about that. Please, darling, take your clothes off and let me worship your sublime body. You know I'm rather good at it."

"Christ, there're enough clothes lying around without my adding to them. Since you never wear anything for long enough to hang it up, I don't see why you always want money for more."

"I'm a vain silly goose, and you're much too good for me. I know that. Still, *something* seems to work right. Let's count our blessings. I wish you'd give back my special one."

Alex's begging revived Phil's determination to play hard-to-get. "You've managed to do without it for the last three days. Let's leave it at that for the time being." He looked around for somewhere to sit, but the only available space was on the sofa beside Alex, and he knew what that would lead to.

"If you're going to punish me, I better do my nails,"

Alex said peacefully. "They're a disgrace. Don't hover, darling. Sit down."

"Where, for the love of Christ!" Phil roared. He gathered up an armful of clothes from the nearest chair and hurled them across the room. A fine manly way to spend a Sunday afternoon, sitting around watching your lover in his cock stretcher, doing his nails. It was the last straw. "We're nothing but a pair of silly old faggots," he shouted. "You may be happy but I make myself sick. I'm going. Don't bother to try to see me again unless you're ready for us to live together and try to make some sort of life with each other. I don't expect you to give up your boyfriends, but I can insist that you keep them in the background of a life with us and not vice versa. That's clear enough. I mean it."

Phil allowed his eyes to linger briefly on beauty—Alex's wide gaze on him, his lips parted, an expression of startled awe filling his extraordinary face. With an effort, Phil turned his back on him and hurtled out the door down the stairs, into the mean streets of the West Fifties, far enough west to be almost slums. Anger precluded thought, until Phil realized that there was nowhere he wanted to go, nobody he wanted to see. His brief outburst had left him with no sense of finality. He'd blown up with Alex often enough before and had always gone back to him. He struggled as usual against regret. For all Alex's shortcomings, they had had periods that had been lightened by a semblance of love. They had achieved continuity of sorts. This was more than he'd found with anybody else since George.

The loss of George had taught him to value love above all else. It was for the glimpses of love he had shared with Alex that he accepted all the frustrations, all the humiliations, all the agonies inflicted on him by this faithless lover. It was for this that he had suspended control, had failed to invoke the steel of his will that had proved so effective against George. Had he deluded himself? Love, to mean anything, worked both ways. Alex had only to say a word to bring him back.

Work saved him. He was about to embark on an extensive promotion of a new line of textbooks. It kept him busy enough for the next month for there not to be much time for tormented thought. At the end of it, he had to admit to himself that Alex had had plenty of opportunity to make a move. He had learned another lesson. He was free. He toughened his will to remain so. It had worked.

He looked at Johnny with a rueful little smile as he remembered. "I think my trouble was that I fell in love for the first time when I was very young, barely nineteen, and I wasn't ready for it to end," he said. "For a long time, all the years doing military service and then getting started in New York, I had the feeling that I'd lost the most precious thing I'd ever have in life because I hadn't put enough of myself into keeping it. I decided that if it ever happened again I'd sacrifice everything to it. When I fell in love with Alex, it never occurred to me that the quality of love can vary. Love was love. Being in love with Alex had to be just as ennobling and rewarding as being in love with a paragon of sanity and virtue. I think if I'd known you after the first few times I left him, you'd've laughed me out of my obsession. There's something very sane and balanced about you, Johnny. I can see the people here feel it. They defer to you. The resident sage."

"That's because I never get carried away by anything. It's really quite boring. I daresay I've been in love a few times, but it's never been an overwhelming experience and it never lasts long. I envy people who live life intensely even if it gets them in muddles. I even envy John Robert and Don for being so *intensely* malicious. Something in me simply prevents me from being completely absorbed into life, a sort of detachment that makes me an observer. Perhaps it's to do with being a painter, but I often feel that something's missing.''

"It seems like something added to me, like wisdom and common sense. My obsession with Alex was a sort of hysteria. Granted, there were times that were pure magic. He could behave himself for as much as a month at a time, when I was almost convinced that there was someone there worth loving. I sometimes wonder if homosexuality isn't basically hysterical. Maybe we shouldn't pretend we're capably of loving seriously.''

"I shouldn't be lured into that dead end if I were you. Not many people can make a complete success of love, regardless of sexual preferences. The capacity to love is what counts. You mustn't try to extinguish it just because you've had bad luck. Maybe it'll help you choose more carefully next time.''

"God. Next time. It's taken me a year to convince myself that I never want to see Alex again. I've finally made it. Let me relax and enjoy it for a while. I enjoy being with you, Johnny. I'm totally content for the first time since I can remember.'' Looking at Johnny's sensible, appealing, humorous face, he thought he might be finally growing up. An essential part of growing up was learning to be self-sufficient like Johnny. George had got him started in life thinking that he'd never be alone. It had taken him all this time to reconcile himself to solitude. Now that he could believe that he had purged himself of Alex, he realized how close he had come on several occasions to going back to George. Whenever they had talked to each other, he had felt that it was all still there, stirring beneath the surface, waiting to be grasped—the instant rapport, the extraordinary identification with each other, the satisfaction and understanding that only they could offer each other, the desire. Maybe. Possibly. Too much time had elapsed to think about it seriously.

Johnny sat forward and put a hand on his knee. "It's probably about time to get ready for the next party," he said.

"What time is it? I've completely lost track."

"Getting on for five."

"Really? What a wonderful way for a day to go. We've been here for only five or six hours? Incredible. Shouldn't we go for a sail? I've got to learn how to handle the boat."

"Quite. I thought we'd take a couple of days to settle down first and give me a chance to get back to work." They stood and wandered around the cabin finding their clothes and getting dressed. "We'll take her out a couple of times so that you're familiar with everything. That'll give us the opportunity to make sure everything's in working order and get any necessary repairs taken care of. After that, we can stock up so we won't have to go into port for a week if we don't want to. Once they know we're ready, I shouldn't think they'd give us much notice to get moving. There's less chance of careless talk if we don't know anything for more than a few hours before we go."

"You sound as if you rescued politicians from jail every day, Johnny. Is that guy Andoni part of your plot?"

"He's Pano's uncle, Pano the chap with the Plaka bar. They're go-betweens with whoever is running the show."

"If Andoni's here and can see the boat for himself, why should they get somebody to tail you?"

Johnny was silent for a moment, looking at Phil thoughtfully. "Come to think of it, it doesn't make much sense, does it? I need you to catch details like that. I'd better have another think."

"Can't you just ask Andoni to find out if they've sent somebody to check up on you?"

"I imagine I could," Johnny said uncertainly. "Do I want to? I don't want to give them the idea that there's something about me that might queer the deal, that I'm being watched by hostile forces as it were. It's impossible. I haven't talked to anybody about it except you. After all, we're on the side of law and order. Anybody who's against us would have to be part of the Colonels' old gang. Except, of course, for the people who put Stavros away without knowing who he is. But that's the government, for heaven's sake. Dear me, you've got me in a frightful muddle. I'm not sure what I should do. Frankly, I rather counted on the money."

"I guess we better wait and see if we notice anything else peculiar." In spite of himself, Phil felt his sympathies and curiosity being drawn into the intrigueIt was the first time he'd been responsible for decisions that might have fatal consequences. Johnny might inadvertently be leading the man he called Stavros into some sort of trap. His imagination roamed. "At least you'll know it had nothing to do with the boat if that guy goes on hanging around," he said.

"And if he doesn't?"

"Then I guess it might only mean that they don't trust Andoni's judgment about boats."

"Yes, that could be it, couldn't it?" He touched Phil's shoulder as they headed for the companionway. "I'm glad we can talk about it, mate. Tell me if you notice anything odd. If we go on being followed, I'll speak to Andoni. I don't want to cause Stavros any trouble. He sounds the sort of chap one wants to help."

"Right," Phil said. Johnny wasn't thinking only of money. Since Phil had been the first to spot the weakness in Johnny's boat-checking theory, he already felt partially responsible for doing the job right.

Nobody was waiting for them when they jumped ashore. They strolled along the quay, observing increased activity where the fishing boats were tied up, pausing occasionally to glance around. When they reached the little church and turned away from the sea, they looked at each other and shrugged. They had seen no sign of the conspicuous mustache. They parted in the steep, narrow street where their houses were, and Phil returned to what was now home to unpack and get ready for the evening.

He rejoined Johnny as dusk was coming on, and they set off for Don's party in the gathering twilight. They both had sweaters around their shoulders; Johnny had warned that it still got chilly at night. Don's house was buried in a garden behind walls on a suburban-looking street that ran from the port to the bustling town they had passed through on arrival. Glimpses of the sea through trees created a romantic atmosphere. The sky was streaked with pink and gold, indicating that the sun was setting. Their host greeted them with plump and fussy cordiality, fluttering his hands over them until he seized one of Phil's and held it.

"Such a handsome lad. I want to hear all about you. What'll you both drink? Whiskey?"

"I prefer ouzo, Don," Johnny interjected. "I left England to get away from whiskey."

"We're all running away from something." Don giggled and squeezed Phil's hand. "What about you, darling boy?"

"Ouzo would be fine," Phil said, withdrawing his hand firmly but as gently as possible. Don patted his behind before turning to a table bearing an array of glasses and bottles. Phil felt a familiar stab of self-disgust for having adopted a way of life that included being fondled by men in public. He glanced at Johnny, whose cool, ironic smile encouraged him to dismiss Don as too absurd to worry about.

He looked around at the guests who had arrived ahead of them. Recognizing faces from the noon gathering made him feel like an established resident. They were settled into comfortable-looking garden furniture set out under old olive trees. The belligerent Anne was there and Sally and Cynthia, without their sewing but with the promised whiskey. John Robert Finlay was with a small Oriental Phil hadn't seen before. His eyes settled on Bryan and Angela, the attractive Australian couple. Without stirring from their chairs, they smiled an invitation and each lifted one arm straight in the air and waggled their hands at him. It was a curiously intimate and irresistible greeting. Phil laughed with delight as Don handed him a cloudy drink.

"There, dear heart." The host beamed cherubically. "What a delightful boy. Enjoy yourself." He turned to Johnny with his drink. "Now, tell me everything Manoli said. I hear you saw him yesterday. Start at the beginning. Did he say why he'd gone?"

Phil didn't wait to hear the answer. He might become one of Manoli's besotted fans when he met him, but so far he hadn't managed to work up much interest in him. He drifted toward the Aussies, who were watching him expectantly, but he was intercepted by John Robert.

"I didn't really get a chance to talk to you at noon," the legend said, getting up as Phil was passing. "You're in publishing. I hear you're with Denton's. A good house. They once wanted to do a collection of my things but I've always liked to publish myself. You must come have dinner with me one night soon. I'd love to hear all the wicked New York literary gossip."

Phil was more aware of his accent than he had been

earlier, a rich mixture of French and British with echoes of the American South. His voice was high and whispery, like a very old woman's.

"Dinner would be fine, but I'm in the textbook division. My gossip is about as wicked as third-grade geography."

Finlay looked at him with a monkey grin. "How delicious. You can give me a scandalous geography lesson. This is Sim, my assistant." His assistant at what? Phil wondered. The small Oriental had risen and was bowing and smiling. Finlay tucked a hand under the younger man's arm and used him as a prop. He gave the impression that he was used to having people to lean on. "Shall we make a date?" he asked.

"Any day. Just tell me where you are."

"Why not tomorrow? Is tomorrow all right for me, Sim?" Phil noted the little show of self-importance. Fair enough for a legend. He didn't think an evening with him would be boring. Finlay's grin was full of malice and mischief. "I'll ask Johnny too. Would you like that? He can show you where the house is. It's quite close to you. Tomorrow evening at eight. A more or less civilized hour for a change," he added with a withering glare at Don.

"I'm sure somebody can tell me where you are if Johnny can't make it."

"You're not 'together' as they say?" His womanish speech mannerisms put quotation marks around the word.

"We're pals. No complications."

"I hope that doesn't mean you're leaving soon. Will you be here for Mardi Gras?"

"I don't know." He glanced over Finlay's shoulder and found Bryan's eyes watching him with lazy speculation. The charge of mutual attraction was humming between them, stronger than at noon and it seemed to Phil still growing as their eyes met and queried each other. He wondered if they would be able to do anything about it, and his eyes moved on to Angela whose cooperation or consent was apparently necessary. Johnny had said they shared. Her eyes were waiting for him, amused and lively with curiosity. He looked quickly back at Bryan while he continued his conversation with Finlay. "I don't even know when Mardi Gras is," he said.

"I never know when anything is, but it must be soon. I know March has started. The girls will know. They're sewing their chaste fingers to the bone for it. It can be simpleminded fun. All the butch boys leap into drag. They pretend to be grudgingly observing the local custom, but of course they're secretly wild to get into their sisters' finery. It's rather a lark. You'll be amused by it."

Phil kept the small talk going while his eyes and thoughts were occupied with the Aussies. He could see that they had come to some sort of agreement about him; they had a charming air of complicity that included him and predisposed him to play along with them. His eyes were as much for Angela as for Bryan. He thought of Helen. She had taught him that he had nothing to fear from women, even though their being women prevented him from falling in love with them. Nothing prevented him from having a good time with them when the rare occasion arose. He had no experience of unorthodox numbers but was feeling so relaxed and at ease within himself that it seemed an auspicious moment to experiment. He said something to John Robert about looking forward to dinner and moved on to the waiting couple.

"Hello there," Bryan said. He reached for Phil's hand and pulled him down beside him into the oversized chair. They both smiled at him encouragingly, as if they expected him to acknowledge whatever plot they were hatching. "We talked a lot about you this afternoon. We've rarely been in such complete agreement. You're our dream boy. Are you going to come home with us later?''

Startled laughter briefly choked him. The idea wasn't unexpected, but having it thrown at him so baldly forced him to face the practical details. What exactly would they do? He would have preferred for it to just sort of happen after a cheerful evening getting a bit drunk together. He looked into Angela's bright, sensible, smiling eyes.

"Wouldn't that be sort of complicated?'' he asked.

"Nothing's ever complicated for two chaps,'' she said easily. "I promise to complicate matters only in the nicest possible way.''

They all burst out laughing. Bryan had put an arm around him to seat him and it was still there. Being pressed against the lanky boyish body gave Phil an erection. Bryan's cock was very visible between his thighs, the cloth stretched smooth over it. Phil was strongly tempted to move his hand a few inches to find out if it was as hard as it looked. Angela of course would know at a glance. He'd learned from Helen that girls were much more aware of such things than he'd been brought up to believe. Helen had been his answer to his rupture with George and had almost convinced him that he'd deceived himself into thinking he was queer. He and Helen had tried hard for a year, but she couldn't help being a woman. It was the only thing that had kept him from marrying her.

He looked at Angela, thinking that she was even more attractive than Helen—cool and direct and quite beautiful in a very civilized way, with cleanly modeled features and a trim, shapely body. He guessed that her naked breasts would be lovely, small enough not to sag or droop. He thought of the three of them lying lazily naked together and looked forward to it. Maybe he could fall in love with a woman if she had a husband who turned him on. He leaned back against Bryan, exerting subtle pressures. Bryan replied with pressures of his own. Johnny. This couple, Bryan and Angela Shackleton. He was beginning to respond again to the people around him after being blind to everybody for five idiotic years of Alex. Crete was waking him up.

They chatted for a few more minutes while Phil finished his ouzo and learned that they were trying to be writers and that they were both on leave from newspaper jobs in Australia.

"We were lucky to hit on this place," Bryan said. They were both drinking red wine and had a bottle beside them on the ground. Angela refilled their glasses while Bryan briefly sketched their current circumstances. "It's so beautifully cheap. We're going to be able to stay a bit longer than we thought."

"It's good for work, I would think. Not much in the way of distractions."

"Only the human comedy. That's better than the telly. Of course you've missed the star attraction, but Johnny says he'll be back."

"Manoli?"

"He's not our favorite playmate," Angela put in.

"He came on very strong with Angie. Real macho. He gives us the giggles but he's very pretty. Not as pretty as you but you're our dream boy. Have you had time to place your bets yet?"

"On what?"

"On Don or John Robert in the Manoli sweepstakes."

"I don't know what's involved."

"Nobody does, but Don and John Robert are in it to the kill. It stands to reason one of them will win."

"OK. I'll take my chances on John Robert, even though I don't know what you're talking about."

"That's par for the course," Angela said, looking at her husband fondly.

"You'll soon see, both of you. I know these things. A sixth sense." He leaned against Phil and they both laughed, although he didn't know why. Maybe just because he felt good and liked the Australian. Don joined them, hovering over them solicitously, his hands floating about ineffectually, looking harmlessly, incorrigibly foolish with his round cherubic face and thinning little curls.

"Does everybody have everything they want? What about the wine? You still have some? Help yourself when you want more. Now really, darling boy." He pounced on Phil's empty glass. "Why are you sitting here with nothing to drink? Just a moment."

Phil pulled himself to his feet and steadied himself with a hand on Bryan's shoulder. He was getting stiff from sharing the seat. "I'll be right back," he said.

Johnny was standing where he'd left him, talking to François, the good-looking Frenchman, and another man Phil didn't know. Don beckoned him to the drinks table with an ouzo bottle. "Was the last one about right?" he asked, pouring. He handed the glass to Phil. "Now, dear boy. Let me show you the house. Not many foreigners own here, but by hook or by crook, this is mine. The Greeks consider Crete part of their frontier, the southernmost island, so there're all sorts of property restrictions. Do you want to see it?"

Phil glanced back at the Shackletons. A couple who'd been with them at noon but whose names he didn't remember were pulling up chairs to join them. He nodded at Don. "Thanks a lot. I'd love to see it. My first private house in Greece."

The facade was obscured by a flaming curtain of scarlet bougainvillea, but once inside Phil guessed that it had been an old farmhouse, elaborately renovated. Floor levels were haphazard; they stepped up and down as they moved from room to room. Bright rough-textured rugs were strewn on the tiles, the bold patterns echoed and elaborated in the brilliant colors of the wall hangings, all of them identified as Cretan by Don, handwoven. The dark, rustic furniture was highly polished wood, the chairs cane bottomed. There was a glow of copper everywhere, pots and vases and curious utensils. One room was lined with books. On another wall a collection of vicious-looking weapons was hung, daggers and swords and battle-axes, all with an Oriental look.

"The Colonels gave me a rough time over those," Don commented. "We were all supposed to turn in our guns, but the police decided I could do quite a lot of damage with these. I had to convince them that I didn't intend to start a revolution. I picked them up all over the East, Malaysia, Indonesia. That one's Indian."

"Magnificent. But everything—the house is stunning." Phil was having second thoughts about his host. This wasn't the house of a silly ass; it had been created with taste and imagination and loving care. He was impressed.

"I'm so glad you like it." Don beamed at him. Phil told himself that he couldn't be as foolish as he looked. "Perhaps you'll come stay with me the next time you come to Chania."

"God knows when that'll be, but I won't forget."

"Shall we seal it with a kiss?" Don suggested with ghastly winsomeness.

Phil's spirits slumped. He was constantly astonished by the confidence quite unattractive men had in their powers of seduction. He held himself stiffly and gave Don a quick peck somewhere in the vicinity of his mouth. Don's grip tightened on him and he abruptly swung away and stared at the first thing he saw that could reasonably claim his attention—the barbaric collection on the wall.

"I suppose you've heard of Manoli," Don said with an arresting shift of tone.

"Johnny mentioned him. Does he live here with you?"

"Certainly not." There was now no mistaking the venom in his voice. Phil took a few safe steps away from him and turned back. The simpleminded benevolence of his expression had been replaced by the thin-lipped malice Johnny claimed to envy. "I'm sure he thinks he'll eventually move in and take over. The young often have delusions of grandeur. He's rather a savage. I'm trying to civilize him, but everybody caters to his worst side."

Phil felt distaste tugging his face into an unfamiliar grimace and turned away with a shrug. He was beginning to get the impression that he wouldn't really know the place until he knew Manoli.

He returned to the garden to find that the evening had acquired a party atmosphere. People were moving about, intermingling. Bursts of laughter punctuated the flow of talk. Phil was apparently the only newcomer but was quickly assimilated as a familar. He fitted more names to faces. Joe and Ray were together. Ed and Nancy had just abandoned their respective legal mates on another island. So it went. As the sky had slowly darkened, lights had come on in trees. Phil had several more drinks and began to feel them agreeably. Two local women brought out food—not quite a meal but more substantial than the usual snacks—crisp fried slices of eggplant, a delectable concoction of bacon and melted cheese, shrimps, chunks of octopus, meatballs fragrant with herbs. Everybody ate heartily, cheating the restaurants out of most of their evening's customers, Phil suspected. The supply of food was replenished. Johnny told him that he'd begged out of the dinner with John Robert.

"Oh? Will I regret it?"

"On the contrary. He's very entertaining, but he only invited me to be polite. You're the audience he wants."

Phil switched to wine and went on drinking, knowing that at the level he'd reached he could drink all night without being bothered by it. Stably pissed, wide open to what was turning out to be a new experience. All these people made him feel that he'd led a very sheltered life, as Johnny had the first night. He'd even been sheltered from being queer for half his life, the working half. All his office associates kept up the fiction of his being straight. He went to a weekly poker game with a couple of guys from the editorial side, a couple from business, all married, all but one with kids. He played his part, going along with the jokes about being a carefree bachelor with a new dame every night. For a long time he had been neurotically cautious about being seen in places that would give him away—and he still felt more comfortable in private gatherings than in gay bars, even though it stood to reason that only gay men were apt to see him in gay bars. It was strange now not to give a damn who saw where he was, or what he did.

For the first time in his life, he was in the majority, not just in a bar but in a whole community. It changed his outlook on life. He felt very close to the strangers in the garden, even though they had escaped all the routine that he accepted as essential to survival. They didn't have to go to an office in the morning. They didn't have to work at any fixed time. They didn't have to cultivate good relations with people who might aid their advancement. Without going further, that was enough to make it unrecognizable to him as a way of life and, he suspected, posed a dangerous challenge. It would be easy to fall apart when offered such total freedom of choice.

As he wandered from group to group and helped himself to more wine, he realized that he'd already made his selection of people who interested or attracted him. The rest were just the extras, the bit players. That was another odd thing about this place: you didn't usually have the whole cast of characters presented to you at once, all lined up like merchandise for you to take your pick from. Usually you met people one at a time, discarding one, retaining another, until you had assembled your circle. This mass confrontation imposed a confrontation with himself, required an answer to the question he hadn't asked himself for a long time: Who am I? He had known once with George, but he had been so twisted and reshaped by his struggle for inner peace that he had become a stranger to himself. Here where everything was so new to him, so different, it seemed important to get back to whatever he really was.

"Has Don showed you the house?" Angela asked when he was once more in her pleasing presence.

"Yes. Amazing. Not at all what I would've expected. I mean, I guess he seems more the type for a villa on the Riviera."

"Exactly, but he'd have to be stinking rich to have anything like this on the Riviera. I've never really had a chance to look at this garden. It's quite beautiful."

They were wandering about hand in hand, in and out of light, finding unexpected little retreats and hideaways among the shrubbery within easy hailing distance of the other guests. "That must be the sea right there. Are people swimming yet?" Phil asked.

"Yes. We started a few days ago. There's a marvelous beach on the other side of town. You can go naked if you want. You look as if you ought to be naked always." Her hand moved lightly down over the front of his slacks, found his cock and closed around it. He'd been groped by women before, but even if it gave him exhibitionistic pleasure, it still offended what he supposed was his old-fashioned sense of morality. He'd been so outraged by his own behavior with Alex that he'd often wondered if he was more fastidious and prudish than he ought to be. He had come to the right place to find out.

He held himself very still, checking an impulse to pull away, to hide himself from her; with relief he felt his flesh stirring and swelling and in another second it became obvious that he wasn't going to be embarrassed by a failure of virility. With that question answered, he shifted on his feet to make himself more easily available and touched her arm to encourage her. She deftly maneuvered his burgeoning erection through the obstacles of clothing until it was free to find its own direction and stand upright. She held it firmly and moved her hand along its length with practiced assurance. "How sweet of it to do this for me," she said. "I haven't been able to take my eyes off it all evening. I don't know what makes it so irresistible. I'm spellbound by it. Turn a bit. There. Some light on the situation. Well, well, well. It looks as if it's going to pop right out the top."

"No such luck. It stops there."

"But it *is* rather big, isn't it?" She slipped the flat of her hand down behind elastic and ran her fingers around the head of his cock. "There, the naked you. Heavenly. So frustrating not to be able to look at it." He glanced over her shoulder in the direction of the house. Shadows moved around them, but he saw nobody and hoped they wouldn't be interrupted; once started he was sharing her enjoyment. She shaped the cloth around it and looked pleased with the effect. "Lucky man. Bryan's is quite handsome too, don't you think, or haven't you found out yet?"

Phil laughed. "Only what I can see with his pants on. I'm sure you're a good judge."

"Women generally are. Penis envy, I expect. I can't wait to see you two together."

"You really want me to go home with you?" he asked, adjusting himself in his trousers when she let go of him.

"Don't you want to? When we find somebody we like, we think we should make the most of it. We don't think marriage should become a closed circuit."

It was the sort of thing Alex used to say when he was being his most infuriatingly reasonable, but maybe here it did make some sense. He was willing to learn. Once more settled into his clothes, he put his hands on her arms and gave them a squeeze. "I'm such a novice. I just can't quite see how it'll work."

"Oh, well, that's up to you and Bryan, surely. He seems to think he knows what you two are after."

"He probably does. Guys often sense it." Their smiling eyes met in the half light and they slipped their arms around each other's waists and wandered back to the party.

Bryan was watching for them. From the depths of his chair, he gave them his curiously engaging straight-armed, skyward salute and slowly uncoiled himself. When he was on his feet, he put a hand on Phil's neck and drew him closer. "Unhand him, woman," he ordered Angela. He grinned at Phil. "Come on. Don asked me to bring a case of wine in from the back. I've drunk most of what there was so that's fair enough. I need help."

They encountered Don near the drinks table, which had also become a buffet. "You dear boys," he said with fussy gratitude when they paused for directions. "The box is just outside the kitchen door. If you can drag it into the dining room, we'll manage from there.''

They were passing the weapons collection when they caught each other's eye and stopped expectantly. They stood facing each other a few feet apart and smiled with understanding as their eyes questioned each other. Phil had the impression that Bryan grew more attractive every time he looked at him. The clever sophistication of his face overlaid an invincible boyishness. His tousled brown hair and wide, guileless mouth belonged to a farm boy. He was a mature, citified Huckleberry Finn. He looked progressively disheveled as the evening passed. His shirt was unbuttoned over the inconsequential scattering of hair on his chest. A shirttail was coming out of loose slacks that looked insecurely hitched around the slim hips. He had removed whatever he'd been wearing on his feet and stood barefoot on the tiles. His lanky body made clothes a pointless convention.

His smile broadened into an exultant grin as he planted his feet wide and thrust his hips out and pulled Phil in flat against him. He laid his hands on him, flat and firm, and moved them slowly back and forth on him, alternately smoothing him and mussing him up, over his hair and shoulders and chest while their cocks thrust up against each other. Phil was aware that his instantaneous erection owed nothing to encouraging caresses; Bryan's wanting him was enough.

Their hands pursued their pleasures. Bryan's clothes didn't interfere with Phil's finding out what the lean body felt like. Bryan continued a firm massage down his back to his buttocks and looked into Phil's eyes. "Like that?" he asked.

"Yes."

"You're bloody fantastic. We'll share a joint and fuck ourselves to death."

"It's the only way to go." They laughed and their mouths abandoned speech in favor of action. Bryan's was big and loose and devouring; Phil's participated enthusiastically. He had almost forgotten what carefree sex was like. He'd been drawn to Johnny more by the promise of friendship than by physical attraction. With Bryan, it was an exuberant outburst of mutual desire, simply satisfied. It was wonderful to feel his desire running free again, capable of relishing variety and choice.

In a moment Bryan was unconcernedly naked. The only two garments he'd been wearing, the slacks and shirt, seemed to drop off when Phil touched them, revealing a slim, agile boy's body with a disturbingly adult erection. Bryan pulled him behind a partly closed curtain into a sort of alcove. Phil was briefly startled by sensing eyes on him and then saw a big Oriental idol—a Buddha?—enshrined in the shadows against a wall. The illusion of privacy, regardless of their still being in full view of the room, was liberating. Phil had hated himself for giving in when Alex had goaded him into indulging in semipublic sex, but he was determined to forget Alex as a point of reference. If Bryan didn't care, what difference did it make if they got caught?

A convenient divan was waiting for them. Bryan fell back on it, pulling Phil to him, and guided his head while his body leaped and writhed with rapture. Phil, aware that he was competing with Angela, dedicated his mouth to Bryan's pleasure and quickly had him gasping and moaning ecstatically.

"Christ, I'm bloody coming," he cried out as Phil's mouth demonstrated the wide range of its capacities. "Jesus, you're fucking marvelous."

The throes of Bryan's gratifyingly convulsive orgasm subsided to the accompaniment of Phil's muffled laughter.

He kept Bryan's cock in his mouth and applied his ingenuity to reviving it after a brief slackening. There were times when he was almost grateful for his homosexuality. A cock was a wondrous device. Guys were so satisfying in their vivid and robust enjoyment of their own satisfaction. He was pleased that he had obviously proved a successful partner to a married man. A first as far as he knew. He chuckled as Bryan's cock stiffened into full erection.

"I'm a selfish bastard," Bryan said lazily, stroking Phil's hair. "I should be doing something for you."

"I don't want to be fucked to death here. I can wait."

"I couldn't, once you got started. You do it so beautifully that I thought you might want to see how easily you can give a guy a hard on." He sat up and ran a hand along Phil's erection. The fact that his fly was open was the only sign that Bryan had taken an active interest in his partner's body. He made a murmuring sound of approval. "Nice. If I know my Angie, I'm sure she was favorably impressed during your little stroll in the garden. She's an expert but you can't beat a fella like you. OK. I'll let go. I don't want Don to catch us. He gives me the creeps."

"What's the hang-up with the East?" Phil rearranged himself in his pants for the second time that evening.

"This is your friendly neighborhood opium den," Bryan remarked, looking up at the idol that loomed from the shadows with Oriental inscrutability. "I'll settle for the wholesome home-grown pot we can get at our place."

Don's gathering broke up soon afterwards. The night was getting chilly when Phil and the Shackletons headed back through silent streets in the general direction of the town Phil was beginning to feel familiar with. He thought they were about to come out on the port, but then they veered off and climbed briefly. They created an unstrained, light-hearted atmosphere together, and Phil liked them increasingly—although he still had some misgivings about what was coming next. He was prone to guilt, and sex unadorned with emotional content often struck him as squalid. He was careful to give each of them equal attention so that Angela wouldn't feel like the odd man out, but he was soon reassured that he didn't have to worry. The Shackletons were a close-knit team.

They entered a small walled courtyard and crossed to a low door. They ducked through, and after Angela snapped on a light, they blinked at each other and gathered together with a flurry of laughter.

"We've got you," Angela announced contentedly. "You've probably guessed what we're going to do with you."

Bryan dropped an arm around Phil's shoulders. "She never could keep a secret." He let go of Phil with a little hug and helped Angela get out wine and glasses. They were in a long, whitewashed, all-purpose room, sparsely furnished with kitchen tables and straight-backed chairs. Typewriters were on two of the tables, with stacks of tyepwriter paper beside them. A bigger round table had a bowl of oranges on it and chairs around it. There was a bed against one wall that evidently served as a sofa. It was an austere working space, and Phil was impressed by the people who found it sufficient for their needs.

"Here we go," Bryan said. "Grab a glass. And now you're going to sample our crop. It's the best stuff we've ever grown."

They went up a few steps to another whitewashed room, small and furnished primarily with a wide bed. Here in the confined space, proximity invited physical intimacy. They sprawled together on the bed, touching here and there, and their hands began to wander. By the time they had shared a couple of joints, the last remnants of Phil's reluctance had been drowned in giggles and his mouth was delighting in

Angela's lovely breasts. Clothes fell off at a touch. Phil and Bryan kept together over Angela while her hands caressed their erections and her tongue displayed its virtuosity.

Later, a fully formed coherent thought pierced the drugged mist of his mind. Could he let Bryan take him in front of Angela? He was straddling her, his cock cradled between her breasts when he felt Bryan move in behind him, pulling his chest back, Bryan's erection thrusting up against his buttocks. His mind rebelled briefly against his body's promptings but lost its grip as his body prevailed. He shouted with the ecstasy of Bryan's possession of him while Angela's hungry mouth awaited his orgasm.

He found himself washing with Bryan somewhere and then they were in bed once more. His body had come into its own and sang with the wonder of erotic release. His cock was a great tingling instrument of conquest. Angela lifted it upright from her belly and brushed her cheek against it.

"So lovely," she crooned. "It looks as if it would feel heavenly inside me, if you'd like to try."

"Try to stop me." He laughed lazily, disentangling himself from Bryan, and rolled up into her. His body was in such complete commmand that he gave no thought to the fact that Angela was only the second woman he had made love to in his life. Every body belonged to him. Angela's eyes widened as he thrust himself into her moist depths, as if she were looking in on herself and was entranced by what she saw.

"Oh Phil, yes," she murmured. She lifted her legs and gripped him with her knees. "It's sublime. No wonder I couldn't take my eyes off it. Yes. Oh yes, love. I'm going to come. Such a beautiful man."

Light was beginning to streak the sky when Phil reached home the next morning. He'd had a long night. The combination of wine and pot left him feeling a little fuzzy around the edges, but the unconventional proceedings had been a complete success.

He stumbled up the unfamiliar stairs in the half light, trying not to wake his new landlady's family and fell into the first bed he came to without bothering with the choice available. His mind whirled and slowed together with his breathing as his grateful body stretched out on the hard mattress. Sleep immediately began to fog his thoughts. He knew that he was launched on an adventure, that he had to be prepared for experiences unlike any in the past, but he couldn't quite remember what this conviction was based on. Something to do with Johnny? He would go see him as soon as he had some sleep.

When he next opened his eyes, bright blue sky was framed in the window. He lay without stirring, reassembling himself. He was in Greece. Crete, Chania. Everything fell into place. He stretched and discovered that he was still fully dressed, complete with sweater. It had been cold leaving the Shackletons this morning. Thinking of his time with them, he realized that he must have been fairly drunk, not to mention high; he didn't usually shed his inhibitions so effortlessly. Booze and pot and the air of Chania. Yes, there was something about the place, something he couldn't quite put his finger on but different from any place he'd ever been. It was just after eleven o'clock. He felt much better than he had any right to feel after six hours sleep.

He sat up, smiling to himself, and pulled the sweater off

over his head. It was going to be another beautiful day. He heard movement below and voices as he went to the room that had a toilet in it. He went on to the room with a basin and makeshift shower in it and only one bed. He put his clothes on the bed and hurried through his morning routine. He hoped to catch Johnny before he went out. He liked having a buddy to check in with. Another first. He also wanted to keep up-to-date on the cloak-and-dagger front.

He stood for a dutiful moment under the rusty shower head in the corner, letting the cold water revive his gratified lethargic body. He went to his balcony and decided that he needn't wear more than a T-shirt and shorts. He checked his money before pocketing it. He'd spent almost ten dollars since leaving Piraeus. A fortune already! Where did it all go?

Kyria Vassiliki stopped him in the stairway on his way out and wanted to know if he'd slept well and offered him breakfast of coffee-milk. He paused in her kitchen to have it, and she agreed to provide it regularly if that was all the breakfast he needed. He felt that he was getting his life organized like an experienced traveler.

He found Johnny standing in front of a canvas mounted on the easel, applying long, casual strokes with a brush. He waved the brush at him.

"The home wrecker," Johnny greeted him cheerfully. "Have you left the Aussies' marriage in ruins?"

"Whew. I don't think anybody could come between that pair. It's amazing. They break every rule I've ever heard of, and it seems to work a treat."

"You see? What did I tell you? Right and wrong—it all depends on the angle you look from."

"More immoral nonsense. You're a menace, Johnny. Still, I should probably make allowances for personal idiosyncrasies. If you're not in the grip of a consuming passion, maybe two people who really like each other shouldn't try to act as if they were in love.''

''Quite. Why do you suppose we Brits talk about being 'fond' of each other? That's quite enough to be going on with in everyday life. One can always indulge in a consuming passion from time to time as a change of pace, like a holiday.''

''Maybe we should get married, Johnny.''

''You're just after me for my money. Isn't it time for a brew?''

''I'll say. I've been up for half an hour. That's plenty long enough.''

''I was out early. I saw our friend with the mustache, but he didn't seem to pay any attention to me. All very peculiar. I decided I should say something to Andoni. The way I put it, I think I'll be hearing from our employers if there's anything we should know about.'' He picked up some keys from the table and left the easel to hand them to Phil. ''I had these made for you. This is for the ignition. This is the cabin.''

Phil took the keys hesitantly. ''For the boat? I wouldn't take her out without you.''

''No, not at first, but you might want to later. Anyway, it's a good idea to have an extra set.''

''Thanks. Now show me your work and we'll be in business.''

''Right you are. The nice thing about me is that I don't insist that you swoon with admiration. Just a polite nod to let me know you've looked will suffice.''

Johnny went to the canvases stacked against the wall and flipped several back to glance at them before selecting three which he pulled out and placed against the walls around the room, face out and at sufficient distance from each other so that they could be studied separately. He returned to Phil's side. "Those are the only three that are finished. I cleared everything out about a month ago."

A quick glance at the landscapes propped around the room prepared Phil to be more impressed than he'd expected, and a longer look confirmed the impression. The landscapes were the work of a skillful professional—boldly composed, figurative but executed with a subtle eccentricity of line that gave them originality, vibrant with an exuberant sense of color. Phil didn't consider himself an expert, but his job had involved looking at a lot of painting and he could tell the difference between the merely competent and the talented. He felt a funny surge of what seemed to be patriotic pride in Chania. Maybe the people here weren't just drifters but were really good at whatever they were doing.

"My God, you're a painter, Johnny," he exclaimed when he had completed his circuit of the canvases.

Johnny chuckled. "I like the subdued note of incredulity in your voice. Thanks, mate. Now that you've done your duty you deserve some refreshment. We'll go find out who's making the tongues wag this morning. You, I expect."

They strolled down to the port under a sun that was beginning to acquire a summer intensity. Johnny teased him about the Shackletons, but Phil switched him onto art. "I wasn't kidding, you know. I think you're damn good. Would you ever consider doing some illustrating?"

"For pay? I say, mate. Haven't I made it clear to you that I'll do almost anything for pay?"

"Wonderful. As soon as I get back I'll look for a book and let you know. Drawings, of course. We can't use much color." Phil was pleased at the prospect of maintaining a working contact with him. It would be a guarantee that the place still existed. He couldn't get over the sense of

unreality that had struck him on arrival, as if the whole
island might vanish the minute he left it—a dream, a
mirage, an accident in a time warp.

Johnny stopped as they turned from a narrow street that
climbed away up the hill. "While we're at it, I might as
well show you where John Robert lives." He pointed up
the street. "Up there. The house on the left with the tree
sticking up over the wall. There you are."

When they emerged from the back streets onto the port,
Phil grew more alert to the people they encountered. There
was no more activity than there had been the day before, a
few men and fewer women wandering here and there with
no apparent urgent business. He saw no conspicuous
mustaches. This wasn't a place where you could lose
yourself in the crowd. As they headed in the direction of
the little humped church, he saw that the chairs around the
long cafe table they'd commandeered yesterday were filling up, already giving the broad quay a small focal point
of festivity.

"Another party?" he asked.

"The daily ritual. They pick up their mail and come
along for a gossip. I have my mail delivered at the house
so I don't come down if the work's going well."

"You take your work seriously despite appearances,
don't you, Johnny?"

"It's a closely guarded secret," Johnny said with a
sardonic glance at him.

They dropped into chairs and were greeted casually. The
Shackletons caught Phil's eye and lifted their hands in
their odd stiff-armed salute. Phil waved to John Robert at
the end of the table. Opposite him, Anne, impeccable in
sweater and pearls, her graying hair carefully coiffed,
looked up from a letter and flourished it at him and
Johnny.

"I'm reading about the snow in London. Nothing makes me happier than hearing about other people's discomfort."

"It *is* fun, isn't it?" Johnny agreed. "Silly cows. Why does anybody stay there?"

Phil smiled at them. His friends. He realized that the midday party was fitting into a routine, a pleasant feature that would become something he looked forward to.

He felt a shift taking place in himself, from being a tourist, a sightseer, to becoming an inhabitant absorbed into a new life. For the first time, he was part of a small, close-knit community. He knew everybody and everybody knew him. Their pasts often remained obscure, but there were few secrets about their current hopes and hates and loves. With a few exceptions, it was safe to assume that everybody was trying to get by for as little money as possible, stretching out their stay. Self-imposed poverty made for economic equality. Phil had never known people who prided themselves on having no money to spare, where sponging became a point of honor. Don was a natural target, and he was valued accordingly. Phil was beginning to get the hang of life here, but he knew this wasn't the kind of life he could lead for long. He had no illusions about his creative gifts; he had none that he could turn into an occupation here and he'd be lost without one. He envied the others' singleminded determination to indulge their individual whims. At least in Johnny's case it was justified.

He had more beer. He talked to everybody. He ate something without paying any attention to the time. He got into a wide-ranging discussion of films with Harvey Feldman. Like most of them, Harvey was about Phil's age, very bright, with a Jewish act he discarded at will. He'd worked in Hollywood and was writing a screenplay for which he had some sort of contract.

When their conversation had run its course, Phil found that his chums had all gone. Don was still there, looking as if he were ready to pounce. Phil made his getaway and wandered off to explore on his own. He discovered a superb sweep of beach beyond the port, presumably the beach the Shackletons had mentioned. It was very wide, maybe as much as a hundred yards, bordered by low-lying farmland dotted with olive trees. Staying close to the water, he couldn't identify the crops but the fields were a pale, tender green with early spring growth. In all the great expanse of sea and sky and sand, he could see only a few figures in the far distance and, much closer, a single body stretched out on the beach. When he got closer, he saw that it was the Frenchman, François, stark naked. He sat up at Phil's approach and greeted him cordially. He reported that the water was still very cold. He explained that he was waiting for a boy from one of the farms behind them who often joined him, and invited Phil to sit. François' naked body was very nice, but it was without sex appeal.

Phil excused himself and went on. After a few minutes, he saw something sticking out of the sand ahead of him, like a broken fence. When he reached it, he saw that it was the fragmentary remains of some sort of shed, maybe a shelter for a boat. Only a few posts were still standing with weathered and splintered planks nailed across them, almost as high as his head—a flimsy wall four or five feet long that had served as a billboard. The planks were encrusted with the tattered remnants of posters that no longer conveyed any coherent message. A convenient landmark useful for hanging up his clothes. He used it accordingly, stripping off his T-shirt and shorts, and, without bothering to change into his swimming trunks, ran down to the sea in his jockey shorts and dived in.

It was cold, bracing more than painful. He swam hard

until he was warm and filled with such profound physical contentment that thought was almost suspended, leaving a warm glow that was closer to feeling than thought, the glow of a deep consciousness of George. He couldn't reach this peak of perfect physical balance and well-being without activating the associations with George that had burrowed into his bones. He had felt like this only with George, or alone. Anybody else spoiled it. Being here alone, cut off from everything he'd known in the past, made him miss George acutely.

Damn George—George, his schoolboy hero, the school's champion athlete and all-around star, two years ahead of him, a remote, glamorous figure with whom he had been incapable of exchanging more than mumbled monosyllables, shy and struck dumb by awe. Whenever he had been naked in the showers near him, he always felt as if his knees were about to give way. George had a superb body and his good looks were unusally distinguished, not in a wholesome all-American-boy way but fine-featured, with big intelligent eyes and a quiet, devastating smile. It was a lean, swift face with strongly marked cheekbones and a firmly modeled but gentle mouth. Phil worshiped him from afar, not yet sufficiently aware of the abhorrent abnormality called homosexuality to fear that he might be tainted by it.

When George graduated and went on to college in the normal course of scholastic events, Phil set out to match his high school record and, in terms of honors and awards, he pretty much succeeded but he'd been uneasily aware of his flaws as a school leader. There was the matter of the basement, for one thing. He couldn't imagine George ever going to the basement, not that it had really amounted to much. It had started when Phil was sixteen and George was having his last months of glory before graduation.

One spring afternoon a classmate of Phil's suggested going to the basement. The secretive air with which he made the proposal made Phil think that it was something he was expected to know about, so he couldn't admit ignorance. He went.

There was a spacious closet in the basement used for storing cleaning materials. He soon learned that it was never locked. Led by his friend, they entered it, leaving the door slightly ajar for light. When he felt his friend's hand on his cock, he followed his example and they jerked each other off into their handkerchiefs. It was astonishing but not disagreeable. It was Phil's induction into a clandestine network; other invitations followed. He was plagued that spring by dreams of going to the basement with George.

Basement sport resumed in the fall, and Phil found himself eventually chosen as a partner by almost half his classmates. With so many participating, he couldn't think of it as anything strange or outlawed. It was just something that guys did at school. He had the satisfaction of discovering that his cock was a bit bigger than many and more or less the equal of others. A few surpassed him but only one was notably bigger. Several guys had told him about Baldwin's before he had a chance to check for himself. It was huge.

They all joked and boasted about their equipment so he didn't think there was anything special about his undeniable interest in size. It was an exclusively male preoccupation not shared by girls. He despised any sign of effeminacy in his classmates.

In his last year, with all of them verging on manhood, Phil began to have qualms about the basement. He caught himself imagining more elaborate play with his favorites, without the impediment of clothes, and he wondered what he would do if any suggested finding somewhere more private so that they would have more scope to experiment. He could no longer close his mind to the implications of homosexuality. It was a word that suddenly seemed to come at him from every direction and he had no intention of becoming a freak.

Mostly, what he heard was reassuring. There were degrees of perversion. He gathered that kids often fooled around with each other without turning into homosexuals— which relieved his lingering guilt about Teddy. Teddy had been his introduction to sex, and they had done things— sucked cock and fucked each other—that only outright queers did. But that had been almost five years before when they had been practically children and they had thought of it as a great joke. What happened in the basement was only a companiable way of getting your rocks off.

All the same, Phil kept a firm check on his thoughts when he caught them straying into dangerous territory, and he assured himself that if any of his partners tried to embellish their routine in tempting ways he would turn them down. He almost turned down Ricky Tellerman when he belatedly proposed a visit to the basement. With only a couple of months of school left, he thought he'd tried it with everybody who was interested, but he'd been told before Christmas that Tellerman had a really big one and curiosity got the better of him.

He was slightly in awe of Tellerman. He was the class intellectual, not bad in the shower—tall and slim and quite good-looking in a sort of scholarly way—but with an aloof manner that seemed to put him above secret schoolboy games. Phil was on edge as they started down to the utility closet, wondering why he hadn't suggested it sooner. Maybe Ricky was shy despite his superior air. Or maybe he'd been waiting for an invitation even though Phil had never made the first move. He liked to be sure a guy was interested.

The evidence was conclusive that Ricky was. Phil was jolted by Ricky's cock. It wasn't the equal of Baldwin's but when he put his hand on it, it sent a shiver of pleasure down his spine. Phil edged Ricky around so that light from the door fell on it. Phil watched, transfixed, his hand moving on a prodigy of male power. The lift and thrust of it made his breath catch in his throat, and his chest labored. It seemed to him a waste of it that they were only going to jerk each other off, but he didn't allow himself to imagine what else they might do. Memories of Teddy were childhood memories and had no relevance to grown men. He tried to make the services of his hand memorable and was excited to feel a special lingering acknowledgment of him in Ricky. They were making some sort of connection.

Phil was scrupulously determined not to take the initiative, but Ricky apparently felt their having connected too and after a few days suggested a second visit. By the time barely a month of school was left, their visits had become a habit and Phil felt it necessary to assure himself constantly that these were no different from all the others. He was spellbound by Ricky's prodigious cock, but he was sure any guy would be. You couldn't ignore it—it was pretty damn flattering to see all that standing up for you. All his training had been closely intertwined with a cult of virility. The emphasis on athletic prowess, the constant systematic development of his body, the ideals of clean living and celibacy and the mild contempt for an effeminate interest in the arts—all contributed to the segregation of the sexes and made him very aware of his manhood. How could he help being stirred by conspicuous concentrated masculinity? It had nothing to do with homosexuality.

Phil and Ricky didn't become close friends in the usual

ways—joining each other between classes, kidding around, sharing interests—but on one of their first visits, Ricky took Phil's hand as they were going downstairs and held it, squeezing it gently, caressing it while they started along the passage to the closet. It was the most vividly erotic moment Phil had ever experienced. His heart raced and he lurched against his companion to steady himself.

After that, they introduced tiny modifications to their touching, modifications that were hardly noticeable but as momentous as if they'd torn each other's clothes off and grappled naked together. Ricky opened Phil's pants to expose him completely, using his hands more freely than was absolutely necessary to achieve their ostensible goal. They stood close together with their foreheads resting against each other. At times Ricky brushed his lips against the side of Phil's face in a faint suggestion of a kiss. Without admitting it to himself, Phil longed for more. He was discovering that his body offered admission to an unknown world of emotion, frightening but irresistible.

He had never cared much who he went to the basement with; now increasingly he wanted it to be Ricky. Ricky touched him with intimations of unexplored love and passion. His imagination grew more unmanageable. He struggled to keep details blurred, but he longed to lie naked in bed with Ricky. Despite his efforts at suppression, somewhere in the back of his mind an image persisted of Ricky and him joining their bodies to each other, of Ricky entering him and taking possession of him. The moment of inexplicable ecstasy with Teddy returned to haunt him. He wished there was some way to find out if everybody had obsessive thoughts about big cocks. It was silly to be upset by his thoughts if they were perfectly normal. School was almost over and he probably wouldn't think of Ricky again.

As if to herald the release from drudgery, summer came in with a rush. Everybody shed jackets and ties and switched to cotton pants. The sudden heat lulled Phil's body into a delicious sensuous languor. Now that he would no longer be in training to be the champion of everything, he had to find a girl. He wanted to make love, really, at last.

When Ricky offered himself once more as a substitute, he accepted with alacrity and had a hard on almost before saying "Let's go." He supposed Ricky felt Phil's readiness because his hands were busy with Phil's scanty clothes the minute they entered the closet. Phil barely had time to register that Ricky was stripping him when they were both practically naked with their slacks and shorts around their knees. Ricky's touch as his hands moved over him was electric with desire; this was the way it felt when a guy wanted him.

Phil imitated Ricky, giving what he'd been given, while blissful sensations raced through him. He was being allowed the intimacy of finding out what a guy really felt like, and he realized with a shock that this was his introduction to adult lovemaking. His heart began to thud with dread. He couldn't make love with a guy. They moved closer to each other and Ricky nuzzled his neck. He felt Ricky's tongue on him. He instinctively lifted his arms and put them around Ricky. They locked themselves together, Ricky's big cock thrust up hard against him. Their mouths somehow found each other and opened to admit their plunging tongues, and their bodies writhed to achieve the illusion of union. Phil whimpered with longing while he told himself that only queers could do what they were doing. He had to stop. He wasn't a queer. He wouldn't be able to go on living if he let himself become a queer. He had to get control of himself.

They broke apart with a gasping breath and Ricky began to move his mouth down slowly over Phil, nibbling his nipples, his tongue a flickering, darting provocation. Phil stroked Ricky's hair, assuring himself that he would call a halt to things even while involuntary little moans of delight escaped him. Ricky's mouth continued its downward progress, finding places where it aroused an almost unbearable erotic clamor. Phil was helpless in the face of Ricky's power to excite him. His muscles tensed and his heart hammered as Ricky's lips and tongue moved along his cock. He thought his legs were going to give way. He stifled a cry as he felt himself entering the exquisitely smooth shelter of Ricky's mouth. He melted with ecstasy while his reeling mind tried to grapple with what was happening to him.

Incredulity paralyzed him. A guy was sucking his cock. He was submitting to the most loathsome act a guy could perform. Ricky was a queer. He waited for revulsion to stir his resistance but his body was gripped by a sublime inertia. He had never felt every particle of it so charged with sensual gratification. He remembered one of the guys—Samuelson?—boasting about letting a queer give him a blow-job in New York. Everybody knew Samuelson had a girl. You didn't have to be queer to let a queer give you pleasure. A question of degree.

He looked down at Ricky as he crouched in front of him in an attitude of adoration, his mouth open wide to welcome his cock, the light permitting glimpses of the great shaft that rose from his groin. It was a vile and abject act but Phil's chest swelled with a sense of his own male power, and he was aware of orgasm pounding up in him. He didn't know if he was supposed to warn Ricky but he wanted to come in his mouth. It built up in him until he felt it was going to rip him apart. He shouted when it struck, forgetting caution, and was almost knocked off his feet. His sight dimmed. When he could see again, Ricky was still there, his mouth working hungrily as if he didn't want to lose a drop of him. How could a guy who seemed perfectly OK be queer?

Ricky relinquished him finally and sprang up. He threw his arms around him and turned him so that he could press himself against his back. He thrust his cock between Phil's thighs under his buttocks and slid it slowly back and forth to let Phil feel its amazing length. Phil worked his muscles to grip him and make it exciting for him. Naturally his partner expected some reciprocation, but Phil dreaded doing the thing Ricky had. Phil dropped his head back and gratefully kissed his chin and neck, swaying with the rhythmic movement of Ricky's simulated copulation, making it feel as much as possible as if Ricky had entered him. It was a thrilling novelty, almost like being joined to him but without doing anything really queer.

"Your body is fantastic," Ricky whispered against his ear. His hands roamed over the front of him as if he wanted to memorize every contour of him. "I've never wanted anybody so much. We've got to go to bed together. I hate it down here. That's why I didn't suggest it sooner. We can't really make love. I want to be in you. You want it too. You're beautifully hard again."

"We can't do it here," Phil whispered, stunned that Ricky seemed to take it for granted that it was something they might do. He exerted pressures to help him reach his climax.

"We'll find a place as soon as school is over. Only four more days. We shouldn't come here again. It'll drive us crazy. All the guys just want to jerk off but I knew right off with you that we could really have something. Oh Jesus, I'm about to come. God, baby, feel my cock. Feel how hard it is. It should be inside you where we both want it. I'm going to fuck you next time. You're the most beautiful guy I've ever seen. You're going to be mine.''

Phil was profoundly shaken. He stumbled blindly through the rest of the day, unable to stop thinking of Ricky. The balmy air continued to lull his senses and seemed to mock him. It was a day for making love, not for being gnawed by guilt. Why guilt? Ricky was a cocksucker. He wasn't and never would be. He had been swept off his feet by a homosexual but he knew now and wouldn't let it happen again. His cheeks burned with shame. A guy had called him baby as if he were talking to a girl. It had made him quiver with delight but that was because it had taken him so by surprise. He hadn't realized that homosexuals could look like everybody else. He couldn't believe he'd gone so far with one. He should be disgusted by him and not having to wonder if he had the strength to resist the next time. The great cock remained in potent possession of his imagination.

He couldn't understand why homosexuality existed. He didn't care if it was wrong. It was senseless. The world was filled with men and women who were made for each other. Why should a guy want another guy? It was like a faulty cog in the works, something to put right. He had plenty of faults but so did everybody else and if you knew what they were, you tried to correct them and overcome your weaknesses. If Ricky thought he was different from the other guys, maybe he had a weakness he was just finding out about. He had tried to avoid thinking about homosexuality because it was too weird to figure out but a temptation might be concealed in it that he should watch out for. He knew how to resist temptation. Self-control had been drummed into him all his life.

When he got to bed that night after a family evening

with his sisters, he felt that life had resumed its normal pattern around him. The next day, Ricky found him to tell him that he'd thought a lot about it but couldn't risk taking him home; was there any chance of their being together at his place? Thinking of his sisters, Phil said no. He couldn't believe that this nice-looking guy had sucked his cock. Phil blushed hotly while they talked.

"I'd rather wait than go down there again, wouldn't you? Don't worry. I'll think of something. I'll call you," Ricky concluded, suspending relations till after school ended.

A couple of weeks passed before he called to say that things were all set, but by then Phil had pushed the episode so firmly into the back of his mind that he couldn't understand why anything about it had seemed important. He made an excuse but took the trouble to sound as if he was full of regret. He didn't want to hurt Ricky.

He had started paying more attention to girls without finding any that he was ready to get deeply involved with. When he imagined being naked with one or the other of them, he was overcome with panic. Sex had always come so easily and casually but all that was over. He resolved that if he found any form of the basement games going on at college he wouldn't have anything to do with them. Girls seemed to make sex forbiddingly complicated, but he would eventually find one who would spur him on to make the effort. Maybe she would suck his cock. If Teddy was to be trusted, girls often liked it. He was glad he'd found out what it felt like even though he would never let a guy do it to him again.

I n his first freshman months at Ann Arbor, his resolution wasn't tested and he went home for Christmas feeling virtuous. For the first time in a couple of years, he'd gone for almost six months without sex. He had finally put childish vices behind him.

His vacation began with bitter Michigan weather and he stopped at a bar on Main Street late on his first afternoon to warm up for the slog home. The first person he saw was George. He hadn't encountered him since George had left school and wasn't sure if George remembered him, so he avoided him and went to the end of the bar and ordered a beer.

Phil couldn't keep his eyes off him. He was more superb than ever and appeared to be alone, although Phil assumed that he wouldn't be for long. George couldn't look much more perfect than he had before, but now Phil was struck by the changes in himself that two years had brought about. He had always felt like a puny kid compared to Geroge, but he didn't any more. They were of about equal height and Phil's body looked as substantial as George's in their bulky winter clothes, but Phil knew he'd never have George's special physical sleekness and opulence, the quality that in the showers had made Phil's knees go weak.

George was a rich boy and looked it. He was the only child of a big dairy farmer and had always dressed beautifully. Now, instead of a beat-up windbreaker like Phil's, he was wearing a short winter coat with a fur collar, perfectly tailored slacks and handsome boots. He looked like a fashion illustration for winter sports. Phil felt the old awe creeping over him.

The bar was busy enough so that Phil didn't think George would notice him. He sipped the beer and stared from a safe distance. George turned unexpectedly and caught him off guard. As their eyes met, there was an instant of blind, naked communication and then George's face lighted up with recognition. Phil's heart was pounding.

"My God," George exclaimed as he advanced along the bar to him. "It's Renfield. Hi there. Sure, I remember. You're Phil. Remember me?"

"Of course." Throwing his arms around him would have been the only way Phil could have expressed his gratitude for the warmth of George's greeting. He took refuge in polite formality.

"This is great. Let me look at you." George gripped his arms and stepped back. "Terrific. You're not a kid any more but you still have those bedroom eyes. Just like Rudolph Valentino. I heard you were breaking all my records at school this year. I wondered when I was ever going to run into you. It's about time."

"I didn't think you'd recognize me." He was flustered and flattered and hoped he wouldn't be struck dumb again. The grip of George's hands had given him an erection.

"That'll be the day." He let go of him and moved in close beside him at the bar with a hand resting on his back where his windbreaker stopped, just above his buttocks. "I always wanted to get to know you, but you know how it was at school. You couldn't have anything to do with anybody who wasn't in your class. That's all changed now. You're at Ann Arbor, aren't you? I'm at Yale."

"Yes, I heard."

"Well, we're free, white and twenty-one. I guess you're *not* twenty-one yet, are you?"

"No, nineteen."

"Nineteen. Twenty-one. That's no difference. We can be friends at last. I hope you're as glad to see me as I am to see you."

"Of course." Phil wanted to tell him that he was happier than he'd ever been in his life. His saying that they were going to be friends overwhelmed him. He felt George's hand move with a slight caress on the small of his back, slipping lower. Phil's erection felt permanent. Would George still want to be friends if he knew? It didn't mean anything; it was just part of his sudden all-engulfing sense of well-being. The world was a wonderful place.

"I know what," George said, giving his back a slight pat. "Let's finish these beers and go home where we can be comfortable and really talk. Do you have a car? No problem. I'll drive you out and bring you back whenever you want. It's only five. How about that?"

"I'd love to," Phil agreed, thinking it the most miraculous suggestion he'd ever heard.

"Great. I'll pay." They drained their glasses and Phil put his hands in his pockets to make sure nothing showed while George gave the bartender a dollar. He took Phil's arm and headed him for the door. There was a flurry of arrivals and departures as they reached it, slowing traffic. Hemmed in by a knot of people, George quickly ran his hand over Phil's bottom and gave his buttocks a squeeze. "God, what a beautiful ass," he murmured, close to Phil's ear.

Phil's knees almost buckled. He reminded himself frantically that he was a man now, not a mixed-up schoolboy. He welcomed the suspension of thought as the cold hit them outside. They almost ran through the busy street to George's car. Phil noted that it was a Thunderbird as he dropped into the leather seat.

"Wow, it's cold," George exclaimed as he climbed in beside him. "A real ball-freezer. We'll have some heat in a second."

They were held up by Christmas shoppers in Newcomers's few commerical blocks, and Phil failed to steer his thoughts away from the look they exchanged in the instant before they'd spoken. He had never known anything like it. He was learning that eyes often said more than words and suspected that George's had been intensely revealing, but nothing in his experience helped him interpret what he'd seen in them. His imagination was probably working overtime; he apparently still hadn't quite gotten it under control. The pat on his behind, the remark about his ass—that was routine kidding around. Why make something of the look?

As they reached the residential district, George accelerated and settled back in the seat. "Here we are together finally. I'm so damn pleased it's happened. I knew it had to, but I was beginning to wonder how long we had to wait. I always felt there was something between us. Do you know what I mean?"

They passed Phil's house, but he didn't see it. "Well, sure. You were always my hero."

"Some hero." George gave a little snort of laughter and pulled off his expensive-looking fur-lined gloves. "I don't need those any more." A somber note crept into his voice. "I guess you know I was starting to cruise you before I saw who it was. That's the way it is. You understand, don't you?"

Phil didn't but supposed it had something to do with the look they had exchanged. He had heard guys talking about cruising girls for sex, but George obviously meant something else. What? He didn't want to close the door on any possibility so he chose his words carefully, making them as noncommittal as possible. "I couldn't take my eyes off you, wondering if you'd see me."

"I couldn't very well help it. You were the only one there worth looking at. I've always thought that, only more so now." He dropped a hand on Phil's knee and exerted a small pressure. "It's all right? I mean, it's the same with you? God, the way you used to look at me. I was wildly jealous when I heard about your little visits to the basement.''

Phil blushed hotly, stunned by the reference. ''Oh, well, that was just—'' he managed before his voice failed him.

''Sure. I know. Same here. I sure as hell thought often enough about us going there together. We used to go in for cock contests too—getting each other hard and measuring to see whose was the biggest. Modesty doesn't allow me to tell you who always won.'' He chuckled and returned his hand to the wheel. ''We used to talk about you younger kids. Everybody agreed that you had the sexiest ass in the world, much better than a girl. It was all just kid stuff, but it was more fun than anything else at school. I soon found out that there were better places than the basement for what I wanted. I guess you did too. Have you got a girl?''

Phil's head was reeling with these intimate revelations. He pulled himself together to reply. ''No, not really. I'm not going steady.''

''I'm in luck. Maybe you'll have some time for me.''

''Of course. Anytime.''

''How about tonight?''

''Tonight?''

''You could have something to eat with me and spend the night. My folks won't be home. You want to?''

''My God, do I ever. I'll call home when we get to your place.''

''Wonderful. We'll be there in a minute and then we'll have all night together. God, I'm glad I found you.'' He replaced his hand on Phil's knee and pulled him closer. He left his hand where it was, allowing his long, strong fingers to stray about deliciously on the inside of his thigh. For a moment, Phil was afraid that he was going to come, but he thought of his call to his mother and ecstasy receded.

He knew his mother was planning a welcome-home dinner with his sisters, but that couldn't be helped. He needed some time to find out what this was all about so that he could settle down into the friend George wanted him to be. His mind floundered in a sea of confusion. George seemed to be telling him things he was failing to grasp. Like the look. Phil felt something sexual simmering beneath the surface but he couldn't pin it down. He looked at the hand on his knee. If anything like this had happened last spring with one of his basement buddies they would have been holding each other's cocks by now. George had dismissed the basement games as "kid stuff," but the only thing Phil knew about was kid stuff.

Except Ricky. Ricky had been a warning. He was beginning to think that maybe Teddy had been a warning too, but as far as he knew Teddy hadn't turned into a queer. There was nothing abnormal about George. He was a paragon of masculine virtue, if maybe not the plaster saint he had imagined. Chaotically troubling thoughts tumbled through his mind as his imagination replaced Teddy with George. His heart was racing. He was imagining the unimaginable.

He had been fourteen, Teddy about a year older, the summer when Phil had gone to spend a week with him on the farm. When his elders had proposed the visit he'd protested that Teddy would think he was too young for him but their parents were friends and it suited their plans.

Actually, he liked Teddy. He was a lively, bumptious guy with an impish face, given to extravagant enthusiasms and outrageous pranks. "Saucy," the old Irishwoman who cooked for them called him. They were both tall for their age and going through a transitional phase when various parts of them didn't appear to fit others. Phil discovered on the first night that Teddy's latest enthusiasm was sex.

He jumped into bed with him, challenging him to a tickling match that soon had them both more or less out of their pajamas. At one moment they were fighting each other off. The next they were locked in each other's arms having orgasms against each other's bellies. It was Phil's first sex with a partner. As the extraordinary sensation passed, he was appalled, prepared for divine retribution, but Teddy laughed contentedly.

"I guess we made a mess. Let's wash up. I want to try things."

By the time they'd washed and dried each other thoroughly, they were hard again. Teddy had a man-sized cock, bigger than Phil's. As Phil understood it, all cocks were the same size and he assumed that his would grow later. Teddy brought a jar of Vaseline back to bed with them. He turned Phil onto his side with his back to him and began to apply Vaseline between his buttocks.

"Hey, what's going on?" Phil protested, starting to pull away. Teddy held him.

"What's the matter? I want to fuck you. You've got to use something. You can do it to me in a minute. We'll take turns. I've heard this is the way guys do it with each other."

Phil hadn't heard that guys did it with each other in any way, but he was ready to learn. It hurt at first but it was much easier than he'd expected. When Teddy was all the way in him, on top of him, pumping rapidly in and out of him, he felt a closeness between them that he'd never known with another human being. Teddy seemed to provide a link with humanity that had been missing before. Phil felt less alien in a world that seemed somehow less mysterious.

"Yeah, that's really hot stuff," Teddy said when the agitations of his body had ceased. "You've got to try it. I'll bet it's really something with a girl." When they'd washed again and reversed positions, Phil no longer felt the closeness. On the contrary, Teddy seemed diminished in some way. Phil was taking something away from him, making him less of a friend. It didn't feel right. They did it a lot in the next few days, but by mutual unspoken consent they didn't take turns again.

Phil thought of it more as an anatomical exercise than sex. They were finding out what their bodies could do, practicing for the inevitable, unimaginable confrontation with a girl, but when Teddy was in him he found himself hoping that he could make it good enough so that Teddy wouldn't think about girls.

The weather was glorious and they swam regularly in the small river that ran through the extensive property. They had to clamber down a steep bank to get to it. The bank was fringed by trees and brush that screened them from above, so they always swam naked, frequently with erections which brought on Teddy's irrepressible giggles.

"You want to suck my cock?" he asked one afternoon lying with Phil beside the sluggish stream after several nights of anatomical exercises had made them familiar with one another's bodies.

"Of course not. Why should I? You pee with it."

"I do more than that with it, you dimwit. Try it. I've heard girls do it. I want to find out what it feels like. Here. I'll do it for you." He rolled over to Phil and showed him what he was talking about. For an incredible moment, Phil lost all sense of identity with his own body. It couldn't be his cock that was generating these stunning sensations in him. He thought he was going to burst. He resumed possession of his body as it was suddenly gripped by impending orgasm.

"Hey. Watch it," he cried. "I'm about to come."

Teddy lifted his head, laughing gleefully. "It's pretty good, hunh? Now you can show me."

He lay back and urged Phil down over him. Phil imitated his nutty friend's performance. He didn't particularly want to do it, but he didn't mind it as much as he thought he might. Putting this private part of Teddy in his mouth added to the closeness he felt when it was in him the other way. He'd never imagined having a friend he could do things like this with.

"Gosh, it feels good, doesn't it?" Teddy said contentedly. "Open your mouth wider so I don't feel your teeth. That's it. I guess my cock is pretty big for you. Yeah, that must be the way you're supposed to do it. I can't wait for a girl to do it. It certainly makes you want to come quickly."

He reached for Phil and pulled him up and held him in his arms. He looked at him with unfamiliarly soft, dreaming eyes. "I love finding out all this stuff with you. You have a great build, but you're pretty enough to make me forget you're a guy. I want to kiss you. How about it?"

"Well, sure. I guess it's OK." Phil didn't know why kissing was supposed to be such a big deal. The brief touching of faces wasn't nearly as exciting as the other things they'd done. He let Teddy draw his head to him and their mouths met. Phil's lips were closed as he started to pull back, but Teddy held him and parted them with his tongue and thrust it between them. Again his body ceased to belong to him as he was bombarded by sensations that he didn't know it was capable of producing. Their mouths opened to each other and their tongues plunged about together. Their bodies began to move and thrash about, and they were no longer wrestling playfully but engaged in a contest to arouse and provoke each other. Teddy's mouth was everywhere on him. Phil was overwhelmed by an ecstatic cataclysm that he hardly recognized as orgasm. His shattered body was limp with a longing to offer himself. Teddy entered him, but this was different from the other times. The way Teddy held him and moved in him made him feel cherished and wanted as he had never been before. Teddy wasn't just trying to make himself come but was leading him on an adventure of shared discovery. Phil seemed to be soaring. He was being lifted out of himself into an ecstatic world that he hadn't known existed. He was sure that what they were doing was called making love, even though he knew that it was impossible for two guys to make love together.

When they splashed into the river to wash and cool off, Teddy was as cocky and prankish as ever. "Boy, we sure have fun together, don't we?" he said, grinning naughtily at him.

"I'll say," Phil agreed, averting his eyes. He was sure it had been much more than that but was shy about the sense of revelation it had left in him.

During the rest of his visit, they did all the things they had learned to do, with refinements and embellishments, but they never recaptured the moment of magical discovery that Phil had experienced beside the river. He held back when he began to feel that he wanted it more than Teddy did. After a few days, he decided that he'd imagined most of it. Guys couldn't want each other in the special way he had felt briefly with Teddy, and he supposed that he had responded so intensely because he had never felt any real warmth and closeness at home. He didn't have a brother and his kid sisters were silly nuisances rather than companions. His father spoiled and favored them, which didn't help.

The visit left him with an enormous prohibition. He didn't understand it, but in spite of his reasoning he knew that there was something in him that mustn't be allowed to surface again. The idea of making love with a guy was ridiculous. It couldn't have any hidden rewards; it was only substitute sex until he was old enough to get girls, just as Teddy said. If there was more to it than that, a darker side, he didn't dwell on it. His life wasn't geared to introspection. He would soon be back at school where he was popular and good at sports and determined to excel. What more was there to think about? At the time, he had never heard of homosexuality.

The next time he saw Teddy, his older friend had started with girls and no reference was made to their forbidden foolishness. When the basement eventually entered his life, he didn't see it as a link with the past. Most of the time he successfully forgot that Teddy had ever existed.

Looking at George's hand on his knee now, he remembered more vividly than he wanted to. The big difference was that he and George were grown-ups. To imagine their doing the things he'd done with Teddy would be pushing fantasy to the limits of the impossible. Whatever ambiguity he felt in George must be in himself. He had to straighten himself out. He'd renounced basement games. He wasn't going to disgrace himself for the sake of a romantic infatuation with his schoolboy hero. He wished his erection would go away.

To his relief, George removed his hand after slipping it under his knee and giving him a squeeze. Phil saw that they were running along the neat white fence that enclosed the extensive acres of the Hudderstone dairy farm. He'd passed it a thousand times wishing that he'd be invited inside.

"Here we are," George said. "You look as if you've been having deep thoughts."

"Not very deep. Just surprised to be here with you."

"I remember that about you. Whenever I spoke to you, you looked as if you were solving the riddles of the universe."

"Just shy, I guess."

"You're not going to be shy any more. I want to hear all about the universe. All about you too. Maybe that amounts to the same thing."

They drove a few more minutes and then George turned in through a gate. The drive curved up for several hundred yards to a big colonial-style house set in trees whose bare branches were silhouetted against the darkening sky. Picture-book farm buildings stood on a rise some distance beyond it. George drove past the front of the brightly lighted house and pulled into the attached garage. There were a couple of cars in it, with room for more. He switched off the motor and leaned back.

"Here we are. This is a pretty momentous occasion." He put an arm around Phil's shoulders and hugged him. "Let's make a dash for it. It's cold."

They ran back along a brick walk to the front door, and George let them into a wide hall. Big rooms opened off it; Phil had an impression of fine furniture and great luxury. George tossed his coat onto a chair and Phil dropped his windbeaker on top of it. George grabbed his arm and hurried him up a curving staircase. They followed a corridor with doors opening off it. George stopped at one of them and led him into a room. "The guest room," he said.

Phil took in twin beds and bright fabric. "Nice," he said.

"I hope you like mine better. That's where I want you, in bed with me. You're not a guest. We belong together."

"It sounds find with me," Phil managed with some difficulty.

"That's what I like about you. You agree to anything I suggest. Don't start saying no."

"To what?"

George looked into his eyes and smiled. "Anything." He stepped close to him and held his elbows and joined their mouths lightly. Phil felt his tongue on his lips and struggled against an impulse to open his mouth and let himself go the way he had with Teddy and Ricky, but George was a grown man and George wasn't queer. He was probably just teasing him. Phil had to make it clear that he wasn't queer either. A tumult of terror and desire raged in him. George let him go with a laugh. "Come on. I'll show you our love nest."

They entered a big room at the end of the corridor, comfortably furnished like a living room except for the big double bed. One wall was largely taken up with a fireplace with armchairs on both sides of it and a big leather hassock on the floor in front of it. George closed the door behind them and Phil heard the key turn in the lock. "I'm going to make a fire. You want to call home? Here." He put the flat of his hand on his back and let it slide down to his behind as he guided him to the head of the bed. It was the first intercom telephone Phil had ever seen in a private house.

"You push this button and then just dial your number," George explained. He left him to cope with his mother's disappointment. Phil turned his back and kept his voice low while he explained with irrepressible pride that he was with George Hudderstone and that they had important matters to discuss that couldn't be postponed. He submitted to her reproaches, which had the welcome effect of subduing his erection. He agreed that he was deeply disappointed too and hung up.

George was crouched in front of the fireplace. In a moment he stood and turned, beaming infectiously, flames beginning to leap behind him. "That feels good. We can get rid of some clothes." He peeled off his expensive cashmere sweater over his head, leaving his hair boyishly ruffled. It was beautiful hair, chestnut, with a slight crisp wave that shaped his head like sculpture. "Making love in front of an open fire is my idea of heaven," he said. "Can you think of anything more exciting?"

"I've never done it."

"You don't know what you've been missing." He'd unbuttoned his shirt and it followed the sweater. George stood at ease, breathtakingly naked to the waist, as superb as he had always seemed to Phil in the shy glances he'd permitted himself at school. His nakedness had always had a special glory for him—smooth skin, smooth muscles, the smooth modeling of the wide shoulders and powerful arms and the curiously erotic taper of his diaphragm down to his slim waist, aglow in the leaping firelight. George lifted his hands to his belt and paused. "At school I was always scared to death that I'd get a hard on when you were near me in the showers. We don't have to worry about that any more, thank God. Go ahead. Get undressed."

Phil couldn't help being aware again of the ambiguity of George's words. Did he mean that they couldn't get excited by each other any more or that they didn't have to hide their erections if they did? He dropped down, unhesitatingly obedient, to unfasten his shoes, wondering what this was leading to. They couldn't be getting ready for bed already. Maybe he was so obsessed by sex that he'd forgotten some perfectly reasonable explanation for taking their clothes off.

George was sitting on the hassock with his back to him, working on his boots. They were barefoot simultaneously. Phil rose and pulled off his rough sweater and managed to unbutton his shirt with fumbling fingers. As he did so, George sprang up and in one swift, graceful movement stripped himself. He stood for a moment shaking out his slacks, his back turned to him, naked from head to foot. He swung around and Phil's mind ceased to function.

His dream of knowing George in all his male splendor had come true. His erection was a magnificence his eyes flinched from. George approached him with a buoyant little spring in his step, his cock angled upward, rigidly immobile. No wonder it had won all the competitions. It was as big as Phil had known it would be, compellingly massive, but he couldn't judge it in comparison to others. It was George's, part of the glorious whole. He moved in close against Phil's side and ran a hand up over his chest under his shirt and pushed it back from his shoulders and removed it.

"You're a slow poke. I'm glad you took your time. I've wanted to undress you for years." His hands dealt expertly with the front of his jeans and closed around his erection. "I guess we turn each other on," he said with a flurry of soft laughter. "You've always had a terrific body but now it's really beautiful."

"I always thought you were the most beautiful guy I've ever seen." Phil could say it finally. The dream of going to the basement with him was coming true.

"It's about time we got together." He held his face close to the side of Phil's and covered it with quick almost imperceptible kisses. He pushed the back of his jeans down and stroked his bare buttocks. "So damn sexy," he murmured.

Phil ran his hand along the length of George's jutting cock. Why had he imagined ambiguity? This was what George had been waiting for and had assumed that Phil knew and wanted it too. His response to the hard flesh that lifted to his hand's caress was frightening. His head swam with desire. He wanted to hold it. He wanted to fill his mouth with it and make it overflow with desire for him. He wanted to feel it against him everywhere and make love to it. He wanted to be joined to him and feel him hugely inside him making his possession of him absolute. Was this the way women felt? It was insanity, a shattering violation of his manhood.

George gave a little tug to Phil's jeans and let them fall to his feet. He moved around in front of Phil and hooked his fingers inside his jockey shorts and slid them down over his thighs as he dropped into a crouch. He kissed Phil's balls and ran his tongue out along the underside of his cock and rolled his lips around its head. He opened his mouth wide and put his hands on Phil's behind and pulled him in. A sort of ecstatic sob choked in Phil's throat. George was sucking his cock. His hero was a queer.

If George was queer, everything he'd been taught to believe about homosexuality was wrong. It wasn't shameful but existed for them so that they could belong to each other and dedicate themselves to each other. They were both queers. That was what George had tried to tell him. His heart felt as if it would burst from his chest with the joy of the unique bond George was forging between them. His legs would no longer support him. He sank down into George's arms.

George stretched him out on the floor with his head and shoulders resting on the hassock. He gripped Phil's wrists, spreading his arms wide, and lifted himself over Phil, slowly lowering himself until the full lengths of their bodies were joined and their open mouths met. Phil's confusions, his half-formed thoughts and repressed impulses, his hesitations, his outraged sense of right and wrong, his longing to conform to the ideal George had offered him for so long, all surged up in him in a clamor for liberation, and his resistance was overthrown. His mouth lusted for George's. Their tongues lunged into each other, seeking to capture each other's essence. He broke George's grip on his wrists and flung his arms around him.

They rolled about on the floor together, pitting their equal strength against each other to find union. Phil felt as if his body had finally come into its own. He was doing things that he'd always tried to imagine doing with girls. Their mouths were on each other everywhere. Feeling George against him was the fulfillment of all his body's needs. He wanted George more than he'd ever wanted anything. He couldn't help it if he'd found his world in a man.

George made a quick supple movement of disengagement and hitched himself up onto the hassock, his cock towering majestically between them, and held Phil's head to guide it. He didn't have to exert any pressure. Phil wanted everything that George wanted. He reached for it with both hands and scrambled to his knees in front of it. He wanted to feel it in his mouth. His mind reeled at acknowledging it, but he couldn't help it: he wanted to suck George's cock.

It was unyieldingly hard and yet its surface was as exquisitely smooth as satin. It was too big to allow him much freedom for exploration, but he sucked and nuzzled it and darted his tongue around it until he elicited gratifying purrs of pleasure from his partner. It was thrilling to be allowed to know this part of the guy he'd always worshiped from afar. He was going to learn to do it well; he was ready to devote the rest of his life to pleasing George.

He was afraid of shocking him by giving free rein to his passion for his cock, but George obviously expected it. He encouraged the efforts of his mouth by stroking Phil's cheeks and lips. Phil saw that he was holding a tube of something and remembered Teddy's Vaseline. He held out his open palm and George squeezed the tube into it. Geroge squeezed more into his own hand, and they both applied the product until George's cock became a sleek, glistening spear. Watching their hands moving on it together, touching and acknowledging each other, was the most thrilling moment of Phil's life.

George lifted a hand to his shoulder and Phil dropped back and twisted over onto his hands and knees. George moved in behind him. Phil's heart began to pound as he prepared for the ultimate consecration of his body by the guy who had already transformed him. He felt the impact of the first enormous entry and stifled a cry. Teddy had prepared him for the initial discomfort, the sharp stab of pain, the momentary sensation of losing control of his body's functions. The wave of bliss that swept over him a moment later was unlike anything he had ever known. George was deep within him, filling him with his masculinity, making them part of each other. In an instant, the miracle had been accomplished. Every particle of him belonged to George. He shouted and his body was flung about in paroxysms of surrender, as all sense of himself as a separate being was shattered.

He lay inert and exultant as George took everything he wanted from the body that belonged to him now. His hands were still hungry for the feel of Phil. They slid around from behind him and found Phil's undiminished erection and pulled him upright onto his knees. George held him against his chest while he stroked it rapidly.

"Let me see you shoot across the room," he whispered against Phil's ear.

Phil swiveled his hips down on the powerful shaft within him. "With you," he begged.

"God, yes. Now." Phil's ejaculation leaped from him and spattered across the floor. George flung him forward and shouted too as he made his final thrust into him.

George lay on top of him without moving, all of his weight bearing down on Phil's back while their breathing steadied. Phil loved George's weight on him. Feeling him slowly diminishing in him drained him of his ecstatic confidence in finally having found a meaning in life. It left him with a desolate sense of loss. He never wanted to feel less a part of George than he did now. He dreaded the moment when they would have to break apart. He had given himself too wholeheartedly to acts that were universally recognized as despicable not to be overwhelmed by shame when the momentary thrill of it had subsided. George had seemed to enter into it with him, but now that he had had what he wanted, he might despise Phil too for being such a willing accomplice. Phil wanted to keep him always but knew that for two guys it didn't make any sense to even think about it.

He twisted his head around so that their mouths were almost touching, risking a rebuff, but George's lips were immediately pressed softly to his, their slack mouths were open to each other, their tongues lolling indolently together as if they were part of the same body. They were grown men with beards that scratched slightly, champion athletes with muscles that had been trained to compete with each other, not make love together. The world had been turned upside down and it was glorious. George's hands began to roam possessively over him.

"It's fantastic," he murmured into Phil's mouth. "I feel as if we've been saving up for this for years. Do you feel it, honey?"

Tears sprang to Phil's eyes at the endearment and his heart seemed to brim over with grateful adoration. "Yes. God, yes. I didn't know what it meant but I always wanted something. You. This. I know now." His heart gave a leap of excitement as he felt George's cock revive in him. It swelled and began to slide into him again, reclaiming him. He worked muscles he was just learning how to use to tighten his grip on George. He thrust his tongue rapidly in and out of George's mouth. He could feel all of George's body being recharged with desire.

"Jesus, baby," George gasped. "You're the sexiest guy I've ever known. Can you feel my cock getting big again?"

"Yes. It's huge."

"For you. Just a second. It's almost there. It feels so good in you. There. That's all of it. Do you feel that? You like it, don't you, sweetheart? We're everything I always hoped we'd be together. We're going to be lovers now."

Phil struggled to come to grips with what was happening to them. George spoke so openly and naturally that he felt it shouldn't be difficult to understand. The endearments that punctuated everything he said suggested that it wasn't just a momentary sexual adventure but something that might have some continuity into the future. "I don't understand much of anything, but I know I love you," he said, hoping that George wouldn't think he was making too much of it. They were two guys, not a couple planning marriage.

"Oh, God, baby, I know that. You're mine. We belong together."

George's conviction added to Phil's confusion while he continued to grope for understanding. Could ties more binding than marriage be created out of their forbidden need for each other? A light seemed to flicker in his mind and fade. All his training warned him that they were engaged in a vile desecration of nature. That he still felt no shame excluded him from the normal moral order; his lack of self-discipline, which he had always been taught was of even greater value than spontaneous virtue, condemned him to depravity.

He could feel no shame when he was exulting in his unsuspected capacity to serve the magnificent demands of George's body. His reward was the breathtaking physcial harmony they were achieving together. He was letting himself adapt to his perversion, but it was impossible to think of it as perversion with George. Homosexuality had nothing to do with it. He was only whatever George wanted him to be.

He moved to the bidding of George's hands, shifting his position inexplicably until he was lying on his back with his legs in the air in an attitude of flagrant abandon, gasping ecstatically as the big cock lunged into him and reasserted its possession of him. George knelt facing him, supporting Phil's legs on his shoulders. Their eyes met in naked, unabashed confrontation. George's face was tense with lust, but his candid eyes were tender and melting with love, unshadowed by shame, accepting him, taking him. They could face each other. There was nothing left to hide. Phil saw no trace of weakness in George's manly beauty, no hint of viciousness or corruption. George remained the irreproachable hero he had always been to him.

Night had crept in against the windows. The room was

in darkness except for the leap and flicker of the flames that played over them and highlighted the splendors of George's torso. They were isolated and alone in a secret world they were building out of the discoveries of their passionate questing bodies.

Phil's breath caught as George doubled over him and lifted his cock to his mouth. Phil prayed that it was long enough to reach. His chest swelled with pride as he felt George's lips, soft and seductive, on it, lingering on it lovingly. George wasn't performing a mechanical act as a prelude to orgasm but was making love to his cock with all the longing he felt for George's. He cried out as the wonder of it struck him. This was George. George was offering his love in defiance of all moral law. Phil was immediately on the verge of orgasm. He cried out again and tugged at his hair in warning. "Look out," he gasped. "I'm going to come. I can't help it."

George shook off his hands and the passion of his mouth intensified. Phil's body careened out of control. His cock plunged wildly into George's mouth as his ejaculation was wrenched from him. He shouted and his hips bucked. George gripped him and soothed him and continued to suck on him, swallowing him eagerly until the ejaculation was spent. He lifted his head at last with a triumphant smile on his lips and resumed his possessive drive for his own orgasm.

George wanted all of him. It was miraculous. He would learn to want George in the same way, even if it made him gag with disgust at first. There was a lot about making love he hadn't expected to like. His resistance stirred against the liberties they were taking even though his body was gripped helplessly by the craving of his desire.

They disentangled themselves from each other and pulled themselves up from the floor. With the passionate connection between them severed, Phil knew that the crucial moment must be coming when they would have to face the consequences of what they were doing. As long as they were in each other's arms, their bodies were their only reality, but they couldn't go on making love forever. He was still afraid that George would suddenly get fed up with him and suggest taking him home. Even if he didn't, what could they hope for? What did he mean by their belonging together? Everybody knew that queers picked each other up in the streets and had sex anywhere, even in men's rooms. That had nothing to do with them, but he'd never heard to two guys actually staying with each other and having some sort of life together. He had never known such intense, heart-stopping happiness at simply touching another human being. Even if by some freak of chance George felt the same way, he didn't see what they could do about it. Would they see each other a few more times during the vacation and let it go at that? He told himself that it would probably be enough.

Hoping for some sign that George still wanted him to stay he trailed him into a luxurious bathroom where George turned on the water in a glass shower stall. Phil lingered at the door while George stood under the water with his back turned and soaped himself. In a moment he turned as if he'd just realized that Phil wasn't beside him and drew him in, smiling gloatingly into his eyes.

Phil's heart leaped up with delight. George's smile reunited them. Everything was all right again for a little while. They stood side by side washing themselves as a deep sense of comradeship enveloped them. Phil thought of the furtiveness imposed by school. He and George could be naked together now and get hard together and do something about it without guilt or shame. Maybe that was what belonging together meant, regardless of what happened to part them. This would be the most amazing afternoon of his life.

George rinsed his own cock by running his hands over it and rolling it around under the water while it lengthened and filled out and finally stood. Phil watched spellbound, scarcely aware that his too was hard again. George's smile broadened and he began to jerk himself off slowly and voluptuously. He wasn't shy about letting Phil see how much pleasure his own cock gave him. It created a wonderful closeness between them. He had often imagined showing off like this for appreciative witnesses, although he had always made himself think of them as girls. Phil wanted to demonstrate that he could give him more pleasure than he could give himself. George dropped his hand to his side and thrust his hips forward to make the most of the display.

"How's that? Is it big enough for you?" he asked with laughter in his voice.

"God, yes. Fabulous."

"I've heard how many admirers yours had. You've got a beauty."

"I beat your record in the broad jump. I wouldn't've gotten anywhere near you in the cock competition." They laughed and Phil sank down over George's chest and abdomen, trailing his hand along smooth muscles, and opened his mouth wide to receive him. George tangled his fingers in his wet hair and brushed his cock over his lips.

"God, yes, honey, suck it," he urged. "I'm dying for you to go all the way with it. I've dreamed of it a thousand times."

Phil quickly mastered the difficulties imposed by size, and his mouth grew more ardent as his dread of climax faded. He could do anything to make George go on wanting him. It would be the ultimate acceptance of the perversion he was discovering he couldn't fight. He wanted George and had to learn how to satisy him in every way.

He felt George's excitement blazing up, encompassing them both. Kneeling in front of him in an attitude of worship with his cock filling his mouth was a final rejection of masculine pride. His need of George was unmasked and exposed to view. He moaned with shameless longing and his mouth begged him to come in it. He heard George's exultant shout and was staggered by the copious force of his ejaculation. It was flung into his mouth in a fierce rush and he had to swallow rapidly to keep it from overflowing. He didn't have time to wonder if it disgusted him until it was over, leaving him longing for more. The pungent taste was a precious gift that George couldn't take back.

George dropped to his knees in front of him. They folded their arms around each other's shoulders and leaned their heads together. "My God, you're fabulous, baby," George whispered.

"So are you. I still can't believe it. I want it to be right for you."

"Don't worry. We're made for each other. Don't you feel it?"

"Yes. God, yes. I couldn't do all this with anybody else." Phil hugged him closer and felt happiness creep through him like an elixir, almost palpable, seeping into his bones and joints. Yes. He was being shaped by George's will. He was going to have to think of himself as a guy who wanted to suck a big cock and be fucked by it. How had it happened? Perhaps he should have decided to stay away from the basement right from the start, but half his class had frequented it and he doubted if they were all queers. If it could happen to George, it could happen to anybody. They were two of a kind. Queers. It felt so foreign to him that he couldn't imagine how it was actually going to affect him, what it would do to him in practical terms. He wished they could remain clasped in each other's arms forever.

The future began when they left the bathroom, the life of small everyday events, the life whose shape he had to learn before he would know what it was like being a queer. George snapped on lights and put another log on the fire. Phil couldn't take his eyes off the stunning naked body. Was this going to be a permanent feature of daily existence, available for his pleasure and passion whenever he wanted it? George opened a closet overflowing with clothes and pulled out two expensive-looking dressing gowns and two pairs of slippers. He dropped the slippers on the floor and handed Phil a dressing gown.

"Our builds are the same. We'll be able to wear each other's clothes," George said fondly. To Phil, it was a hopelessly optimistic promise of a life together—how could they wear each other's clothes when they were off at different schools?—but at least it told him that they could think of more than one night together. Pulling the other dressing gown around him, George went to the phone and talked to somebody downstairs called Emma. They joked and laughed and discussed food.

"That's OK," George said. "I know how to cook a steak. We'll be down in a minute. You go watch TV. Sure. Leave your scalloped potatoes in the oven. I won't let them burn." He hung up and turned to Phil and his eyes lighted up with admiration. "God, you're handsome. I'm really nuts about you. I don't think I'll let you keep that robe on for long. We better get moving if you want to eat." He went to Phil and gave him a quick kiss and put an arm around him and led him to the door.

The little click as it closed behind them ended Phil's

dream. This was the ordinary world. He and George had become ordinary friends. That was miraculous enough. He almost wished that he'd imagined the rest of it. George didn't seem to be aware that everything they'd done made them outcasts. Guys couldn't call each other "honey" and "baby." Guys couldn't roll around on the floor together in paroxysms of ecstasy. Did George think they could keep it a secret? People would begin to wonder if they didn't have girls, and he didn't see how they'd ever have girls if they welcomed what had happened to them.

They should be overcome with remorse, swearing not to let it happen again, even deciding not to see each other any more. George was so relaxed and casual about it. Maybe experience had taught him that the sex part didn't last long and that they'd be devoted, platonic friends in a few days.

They went down through the imposing house, passed through a spacious dining room and entered an immaculate modern kitchen. Two places had been set at a table in what Phil supposed was called a breakfast nook. George took charge competently. "Do you like your steak rare, honey?" he asked.

"Yes. Practically raw."

"I thought so. Same here. There's a potato thing in the oven. She told me to cook the string beans just so, but I wasn't listening very carefully. Beans are beans. I guess I can cook them. You want a beer while we wait?"

"Sure, if you do."

George poured beer and they sat opposite each other at the narrow table, their knees pressed together. "That robe is perfect for you. Keep it. It's a Christmas present."

"You mean it? I'll never be able to give you anything this beautiful."

"Oh, yes you can. You have. You. That's all I want."

"But George—"

George leaned forward and silenced him with his mouth. Their kiss lengthened and deepened while their knees thrust up against each other and their hands became active under the table. George pulled back with breathless laughter. "I can't pretend I've been sex starved. I guess I'm starved for you. I told you I didn't think we'd stay down here long." They looked at each other and took long swallows of their beer. "Those potatoes should be ready. I'll give the steaks my personal attention." He pulled the dressing gown closer around him as he rose.

Phil watched enthralled as George busied himself with pots and the stove. This was normal enough—two guys fixing steaks together. The fact that one of them was George Hudderstone should soon seem normal too. If they could keep their hands off each other long enough, it might even begin to seem real.

George served their plates at a counter and brought them to the table. He put two glasses of milk in front of them. "Wine from our own cellar," he said and sat. "I hope I haven't ruined our banquet. We're beginning to live together, darling. Happy?"

Phil had trouble breathing. There was a block in his chest. Living together? Did George expect him to move in? They had to talk. Sex turned everything into a dream. "I love being with you," he managed.

"Same here. You've got that faraway look in your eyes again. What're you thinking about?"

"Nothing much. I'll tell you after we've eaten."

"OK. We've got to tell each other everything. Don't forget that. I want to hear about Ann Arbor."

They ate ravenously. They talked about college and what they were planning to do with their lives, but all the steps that Phil had taken for granted as inevitable—law school, marriage, a family—could have no meaning until he came to grips with what had become the central fact of life. He'd never heard of a queer lawyer. He began to understand George's carefree attitude. He was going to take over the family dairy business. Nobody would wonder much about a bachelor farmer. He suspected that he would have to fight a solitary battle if he hoped to save himself; George wouldn't help him.

They scraped their plates clean and looked at each other and laughed. As their eyes held and questioned each other, their smiles faded. George rose abruptly and circled around behind him and pulled his shoulders back against him. Phil felt the surge of George's cock under the dressing gown as he let himself go to his embrace. It hardened and quickly acquired its prodigious size against the side of his face. George's hips stirred invitingly.

"My God, baby," he muttered. "You're such a sweetheart. I'll never get enough of you."

Phil's erection lifted between his thighs. He held himself still, trying to get control of himself. If he hoped to preserve some semblance of manhood, he had to stop swooning like a lovesick maiden at George's advances. Everything had happened so suddenly and unexpectedly; he had time now to pull back.

Fingers moved enticingly along his neck and over his cheeks. Against his head, he felt the insistent stirrings of George's wanting him. He knew it was one of the rarest wonders that life offered. Happiness seeped deeper into him, filling him. It might begin to pass by tomorrow. Pulling back would be easier in the morning. He couldn't help it if George thought he was going too far. George had started it.

Phil swung around in his chair and flung his arms out to hold him. He pressed his face to the astonishing focus of all his need and desire. It lifted from the dressing gown and soared up to Phil's expectant mouth. His lips parted on it and his tongue caressed all its length. His worship of it was an insanity that felt incurable.

"Come on, darling." George's voice cut through the mist of Phil's helpless surrender. His laughter was soft and eager as he tousled his hair with his hands. "Isn't it about time we went to bed together? You're sensational on the floor. Bed might be an interesting novelty."

At the prompting of his hands, Phil was on his feet. Their robes were open. Their arms locked themselves to each other in a powerful grip. Their tongues invaded their open mouths and plunged deep with exploration and possession. They flung their bodies against each other and vied for domination. Phil was thrilled to feel that they would be equals in a test of strength. They broke apart simultaneously, breathing heavily.

"Jesus," George gasped. "Emma's going to find us doing it on the kitchen floor next if we don't watch it. Let's go. She'll take care of everything. We haven't made much of a mess." He took his arm and headed back toward the staircase, their cocks swinging out boldly in front of them. Phil made an attempt at modesty by tugging at his dressing gown but the attempt ended when George stopped in front of a big floor-length mirror in the entrance hall and lifted it from him. He shed his own and tossed them onto a chair and turned to face the mirror. "There. I wanted to see us together." He ran a hand along Phil's shoulders and down to his waist and held them side by side. "All those measurements they were always taking, height and weight and chest and the rest, I bet they're practically the same. I feel sort of as if I were in love with myself. You've got to admit we're pretty damn beautiful."

"We're alike, all right," Phil said. He was so used to thinking of George's body as a model of perfection that he was astonished that his stood up pretty well to comparison. Seeing their cocks thrusting together gave him a tingle of delight. George's was much bigger, of course, but it didn't make his look ridiculous. Their eyes met in the mirror and they burst out laughing.

"Fancy meeting you here," George said. "Isn't it weird? It's like looking at ourselves from outside somehow. You're Phil Renfield. You've got a sweet ass. I want to go to bed with you. How about it?"

"I wouldn't mind, except you're a guy. I've been told I shouldn't go to bed with guys." He was slightly shocked at himself for being able to laugh about it.

"That's a good rule, but you can make an exception for me. We went to school together."

"I'm glad you thought of that. It makes all the difference." They laughed again and dropped the game and turned to really look at each other. "You're much better looking than you are in the mirror."

"So are you." George stepped in closer and hugged him, moving his hands over his back in an oddly tentative way, as if he were trying to find places he hadn't touched before. "Our first night together. God, all night in bed with you. Race you to the room."

They broke apart and George snatched up the robes and they pounded up the stairs. They were in each other's arms, laughing breathlessly, before the bedroom door was closed. They lurched and staggered to the bed while they clung to each other, their mouths joined. George freed an arm to pull back the covers and they landed in a heap of thrashing limbs and heaving torsos. As they recovered their breath, they began a studied search for ways of pleasing each other. They were able to let go of each other and draw back enough to look at each other. They burst out laughing when they discovered tricks that aroused unexpected responses. It was unlike any lovemaking that Phil had imagined. It was fun. There was nothing physically shy or reticent in George. He was obviously proud of his body and pleased to show it off, but Phil sensed no vanity in him. He made Phil feel that he had reason to be proud of his own. His tendency to hide himself against George passed. Girls had never given him confidence in his body's attractions, only guys. This realization contributed to his beginning to understand what was happening to himself and to accept it as almost inevitable. The sacrifices he'd made to perfect his body and turn it into a finely tuned instrument had made him hyperconscious of it. It demanded attention. The discovery that it could inspire passion, even if it happened only with guys, was a long-awaited revelation. He wanted to use it fully and offer it for others' pleasure. He wanted to find his own pleasure in it. A phallic fixation had somehow got tied up in it. It had probably been the same for George. They were made for each other.

George encouraged his infatuation with his cock and unselfconsciously demonstrated his own delight with Phil's. Even though he was almost convinced that it wasn't shameful to be queer, Phil knew that he still had inhibitions to overcome before he could match George's frank, ardent lovemaking. He forced himself to abandon restraint as they led each other to simultaneous orgasms with their mouths.

He lay with George's head on his stomach wishing that he would never have to move. Joy coursed through his veins. He was challenging the most powerful taboo that existed in the world he had grown up in, but he couldn't stop himself. He was ready to defy Biblical plagues or eternal damnation for the sake of having George, but he knew that if they expected it to be more than a wild night of fucking they were going to have to try to make sense. It seemed to him that they were getting in so deep that they were soon going to be beyond words. He didn't know what to say without spoiling it. After a silent moment, George pulled himself up and kissed him gently on the mouth before jumping out of bed to poke the fire into a cheerful blaze. When he came back, he lifted the covers over them and stretched out against Phil with a hand on his chest, looking down at him.

"Tell me what you're thinking, baby," he urged.

"Not exactly thinking, really." Phil's heart accelerated. He had to find out what this meant to George. He was still afraid that it was all going to turn out to be some sort of grotesque misunderstanding. "I'm not sure how to say it. I'm going to sound stupid but I can't help it. You obviously know more about everything than I do. When you asked me home with you, did you think I was—well, a homosexual?"

"Oh." George shifted slightly and took Phil's hand. "I hoped you were, naturally. When I told you I'd started to cruise you, it was to make sure you wanted it. You understood what I was driving at."

"No. I didn't."

"You don't know what cruising means? Well, it has to do with the way you look at a guy when you're trying to pick him up. It's called cruising."

"You've done that?"

"Sometimes."

"I haven't, but I see I gave the impression that I knew what it was all about. I guess you think I'm a homosexual now."

"Well, sure. *I* am. None of this could've happened if we weren't."

To hear George explicitly accept the word as a description of either of them was a brutal shock. It seemed to close doors and cut off escape. Phil's hand felt numb in the hand that held it. He couldn't deny that they had performed every unspeakable act that he had ever heard of, but he clung to an irrational hope that George could explain it away in some other terms. The way he talked about there always having been something special between them seemed to invoke fate. The usual words didn't apply to them. They were ordained by fate to belong to one another but that didn't mean that they both couldn't eventually get married like everybody else. He hadn't had time to find out if girls were capable of wanting him passionately the way George did, the way Ricky and even Teddy had. He had trouble speaking and he was glad he didn't have to look at George. "You admit it?" he asked slowly.

"Not to everyone, but there wouldn't be much point pretending with you."

"Doesn't it terrify you?"

George made a little dismissive snorting sound. "Not particularly. I've always known about myself. I guess I'm used to it."

"What if your family finds out?" A chill of horror crept over him as he thought of his own.

"My mother knows."

"Doesn't she care?"

"She doesn't want Dad to find out. She worries about later, if I fall in love and all that. She's afraid I'll get mixed up with the wrong guy."

"Is it possible for two guys to fall in love with each other?"

"Why not? We're human. It almost happened to me the first year at Yale. He was a wonderful guy, but I couldn't stop thinking about you and I knew it wouldn't be the same with him. It's really happened now."

"Falling in love? You mean, you're going to get married?"

George pressed his hand with a gurgle of laughter. "I would if I could. Not a girl, silly. With you. I'm in love with you. I always have been."

"You mean it?"

"Of course. You're in love with me, aren't you?"

"Oh, George." They were in each other's arms, their cocks thrust up hard against each other, their mouths open to each other, their saliva mingling. Phil struggled free, his eyes blurred with tears, tears of relief and gratitude and love. They weren't plunging blindly toward disaster. George was prepared for him, had been waiting for him. Being in love overturned the rules, and George created rules of his own. He had the serene confidence of a born leader. A champion. He couldn't help thinking of himself as a winner even when acknowledging his perversion. He needed George to reconcile him to his own nature. He swallowed his tears and spoke. "I've been trying to talk to you about it. How can guys like us be queer? If we're not queer, we can't be in love with each other, can we?"

"Well, no. I guess not," George said with a little twitch of amusement at the corners of his lips.

"What does it mean? What're we going to do about it?"

"Everything. We've got to plan things so we do everything together. I guess we'll have to spend most of Christmas day with our families, but there'll still be an hour or two when we can have our own Christmas. We can sleep together most nights. It'll be like being married. Now that I have you I won't want to fool around with other guys. We'll be just for each other. I told you. We're starting to live together. That's what we want, isn't it?"

"Will everybody know?"

"They'll know we're friends. There's nothing wrong with that. It's not like New York. So many guys are gay there that people take it for granted unless you make a big thing about chasing girls. Nobody thinks about it here. You've done it with lots of guys, haven't you? Has anybody suspected anything?''

"No," Phil protested indignantly but realized that George had probably been promiscuous. "I mean, there's been nothing to suspect. You know about the basement. That didn't mean anything except once when it might've turned into something if we'd been somewhere else. That's all. There was one other time long ago—five years ago.'' Telling George about Teddy and Ricky, he thought about others. He could admit now that it had been growing in him for the last couple of years, the hunger for guys, a dread bottled up deep within him so that he could live with it. He could say it all to himself in plain words now. Hard cocks excited him. He worshiped George's. He wanted to suck it. He wanted George to fuck him. He'd get used to being a homosexual. He wondered if he'd have to do it with other guys before he could be sure. If he were a homosexual . . . If he were a homosexual, it all made ecstatic sense. He would become a part of something he hadn't known was possible and spend the rest of his life with George.

"My first was an older guy, too," George said, stroking Phil's hair as he told his brief story. "It was a first for both of us. I seduced him and knew immediately that that was it."

"You make me feel as if I should've known, but it still seems strange. How does anybody get that way?"

"Who knows? My mother made a sort of study of it when she thought there might be something she should do for me. She thinks most guys are naturally that way; that is, at least bisexual, but the social stigma forces us to be straight. It doesn't always work. Some of the greatest men in history have been that way. Alexander the Great and his lover went all over the world together and were treated like gods, but you know all that. When the Greeks talked about love, they meant between men. Women were for having children and taking care of the house. Of course things were different then, but it makes sense to me in a way. Guys understand each other in ways that women can't know anything about.'' He shifted again and their hands curled around their hard cocks. They stiffened perceptibly. ''Feel that. We're so close, darling. We're the same. We're finally together. There's nothing terrifying about that.''

''I'm not terrified when I'm with you, but vacation isn't going to last forever. What'll we do then?''

''Easter's coming. After that, we'll have the whole summer together. We'll write to each other all the time. I don't see why we can't meet in New York for a weekend if we get really desperate.''

George had it all worked out. Their meeting hadn't been entirely accidental; George had been waiting for it. He was planning a real life for them. ''I never have any money,'' Phil said realistically.

''I can pay for your ticket. Nothing else will cost much. I know guys in the city where we can stay. We can do it after midyear's. We'll only have to go for about a month without seeing each other.''

''That sounds wonderful. It helps to talk to you, but there're still things I don't quite get. Don't queers wear makeup and act like girls?''

''Those are the queens. I've been to places in New York where they go. It's sort of peculiar at first, but they make a big joke of it. You get used to it. You'll see.''

''I'm not sure I want to. It sounds weird. But if it can be like you say, that it's not sick for us to be in love with each other . . . How did your mother find out about you?''

"Oh, that." George looked at him with a guilty little smile. He threw the covers back and jumped out of bed. His cock swung out proudly as he started across the room. He went to the shelves beside his desk and extricated a manila envelope from under a pile of books. He returned with it and dropped down on his stomach beside Phil. "I left these spread out on my desk. It's the stupidest thing I've ever done. My mother found them. She wasn't snooping or anything. She couldn't help seeing them." He shook a sheaf of photographs out of the envelope and handed them to Phil.

They were standard-size glossies, and Phil studied one for a moment before he could believe what he was looking at. He stared, his eyes widening. His scalp contracted. His cock became a taut ache of lust. He gripped it to ease the strain of a gathering orgasm.

He slowly turned over the photographs, his eyes lingering on details. A younger George and a willowy blond Adonis, both naked with erections, were intertwined in a series of flagrantly erotic poses, attention drawn to genitals by skillful lighting and striking angles. Phil was shocked and hyponotized. He was prepared to find the sight of copulating males obscene, something that would make him avert his eyes with shame and disgust, but there was nothing obscene about these two. They radiated beauty and grace. He didn't understand why he had ever doubted his homosexuality. He looked at the two beautiful bodies and wanted both of them. He was going to have a sex life at last. Life would be transformed.

His mind reeled with an explosion of erotic images. He regretted that his lack of experience confined them to fantasy. He imagined the crowded shower room at school erupting into an orgy. He thought of guys he had been to the basement with, all of them stripping and really making love. Thinking of naked guys, he was aware for the first time of the power of his unleashed unnatural lust. He felt it as a threat, something he would have to curb, as he had been taught he must curb all powerful impulses. He returned his attention to the photographs. George's heroic cock imposed its will almost visibly on the more modestly endowed stranger. All of Phil's body was gripped by his need for it, a wrenching need to submit to it. The photographs were a revelation. He wouldn't let anybody take George away from him.

"Jesus," he muttered.

"Are you shocked by them?"

"I guess so, but they're fascinating. I've never seen two guys together before."

"That's Danny. He's a photographer. He took the pictures with a timing gadget. I guess it's obvious we were having a big affair. It was certainly obvious to my mother. Actually, she was pretty wonderful once she got used to the idea. If you're shocked, you can imagine what she must've felt."

"I'm shocked maybe because I find them so exciting. They almost make me come. You're more or less the first guy I've ever made love with, don't forget. I hardly know yet what's happening to me. I know I don't like seeing you like that with another guy."

"It was almost two years ago, baby. You know what I'd like? I thought of it downstairs when we were looking at ourselves in the mirror. When we go to New York, we should let Danny take some pictures of us. It would be wonderful to have them when we have to be apart."

"Like these? You mean, he'd see us practically making love?"

"I don't think we could expect very good results if he's blindfolded," George said with laughter in his voice. "It's all right. I'm hardly news to him, and I won't let him try anything with you. He's a pro. He'll be concentrating on the job.''

Phil told himself that lack of experience made for prudishness, but something in him was outraged by the suggestion. His sense of decency? Wanting what amounted to filthy pictures of a lover struck him as distasteful and corrupt. He had only to look at George's lean, swift face to doubt his own judgment. The candid eyes were clear and direct, shining with virtue. The strong modeling of the cheekbones, the humor playing around the seductive curves and fullnesses of his lips were compounded of sensitivity and refinement. He could trust George as his guide to an unfamiliar world.

He glanced at George's partner. Full, soft lips and heavy-lidded, inviting eyes. He hoped Danny wasn't quite as irresistible as he looked in the photographs; he didn't see how he could have a hard on in front of him without things happening, but George would probably know how to handle it. George and Danny. His fingers flicked the picture of a slim, shapely cock lifting to George's mouth. Two years ago. George was his now. Phil's cock swelled into an aching knot of lust.

He kicked the sheet back and lunged up to his knees, his cock a rigidly upright statement of his need. ''I'm going to come,'' he exclaimed in a strangled voice.

George immediately pulled himself up and crouched in front of him, sliding his tongue along his hard flesh to lead him to ecstasy.

''It's bigger than his, isn't it?'' Phil demanded.

''I'll say. It's a honey.''

''My God. Now,'' he cried. He caught a blurred glimpse of George opening his mouth wide to receive him and thought of Danny. His orgasm gathered force in him and crashed over him like a wave. When it had spent itself, he broke from George's grip and rolled onto his stomach. "Take me, darling," he begged in a dreaming voice. "I want you in me. Fuck me. I want to belong to you." It could happen between two guys, he thought wonderingly as George moved slowly into him. Love went beyond the limits of gender. They were being as completely joined as male and female, but he felt no loss of self. He didn't have to have an erection to find an overwhelming satisfaction in satisfying the man who filled him so sublimely. They were in love in defiance of logic or natural law. Phil knew that only George could make it feel right but wondered if even he could protect him from the shame that he had kept at bay so far. It was bound to hit him sooner or later. Nobody could help being ashamed of homosexuality.

When morning came, Phil woke up at peace, not a guilt-ridden victim of his unnatural appetites but blissfully content in the comforting arms of his lover, a massive erection pressed against his buttocks. The next few days proved that George had been right; life continued on its even course. They hadn't become outcasts overnight. They were still popular, good-looking young members of the local elite, their athletic records confirming them as models of upright, clean-living American boys. Prepared to make enormous adjustments in a struggle to adapt to thinking of himself as a queer, Phil began to wonder why people made such a fuss about words. He just happened to be in love with a guy. Nobody expected him to get married yet, so what difference did it make if he didn't have a girl at the moment? Nobody knew what the future would bring. The only transformation was within themselves, in the radiance of their shared love.

They felt as if they had always been together and acted accordingly, naturally and without self-consciousness. The first and last awkward moment was Phil's meeting George's mother. Phil was tense and embarrassed, knowing that she knew everything, but she was a brisk and busy woman who was cordial without making him feel that she was taking a special interest in him because he was her son's lover. She treated him casually, as a member of the family, and left them to their own devices.

George led a much more active social life than Phil was used to, but George arranged for him to be included in everything. They went to parties where Phil was often the youngest guest, but the age difference wasn't great enough to matter. They had a plausible excuse for spending their nights together. They were going to be out late. George had a car. It was more convenient to use George's place as a base.

As George had anticipated, they didn't have much of a Christmas together but managed an hour in George's room in the late afternoon when they made love and exchanged the heavy silver chains that they'd shopped for together. Phil's didn't look quite the same as the one they'd seen in the shop; years later he discovered that it was platinum. They put them around each other's neck and swore to wear them always. Their wedding rings.

"Our first Christmas, but the last that's going to be like this," George said when their time was up and they were trying to let go of each other and get out of bed. He fingered Phil's chain. "It looks great on you. Mom's really happy about us. She says that if I have sense enough to stick with you for a year, she's going to make Dad accept us—not exactly as lovers maybe, more sort of like brothers. She says he always wanted a brother for me, but she couldn't have any more after me. Anyway, she wants him to know that we love each other and will probably live together sooner or later until we get married." George laughed and brushed his lips against Phil's. "Those imaginary wives they've all got picked out for us. Next year you'll be with me for all the family stuff."

"That'll be wonderful." Phil snuggled in closer against him. Their night together had lengthened into a year. George was amazing.

"I've talked to her about living on my own in town after I graduate. That's not much more than a year away. I figure it'll make more sense to your folks for you to stay with me when you come home if I have a place of my own. It's natural for guys to room together."

"Oh, God, George, I love you so." He was limp with love. They would never let each other go. George was thinking of everything. He was setting them up for a lifetime together. There wasn't anything that wasn't right between them. They had shared so much that it was practically the same as having grown up together. Their bodies were made for each other. George had known it. They belonged together. It would never be like this with anybody else. He was safe and secure and in love for life.

George had dates for several of the bigger parties, including the New Year's Eve party, and for appearances' sake they agreed that he shouldn't break them. He had another family obligation on New Year's Day, a midday gathering some thirty miles away, and would have to get up quite early, so they decided reluctantly to spend another night apart. The New Year's Eve party was in a big private house belonging to one of the richest families in the area, and George had arranged Phil's invitation. As the owner of Newcorners's biggest insurance agency, Phil's father knew everybody, but there was an upper stratum of the rich with whom the Renfields weren't socially intimate. George had a spare dinner jacket for him to wear. Accustomed already to sharing George's lavish wardrobe, Phil was getting used to looking as elegant and glamorous as George had always been.

At the stroke of midnight, they pushed their way through the crowd to each other and tugged secretly at the chains under their shirts and looked deep into each other's eyes, pledging themselves to a new year while horns tooted around them. It was almost as thrilling as the kiss they wanted to share. The party moved into high gear, with the stereo pounding, but George took his date home quite early after checking with Phil about their plans for meeting the next afternoon.

Phil danced, taking time out from time to time to catch his breath and have a glass of champagne, which was making him a bit high. Having been in training for years, he and George didn't drink except for an occasional beer. He hoped the champagne would help him sleep soundly. Sleeping with George had become a habit, and he hated going to bed alone. He noticed that a guy called Howie, who had been very friendly all evening, was beginning to turn up at his side whenever he left the dance floor. Howie was attractive. He was from out of town and had been staying for several days with friends of George, the Millers. When he laughed, which he did frequently, beguiling dimples appeared in his cheeks. His eyes were playfully flirtatious and Phil became aware that the young man was finding excuses for touching him a lot, deliberately and insinuatingly. With a little flutter of excitement, Phil came to the conclusion that Howie, who was pretty old, maybe over twenty-five, was after him. He began to get an erection whenever Howie approached. For the first time, his new sexual alignment was making itself felt with a stranger. He had wondered if he would ever be attracted to other guys; Howie had a lush, fleshy look that was very sexy. Nothing could happen here so it was quite harmless, but wondering what a guy would be like in bed was a new experience and added interest to the party.

"If I drive you home, will you invite me in?" Howie asked with a comic leer, showing his dimples. He'd just learned that Phil had no plans for getting home.

"There wouldn't be much point. The place is swarming with my family," Phil said, acknowledging the attraction between them.

"Right. I guess we know what we're both thinking." Howie smiled into his eyes long enough to dispel any doubts. "Well, I can't very well take you back with me to the Millers. How about it? Shall we go see how the land lies here?"

"How do you mean?" Phil asked, growing wary.

"This is a big house. I'll bet we can find a bedroom upstairs where nobody would bother us for half an hour."

"I don't know." He and George hadn't talked much about fidelity, but they didn't have to. They wanted each other, nobody else. He wasn't going to be like the queers he'd heard about who could be had by anybody. He didn't even know how queer he was but Howie tempted him. That was one question answered, but being tempted wasn't the same as actually liking it with anybody but George. He probably shouldn't want to find out. "I guess we better not," he said indecisively.

"This is getting interesting," Howie said merrily. They had wandered away from the dancers to the side of the room. They were standing in front of a door. Howie opened it and led him into a deserted library and closed the door behind them. "You're gay, aren't you?" he asked.

"I'm not sure. Sort of, I guess."

Howie stepped closer and put a hand on Phil's crotch. He laughed with an irresistible display of dimples. "You've got a hard on. Are you waiting for somebody to bring you out?''

George had explained what that meant too. He found Howie's erection. It felt like a good substantial one. He wished he could see it, thinking the temptation would end there. Obviously he was queer enough. It wasn't just an idea George had put in his head. Another question answered. They smiled playfully at each other while they investigated the dimensions of their cocks. "I guess I've come out," Phil admitted.

"I'd gladly help if you have any doubts. Are you sure you don't want to have a look around upstairs?''

"We might get caught.''

"It's possible. We don't want to cause a scandal. I'll drive you home anyway. I hope you don't live too near.'' He put a hand on Phil's behind as they started back to the door. "That's awfully sexy looking when you're dancing.''

Howie joined him again an hour later as the crowd began to thin. "You ready?'' he asked.

"I'm ready for you. I wish we had some place to go.'' Phil was drunk in a manageable way and had thrown caution to the winds. He had resisted temptation and felt virtuous. Nothing much could happen on the way home even if he wanted it to. He was glad for the opportunity to test himself alone in public as a queer, or a gay if that was what he was supposed to call it. It was a peculiar word for it, except that tonight he felt gay in every sense of the word. Giddy and gay, equipped with an unfamiliar set of sexual appetites.

They said good night to the proper people and collected their coats, Phil's a shabby sheepskin of his own, and went out to the car. It was cold but the dark was thinning, diluted by the approach of dawn. Phil gave directions for the short drive and they started off in silence while the heater slowly warmed them. The warmth revived their attraction to each other. Their thighs stirred. Phil's cock hardened agreeably, and he moved his arm along the back of the seat and touched Howie's shoulder.

"It's damn decent of you to go out of your way for me," he said. "The Millers are in the other direction."

"I've been watching you dance for the last hour. What a body. I'd drive almost anywhere to get my hands on that ass."

"You did."

They both laughed. "I wasn't thinking of just giving it a pat. Did you say the next left?"

"Yes. We're almost there."

"You're full of bad news. I'll go in and liquidate your family if you want."

"That's what they get for having a son with a sexy ass." Phil was amazed at feeling so at ease with his new identity. He could laugh and enjoy himself. He wasn't worried any more about being turned on by an attractive guy.

Howie laughed with him and made the turn. The residential streets were deserted. "Do you have a hard on?" he asked.

"How did you guess?"

"Just wondering. Let me see it."

Phil obliged, feeling only slightly guilty. It was nothing but a basement game. Kid stuff. Being fully clothed in a car, even with his cock out, couldn't count as an infidelity. It got very hard while he extricated it from his clothes, and it felt wonderful when it was free. He didn't know what he would do if he ever caught George doing anything like this, but George wouldn't let himself be caught. That was where caring and consideration came into it. George had showed off his cock to lots of guys and undoubtedly would again. It couldn't hurt him if he didn't know. He was sure neither of them would ever be careless about it.

Howie ran his hand up and down on him. "Nice," he said. "It's time for the pause that refreshes." He pulled over to the curb and stopped. He switched off the lights and the motor. He twisted away from the wheel and dropped over and drew Phil's cock into his mouth. Phil uttered a little startled cry. It still took him by surprise. He had to remind himself that he was gay now. This was something gay guys did together. Howie did it very well. Phil was rapidly approaching his climax.

"I'm going to come," he warned. Howie continued his thrilling mouth-play. Phil twisted his fingers in his hair and grunted and gasped and released his orgasm into his mouth. Howie continued to suck on him eagerly. He and George weren't the only ones who swallowed it.

Howie sat up. "That was worth the detour," he said with merry satisfaction. He pushed his coat out of the way. "It's all yours." Phil saw that Howie's fly was open, his cock thrusting up from it. The gray light was dim, but he could see that Howie didn't have to be shy about showing it. He put a hand out to it and confirmed that it was everything it appeared to be. He couldn't avoid what was expected of him after what Howie had done for him. He shouldn't have got started on something he didn't want to finish. Guilt clawed at him as he shifted into position and opened his mouth wide and put the substantial cock in it. Guilt was swept away by a blazing rush of desire. He rolled his tongue around it and opened his mouth wider for it until his lips brushed pubic hair. He felt as if he would gladly choke to death on it if Howie asked him to. He thought he had overcome his distaste for the act only with George, because George wanted it, but he couldn't kid himself any longer. His mouth craved cock, George's most of all, but Howie's too and Ricky's and all the ones he'd jerked off in the basement, back to Teddy's. It had become an obsession since the first time with George—feeling the close, intimate contact with the source of life-giving male power, knowing that he could satisfy the hunger of the mysteriously rigid flesh that demanded relief from his lips and tongue. He was a born cocksucker. A lot of questions were being answered tonight.

He tugged at clothes until Howie's trousers were down around his knees and his shirt hitched up around his chest so that he could hold his balls and freely worship all the area of a man that made him a man. Howie laughed and crooned and let out short yelps at his uninhibited improvisations. Phil had a hard on again when the warm rush of fluid filled his mouth. Howie stroked him when Phil sat up.

"You're sweet," he said. "I'd say there's not much doubt about your having come out. You certainly don't have anything more to learn about what to do with a cock. A champion. Do you want me to suck you off again? You've taught me some new things."

"It's getting cold. I better go."

"I'll be watching for a chance to get you into bed in comfort. Do you like to be fucked?"

"Maybe."

"I'll bet I can make you like it."

Phil giggled, thinking that Howie had a long way to go before he could kindle the frenzy of passion that George aroused in him. "Be careful. I don't want anybody to get ideas."

"Naturally. I won't do more than glance at you. The door will be locked. Thanks for ending the evening so beautifully. You must be incredible when you get your clothes off."

They covered themselves and in another few minutes Phil was home. He thought over the evening as he prepared for his lonely bed. It hadn't been much of an infidelity, but it could have been if circumstances had been more favorable. He'd learned that he could be tempted more easily than he thought. He couldn't condemn himself for wanting to find out what he was all about, but he was going to have to be careful. No further involvement with Howie, for one thing. Circumstance didn't have to be very favorable to satisfy his craving for cocks. A few minutes alone with a guy in a car or any secluded spot was enough. There were probably plenty of guys, even straights, who wouldn't object to having their cock sucked.

He wished he could tell George about it and find out how important he thought fidelity was, but he didn't see how he could talk about it openly without sounding as if he wanted to play around. He didn't. He'd discovered something about himself that he had to learn to keep under control. He could tell himself that it was disgusting, but that didn't help much when he wanted it so much. He was frightened, most of all, of becoming effeminate in his manner and in the way he responded to people. He had been taught to despise sissies, but there must be something new about him that had invited Howie's frank approach. It had never happened before. He supposed his eyes gave him away. He was going to have to watch out how he looked at guys. The problems of being queer were just beginning.

Later in the day, when George had escaped his family, they talked about the party. "Did you have a good time after I left?" George asked.

"I danced a lot. I liked it better when you were there. I sort of made friends with a guy called Howie, that friend of the Millers. He's gay, as you call it."

"I thought he might be. Was he after you?—not that I could blame him. He's very attractive."

"I've never let myself think about it with guys." He seized the opening to tackle the subject that preoccupied him. "I guess it'll be different now. You wouldn't mind if I was attracted to him?"

"Oh, honey, we're going to be attracted to other guys, or vice versa. That's natural. It shouldn't be any big deal. Did he make a pass at you?"

"He asked me if I was gay at the party. I sort of mumbled something about not being sure. He offered to give me a lift home."

"You accepted? Did he make a pass in the car? You don't have to tell me if you don't want to."

"I do. You said you wanted me to tell you everything. He asked me if I was going to invite him in and I said I couldn't, naturally. He said he couldn't ask me to the Millers' and that was the end of that. I was sort of worried about how you're supposed to turn a guy down. What would you have done?"

"With Howie or generally? We're still pretty new to each other, but I don't think I'd've been interested. I'll be honest with you. Before you came along, I would've jumped at the chance. I like sex, as you may have noticed. So do you. As long as we want each other as much as we do, who needs anything else?"

"You mean you're going to be faithful to me?"

"Only because I want to be, baby. I hope I'll make you want to be faithful to me. We shouldn't even have to think about it."

"You're right, of course. It's all so new to me. It helps for you to tell me how we're supposed to behave. I used to think about having real sex in the basement, but it always had to do with guys taking me. Well, like Teddy and what almost happened with Ricky. I never dreamed I'd—you know. I didn't know I'd want to—to suck your cock the way I do."

"Thank God you do. Guys often make me feel that it's an awful sweat. Maybe that's why I'd almost mind it more if I found out you'd sucked a guy off than if you'd been fucked. I don't think we have to worry about it. We're alike. We know how to behave. I'll try not to have jealous fits if a guy looks at you. They say it's easier to find a lover than to keep him. I'm going to learn how to keep you."

"You won't have to learn very much. I want you to keep me. I want to keep you. Forever."

Phil supposed that they'd covered adequately the question of fidelity. It couldn't be a problem because they'd never let it be a problem. He hoped it was as simple as that. He'd learned at least that his infidelity last night had been more serious than he realized. He didn't see how George could ever find out about it. Now that he knew what it meant to him, he'd have to make sure that it never happened again. He had to be worthy of George's love. It was amazing. They were really in love with each other in a way that was going to rule their lives. He'd found something that required his total dedication.

"I hope you don't forget you want to keep me when we have our weekend in New York," George said teasingly.

"Why should I?"

"Oh, honey, everything's so different there. Anything goes. Here everybody has to be so careful. We probably know guys who're queer without ever suspecting it. Well, like what happened with Howie, for instance. He doesn't live here so he can afford to take a risk, but you had no place to go together even if you'd wanted to. That wouldn't be a problem in New York."

"What difference would that make? Can you imagine me saying good night to you and going off with another guy? Are you still thinking about asking that friend of yours to take pictures of us?"

George laughed. "Danny turns you on, doesn't he? On second thought, I think we'd better stay away from him. Why ask for trouble?"

"Shall I tell you the truth? I was sort of shocked by your even suggesting it. It seemed so sort of cheap when there's so much more to love than what we do with our bodies."

George sobered and his eyes were suddenly brimming with passionate tenderness. "You're so wonderful, my sweet baby. You're right. That came out the first night, before I had time to realize what was happening to us. Nobody could take a picture of what it means for us to hold each other."

Phil's throat tightened with an ache of adoration. "I'm glad you understand. I knew you would. We agree about everything. We don't have to think about infidelity again. That business about the pictures made me think that being faithful to me was the last thing you wanted." He was soon to have reason to give more serious thought to the problem of infidelity.

———

Phil ran up out of the sea, trying to shake George out of his mind, his eyes sweeping the length of the beach as he emerged. He could still see some figures at the far end. In the other direction, toward the port, the speck on the sand was probably the Frenchman. His private beach. He needn't have bothered with his jockey shorts. He pulled them off and hung them on his fence. It didn't matter that the sun and air all over his body, coupled with memories of George, began to give him a hard on. The fence provided additional privacy. Imagining being here with George was really putting the icing on the cake. They had had plenty going for them without throwing in a touch of paradise.

If the circumstances of their parting had been avoided for another year or two, Phil probably would have had sense enough to give them a chance to patch things up, but in the long run it probably wouldn't have made a difference. His thoughts fell into a well-worn groove. He wasn't made for a homosexual marriage. He cared too much about what people thought. He hated to be treated like a misfit or an oddity and felt the strain of the deceptions that were constantly imposed on them. Homosexual marriages rarely worked anyway. Forget it. Stop dreaming of romance like a kid. His older colleagues seemed to find fulfillment in their work. He was sure he could too. The groove stopped there. For some reason, he didn't find himself very convincing today.

Using his T-shirt as a pillow, he stretched out on the sand as naked as the Frenchman. The sun caressed him like a hundred hands and the tentative beginnings of an erection became the real thing. He led his thoughts into another groove: the blessings of a solitary, unattached life. His erection told him that it would be very pleasant to have a companion. While he was at it, he might as well admit that he knew who he'd like the companion to be still. Now that he'd freed himself from Alex he was right back where he'd started.

He dozed and awoke with a start. Was it only this morning that he'd come home at dawn? He'd probably had enough sun for the first day. A real nap in a bed wouldn't do any harm if he expected to be his usual scintillating self tonight.

He almost slept through his dinner date with John Robert, and when he found the house, the women, Sally and Cynthia, were already there, sitting serenely on the floor of the upstairs living room with their mysterious sewing. The ground floor he'd come through, like the houses where he and Johnny were staying, was a deep, cavernous arched cellar. John Robert directed him to a decrepit wicker armchair overflowing with limp cushions. There were other wicker chairs in the crowded room, a couple of lumpy sofas and a number of tables piled high with books and magazines. The walls were closely hung with pictures, a few framed, most of them tacked up in careless disarray. The room created an effect of intense intellectual and artistic activity, with no time to spare for style and very little for comfort.

"They're making a costume for me," John Robert explained. "Not for me to *wear*. Friends of mine in New York are going to do one of Sim's plays, and I'm supposed to do the costumes. It's a brilliant play. Do you know the Acorn Theater?"

"No, I don't think so."

"It's very off Broadway, naturally." He handed Phil a sketch as Sim silently presented him with the ouzo he'd been offered on arrival. The sketch was the only example he'd ever seen of John Robert's work that he could make head or tail of, but just barely. It was a fanciful costume, almost a dress, but with full trousers gathered at the ankles and an elaborate crownlike headdress. Phil thought of the Oberon in a production he'd seen of *A Midsummer Night's Dream*.

"Won't you have to go to New York if you do the costumes?" he asked.

"We'll be going in the fall. I'm sending this one to show them what I'm planning. We've made it to fit Manoli so we'd have a model. Would you model it for us?" He turned to Sally, who was apparently the leader of the sewing team. "Do you think it'll fit him?"

She looked at Phil for a long moment, her eyes moving over his body, a guilelessly innocent study without a trace of coquetry. "He's built like Manoli, isn't he," she decided. "I took some of his measurements just to get me started. Men are such a different shape 'than girls."

"They have that tendency," John Robert said with a giggle. He lifted his glass to Phil. "You'd be an angel to try it on for us. They'll have it finished tomorrow or the next day."

Phil looked dubiously at the yards of colorful gossamer cloth, the flowers and the garlands, and thought he'd look pretty silly. Sally's eyes lingered on him a moment longer and then she gave her head a little shake. "It's bad luck not to wait for Manoli, unless you think he's never coming back. Do you?" she asked forlornly, sounding like a bereaved child.

"If he doesn't, we have only Don to thank," John Robert snapped. "I'm going to put an end to it if he does come back. I've made up my mind about that." His voice dripped with venom. Phil found him rather frightening in a sort of absurd way; he wouldn't want him for an enemy.

"I suppose somebody should do something, but what?" Cynthia demanded.

"I'll manage it. I'm a match for that aging Canadian buffoon."

Phil couldn't guess what it was all about and was trying to think of a question that wouldn't sound prying when Sim reached for his glass and asked if he wanted another drink. As Sim turned away, he heard John Robert finishing a sentence.

"—done that, I don't think we'll hear much more out of him." John Robert sat back, looking malevolently pleased with himself while the women leaned to each other with scandalized laughter. John Robert looked at Phil, his expression clearing. "I get too absorbed in other people's lives here. Tell me about the books you do."

Phil suspended curiosity, hoping there would be more local gossip later. "The books that interest me, I'd have to show you for you to understand. I'll show you when you come to New York. Tell me more about the play. I didn't know you did anything so—well, so down-to-earth as costume design."

"Yes indeed, although I hope the play won't be all *that* down-to-earth. Cocteau and I used to dream up *the* most divine follies for Winnie de Polignac's soirees. I know what you mean, of course. Some of the poetry is lost when you turn an image into a thing. Cocteau and I used to argue about it, but he was basically more of a showman than a poet."

Phil was quickly caught up in John Robert's reminiscences of prewar Paris, and his curiosity faded into the back of his mind. He didn't really care much about Don and his involvement with a local boy. Sally and Cynthia bowed over their work, conferring together in whispers. Phil encouraged John Robert with questions. Sim came and went, refilling glasses, a neat, discreet houseboy. Eventually, he told John Robert that dinner was ready whenever he wanted it.

It was after eleven when Phil left with the women. He had enjoyed the evening, including Sim's highly spiced meal, and was inclined to be impressed by John Robert even though he didn't like what he knew of his work. The trio had taken only a few steps down the narrow street toward the port when Phil almost collided with the mustachioed man. He was so startled that he started to speak to him but checked himself as the man brushed past. Had he been waiting just outside John Robert's front door? Whatever he was up to, he obviously wasn't concerned about keeping himself out of sight. Failing to find any rational explanation for the man's being there, he wondered if it had been simply a chance encounter. That was as good a guess as any. Maybe Johnny would have an idea.

He stayed with the women past his own street and stopped to say good night when they told him their house was off to the right. They left him with friendly hugs and he went on down to the port, hoping to find Johnny. He couldn't remember when Johnny had last mentioned the man. Yesterday? Something, maybe the sleep before dinner, had turned time upside down. He had to think a minute to be absolutely sure that he'd had his swim today. It seemed like several days ago. This was the first time he'd been on the port at night.

The cafes were brightly lighted, but it was too chilly for anybody to be sitting out in front of them. He heard music, the fast, swirling music he associated with Greek dancing, and followed it to its source in the cafe next to the one they went to at midday. He entered a big bare room, full if not crowded with Greek males, predominantly young but with an admixture of older men at several tables. Most of them had metal measures of wine in front of them. The musicians were at the far end of the room, and in a cleared area in front of them five or six young men in a row, linked by handkerchiefs, were dancing. It was the sort of intricate dance with much stamping that his Greek friend had taken him to see in New York, but he'd seen nothing like it in Athens. There, everybody had opted for the West.

He saw the Shackletons across the room sitting with Anne and Harvey and a very tall young black man. Phil had noticed him around, but they hadn't spoken. His eyes continued to search for Johnny as he started forward. He was aware of a boisterous group of Greeks at a table, waving and calling out to him. As he was passing them with a friendly smile, one of them reached out to him and pulled him into a chair beside him. The others laughed and cheered. They were all dressed alike in bulky dark high-necked sweaters and thick dark pants, a vaguely nautical uniform. The one next to him, the one who had commandeered him, was almost handsome; the others were rough, nondescript-looking guys but their youth and cheerful high spirits were disarming. The one next to him told him his name was Pavlo and put an arm around him in an embrace that bordered on being amorous. Phil's cock registered pleasure. The others eyed him with laughing appraisal, and their bawdy remarks hinted that they were all thinking of propositioning him. He took a swallow of the retsina he'd been handed.

Andreas, his friend in New York, had told him that it wasn't unusual for young Greeks to hunt in packs looking for a boy who would accept the passive role in communal copulation. The idea didn't appeal to him, and Phil wasn't even sure he should be sitting with them. Eyes might be watching from the crowd. He didn't want to do anything that might compromise Johnny; a guy with questionable sexual tastes could be considered a liability to the rescue operation. He started to pull away, but the Greek held him as if he intended to keep him.

"You're very handsome," Pavlo said. "I love you."

In Greek, the declaration wasn't as startling as it

would have been in English. Phil knew that the verb was used to describe feelings for casual friends as well as lovers. Pavlo seemed ready to be both. He took Phil's hand and put it on his crotch. Phil let his fingers stray over thick cloth and felt the hard core within. There was too much bulky cloth for him to gauge it accurately, but there seemed to be quite à lot of it. Groping seemed to be the fashion this season.

"You like it?" Pavlo asked confidently.

"Very much," Phil said politely.

"You'll like what I do with it. You come with us. We'll have some fun. You have someplace we can go?"

"No." The music swirled around him. Voices dinned in his ears. The others looked at him with an expectant glitter in their eyes. He supposed they were all planning to fuck him. Four of them and Pavlo made five. The more the merrier. If he thought he could be so thoroughly fucked that he'd never want to be fucked again, he might consider it. He exerted pressure on the flesh he held and felt it swell against the thick cloth. Pavlo smiled approvingly. "We get you into the barracks. We have a friend with a taxi. He'll take us. A beautiful boy; everybody will want you."

Beautiful was another word that was used loosely to cover everything that didn't actually offend the eyes. It turned out that "everyone" were cadets at the naval base in Soudha Bay, like his present companions. He'd heard of Soudha Bay but hadn't known that it was only a couple of miles away. They wanted to turn him loose in the barracks. He had tried for years to lure Alex into fucking him. Now he was being offered the Greek Navy.

Andreas had told him a lot about Greek attitudes toward homosexuality. Although it was taken for granted that normal guys had sex together, their lovemaking was hemmed about with taboos. They didn't kiss. They regarded cocksuckers with contempt. They made it a point of honor to prefer the active role, although in the nature of things there had to be some give and take.

Pavlo's smile was complacent, tinged with scorn. "Are you a *pousti*?" he asked.

Phil recognized and accepted the derogatory equivalent of "fairy" or "faggot." For once, he didn't feel like lying. He met his eyes and shrugged. "Yes," he said firmly.

The Greeks looked at each other across the table and Pavlo nodded. He poured Phil more wine and spread his legs wider to allow Phil's hand more scope. "You feel how big it is?" he asked.

"A big man," Phil agreed. He drank some wine and straightened and leaned slightly to one side to check the Shackletons, thinking of them as a line of retreat. They were gone, taking with them his tenuous ties to his new community. The fast, lilting music was an infectious celebration of his independence. He'd just discovered that he could tell anybody that he was a faggot and the hell with the sneers, the jeers, the pitying looks. It gave him a feeling of proud self-assurance and the thought that there must be better things to do with it than groping a moderately attractive young tough, no matter how big his cock was.

"You go with me?" Phil asked, more to find out if Andreas had been a reliable informant than from genuine interest in Pavlo. "I have a place I take you. Not others."

"You and me? Only two is no good. I want us to stay with my friends. Maybe it's different for a *pousti*."

"That is so." He wondered why he'd always shrunk from telling people that he was a faggot. It had a stimulating effect on Pavlo. He grew more amorous and even went so far as to touch Phil's quiescent cock.

They ordered more wine and Phil was shouted down when he tried to pay. The retsina had begun to make his head swim agreeably. The dancers left the floor and Phil's companions stood up. Pavlo, adjusting his crotch, pulled Phil along with them.

They made their way through the tables and lined up in front of the musicians, linked to each other by corners of grubby handkerchiefs. They began to move to the music, but the rhythm was more intricate than Phil had realized. There was a hidden beat in it that he hadn't heard and that kept eluding him so that he got caught on the wrong foot at critical moments. The retsina might have something to do with it. After a few more failures, he let go of the bit of handkerchief and withdrew amid laughter and cheers.

He watched the line advancing and reversing, the dancers moving in unison, leaping, dipping, stamping their feet, effortlessly expert. It was an impressive show, almost impressive enough for Phil to let them all fuck him.

He drifted farther back among the tables until he reached the one they had vacated. Standing beside it, he took a swallow of the wine he had left and checked the dancers. Nobody was paying any attention to him. He put down the glass and turned and quickly slipped away.

He walked briskly around the port, keeping an eye out for the guy who still seemed to have them under surveillance. He was pleased with himself for not doing anything that might embarrass Johnny.

He turned into his narrow street and after a few moments peered up at Johnny's house, prepared to go in, but no lights were showing so he continued the short climb home. Alone as usual. A dose of debauchery might be good for him, but it wasn't in his nature. He was as free as air, free to do anything he chose, but freedom included the right to say no. He had never gone in for the seamier side of sex, the street pickups, the fun and games at the baths, even the more respectable orgies that some of his friends organized as social events. Maybe he was a prude but it was a real part of who he was. At least he had got around at last to admitting that he was queer. That had felt good.

K yria Vassiliki had his hot coffee-flavored milk ready for him in the morning and as soon as he had drunk it, he headed back to Johnny's house. This time, he climbed up through the house to his room again without success. Questioned, Kyria Katerini said she hadn't seen him since the day before. She wasn't sure whether he'd spent the night there, but if he had he must have gone out very early.

"Mr. Johnny, you never know with him," she said roguishly. "He has his secrets. He doesn't tell me all of them."

Phil thanked her and left. He was sure Johnny wouldn't go anywhere for long without letting him know, so he assumed he'd turn up for the sacrosanct midday gathering. Hesitating under the blazing sun, he decided on a swim before allowing himself a beer. He returned to his beach without encountering a soul. He was amazed that the magnificent sweep of sand and sea didn't draw a crowd; anywhere else you'd be picking your way over the bodies.

He walked along the edge of the sea, discarding clothes as he went, first his T-shirt, next his sandals and shorts. It seemed ludicrously modest to wear anything, but on the off chance that somebody would suddenly materialize out of nowhere, he settled for rolling down his jockey shorts to the line of his pubic hair. He wanted to get rid of the white patch around his middle. He tanned quickly and the rest of him was already a gratifying coppery brown.

He approached the jagged bits of his ruined shed and hung his clothes on the convenient planks. Stretched out on his back on the sand, he spread his legs and rolled his jockeys still lower so that only his cock and the parts of him encircled by elastic were unexposed. Next time he must remember to bring a towel to cover himself in an emergency without having to actually wear anything.

He exhaled a long, contented breath. His beach. His sun. His sea. He was very aware of his freedom. Nothing but a sense of his own identity—that was the way to travel through life. He needed nothing more. The only thing he could think of wanting at the moment was a sail in Johnny's boat. He couldn't bother to think back and divide the time he'd been here into days, but surely it had been long enough for Johnny to have settled down again. Maybe he'd been out early this morning getting her shipshape. If they didn't run into each other beforehand, he'd go look later. He moved his arms to expose their underside to the sun.

The clan was settling down with their mail at the big cafe table when Phil returned from the beach. The Shackletons gave him their funny straight-armed salute. He stopped behind John Robert with a hand on his shoulder and thanked him for dinner. Johnny wasn't there. The Shackletons were watching him expectantly and he went around to them. They pulled a chair around between them and he sat.

"You have to be between us so we won't be jealous," Bryan said. "What a stunner. You're getting as black as a native. That is, if we had black natives here." He ran his arm over Phil's back and shoulders in a long exploratory caress. "Crikey, that turns my legs to water. Your body knocked us both for a loop. It's a living, breathing work of art. Angie wants to take charge of its care and feeding. Will you let her cook you dinner tomorrow night? We can roll a joint and generally misbehave. Our theory is that you can't have too much of a good thing."

"That makes sense." He indicated the next cafe. "I saw you at the ball last night. You were with a black guy."

"That's Lester, Harvey's boyfriend. Why didn't you join us?" Angela reproached him.

"I was about to but I got waylaid by a bunch of jolly tars."

"Did they abduct you and take turns having you?" Bryan asked as if it were an ordinary occurrence.

"No, but they suggested it. I was sort of interested in one of them."

"That won't get you anywhere here. The poor dears are terrified of doing anything without half a dozen of their pals in tow."

"So I've heard. Very peculiar. Speaking of which, why doesn't anybody go to the beach?"

"Which one do you go to?"

"On out that way, beyond those houses, the one I thought you mentioned."

"Yes, we go there, but first thing in the morning before we go to work. The social swim is over there from those rocks on the other side of the entrance to the port. There's plenty of group activity there, but it's a bit early in the season for it."

"That suits me. I feel as if the beach belongs to me, but I'll let you use it."

"We don't wear anything. If you were with us, I think we might frighten the horses."

"I haven't seen any horses." Phil's deadpan delivery

made them laugh. "I haven't seen Johnny either. Does anybody know what he's been up to?"

"He's around. We saw him this morning, didn't we, angel?" Bryan looked at his wife for confirmation.

"This morning? That was yesterday, wasn't it?" she said vaguely.

"Perhaps so."

Phil wasn't the only one who couldn't keep the days straight. Before the question was settled, Don joined them, taking a chair opposite Phil and placing a small sheaf of letters in front of him. "Greetings all." He beamed plumply at them.

"I hear Manoli is back," Bryan said.

"Not yet. Any day now, I imagine."

"Somebody told me they'd seen him," Bryan said lazily, with enough of a smile lurking behind his eyes to make Phil think he might be teasing the Canadian.

"Nonsense," Don snapped testily. "He'd come to me the minute he got here. Who told you?"

"It must've been Sally."

Don leaned forward and called down the table. "Sally, have you seen Manoli?"

"I'm not sure. I thought I caught a glimpse of him at the end of the street when I was going into the post office. I may've been mistaken."

Don sat back, his good temper restored. "There you are. I was sure you were wrong. I'll let you know when he's here."

Johnny still hadn't appeared when the gathering began to break up. Phil offered to buy the Shackletons some lunch and share a bottle of wine with them. A more expansive invitation seemed inappropriate here. He talked to them about their work and about New York agents and publishers, and a warm feeling of friendship was created between them, seasoned invitingly by sex. They parted when they'd eaten lightly, the couple for home, Phil to go look at the boat. He saw no signs of any alterations having been made on it and went home for a nap, hoping that Johnny wasn't going to turn out to be as elusive as Manoli.

He prepared for an afternoon visit to his beach by putting on his brief swimsuit under his shorts and rolling his suntan oil into the big beach towel he'd brought with him. He was passing the last buildings that bordered the beach when a man turned into the street in front of him and headed in his direction. Phil's heart skipped a beat and his scalp tightened as he was gripped by thoughts of George. It was only a fleeting seizure. As they passed each other, a furtive glance told Phil that only a trick of light falling on the man from behind had made him see the set of George's head and shoulders. Manoli again? He hadn't really seen him with Johnny in Piraeus, but there too it had been the set of the head that had reminded him so vividly of George. Maybe Sally had been right. Maybe Manoli had come back without letting anybody know. Or maybe he'd gone straight to Johnny and they'd been doing something together. The guy he'd just passed wasn't as young as he initially expected Manoli to be, closer to thirty than twenty, but strikingly handsome, which fitted. It required a small effort of will to stop himself from turning to look back at him.

He didn't look back until he had reached the scraps of ruined shed and hung his T-shirt on what he thought of as the fence. Before taking anything else off, he surveyed the vast expanse of sand in both directions. As before, he could see figures at the far end, moving in a way that suggested organized activity. Some sort of game? In the other direction, toward the port, a figure was sitting where nobody had been when he'd passed a few minutes ago.

Somebody had come along after him, but it wasn't the guy he'd decided must be Manoli. For one guy to remind him of George was fair enough, but there had to be a limit, unless he was going nuts.

Smiling to himself, he stripped off shorts and swimsuit and felt the sudden caress of sun and air on every part of him. Pure bliss. He planted his feet apart and stretched, reaching for the sky, and his cock immediately swelled and lengthened into partial erection. He was free and naked, his pleasure in his own body gathering into a tingling in his groin.

He lowered his arms slowly and let his hands stray teasingly across his chest and abdomen while his cock continued to harden and lift until it stood upright. He dropped his hands to his hips and thrust them forward and looked down at himself. Not bad.

Being out-of-doors like this, naked and aroused, turned him into whatever the opposite of a prude was. If five sailors wanted him now, they could have him. His hands crept to his hard flesh, delighting in the feel of it. He was more tempted to masturbate than he had been since he was a kid, but he thought of the forlorn aftermath and resisted. It felt too good the way it was now, full of the potential for ecstasy.

He took another look around him. Everybody was keeping his distance. His cock would have to be even bigger than he'd like it to be for anybody in sight to see what it was doing. He could make a dash back for his towel if modesty were unexpectedly required. He took his shorts with him in case of emergency and strolled down to the edge of the sea, his cock swinging out in a wide arc in front of him with every step. Its air of flaunting itself, of calling attention to itself made him smile.

He stood facing the sea but keeping his feet dry to savor

for another moment the joy of his priapic nakedness. He knew that the cold water would bring his games to an abrupt end. He provoked and toyed with himself while his body seemed to sing in harmonious communication with nature. When he had strained his control almost to the breaking point, he took a deep breath and tossed his shorts behind him and plunged in. It was an exhilarating shock, a different sort of physical harmony, and when he came splashing back to the beach his manhood was sadly shrunken. He snatched up his shorts and trotted up to his towel, much more inclined to hide himself now than when he'd been committing a public indecency.

A vigorous rubdown set his blood circulating again, and by the time he'd dried his crotch thoroughly he no longer felt like a eunuch. He spread the towel, lay out on his back, and arranged his brief swimsuit over his cock, not so much for modesty as to protect it from burning. The sun was still high and stung him more penetratingly than ever before. Another few days like today and he'd be able to stay out on the boat for a week without suffering any ill effects. He really must stir Johnny up about taking a sail.

His thoughts began to blur and run into each other. Was he going somewhere on a boat with George? No, that was Michigan. They'd done a bit of sailing on a lake. Maybe George would like to go for a sail when . . . . He slept.

He stirred and rubbed his nose and realized that he had a hard on again. He smiled and moved a hand down over himself, feeling for his swimsuit. The little scrap of cloth was still there, but it was no longer doing a very efficient job of covering him. It had slipped to one side and his cock was lying naked on his belly. His smile broadened as he ran his hand along it. Hard as a rock. He flattened his hand under it and pushed it upright from the base. It felt as if it were soaring to the sky, sending the first signs of orgasm shivering through him. His eyes fluttered open to see if it looked more impressive than usual. A cry broke from him and he jerked upright, covering himself, his heart pounding.

Manoli was standing a few feet from him, naked except for scanty trunks that could barely contain the erection curving up against his groin. He stood looking down at him, his back to the fence. Their eyes met and Phil took a quick breath. He didn't doubt for an instant that this was Manoli. He sensed inevitability in their meeting. He could see danger in the other's dark stare, the fire of suppressed violence. He felt threatened, hypnotized. Manoli's handsome face was cold and expressionless. His hands made a quick movement on his trunks and his cock swung out and lifted over him. The trunks fell to his feet and he kicked them aside. He took a step forward.

Phil moved in a dream, as if everything they were doing had been rehearsed. He lifted his bottle of suntan oil and their hands touched briefly as Manoli took it. Phil rolled up onto his hands and knees and lowered his head, submitting. Manoli dropped down behind him. He felt something brushing against his buttocks and then Manoli gripped his hips with oily hands and entered him masterfully. Phil moaned in rapturous welcome. There was no warmth of intimacy in the joining of their bodies. Phil was being taken and used mercilessly. He felt as if he were being subjected to some unnameable indignity. He was being fucked with contempt. Resentment seethed in him, but he was powerless, unwilling to express it in any way. Manoli held him in an iron grip of desire.

Phil had never felt anybody so charged with sexual energy; it crackled all through him. He was being taken as he'd always wanted to be taken, with a driving will to demolish his shame and every other barrier of resistance in him, reducing him to a grateful instrument for male gratificiation. He had seen Manoli's cock without being struck by its size, yet its relentless power was devastating. He was enslaved by it.

Phil dissolved in the rising tide of his orgasm. He clutched his swimsuit against his straining erection and moaned with the rhythm of Manoli's coldly triumphant possession of him: He cried out as his climax broke and his body shuddered and buckled with the successive waves of his release. Manoli flung his weight forward and bore down on him with his hands on his shoulders, slamming his hips in hard against him. Phill shouted with his own bitter triumph as he opened himself completely to Manoli's extravagant demands. He had cheated the conqueror of victory; instead, they were joined briefly in an equality of giving and taking. From Manoli came a strange despairing sound, and heaving with the throes of orgasm, he delivered himself into Phil. The two remained for a moment, suspended in stunned immobility and then Manoli withdrew roughly and sprang up. He grabbed his trunks and ran down the beach and plunged into the sea. Phil wondered if he kept score. Add another foreign faggot to the list. Phil felt destroyed by the encounter. Something irreplaceable had been taken from him.

He pulled himself slowly to his feet, holding his sodden swimsuit rolled into a ball, and followed Manoli to the water. Walking naked under the blazing sun, he was only now becoming aware of the folly they had committed—but nobody had approached. He supposed people fucked on beaches all over the world and got away with it, but he was surprised that what he thought of as his fastidiousness hadn't prompted at least a moment of shocked resistance. On the contrary, he'd acted as if he'd been waiting for it.

After Alex's soft devious passivity, there was something

bracing about the Greek's downright self-assertion. Even his contempt aroused Phil's begrudging admiration and challenged him to prove himself. Something had happened at the end to redress the balance between them. He didn't understand it and doubted if Manoli did either, but he must have felt it too. He suspected that the Greek had been taken unaware by the strength of his own desire.

He wanted to be with him now to see if anything had emerged from the cold-blooded encounter, but Manoli was swimming quite far out and he'd be damned if he'd chase him. He walked through the small breakers and stopped when the numbing water was up to his waist. He opened out his swimsuit and swirled it about, rinsing and wringing until all traces of what he'd used it for was gone.

Manoli headed in toward him and Phil's heartbeat accelerated. He watched for a look or a touch that would acknowledge him. When he was close, Phil rose from the water and stood a few feet from him. Manoli had put his trunks on. Their eyes met. Manoli's were wary and in their depths Phil detected incredulity, as if he expected to find somebody else there. The Greek's head was beautifully modeled and the high, flat cheekbones and straight nose carried the reminder of George's keen refinement. Phil wanted to reach out and hold him. All the nonsense about his own body being a work of art applied equally to Manoli's. He appeared to be a shade shorter than Phil, but his shoulders were wider, lightly balanced, and his smoothly muscular torso was hairless, an even dark honey-brown everywhere. A statue. A body he could worship if he let himself. In spite of the numbing cold, Phil's cock jutted forward, buoyed by the sea and magnified by it. Manoli's eyes didn't drop to it. He nodded faintly.

"I'm Manoli. I'll see you later," he said in a neutral voice. He turned away and splashed up out of the water and continued on across the beach, past the fence, toward the cultivated land beyond. Phil watched his departing back, mesmerized by the flow of muscle, from the wide graceful shoulders to the compact buttocks molded in the tight trunks to the spring of his calves as he made his way over loose sand. The poetry of power. He must have been heading for a path because when he reached the greenery he turned aside and quickly vanished. Phil felt a sharp wrench of loss.

He would see him later? Very probably but maybe not in the way Manoli meant. He was going to have to avoid Manoli if he hoped to preserve his newfound peace of mind. As far as he was concerned, Manoli was dynamite, to be handled with great care. He wondered when he was going to make his official reentry into the life of the port. He hung his swimsuit around his neck and pushed off for a brisk swim.

B y the time he had showered and dressed for the evening, he knew that he was working himself up to making a fool of himself again. All his remaining time on the beach had been haunted by sensual memories of Manoli, by his dangerous eyes, the feel of his body against his. He had longed for Manoli to be in him again. All during the walk home, he had looked for Manoli everywhere, had seen him a dozen times, had almost called out to him. He relived every moment they had been together. His heart raced when he thought of Manoli's hands moving to his trunks and releasing his cock. *I'm Manoli. I'll see you later.* The only words he'd heard him speak. He'd heard the flat neutrality in his voice, but he was sure that there had been a special message in it, a pledge, a promise, the declaration of a pact between them. They were going to belong to each other. Later. He was going to find a way to be with him later.

Phil shook his head. He was stark raving mad. Certifiable. He couldn't let himself fall for another shit. He'd just been through all that. Johnny had as good as told him that Manoli was a whore, and even if he wasn't he'd been behaving whorishly with Don and maybe with John Robert too. Don had a knack of making everything sound distasteful, but he wouldn't be able to if Manoli hadn't given him some reason to. What's the matter with the brain you presumably were given at birth? Phil asked himself. A Greek had seen a more or less presentable guy naked on the beach and had fucked him because he had nothing better to do. Hardly material for a great romance. Nothing to build a life on. For a moment Phil felt as if he might have recovered his sanity. Stick to the facts. He'd been ready for a good fuck. The same with Manoli. That was all the afternoon had added up to. If Phil kept reminding himself of that and got his evening moving, by morning he would've forgotten everything else. He snatched up some money and hurried out. At least he didn't have to waste time making plans. This place was like a club. There was always someone around to have a drink with. Or have a fuck with, as far as that was concerned. First, he wanted to try to find Johnny.

He was only halfway down the stairs when his steps slowed. Manoli might come here looking for him. He didn't want to risk missing him. He took a few more reluctant steps and paused at the top of the last flight. Did he intend to stay here waiting for the rest of his life? Hadn't he just decided he didn't care if he never saw

Manoli again? Even if he changed his mind, he knew meetings here always took place on the port. People didn't go to each other's houses unless they were invited. Christ, he was letting his madness get a grip on him again. He was wretchedly familiar with the state of mind he risked getting into. He had spent enough hours of his life sitting beside a telephone that never rang. He was a blasted idiot. Get moving, he told himself viciously.

He forced himself down the stairs and into the street. He almost ran down the short distance to Johnny's door, as if he were afraid of being grabbed and dragged back. The door was unlocked as usual, and he took the stairs two at a time. He wanted to make his meeting with Johnny quick and get down to the port. Manoli would find him easily there. He called as he reached the top of the last flight and there was an answering call from the room. Johnny turned to him from his worktable when he made his breathless appearance.

"Howdy, stranger," Johnny said in his best movie Americanese.

"Howdy, yourself. You disappeared. Where've you been?"

"Harry Whitelaw turned up on his yacht late yesterday afternoon. I hitched a ride with him to Heraklion. It gave me a chance to travel in style and get some business done. I just got back on the bus."

"Who's Harry Whitelaw?" They stood close to each other, giving each other little pats of welcome. Johnny squeezed Phil's buttocks appreciatively.

"Harry? I thought you might know. I'm told his father was famous in the States for some great political scandal in the twenties. It was to do with oil, I believe, but teapots somehow figure too. I find American politics baffling. The part that isn't baffling is that he skipped the country with vast sums of money that didn't belong to him. It's all Harry's now, bless his simple Yankee heart.''

Phil laughed and draped an arm around Johnny's shoulders. Johnny continued to toy agreeably with his buttocks. It was a comfort to be with Johnny again. ''There was something called the Teapot Dome Scandal. Maybe that's it. I don't know much about it. Like Watergate, only it was all about some big financial swindle. You had business with Harry?''

''No, indeed. Dear me, no. Wait till you meet him. He's coming back sometime tomorrow. We're invited on board for dinner tomorrow night.''

''Tomorrow night? I think that's when I'm supposed to go to the Shackletons.''

''Not to worry. There's a tradition here that all other engagements go by the board when a yacht comes in. The Shackletons will understand. Manoli will probably be with us. He's back. He drove up in a taxi with Hilda just as I was getting out of the bus. I told him that Harry had sent Don an invitation that included him. Harry hasn't met Manoli. No more have you, now that I think of it. It should be an interesting evening.''

''Manoli? *The* Manoli?'' Phil managed, his mind whirling with conjecture.

''God forbid there should be two of them,'' Johnny said dryly.

''When was this? When did you get here?''

''Just now. Half an hour ago.''

''I see.'' He broke away from Johnny and took a few steps around the table, breathing deeply to control the alarming activity of his heart. It felt as if it were performing somersaults in his chest. What was the matter with him now? Did he resent Manoli making a mystery of his return because in effect it made a nonevent of their meeting? Was

he angry with Johnny for offering the Greek to a rich
American with a yacht? Was he outraged by any mention
of Manoli as a trespass on his private domain? His insanity
had taken a turn for the worse. He forced himself to listen
to Johnny, who was speaking of his own adult world.

"—in Heraklion. I think I found out all I wanted to
know. I thought we might take the boat out tomorrow."

"I was going to ask you if it wasn't about time. I've
come by several times. I wanted to tell you that I found
our tail waiting outside John Robert's house the night—
last night, I guess, after I had dinner there."

"That's what I'm trying to explain, rather. We don't
have to worry about him. He's on our side. He's secret
police. Very secret. You might say that he's looking after
us, me mostly, but you too now that they know you're in
it. They want to make sure that nobody takes a sudden
unhealthy interest in us. We can forget about him and let
him get on with his job. He may be around until we take
off."

Phil felt his sanity returning. This was something he
could think about reasonably, not a fuck on the beach. He
turned to Johnny and looked into his appealingly homely
face, lively with irony and humor. Johnny was the reason
for his being here. They were partners in a serious under-
taking. "Have they said anything more about dates?" he
asked to prove to himself that it was important to him.

"For our big voyage? No, but I have the feeling it'll be
pretty soon. The fuel tanks are full. I'll top up the water
supply in the next couple of days. We can start taking on
provisions. I want to be ready to leave within a few hours'
notice. I don't think they'll give us more than that. They'll
be watching the weather reports. I'm pretty sure we have
another week. After that, it could be any minute."

Phil's interest focused. This was what he needed—activity,

something to keep his mind occupied, rational priorities. Going off for a week on a boat with Johnny was going to be damned exciting, complete with good times in bed. He had learned that promiscuous sex didn't work as an antidote to infatuation, but Johnny would be a real comfort, a friend who offered him affection as well as the satisfactions of his handsomely endowed body.

"I can't wait to learn how to handle the boat," he said. "You can't work in the dark. Come have a drink."

The sun was getting low in the sky when they headed down the street toward the port. Phil's heart was beating so erratically that at moments he had trouble catching his breath while he kept up with Johnny. He had to see Manoli. He didn't care if they didn't have a chance to really talk. To see him, to look into his eyes would tell him how he was going to have to deal with him. He might discover immediately that he could dismiss him from his thoughts without any difficulty. It might have been simply a sexual shock that would have no repercussions. At worst, he would steel himself to resist the attraction. He wasn't going to let a Greek hustler turn his life upside down.

"You said Manoli came with Hilda," he reminded Johnny. "Who's she? Does he have a girlfriend?"

"If he has, it's definitely not Hilda. She's nobody's girlfriend. She's one of the world's great femmes fatales. I think you'll be fascinated by her. I am."

"She lives here?"

"Like I do. As much as she can, with enforced retreats to greener fields to forage for supplies. She has husbands."

"Plural husbands?"

"I believe she's careless about divorce. She has several who're eager to pay her to leave after she's been with them for a month or two. They forget what a fiend she can be when they haven't seen her for a while. At least, that's her story. I suspect they're so dazzled by her that they fall in love with her all over again and give her anything she asks for. She's been gone for four or five months this time. God knows where she found Manoli.''

Right here, Phil thought, where he's been since noon or earlier, waiting to pretend that he'd just arrived. He knew that it was ridiculous of him to feel it as a personal affront. ''She sounds like quite a lady,'' he said, not sure it was an appropriate response to anything Johnny had said. His attention span had shrunk to a matter of seconds.

''You'll see. Everybody was gathering to give her a big welcome when I left her.''

Nearing their cafe, Phil saw that all the familiar faces were present, but they hadn't commandeered the big table this evening. They were scattered about in groups. His eyes came to rest on a group of five sitting in front on the corner. Don. John Robert and Sim. A striking-looking woman. The back of a dark head that reminded him of George. There was only one Manoli and he was here. Phil felt everything go slack in him. He felt as if a great weight had been lifted from him. The beating of his heart subsided and smoothed out. His breathing returned to normal. All the odd pressures, induced by nothing he could name, that had distorted the natural functions of his senses—all were gone.

Don saw them approaching and waved a pudgy hand at them. ''Come join us,'' he called. ''You're just the pair we've been looking for.''

They stood beside the table while they all greeted each other. Phil's and Hilda's names were pronounced, and she offered him a strong but elegantly formed hand and gave him a firm grip, accompanied by a smile of touchingly tender charm, a very feminine smile. It was Manoli's turn.

He grunted something and looked up at him with eyes that were cold with warning. Their handshake was so fleeting that it might have been thought that they instantly found each other physically repellent. Chairs were pushed around and they sat, Phil between Hilda and Johnny, with Manoli opposite him. Phil felt no great compulsion to be beside him, to make contact with his body or his eyes. *I'll see you later*. This meeting was hardly worth making a point about. Later was yet to come. He turned to Hilda.

"Everybody tells me about Johnny's thrilling new friend," she said. "I knew it was time to come see all my babies. I'm very emotioned to be back." Her English was heavily flavored with a Middle European accent but fluent and relatively flawless, tripping over an occasional word. Phil was immediately spellbound by her. She had a head off a coin, a Byzantine empress's head, with a jutting nose and a full, sensual mouth. Her enormous greenish eyes gazed at him with candid warmth and interest.

"I hear you three all arrived at the same moment," Don said to Johnny.

"Practically hand in hand."

Phil glanced at Manoli and again caught the warning look. What was he afraid of? Did he think he was going to say, I liked the way you fucked me on the beach this afternoon? It seemed to him that their secret was reasonably safe. A waiter he hadn't seen before paused at the table and Phil leaned forward. "Order drinks, everybody. This is on me. It's about time I said thank you for all your hospitality."

"No, no," Hilda protested. "The party is mine. I've dreamed of it for months. Every day, trudging through the snow in Paris, I dream of this evening. Everything is so cheap here. Tonight, I'm a millionaire."

Her accent was exotically evocative; she made Paris

sound like the steppes of Russia. There was a husky gurgle
in her voice that shifted easily into laughter. Her smile was
radiant despite imperfect teeth; Phil noticed a gap at one
side that showed frequently. Her abundant auburn hair was
streaked with gray. She seemed to be wearing no makeup
and her skin was unlined, but he guessed she might be
well into her forties. She was simply dressed in slacks and
a bulky loose-knit sweater with a no-nonsense rolled collar, but he found her enormously glamorous. She seemed
to put them all on their mettle. He felt a lift in the air, a
febrile gaiety that emanated from her to include the tables
around them. He realized that they were the focus of
everybody's attention; when he glanced around him he saw
eyes on them. Even Manoli seemed less self-enclosed,
more vulnerable. He caught a look of almost youthful
admiration in his handsome face when he glanced across
the table at Hilda.

While they all ordered, repeating their orders as the
waiter grew increasingly confused, Phil noticed a small
donkey wearing a straw hat tethered to the stanchion that
held the awning up behind Hilda. A wooden saddle was
strung with brightly colored local woven bags. "A friend
of yours?" he asked her, indicating the beast.

She glanced back and uttered her enchanting laughter.
"Of course. That is Animal. He's mine. I call him Annie
for short. He's a boy donkey, but he doesn't mind. He's
very sophisticated for a donkey. He has to be to live in a
place like this. How would I get my Vuitton luggage home
without him?" She laughed again and laid a hand on Phil's
forearm, looking at him as if he were the only person in
the world she wanted to look at. "You are the most
beautiful color I've ever seen."

Her eyes and her hand were on him as if he belonged to

some charmed inner circle. "I've been sunbathing naked on the beach," he explained.

"You must tell us where. We'll all come look. I think it must be a lovely sight."

A knee was pressed to his. It was placed wrong to be Hilda's. He looked quickly around the table. It could only be Manoli's. Their eyes met briefly. The knee moved up and down against his and was withdrawn, leaving Phil with an erection. He was stunned. A blatant sexual tease was the last thing he would have expected from the macho Greek. It excited him but he was obscurely disappointed in him. He had seen again what he had thought of earlier as incredulity in his eyes, more like bewilderment this time, as if he didn't know what to make of him or of his own reaction to him. It didn't fit the picture he had formed of him as a sexual thug. It was more what he would expect of a silly, mixed-up queer like himself. If Manoli turned out to be a closet *pousti,* he could feel a little healthy contempt himself, and insanity would be cured before the evening was over.

Hilda was the most effective antidote he could have hoped for. She would have kept him delighted and amused even if he'd been undergoing major surgery. She talked about Paris and various husbands, uttering her lovely gurgling laughter. Even sexually she didn't leave him indifferent. She gave him the impression that if she wanted a man she would make him feel like the most wanted, most admired, most cherisehd man in the world. If she ever showed any interest in him in that direction, he doubted if he would resist finding out where it led. He didn't even notice that no drinks had been brought until Don began to twist around in his chair, waving his hands and snapping his fingers. "Really, the service here sometimes makes me wonder why they open for business," he exclaimed petulantly.

"No doubt in Canada you're accustomed to an army of flunkies to do your bidding," John Robert said in his thin, womanish voice. "Unfortunately, the Greeks don't know what an important man they have in their midst."

"At least I can pay my bill if I run one up."

"Oh, we know you can buy us all if you choose, but you're careful not to let it get to that point, aren't you."

Don seethed. Phil could almost hear his rage bubbling in him. It had suddenly become an obscene confrontation, spiteful and spinsterish, although the words that had been exchanged seemed only mildly taunting. "Hilda has been kind enough to offer us drinks," Don said, apparently shifting his ground. "I think it only common courtesy to see that they serve her order."

"I'm sure Hilda can get all the service she needs without any help from you."

"Then what're we waiting for?" Don snapped. "Manoli, go see that they serve our drinks."

"Why should he?" John Robert demanded rudely. "He's not a waiter." Phil mentally applauded.

"He knows all these people," Don persisted. "He can get the drinks himself. Manoli, you heard me."

The note of command was shocking. Phil immediately allied himself with Manoli. He looked across at his hands on the table doubled into fists. The knuckles were white. His head was slightly lowered over them. Phil held his breath. He had seen the potential violence in the Greek's eyes. With infinite sweetness, Hilda leaned across the table and gently touched Manoli's cheek with her fingers. It was so nearly what Phil wanted to do that it gave him goose bumps. Manoli lifted his head and looked at her with touching gratitude. She murmured something that

Phil didn't hear, more a movement of her lips than speech. He saw the communion of their eyes deepen, and all the signs of stress faded from his face. Phil realized for the first time that his mouth was capable of tenderness. He saw them exchange a slight nod and then Manoli sprang up and flung himself away from the table. Everybody seemed to slump with relief in their chairs except Don, who continued to look peevish but pleased with himself.

"Don't be naughty, darling," Hilda said to him. "Be sure to thank him nicely."

Phil found the whole scene incomprehensible, although it was clear that there was something to be understood from the way Hilda had controlled it. Obviously, Don had some hold over Manoli and was willing to humiliate him publicly to prove it. His daring seemed foolhardy. The Greek's pride was almost palpable. Don was asking to have his plump face bashed in. Maybe it was as simple as that. John Robert was bitchily ready to aggravate an antagonism wherever he saw one. The exchange had left Phil feeling nervous and uneasy. He waited for Hilda to restore the party atmosphere.

In another moment Manoli returned and dropped into his chair. Phil noticed that his clothes didn't look local, more like American "leisure wear" that could be expensive—well-cut washable pants, a becoming sports shirt, a lightweight combination jacket-windbreaker. He wore them with style. He was followed by the waiter, who laboriously served the drinks.

"There. What did I tell you?" Don said to John Robert. "Manoli knows how to deal with his own people. If we left it up to you, we'd sit here all evening without a drink."

Hilda lifted her glass to Manoli. "Thank you, darling," she said, filling her words with resonances that went far beyond the drink. Phil avoided looking at him, embarrassed at being a witness to his surrender. He hadn't expected to see him as an underdog; it made Phil more susceptible to his attraction. He wanted to say or do something that would show him that he admired him for taking Don's behavior in his stride. Jesus, how complicated it could get justifying wanting a guy who spelled trouble.

Hilda's gaiety prevailed. The force of her personality compelled response, weaving them into an ensemble like an orchestra conductor. Their music was sweet despite the sour notes sounded by Don and John Robert. She had been away. She had come back. She required them to make her glad that she'd come back.

Although reserved, Manoli was more animated than Phil had expected. He had his slightly fierce charm. Whenever he felt that Manoli's attention was fixed on somebody else, usually Johnny or Hilda, he let his eyes linger on his mouth. It was very firm but not hard or cruel as he had imagined it must be that afternoon when he'd been too agitated to truly look at it. It was well shaped, with seductive red lips. He wondered if he ever made love, if he only fucked. With a woman sometimes, maybe. Maybe with Hilda. The thought made him jealous of both of them. Manoli caught his eyes on him once or twice and smiled faintly, not a notably friendly smile but without contempt.

Hilda urged more drinks on them, and this time Manoli checked what they were all having and got up without waiting for an order. Phil was indignant for him. Why should he let himself be treated like a servant? He must detest them all. He was strongly tempted to follow him to lend a hand but wasn't sure the gesture would be welcome. To his surprise, John Robert rose and disappeared into the cafe. He returned with a single drink which he placed in front of Hilda with a courtly bow, to a burst of laughter and cheers. Don looked as if he would gladly bash John Robert's face in. A peaceful little community. With Hilda's support, Manoli had come out ahead for the moment, but Phil doubted that Don had sense enough to leave well enough alone.

Manoli was almost genial when he resumed his seat, but he made no further contact with Phil. They were just a couple of guys with friends in common who had no reason to pay any particular attention to each other. Phil didn't care. Without attempting to examine his confused and turbulent feelings, he was content to absorb the feel of his presence, learn the look of him, find the flaws that would prevent him from falling helplessly for him. Hands. Clumsy or lumpy sausage-fingered hands turned him off. Manoli's nervous, sinewy hands didn't. He had already discovered that he could find no fault with any other part of his body. In motion, it had the quick, assured masculine grace that to Phil was the epitome of nature's beauty. He waited for Manoli to do something so offensive (why did he suppose he would?) that he could conveniently dismiss him as a hopeless case. Not that gross offenses had weighed much in the balance when Alex ruled the roost.

Additional drinks arrived unaccompanied by drama, and they all got mildly, cheerfully drunk. Phil was listening enchanted to Hilda's laughter, pleased and flattered that something he'd said had provoked it, when he heard Manoli say, "—the first night she back." His English was haphazard but unselfconscious.

"And *your* first night, my dearest boy," Don cajoled. "You've been gone—"

Phil stopped listening to resume his fun with Hilda. Don and Manoli provided a background duet. He was aware that it was developing into an argument as the duet became more stubborn. It came to an abrupt end.

"I don't intend to discuss it further." Don's voice was harsh and peremptory, brooking no interference, the voice of authority silencing a disrespectful subordinate. It brought all conversation at the table to a halt. Everybody toyed with their glasses and shifted in their chairs. Phil told himself to stay out of it. It had nothing to do with him. He glanced at Manoli. Eyes closed as if he were counting to ten. Clenched fists white-knuckled again. Why did he put up with it? Because he was a whore? Phil welcomed the contempt that the word revived in him. He was damned if he was going to feel indignant for him.

"Good night everybody," Don said blandly and then looked at Manoli with a little gleam of triumph. When he spoke to him, it was to issue orders. "Come. Thank Hilda for the drinks. Finish up what you have there. I want to go home. Let's go." He gave the top of the table a decisive pat with his outspread hands and pushed himself to his feet. Manoli leaped up and strode off along the quay. Seeing that he was being abandoned, Don stirred his ample body into unaccustomed action.

"He's mad," John Robert commented, watching him go. "I declare he's suicidal. What makes him think he can get away with it?"

"He does it just to prove to you that he can, I should think," Johnny said. "If you two go on playing your games much longer, we're going to have a very dangerous young Greek on our hands."

"I can't imagine why you think *I* have anything to do with it," John Robert protested innocently. "What do I *do*?"

"You know very well what you do. You're a wily devil. I daresay I see only half of it but that's quite enough."

John Robert beamed contentedly. "All I do is encourage him to stand up to that overblown Canadian windbag. What's wrong with that?"

"That isn't *quite* all, darling," Hilda interjected. "At least it wasn't at the beginning. You were very much the dog in the—where was the dog, darling?" She leaned forward to ask Johnny's help.

"In the manger, as a rule, although I haven't the faintest idea what he was doing there."

"No matter. I know what I mean." She turned back to John Robert with gentle maternal reproach. "You maybe didn't want him very much for yourself, but you very much didn't want Don to have him."

"That was only common humanity," John Robert said, enjoying being cast as an incorrigible child. "Nobody would wish Don on his worst enemy."

Phil sat back with an enormous sense of relief, as if some catastrophe had been narrowly averted. He was getting neurotic in his old age. The suppressed hostility seething around the table had filled him with irrational foreboding. People here weren't subject to the controls and restraints that kept the ordinary working world in order. They shed their guards as casually as he had shed his clothes on the beach. Anything could happen. He saw the white-knuckled fists clenched on the table and shook the image out of his mind. Why was he overdramatizing? What difference would it make if Don got a fist in his foolish face? It would probably do them both a lot of good. He skirted the question of whether he could still look forward to later and concentrated on his companions as Lester and his friend Harvey paused at the table to greet them.

"Come have a drink with us to welcome me back." Hilda waved to the vacated chairs and the newcomers sat.

The waiter immediately appeared at her side and they all ordered drinks. "You had to buy me a farewell drink when I left. All winter I've been with my Egyptian husband saving his money so that I could buy you one when I come back. I hoped you would wait for me."

"I'll always wait for a lovely lady," Lester said with a placidly good-natured flash of white teeth. "I just got back a day or two ago myself. Some cats from the States took me sightseeing. . . . Knossos, those places. I've been getting me some culture."

"It won't come amiss," Harvey commented.

"Watch who you're calling a miss, Feldman," Lester retorted, camping outlandishly. The others welcomed the friendly banter with laughter, and the cloud remaining from Don's peevish outburst quickly lifted. Phil was particularly grateful for an amiable new face. He had had enough of simmering passion, his own and everybody else's. He had wondered too often about his failure to find anything but pain in passion to expect to make any sense of it at this late date. He hoped only to avoid it. He held his hand out across the table. "I've seen you around a couple of times, but I guess we haven't really met," he said to Lester. "I'm Phil."

"Sure. I've heard about you. A *lot*."

"Then you better tell me a lot about you. All I know is that you've got the biggest goddamn hands I've ever seen."

"Yeah, I'm black too. I'll bet you didn't know that."

"Now that you mention it, I thought it was a bit early in the season for a tan like that." They both laughed, friendly relations established. For no reason Phil could think of, he had never had any black friends and was pleased that his slight self-consciousness had passed so quickly. Lester was very tall; even sitting, he seemed to tower over everybody else around the table. He had a lean frame and his shirt, open loosely to the waist despite the evening chill, revealed a pleasing expanse of brown chest. Phil caught himself thinking that Lester didn't look very Negroid. His lips were seductively full but not thick, and his nose wasn't flattened. Phil decided that this was racist stuff and willed himself to be attracted without racial references.

When questioned, Lester explained that he had wanted to be a dancer but his height was a professional handicap.

"I'm too tall for a dancer, except the eccentric specialty stuff, and too short for professional basketball. What else can a poor black boy do? I decided to become a millionaire instead." He told Phil about the chain of Lester Langley Dance Studios on the West Coast. "I'm being robbed blind while I'm over here, but I don't care. I like it here. They don't seem able to tell the difference between a nigger and real people."

"Niggers are a prettier color. I've been working on it." Phil slid his arm across the table against Lester's. There wasn't much difference between them.

"Yeah, you're all right." He gave Phil's forearm a squeeze with his enormous hand. "You can always tell, the way honkies say that word. We get a good class of people here. I'll be sorry to go."

"You're going?"

"Old Harvey can't stay much longer. He's not a millionaire but he will be. He's a red-blooded American, same as the rest of us. Of course he's Jewish, but we have to try to be tolerant in this world. He's not so bad, considering."

"I can see you're a very broad-minded person. I'll try to be nice to him."

"You do that." Their lips twitched and they burst out

laughing. John Robert beamed at them benevolently. Hilda's welcome-home party was finally gathering some momentum.

They had more drinks, the waiter serving them efficiently, and eventually John Robert swayed a bit unsteadily to his feet. "We have to go before Sim has a fit. You wouldn't believe how possessive he is. I tremble in my boots. Such a *he*-man." He embraced Hilda and went skipping off with childlike steps, followed by the docile Oriental.

The four remaining men gathered closer around Hilda, basking in her incandescent charm. She made them laugh simply by seeming to be so amused by herself. The lights came on around the port. She ordered food lavishly and they all switched to wine. Time flowed effortlessly. Food arrived—grilled lobster with an egg-lemon sauce, a platter of delicately fried whitebait, another of fried potatoes, a big mixed salad studded with black olives and white feta cheese. They shared a communal meal, all of them forking bits directly from the platters.

"In Paris they think I'm mad when I say I miss the food here, but where else can you find lobster that is plucked from the sea an hour ago? It's all so *good*. We will have more so that we get very fat. My babies must be fed."

Other members of the club were leaving, and the old-timers stopped to tell Hilda how glad they were that she was back. They dropped into the vacant chairs and picked absentmindedly at the replenished food and drifted on after receiving the blessing of Hilda's laughter. Music started in the next-door cafe. It rose to the glittering sky, teasing, mirthful, plaintive, full of sun and the sea's melancholy. Phil felt as if something in him was bound to give way if anything increased his sudden sense of well-being.

"What time are we going out tomorrow?" he asked Johnny.

"Not too late? Why don't you come pick me up about

ten? We'll take some food and plenty of beer and stay out all afternoon.''

"Wonderful. I'm really looking forward to it."

Johnny studied him for a moment with a bemused little smile. ''You're getting younger and younger. You should think about staying forever, you know. You'll live to be two hundred.''

"I wouldn't mind if I could go on feeling the way I do now. I love everybody, especially you and Lester and Harvey. Hilda's different. I worship her.'' He didn't want to examine himself too closely, but he felt sure that he wouldn't be plunged into despair if he didn't see Manoli again tonight.

Johnny's smile broadened with affectionate approval. ''That's the way. Have some more wine.'' He emptied another bottle into their glasses, and it was quickly replaced in the ice bucket.

Their high spirits didn't flag. Having disposed of all the food Hilda had had set before them and restraining her from ordering more, they didn't stint on wine. It made them prone to laughter but with no other noticeable effect. It was almost midnight when Hilda sighed contentedly and brought the party to an end.

"I am so much loving being here with my babies, but it's long past Annie's bedtime. The poor thing has been sound asleep for hours. We must go.''

"I need a stretch," Johnny said. "I'll walk you home.''

"We'll all walk you home," Harvey suggested.

"That will be lovely.'' Hilda picked up the idea and made it seem like the only way to end the evening. ''I have some wine. Annie will have some lovely hay. It will be my housewarming party and a special welcoming party for Phil. So handsome. Come along. A walk is just what we need to make us thirsty again.'' She signaled the waiter and rose and untethered her donkey. Phil could see now that she was taller than average, big boned, with ample, womanly hips, her body fitting the image her personality created of womanly warmth and generosity, with a natural elegance that had no need of studied, urban artifice. She looped the rope around the animal's neck and it set off with dainty little pattering steps, lightly carrying its burden of roughly woven peasant bags. They all followed in a straggling group.

When they reached narrow streets, Phil and Lester dropped back a few paces. Side by side, Phil felt dwarfed by his new friend. "Jesus, you *are* tall," he said, looking up at him. "How tall do you have to be to be a basketball player?"

"I'm about six four. That's nothing. Those cats are six seven, six eight. Besides, I hate basketball. I wouldn't be caught dead in those little outfits they have to wear. Give me tights any day. They make you look real smooth and sexy." He laughed and threw an arm around Phil's shoulders and hugged him. It sent a pleasant little shiver down Phil's spine, the awakening of sexual awareness. He wondered if they might be headed for bed together. It was impossible not to think about sex here. He hoped he wouldn't discover a racial block in himself that he'd never been aware of. He liked Lester and thought him physically attractive. That he was black seemed only incidental.

They left the narrow streets and followed a path up a hillside, rocky and bare except for an occasional clump of trees. Small whitewashed houses were dotted about, all in darkness. A segment of moon was low in the west, but the clear night sky blazed with stars. Phil had never seen so many stars, all of them blinking and pulsating as if they were hooked up to a faulty power line. Music drifted up to them from the port. Johnny began to sing in Greek in a light, sweet baritone, and Hilda joined in, humming when she didn't know the words, coming in strong when she did. The star-bright sky, the little donkey pattering along wearing its hat, the man and woman singing on either side of it created a potent if slightly comic magic in the night.

The climb grew steeper and Annie slowed down. They all adjusted their pace accordingly. Johnny broke off his song as they all began to breathe more heavily. The sea came into view, stretching off to the horizon, dark and motionless under the stars.

"Have you tried the local dancing?" Phil asked Lester.

"Sure, I really dig it. It's great."

"I tried it last night and made a complete ass of myself. Were you still there?"

"We were just going. I almost joined you but decided not to. I wasn't sure I'd be welcome. You never know with our compatriots."

"Jesus," Phil muttered.

"Yeah, but it's something you've got to think about. I like it here too much to run the risk of stirring up that old shit."

"Well, now you know."

"Yeah, now I know." He touched Phil's shoulder and sent another agreeable little shiver down his spine. They climbed a few more minutes, approaching a small whitewashed house like the others they had passed. It was surrounded by a low whitewashed wall and a big fig tree stood near the door. Phil recognized the leaves even in the dark; fig leaves were unmistakably fig leaves. Annie pattered through a gateless opening in the wall and stopped under the fig tree. Hilda went on to the door and opened it and snapped on lights before turning back for her possessions. They all gathered around and lifted off the bags that were strung on the wooden saddle.

"There, you poor faithful creature," she said to the donkey. "Go on around to your house and eat some hay." She gave his rump a pat and he ambled off indolently, as if he knew he was no longer on duty, and disappeared around the corner of the house. Hilda led the way to the door.

They entered a kitchen that appeared to occupy the whole ground floor. The working elements—stove and sink and big butcher's block as a table—were at one end. The rest of the room was colorful and inviting—cupboards, pottery on shelves, gleaming copper pots hanging on one wall, big bunches of herbs and a loop of garlic sprouting from the ceiling beams, a long dark wooden dining table surrounded by benches and cushioned wooden armchairs. Several boldly patterned local rugs were scattered on the polished tile floor. It was picturesquely rustic without being quaint, a room for hot days or cold nights.

They piled Hilda's bags on one end of the table as she brought out glasses and a big wicker-covered jug. "You know how to do that, darling," she said to Johnny, putting everything down in front of him. He slung the jug over his shoulder and, using himself as a fulcrum, deftly filled the glasses with red wine. They all took a glass and toasted their hostess before settling down around the table, Hilda at the end, Phil and Lester on one side, Johnny and Harvey on the other. Sitting next to Lester gave Phil a welcome opportunity to show him that the last thing he wanted was to avoid contact with him. Hearing that he'd been afraid to join him on the dance floor had been a shock. He despised race prejudice, and it had never occurred to him that he might be suspected of it. The fact that he had never been to bed with a black was an accident of circumstance; the occasion had never arisen. There was no reason to suppose that it would now. Lester and Harvey appeared to be happy together, and Phil had always been scrupulous about not poaching on other people's territory. He wanted only to act with Lester exactly as he would with any attractive guy, no matter the race.

When their arms or legs touched casually, he didn't draw back. He put a hand on his arm occasionally when something they said made it seem like the natural thing to do. They made their own small connections openly and straightforwardly while remaining part of the group. After performing his trick with the jug a few more times, Johnny put his empty glass down with a definitive little click.

"I'll have to get up early if I expect to get some work done before we go out. Let's try to make it at about nine," he said to Phil. "Will anyone think me a spoilsport if I pack it in for the night?"

"The voice of reason," Harvey said. "You make sense about everything except film. I don't understand why a painter can't see—"

"Hear, hear," Johnny cried. He laughed and got to his feet, ruffling Harvey's hair. "If you get started again, we'll never leave. Come along. Say good night to the lady and we can argue all the way down the hill." He held out his arms to Hilda while they all stood. "It's good to have you back where you belong," he said, holding Hilda in a fond embrace. They kissed lightly on the mouth. "Thank you for a jolly marvelous party."

Harvey followed with his thanks and good night and had resumed his argument before he and Johnny had reached the door. Phil heard their good-naturedly argumentative voices in the night when Hilda stopped outside at her wall with her two remaining guests.

"You must tell me," she said, holding their arms. "Is everybody planning to dress up for Mardi Gras?"

"I don't know," Phil answered. "I've heard people talk about it. I don't even know when it is."

"Today is Friday? No matter. It is next Tuesday."

"I've heard Mardi Gras means Fat Tuesday," Lester said. "Is that right?"

"Yes, fat because you can eat all you wish before fasting for Lent. I think we must all dress up. The people expect us to make them laugh."

"I'll dress up if you tell me what to wear," Phil promised.

"I'll think of something, something dashing if not funny. Not a woman. You're too handsome to be a woman."

"Thank God I don't have to be a woman. You say the nicest things. No wonder I'm mad about you."

They hugged and kissed her and watched her go back into the house before they set off into the night. They heard the voices ahead of them, quite clear but too faint for them to hear what they were saying. It was difficult walking downhill in the dark. They kept tripping and sliding on loose rocks and grabbing each other for support.

"Do you suppose I'm drunk?" Phil wondered.

"No way, man. We've only been drinking for four or five hours. How could you be drunk?"

"Exactly. You have a clear, logical mind, Lester."

They went on and in another few minutes they both almost took a spill. They flung out their arms and held on to each other to recover their balance. Phil gripped Lester's biceps and felt Lester's hands slide down to his waist. The hands moving on him gave him the sturdy beginnings of an erection. He wished Lester would find it as proof of his interest in him. He gave Lester's biceps a squeeze, aware of silence. "Do you still hear them?" he asked.

"No, but they must be just ahead of us. They had only a minute head start and there're no cliffs around here for them to fall off." He gave Phil's waist a pat and they let go of each other and continued their treacherous descent.

They came to a fork in the path and Lester stopped and shouted, ''Hey. Harv. Johnny.'' There was no answer. Lester waved off to the left. ''It's shorter this way to your place. Shall we try it?''

''OK. You know where I'm staying?''

''You're in that place with all the beds, aren't you? A friend of mine was there before Christmas. Let's go.'' He put a hand on Phil's shoulder and guided him to the left. Phil stayed close to him so as not to break contact. After another five minutes they skirted some houses and came out into a street without having caught up to the other two. ''Do you see where you are now?'' Lester asked.

''No. Should I?''

''We're almost there. Your house is right down there.''

''Is it?'' He peered ahead of him. ''Oh, sure. Now I see. I was turned around. I've never been past the house in this direction.'' They were approaching it from above and stopped when they reached it. ''You want to go down to the port for a nightcap?'' Phil had to restrain his feet; they were ready to keep going. Manoli might be there. Phil didn't think he and Don would last the whole evening together.

''It's an idea,'' Lester said with a lazily knowing smile, making no move to go. The street was well enough lighted so that they could communicate with their eyes. Phil wasn't indifferent to what he saw in Lester's. ''But I must admit I'm not thinking much about a drink right now. Bryan says you have the most beautiful body he's ever seen.''

''You shouldn't believe everything you hear.''

''No. That's true. I like to find out certain things for myself. Harvey and I allow ourselves a certain amount of leeway, in case you've wondered.''

''Well, it has to be considered unless you're asking for

trouble.'' They looked at each other, laughter beginning to ripple between them. Why should he go wandering around the port hoping that an arrogant Greek would do him a favor? Lester wasn't too proud to let him know that he wanted him. If he held back, he would always wonder if it were because Lester was black. "I didn't want to be the one that started anything," he said.

"It's a deal?"

"You talked me into it.'' They leaned to each other, laughing, and gripped each other's biceps. "You're such a tall son of a bitch. I want to get you down to my level. Come on.''

They took care to tread lightly as they mounted the stairs. Lester stayed a step behind him with a hand on his buttocks, sliding over them as they moved and giving them little syncopated pats in time to their climbing feet. His touch was playful but full of erotic innuendo. It gave Phil a hard on. He had had sense enough to stick with a guy he really liked instead of making a fool of himself on the port. Thanks to Lester, the Manoli crisis was passing. The tug to the port was almost gone.

As they turned at the landing and started up the last flight, Lester put his other hand on Phil's erection and applied pressures fore and aft. "Yeah, man. You're good,'' he murmured appreciatively against Phil's ear.

Phil slipped a hand through the arms that encricled him and landed it on Lester's cock. It was as hard as his own and felt twice as big. "You're better,'' he said. When they reached the top of the stairs, they were laughing silently together.

Phil snapped on the dim bulb that hung on a cord from the middle of the ceiling in the front room. The preliminaries in the stairway got them off to a gleeful start. Lester pressed his soft, full lips to Phil's and engaged their tongues. Lester undressed him with humorously languid assurance and took his time to play with bits of him as he uncovered them. His big hands were wonderfully gentle. The warm, capacious velvet of his mouth made Phil want to leave his cock in it all night until it moved on to other parts of him. The lingering process made him feel gloriously naked when the clothes were gone. The long brown body that was coiled around him was adroitly naked too.

"My, oh my," Lester said with muffled laughter. "I can't quarrel with Bryan. You've got a *body*, man."

Lester's cock swung into view for the first time. Phil stared at it for a horrified moment before flinching from it. He cursed himself. What color did he expect a black man's cock to be? Some deep-seated atavistic revulsion gripped him momentarily, but he was determined to overcome it. It had been a struggle to accept being a faggot, but he'd never forgive himself if he was a racist faggot.

He flung himself forward and tipped Lester over onto the bed beside them. He nuzzled his nipples, desperate to prove to himself that he was worthy of being wanted by a black man. His hand assessed the massive dark cock that he couldn't look at. He willed himself to want it in him. He slid down to it and held it upright in front of his eyes, and forced them to travel slowly over it. He had found George's match at last. He ought to be celebrating. In the dim light, he couldn't judge nuances of color. It was all in the mind.

He closed his eyes and moved his mouth to it, gripped by a strange dread, as if he were transgressing some primordial law of nature, irrational and appalling. He felt his erection dwindling and commanded his lips and tongue to perform their usual services. He couldn't will himself to stay hard but he could force himself to enact the familiar ceremonies of lovemaking. He despised himself for the resistance in him.

His mouth exulted in the sheer size of Lester. It made Phil almost feel as if he were with George again and restored his erection to some measure of its customary vigor. Lester's big gentle hands on him everywhere pushed his misgivings into the back of his mind. Phil's mouth was generous in demonstrating his desire. He wondered if Lester had to make an effort to adapt to a white and was glad that his tan made them almost the same color. Their need for consummation became urgent and Phil rolled over onto his stomach.

"You got something, baby?" Lester asked.

"Yes. I'll get it."

"Don't you move. Tell me where."

"The next room. Sort of the bathroom. You'll see it on the table." Phil's heart began to hammer. He pitted his will against the knot of protest that was still in him. He heard the dancer moving around the room. In a moment his footsteps brought him back to the bed. He dropped down on him, straddling him, pinning him down. Phil's breath was coming in gasps. He uttered a strange beseeching whimper. Big hands gently arranged him the way they wanted him and moved to his buttocks. His whole body began to tremble at the imminent violation of his blood's prohibition. Greased fingers slipped into him, preparing him, and he groaned.

"You want me to fuck you, baby," Lester said soothingly.

"Yes," Phil cried in defiance of the taboo that made a black man untouchable.

"Yeah. I guess I'd have to rape you if you said no." He steadied Phil's hips and took what was offered him, sliding into him in enormous possession of him.

Phil shouted and tried to wrench himself free. "No. Oh, Christ. I can't—"

"Easy, baby. Nice and easy." Lester gripped his hips and continued his implacable advance. "Jesus, did I ever want you. I've got you now, honey. My, oh my, I've really got you. Just feel that. I'm in you. More and more, baby. Slow and sweet. God, what a sweetheart. You make my cock feel like God Almighty."

"Jesus. Oh Jesus, Les. It's big." He tried to close his mind to the picture that was lodged in it of the big black organ forcing itself into him. He had always thought of the act as a submission, a voluntary surrender of himself but never as servile and degrading. It was insane. Reason must count for something. He was being taken the way he wanted to be taken; the color of a guy's skin didn't alter the nature of the physical act.

Slowly, he felt himself entering into Lester's ryhthm. Everything was working right between them. Lester was superbly establishing his male presence deep within him, moving smoothly but with unyielding purpose, displaying a touching concern for Phil's desires. He cradled him in his arms and his hands made Phil's body feel as if it were the source of infinite delight. He demonstrated the depth of his possession by withdrawing from him slowly and repeating his long, triumphant entry while they crooned a tuneless little song of mutual satisfaction.

Phil cried out ecstatically as he felt orgasm gathering in him and became aware of a shift in his mind. He was no longer trying to prove anything to himself; he was simply giving himself to a guy he wanted. He tilted his head and looked up at the dark, intent face, his eyes noting the African cast of his handsome features. This wasn't an experiment in race relations. It was a basic human exchange. He had conquered the taboo.

He moaned with his approaching orgasm. "I'm going to come," he murmured.

"Yeah, baby. You come." Les handed him the towel he'd brought to bed with him. "I want to watch you getting hard again while my cock is showing off for you. We'll come together later."

They lay still eventually while their spent bodies slowly relinquished each other. When Les slipped out of him, Phil headed him for the shower and lay back to savor his victory over himself. He'd been had by a black man. He could count on his will. He had willed himself to renounce George. Alex had been a painful struggle, but his will had prevailed in the end. He thought of Manoli. The Greek had given him a scare, but that was under control now. Control. He had never been crazy about the cards fate had dealt him, but at least he'd learned something about controlling them. He hadn't known racial prejudice was one of them, but that was happily disposed of.

He rolled out of bed and joined the dancer in the next room. He was a comic tangle of long limbs under the inadequate shower. He couldn't see anything about him that he didn't like to look at. He regretted having led such an involuntarily segregated life. He crowded in beside him under the shower and was welcomed by a winning flash of white teeth. "That was good, baby. I hope you agree." Les put an arm around him to draw him in and handed him the soap.

"I'll say. It was great." Phil ran his hand down along Lester's cock and was thrilled by the power he awakened in it. It instantly swelled and straightened and jutted out at a downward slant, almost achieving its maximum dimensions.

Les chuckled. "Thanks, honey. You know how to keep it looking pretty. I wouldn't mind having more but it's against the rules. Harv and I have agreed to back off if we feel we're getting into something that could become a problem. If ever I saw the makings of a problem, you're it. I don't think it would be an exaggeration to say that you're one of the greatest fucks I've ever had. I mustn't kid myself that it's more than that.''

''Sure, but thanks for telling me I was good. You can't guess how much it means to me. I mean, you of all people. You're not a fuck I'm apt to forget.''

''Your first nigger?''

''How did you guess? Not the last, I hope.''

They looked into each other's eyes and laughter bubbled up in them. They brushed their bodies against each other lightly, playfully, and turned away to rinse themselves.

Dry, Phil hitched a towel around his waist and they went back to the bedroom. Les gathered up his clothes from the ones scattered about. He dressed quickly but relaxed when he was ready. ''I've got to get away from you while I'm still making sense,'' he said with a tranquil smile. ''What a beautiful problem you'd be.'' He reached for him and pulled him in close against him.

Phil put his arms around his neck and drew his head down, feeling as confidently at ease with him as if he'd always had black lovers. ''I can see you're going to lose lots of sleep over me.''

The captivating smile widened. ''*À demain,* baby.'' Lester gave his cock a little squeeze as Phil opened the door for him. ''That feels as if I'm leaving you something to remember me by. How about me?''

They smiled and waved as Lester started lightly down the dark stair. Phil closed the door and was still smiling as he turned back into the room. His body gave a leap and he gasped and stood rooted to the floor, his heart thumping with the momentary terror of discovering that he wasn't alone. Manoli stood in the other doorway naked, his feet

planted squarely, his pelvis thrust forward, flaunting his
erection with his hands on his hips. Phil pulled off his
towel as a great flood of joy surged through him. He hadn't
realized that he wanted so desperately to see him. He made
a rush for the intruder and flung his arms around him.
"You're here," he exclaimed incredulously. He leaned
forward for a kiss but Manoli jerked his head away and
gripped his arms, keeping his distance. To soften the
rebuff, Phil reminded himself that Greek guys didn't go in
for kissing. If he wanted him enough to make this unconventional appearance, kissing could wait. He was just
beginning to take it in. Manoli was here. His hands held
him. His cock was brushing against him. He was naked
and wanted him. "How did you get in?" he demanded,
beginning to recover his faculties.

"I know how." The Greek's eyes were cold, his expression sternly set. "Why did you let him have you?"

Phil's numbed joy turned abruptly to indignation as he
realized what he might have seen. Manoli had broken in,
invaded his privacy, shed his clothes as if he belonged
here, taking it for granted that he could have him whenever he wanted him. It was outrageous. He tried to shake his
hands off but their grip was firm. "How long were you
here?" He made it an accusation.

"Long enough. You let him have you. Why?"

"You see his cock?" Phil taunted him. "I wanted it."

"You want me. You're in love with me."

"Why you think that?" Phil was determined to stand up
to him, but he didn't want to drive him away.

"I saw it this evening. Men have been in love with me.
I can tell."

"Are you in love with me?"

"I don't fall in love with men."

"You want me."

"Yes. I came for you as soon as I could. You knew I would. I have a man's cock. Is as big as yours." Manoli ran it along Phil's groin. Phil clenched his fists to keep himself from reaching for it.

"Mine is nothing much," Phil said. He was falling again under the spell of the physical magnetism that he'd felt in Manoli the first moment he'd seen him. He felt as if his eyes must be burning into him; he couldn't take them off him. He gave up trying to control his hands. He lifted them and ran them over him and forgot his outrage. *You knew I would.* Could he mean that he recognized and accepted the extraordinary current of attraction between them?

He made his hands as provocative as he knew how and used his nails when he found sensitive areas. He felt Manoli succumbing to his caresses. The grip on his arms loosened and his body edged closer. His eyes softened and the fierceness faded from his expression. Phil felt unexpected tenderness in the hands that stroked his shoulders as Phil lowered himself slowly down the front of him, nibbling his body with lips and tongue. Wanting Manoli didn't have to be a madness; Phil would keep his balance for once and find something good with him. Manoli had said he'd come to him as soon as he could. He too must have felt that a connection had been made between them that went beyond quick, casual sex.

Phil opened his mouth at last on the cock that he'd tried to exclude from his thoughts all evening. He ran his tongue along its rigid length and shivered with ecstasy. It made him think of swift, lethal things. It was an arrow in flight, a bird of prey plummeting for a kill. He wanted it to pierce him and spend itself in him. He held it against his cheek and felt the unyielding will in it. He buried his face in his pubic hair and closed his teeth lightly on its thick base. He felt the leaping strain of need in it and wanted to offer himself for its satisfaction.

"Is it big enough for you?" Manoli asked above him.

"I can't complain if it's as big as mine," he said with irony that he immediately regretted. The last thing he intended was to make fun of him.

"It is, isn't it?"

"Yes, they are much the same." He spoke with his lips on it, touched by the childlike plea for reassurance about his manhood. Without his having thought about it, he realized that they'd adopted a mixture of Greek and English as a language that suited them both.

"Yours is big. You and me, I think we are bigger than most men."

"A little, perhaps." He opened his mouth for the object of Manoli's concern and drew it in until his lips brushed pubic hair again. He wanted him to feel the joy it gave him and make him as proud of his cock as if it were the biggest in the world. He performed on it with all his considerable skill and slowly withdrew from it. He pushed it upright against his belly with his forehead and rolled his tongue around his balls. His daring jolted the body he wanted to satisfy without transgressing acceptable limits.

"I please you?" Manoli asked almost shyly.

"Yes. I want to please you." He pulled back and let his cock drop down into his mouth once more. He didn't expect Manoli to reciprocate, but to Phil's surprise he didn't seem shocked by what he was doing. On the contrary, he participated in his fashion by stroking his face encouragingly and holding himself to show him how it was best for him. He didn't let making love to him become a one-way service.

At Phil's prompting Manoli moved his hips in a facsimile of copulation. Phil felt Manoli's excitement mounting and longed for him to reach his climax in his mouth. Would Manoli feel cheated if he didn't have him in the customary way? He was terrified of offending the sensibilities of a guy who thought he couldn't fall for a man.

He sprang up prepared to fling his arms around him and kiss him, but remembered in time and turned and pulled him in against his buttocks. "Take me quickly," he urged.

Manoli's hands did everything Phil wanted them to do, holding his cock while pressing in against him, sweeping up over his chest and bringing his shoulders back so that the sides of their heads lay against each other. "I've wanted you all evening—ever since this afternoon," Manoli said against his cheek.

"You hide it very well."

"You understand about that."

"Not really, but you can tell me later if you want."

"I will tell you everything if you become my lover."

It sounded as if an official post were waiting to be filled, and Phil broke away to forestall laughter. He snatched up the lubricant and intercepted Manoli as he started for the bed Lester had just vacated. He turned him back toward the room he thought of as the bathroom. His new home was ideally equipped for the varied sex life Phil was apparently embarked on. He was beginning to feel like a call boy, turning a trick every hour on the hour. New York was never like this. It sounded as if becoming Manoli's official lover might curtail his activities. He was willing.

He pulled the cover off the bed in the bathroom and found a clean sheet under it. He prepared them both, liking having the conveniences so convenient. The toilet was installed in a room of its own so it didn't look too much like a bathroom. He tossed a towel onto the bed and stretched out on his stomach for a conventional coupling. If there were going to be any frills, Manoli could initiate them. Feeling him moving in over him almost brought Phil to orgasm. He hadn't felt such exciting promise in an encounter for years. The chemistry between them was right. Maybe some people really were sort of made for each other.

Manoli entered him. For a stunned moment, Phil didn't know what had happened to him. He was bewitched. He was possessed by demons. He had lost his bearings in time and space. Fireworks were going off in him somewhere. It was terrifying and sublime. Manoli began to move in slow possession of him. Phil was having the most electrifying physical experience of his life. Manoli was his body's mate, absorbing and fulfilling all the longing that was in him, completing him and restoring him to vibrant life. He was reliving the first moments with George, confronting his destiny.

He lifted his hips to deepen their union. "Oh God, take me," he moaned.

"I take you. I'm in you where you want me. You're mine now. Why did you let Lester have you?"

"You left. I not know you want me to wait," Phil answered in his pidgin Greek.

"You must have known. We knew everything this afternoon. Are you sure it's not because you want only an unnaturally big cock?"

"Is no matter how big. I love yours. You don't feel that when it is in my mouth?"

"It was very wonderful. I let you do it because you're in love with me. Say it. Tell me you're in love with me."

"God, yes. I'll say anything you want. I'm in love with you."

"I'm glad. You're the only man I've ever wanted to be in love with me. I don't want to share you."

"You don't have to. I don't want others."

"I believe you. I think we're very good together. I didn't know it could be so good with a man. I want you very much. You're mine."

"God, yes. Make me yours."

They rode a wave of ecstasy that carried them to simultaneous orgasms. They lay panting together while Phil tried to reassemble his wits. What commitments had they made to each other? He felt as if he'd been struck by lightning, shattered and consumed by flame. Whatever had prompted his declaration of love had been burned out of him in the roaring climax of their passion. Who and what was Manoli? How could he have said he was in love with him? What did he expect to do about it? Go sailing away with Johnny and leave him here? Holidays ended whether you liked it or not.

They crossed the room and showered and dried themselves while their eyes remained fixed intently on each other's bodies. It was the one thing Phil was sure of; he was spellbound by Manoli's. When they were dry, he moved to him until their faces were close enough for them to feel each other's breath. They looked at each other and Phil moistened his lips. Making love without kissing was inhuman. It would drive him crazy. He put his hands around Manoli's neck and felt his shoulders straighten and saw his eyes turn wary. Phil gave his head a little shake. "It's all right. I won't do anything you don't like. What you want to tell me?"

"Tell you?"

"You said you tell me everything. Why do you let Don treat you like his servant?"

"Why do servants do what they're told? For money, of course."

Phil was familiar with self-loathing and saw that Manoli was seething with it as he spat the words out. It was the source of the violence he had felt in him. It struck a chord of pity. Phil moved his hands comfortingly along Manoli's shoulders. "Servants don't usually sell their bodies," he said gently. "Are you a whore?"

"No," he protested vehemently. His eyes were fierce and he shook Phil's hands off. "You don't understand. You don't know what it's like here. This is a bad place. You shouldn't stay. You must go and take me with you."

Phil's mouth dropped open with astonishment. He was struck dumb. He stifled a wild burst of laughter. Manoli was mad. He put an arm lightly around his waist and they started for the bed, shoulder to shoulder. After Les, it felt good to be with somone more his height. "Where do you wish me to take you?" he asked.

"To your home. To New York? John Robert wants to take me to New York but not until six months, when he goes."

"What would I do with you in New York?"

"I would be with you."

They reached the bed and stretched out on it. It was big enough for both of them if they didn't stray too far from each other, which Phil had no inclination to do. Manoli propped himself on his elbow over him and put a hand on his chest. "You're in love with me, my Philip," he said, as if reminding him of an essential fact.

Phil heard his name echoing in his ears. The way Manoli said it was an ultimate intimacy, an acceptance of him, a blissful shock of communication. It made him want to believe that it was true. He covered Manoli's hand with his own, another perfect fit. Their faces were so close that the meeting of their mouths seemed inevitable. How could anybody resist? He traced Manoli's features with his index finger—the sweeping arch of his brows, the straight nose, the firm but sensitive and shapely lips that he longed to feel pressed to him. "Even if I *am* in love with you, what's the good?" he demanded. "Why do I want somebody who can't love me?"

"You're a *pousti*. I understand. I am a man for women, but I can satisfy you. You want me with you."

"Do you think I am hungry for sex? Why do I want you with me without love?"

"Don wants me, and I truly don't love him."

Phil dropped his hand and turned his head away. To be measured against Don was enough to bring even him to his senses. "Maybe he likes to suffer," he said. "I don't. I don't wish to pay for your body. I hope he gives you much."

"Very little but words. In the beginning, last year when the Colonels were gone and I could come home, he promised me very much, but he always has a reason to delay. He wants me to beg. He's waiting to see me crawling in front of him."

Phil's eyes were drawn irresistibly back to him, and his hands reclaimed him. "How much?" he asked.

"Ten thousand dollars. With that, my mother would be rich. My sisters would have dowries so that they could find good husbands. I could go away and find work. He would give it to me if I do everything he wants me to do. I'd rather go with you for nothing."

"Or John Robert?"

"Yes, but there would be nothing for my mother and sisters. I'm bound by honor to do everything I can for them."

"I have no money. I can do nothing for them."

"I think with you we could find a way. You would want to help me. John Robert wants only to use me to play a game with Don. He asks little of me. He draws pictures of me naked. He likes me to—it's an expression—jerk off in front of him. He gives me presents, but I think in New York he would have no more use for me."

Phil closed his eyes to give himself a moment's respite from the painful beauty of his tormented face. He was getting more than he'd bargained for. Manoli shocked but moved him. He was obviously spoiled, misled, misguided, easily corrupted and probably a lot of other things that were far from admirable, but he felt an untouched core of strength and decency in him. He couldn't imagine Manoli doing anything evil. He slipped his arms around him and hugged him close. Manoli dropped his head against his neck. Phil's breath caught and broke from him with a sound like a sob. He was letting his resolutions be undermined by a Greek male whore. Facts were facts. He couldn't claim that Manoli had deceived him. He stroked the body he held, the body that he wanted, and forced himself to speak cold-bloodedly. "Why can't you see that you speak as a whore? I don't mean pictures for John Robert, but you give him sex pleasure. That's not a model. That's a whore."

Manoli struggled free of his arms and lifted himself over him again. He erupted in a torrent of angry self-justification. "Am I a whore only when men pay me? I have a friend. He had fine clothes. He met rich women in the big hotels in Athens. One of them took him to a place called Denver and married him. Lots of men marry to get money. Are they whores? Rich women don't come here, not the ones who want to get married. Maybe it will be different in New York."

"Is that why you want to come with me? Many handsome young men in New York. You find a rich wife but she probably much older and not very good to look at."

"My friend's wife is old, but he doesn't care. He has all the young girls he wants."

"Do you think that sounds nice?"

"Nice? What is nice?" He blazed with rage, his face wonderfully animated by anger and devastatingly handsome. "You don't know nothing. I was born when the war ended so I didn't see that, but when I was a little child it was still like the war. Everybody said so. Not enough to eat. A civil war. People getting killed and being taken away. I don't remember my father. I couldn't go to school after I was eleven. My mother needed me to help. I did anything to earn a few drachmas. When I was older I worked on ships. You don't need an education for that. I was fucked by men who were bigger than me, and I sent all my money home to keep my sisters from starving. Don gives me hope for better life. I take what I can get."

Phil was moved by him again. The flaw in Manoli's reasoning was obvious, but he was ashamed of himself for judging him too glibly. He ran a hand over his dark hair, knowing that he was taking advantage of his helplessness. He hadn't the right to give himself the pleasure of fondling him. He dropped his hand and spoke hesitantly, suspecting that anything he said would be wrong for one or both of them. "It's true I know nothing about hardship, about the life you had, but what of the others who are the same? They're not all whores. To be a whore is not a better life. You will hate yourself. Hardship didn't stop you from turning into a beautiful man. What if you are ugly or deformed? You would have to live somehow. Men then don't offer you ten thousand dollars to crawl for them."

"I won't crawl," he asserted, "but if I were ugly and deformed I wouldn't know there was anything to hope for. I wouldn't have you."

Phil gripped Manoli's arms. There was such a ring of gratitude in his words that Phil was ready to offer him anything, but he was lost in a maze of contradictions.

Perhaps he was dealing with a culture so alien to him that he couldn't hope to understand it. His uncertain grasp of the language didn't help. How could men who made love with other men deny their homosexuality? When was a whore not a whore? "You have nothing to hope for from me," he said, quelling his protesting feelings. "How did you find me this afternoon? Did you follow me?"

"My mother's house is near there. I watched you. I saw you naked with your big cock standing up in front of you. I thought you were only another tourist looking for Greek boys, except that you had a beautiful body and were very handsome. When I took you I knew that you were different in some way, and when we were with the others this evening I saw why. You're a good man, like Johnny, but Johnny cares for nobody. He watches. He is contained in himself, if that means what I think. You give yourself. You gave yourself to me." He shifted his elbow to let his hand fall and toyed with Phil's hair and ear. Their eyes searched and probed each other. Manoli's other hand crept tentatively across· Phil's chest while his eyes seemed to question what he was doing. Phil struggled for breath and his lips parted as the hand crept lower, fingers stirring on him. His cock surged up across his belly to meet them. The hand closed around it. Phil grabbed his wrist and wrenched it away.

"Don't," he cried, almost weeping with self-denial. "Why you do that? You're not a *pousti*. Whores have tricks. How do I know why you do anything?"

The sudden stillness of Manoli's body seemed menacing. Phil was appalled by the hurt in his face. "Is wrong to say that," Manoli reprimanded him quietly. "You must never say that. I want nothing from you but what you want. I'm not a *pousti,* but you give yourself to me. Your body is mine now. I will go with you. Even if I get married, you will always be my friend. We will be together.''

''But listen—'' Phil broke off, defeated. He was faced with an irrational child. Manoli spoke as if his faith in his fantasy was unshakable. Phil sensed a surprising lack of practicality in him, as if he were used to others solving problems for him. The whore's mentality? Even if Phil willed himself to break the spell the Greek cast over him, he didn't know how to convince him that he couldn't accept responsibility for him. Phil reached for his hand and returned it to his cock. It leaped up into full erection at his touch. He watched his face for signs of distaste, but his expression cleared. Manoli stroked it experimentally, as if he were getting used to the feel of it.

''You see? I make it hard very easily,'' he said as his hand grew bolder. ''I know how to make you happy. You want me with you.''

''But don't you understand? If you tell me you love me, even then I don't know what we do. I tell you, I have little money, but that's not it only. It's very difficult to get into the U.S. Your friend gets married. That's different. For you it's very difficult. You're not allowed to work. It takes much time to arrange everything.''

''You'll tell me how. I know other ways. Sailors know how. They call it jumping ship. I can get work on a ship and be there quickly.'' He gave Phil's cock a long, posses-sive caress and smiled with thrilling complicity. ''I think you will want me there quickly. Don promised me again tonight that he would have the money soon. If I get it, I'll keep enough to go with you. When we get there, you will take care of me at first. If you give me money, you don't give it to a whore, you give it because you love me. You don't want me to be a whore. I'm not a whore.'' He paused, the muscles of his jaw working, and went on with an effort. "I must get away. Now that I have you, we can—" His voice broke suddenly and a spasm of despair contorted his face. Tears welled up in his eyes.

Phil rolled over to him, shocked into an agony of love and compassion, and forced him back onto the pillows. He gathered him into his arms and kissed his eyes, tasting his tears. Manoli's lips were parted, and Phil plunged his tongue between them. Manoli opened his mouth and he took it, teeth clashing against teeth, tongues vying with each other in an ecstasy of exploration. Their kiss lengthened until their mouths seemed to belong to both of them. They clung to one another, their hard cocks driving in against each other, their legs thrashing, their bodies totally abandoned to each other. If Manoli was practicing whorish tricks, he was sublimely good at them.

Their lovemaking expanded into a greater awareness of each other. Manoli's unconditional surrender of his mouth allowed Phil to hope that eventually Manoli would accept him as a lover in every way, denying him nothing. He dropped his cautious restraints and hitched himself around so that the availability of his cock might tempt Manoli into making an experiment. He shamelessly demonstrated his skills as a cocksucker. Manoli didn't imitate him, but his hand had become a willing substitute. He could feel Manoli's orgasm approaching and knew that he couldn't delay his own much longer. He was eager to allow his mouth free rein to the end, but he thought of the electrifying fulfillment of being taken by Manoli and altered his rhythm, waiting for a signal from his partner.

"Don't stop," Manoli murmured.

Phil's heart lifted with the joy of another victory, and he reveled in their close collaboration as they rushed to their climax. Manoli cried out and Phil's mouth was flooded with his pungent essence. He swallowed it with undisguised satisfaction, risking Manoli's contempt, and felt Manoli directing his own orgasm onto his chest. It was beginning to seem less inconceivable that Manoli might soon want to take it with his mouth.

He continued to suck on Manoli's cock while it dwindled. He was aware of Manoli wiping himself with the towel. He relinquished him finally and swung himself around and stretched out beside him. He stroked his hair and kissed his mouth gently. His lips were soft and receptive.

"I have never let anybody do that," he said, looking into his eyes. "It's very wonderful to be loved by you. I'm almost like a *pousti* with you. It's very strange to be kissed by a man. I don't like your beard, but your mouth is very exciting."

"Yours too. What made you cry?"

"Because I want you. I want so much for you to love me. I'm frightened that something bad will happen. This is a bad place. We must go away. I've never known a man like you. I need you. I've always needed a friend who will help me."

"We all do."

"Do you? You know much that I don't know, but you don't know how hard life is alone. I am always alone. In what way can I help you?"

"I don't know. I'm always alone too. Maybe little by little if you are more like a *pousti* with me, you can help me. We only begin to know each other."

"I don't feel that. I must go now."

"Where? To Don?"

His expression hardened. "I don't sleep with Don. I go to my mother's house." He pushed Phil from him and climbed out of bed and went to the washbasin.

Phil sat up and threw his legs over the side of the bed,

startled by the abrupt shift in his mood. He stood and
drifted closer to him, watching him splash water on his
chest and abdomen.

Manoli glanced at him with a sweet fleeting smile. "You
are on me still. You swallow me?"

"Of course. It's you. I want it."

"I can never do it. It's something we don't do here,
only bad women sometimes."

"You don't act as if you think it's bad for me to do it."

"No. You're a foreigner. All foreigners do it. It's
strange but you give me much pleasure."

"I'm glad. It's pleasure for me too." He paused,
reluctant to stir his anger. "Are you afraid of Don?"

Manoli's smile vanished, but he looked at him with
serious concern rather than anger. "I'm afraid of what he
might do to us. He mustn't know that you're my lover. He
will know I've had you. Everybody knows everything
here. I don't know how. That doesn't matter, but he
mustn't know that it's important."

"Will he know if you stay? I want you to sleep with
me."

The smile returned accompanied by a knowing little
gleam of mockery in his eyes. "Yes, you want me with
you. I too want to sleep with you." Manoli leaned forward
and kissed his lips, not waiting for Phil to provoke it. He
squeezed his hand as he let him go. "I'll go to the toilet."
He went through the door that led to the back rooms.

Phil felt such an easy familiarity in his being here that
he wasn't surprised that Manoli knew his way around. He
realized that he hadn't bothered to find out how Manoli'd
let himself in. It didn't matter. Manoli was the sort who
didn't stand on ceremony and ignored physical obstacles.
He wanted to come in. He came in. Phil smiled to himself.

As he brushed his teeth, he wondered where he was

headed. He seemed to be in control still. He felt no need to set his will against his desire. Manoli was proving an accommodating lover, ready to adjust to novel sex. Phil was pretty sure he'd made it clear that he intended to go slow before getting heavily involved. It was so unlikely that Manoli could get to New York that Phil didn't even want to think about it yet. Making love with him here for the next few weeks would tell him if they wanted it to go on somewhere else. He thought of his date with Johnny in the morning. Their secret mission would give him an excuse to get away from Manoli for a few days and find out what that felt like. He wasn't going to let himself get carried away.

Manoli returned and stood behind him, looking at him in the mirror as he finished with his teeth. "You are very handsome, Philip," he said. He trailed his fingertips tantalizingly around his buttocks. Tremors stirred Phil's cock. "Here is beautiful. I think I will have more sex with you than with any other man." He moved in beside him and reached for the toothbrush. "I need that too."

Phil had heard somewhere that a sure way of knowing you were in love was if you could share a toothbrush. He handed it over without a moment's hesitation, glowing with the wonder of their unlikely intimacy.

When they had both completed their bedtime preparations, Phil turned the lights out and found the bed in the dark. Manoli was waiting for him and reached for him and brought him in beside him. He arranged Phil on his side with his back to him, folded in against him. He kissed his ear and tickled it with his tongue. Phil giggled and his cock began its jubilant transformation. It was as big as it would ever get when Manoli's hand found it and curled around it. They laughed softly.

"You have a fine cock, my Philip. Is always hard."

Feeling very daring, Phil joined his hand with Manoli's and showed him how he wanted to be held. He felt no resistance to his guidance. Manoli was beginning to enjoy fondling a cock. "You too. We are big. We will sleep and want each other all the night."

"And in the morning I will give you a big fuck. You must sleep, my Philip. You go sailing early with Johnny."

Everybody knew everything here. "Yes."

"You go away somewhere with Johnny soon?"

Phil wondered about the secrecy of Johnny's plans. "No. Maybe later for a day or two around the island."

"I will come with you?"

"It's something that pleases me. I must ask Johnny. I think he has friends who come with him."

"You will take me with you," he sighed peacefully.

To his relief, Phil heard drowsiness slurring his speech. He must check with Johnny about what he was supposed to say. Sounding mysterious would be as bad as saying too much. He was almost sorry that he was committed to Johnny's project. What he had thought of as a splendid adventure yesterday seemed tame compared to the adventure of being with Manoli. He nestled in against him and felt him drifting into the limp defenselessness of sleep. Not being able to see him made it even more difficult to believe that he was real. Their public indecency on the beach had led to this sweet, tender union of their bodies. A likely story. He was dreaming. He felt Manoli's breathing becoming deep and regular. Another dreamer.

They would dream that they were awake and in each other's arms in the morning. He hadn't felt so content and at ease with himself since the last time he had slept with George. So long ago. So much loss ago. The troubling resemblance to George that he'd caught in his first glimpses of Manoli had vanished with their growing familiarity. A feeling rather than a physical resemblance remained, something that had been strong and secure with George, built into his discovery of himself and his place in life, a constant. With Manoli, it could only be an ephemeral intimation of what might be, but it was the first time he'd felt it with anybody but George. Stranger and stranger. Manoli was straight, whatever that meant. Manoli was on the make. They could hardly talk to each other, even though they were developing a private language that worked surprisingly well, Phil's labored Greek bolstered by Manoli's English. Language problems could be solved, but it was ridiculous to feel anything sure and durable with him, even momentarily, compared to what he had known with George, who had declared his love for him within an hour of their first passionate encounter and who wanted to give him money, not take it away from him. If everything had been so wonderful with George, why weren't they still together? That was the question.

George had arranged for the two of them to stay with Charlie, one of his ex-lovers, when they had their first weekend in New York shortly after New Year, as promised. It seemed to Phil in retrospect that the seeds of discord had been planted then. In the euphoria of his reunion with George, feverish with the anticipation of the end of a month's chastity, Phil hardly noticed their host when he went to the apartment straight from the airport. Charlie tactfully left them for the evening after a few minutes of polite greeting.

When he came back quite late that night, he caught them in the living room during a lull between their hectic sessions in bed. Phil heard him at the door and sprang up from the sofa, where they'd been sitting with their dressing gowns carelessly draped around them. Phil was still shy of any public display of physical intimacy between them, even with a guy who would understand. Charlie came breezing in and made them laugh for the next half hour with nonsense about his activities around town, all of it what Phil had learned was known as camp. He referred to friends with names like Al and Herbie as "she" and to himself as "Mother." It made Phil uncomfortable, but he supposed he'd get used to it. It was particularly incongruous coming from Charlie, whose good looks were broodingly poetic. He had great limpid eyes and a provocatively sensual mouth. He was beautiful when he wasn't camping, and reminded Phil of Montgomery Clift.

"Time for Mother to get her beauty sleep," he announced eventually. "I'll finish with the bathroom and leave you honeymooners to it." He planted a good-night kiss on George's mouth, which gave Phil a turn. "I get to kiss the bride," he said, standing over Phil. "George has always known how to pick 'em. Look at me." He leaned down and kissed him. It was a quick kiss and Phil supposed it looked decorous, but Charlie had let him feel his tongue between his lips. It made Phil's heart flutter and left him with the start of an erection. He knew Charlie was going to have him. He hadn't learned yet when he was supposed to say no.

It happened the next morning as if they had all conspired to arrange it. George had to go out early on some business for his father. Phil dozed late and took his time getting ready to join him. Charlie came home unexpectedly from work. Phil heard the door slam as he was finishiing his shower. "George?" he called.

"Your genial host," Charlie called back.

Phil was drying himself when Charlie called again from the other side of the door. "Can I share?"

Phil assured himself that it was no big deal being naked with a guy in the bathroom and held the towel modestly in front of himself. "Sure. Come in," he called.

Charlie burst in grinning, wearing only a carelessly tied dressing gown that left a lot of his naked torso exposed. He paused dramatically on the threshold and shook his head with regret. "Shucks, I missed it. I wanted to see water cascading over your glistening limbs." He approached, his hands in the dressing gown's pockets holding it closed. He stopped in front of him, his eyes inviting. "You're the sexiest thing I've ever seen even with that towel draped over the main attraction. Is George coming back to collect you?"

Phil tried to go on drying himself while hiding what was happening to his cock. "No. I'm supposed to meet him somewhere on Fifty-seventh Street at twelve-thirty."

Charlie's grin broadened. "More than an hour? Silly old George for leaving you at my mercy. Of course we didn't know I was going to have some time on my hands this morning and that you'd be here naked and waiting for me so I suppose we could call it fate rather than gross negligence. God, what a bod. You and George are too much. It wouldn't be fair to me not to have you both." Charlie drew him into his arms and resumed the kiss of the night before, which had been only a hint of the marvels of his mouth. Towel and dressing gown slipped away. The eagerness of Phil's body to feel Charlie's against him made it a real infidelity. In a stunned fragmentary instant, he realized how radically he had altered in less than two months. He could no longer think of being naked with a friend as innocent. He was still thrown off balance by the abrupt transformation of sex from almost impersonal play in a closet to a total commitment of his body, the unrestrained satisfaction of physical passion. He and Charlie were naked, their cocks straining up against each other with the unequivocal urgency of wanting all of each other.

They broke apart, panting, and Charlie ran a hand along Phil's cock. "Big but not gaudy, thank God," he told Phil approvingly. "George's can wear a girl out. You don't make me feel like a dwarf."

"Some dwarf," Phil said. Charlie's cock was almost as big as his own so he didn't want to think of it as dwarfish. His body would have been a disgrace in any self-respecting gym, nicely formed but angular and undeveloped and hairless as a boy's, yet puzzlingly, mysteriously desirable. Phil was aware of dislocating inner tremors as the urge surfaced in him to submit to male will. It was extraordinary that the nondescript physique could convey such a sense of indomitable virility.

"We better find out more about this in bed," Charlie said. "You wouldn't be with George if you don't like to be fucked. I do too, but I'm branching out. Are you going to let me have you?"

"Well, I—"

"Of course you are." He hurried him into his bedroom and they fell onto the bed in a tumultuous meeting of bodies. Phil abandoned himself to pleasure while he found justifications for himself. George had wanted Charlie. It was natural for Phil to want Charlie too. It was like having more of George. It flashed through his mind that Charlie was only the second guy he'd actually gone to bed with— Teddy hardly counted—so it made sense to pick up more experience. George had had a lot. Phil remained so unfamiliar with homosexuality that it still startled him when a guy wanted him. It couldn't seem completely natural and right with George unless it seemed natural and right with others. He sucked Charlie's cock with the passionate dedication that he'd learned was part of him, but he wouldn't know if his compulsion to give himself to a man was equally a part of him—something he would have discovered even without George—until Charlie took him.

When he did so, it was without the sublime shock of George's possession of him, but he felt it satisfying the need that George or maybe even Teddy had revealed to him. A guy wanted him and was taking him. A guy's cock was moving in him and finding its pleasure in his submission. Something in him compelled him to accept its domination. He worshiped phallic power. A guy who attracted him turned him into a girl. It was incomprehensible but true. His breath caught as Charlie's thrusts became more determined and he uttered a long moan of acquiescence.

"You like my cock in you, don't you, hon'?" Charlie murmured. "Aren't you heavenly. Are you almost ready? If we come quickly we'll have time for another."

When they were back in the bathroom under the shower, Charlie looked at him with a conspiratorial smile on his beautiful lips. "Mother's rather new to it, but it seems to me you're pretty sensational. After what you're used to with George, I was afraid you'd dismiss me with contempt."

"Because his cock is so big? I didn't fall in love with him for that. I almost fell in love with you when you were in me. I don't think I'll ever want to branch out."

"You're my honey child. It's too ghastly to think about, but I'm seven or eight years older than you. A lot can happen before you're an old man like me. Would you consider a weekend of our own?"

"How can I? I couldn't afford it."

"What's to afford? I think I can manage the plane ticket. The rest is chicken feed."

"Wouldn't George find out?"

"Why should he? I don't intend to let you out on the town. If you're worrying about cheating, don't bother. Fidelity isn't his strong suit."

"It isn't?"

"Wait a minute. Don't get me wrong. Maybe he really is a reformed character. We made it when he came through on his way back to school a month ago, but he told me all about you. He said you were it. No more fooling around."

"But you went to bed together after our vacation?"

"Well, that was probably just habit. We've been doing it since he was a freshman, but I was one of millions. That cock of his is famous. I was at a gang bang with him once when he had six guys in a row and a few others before and after. Now that I know you, I believe him when he says he can't be bothered to look at anybody else, but don't be upset if his old ways catch up with him every now and then. Fidelity isn't everything."

The images Charlie had conjured up in his mind were giving Phil a hard on again. He didn't care about George's past except to envy some of it (not the shocking gang bang) and didn't think he even minded very much George's having somebody since they'd been together, considering that Charlie predated him, but he had to get himself straight about what he'd suspected all along was an important problem. If George couldn't or wouldn't fix the rules, he was going to have to figure them out for himself. He certainly couldn't expect Charlie to be any help.

He saw that their cocks were keeping pace with each other, both slanting out in front of them and beginning to lift. Charlie turned him and moved him out of the stream of water and closed in behind him. His hard cock thrust up against his buttocks. Phil's was fully erect when Charlie's hands reached it.

"Lordy, I didn't know your Mother was such a potent

lady.'' Charlie's voice shook with laughter. ''If you don't dawdle over dressing, we still have time. Shall we try for the jackpot?''

''I can get dressed in no time. Put it in me.''

Charlie did so, and they sank to their knees together, remaining joined. Their bodies rocked to the rhythm of their copulation. ''Are we going to have our weekend, honey child?'' Charlie asked, his voice jubilant with possession.

''I want you so damn much. I can't believe it. Oh God, yes, like that. Your cock is fantastic. It feels as big as George's.''

''It's almost as big as yours. That's not bad.''

''I didn't know I wanted it like this with anybody but him. I don't want to cheat on him. You're the only other one.''

''Don't worry. It's all in the family. We'll share you. I'm the second?''

''Yes, except once when I was a kid.''

''Oh, hon, you're such a sweetheart. Next time we'll spend three days in bed.''

''You mean it about paying for my ticket?''

''Of course. You're my honey child. Tell me if you need more.''

It was amazing that guys were ready to pay to have him with them. George's generosity had prepared him to accept it. He hoped he wasn't turning into a whore. ''You're making me come,'' he exclaimed ecstatically.

''Me too. You won't be late for him.''

It was a bit of a strain being with two guys he wanted so much, but fortunately Charlie was out a lot. Phil had impossible visions of them all in bed together, of both of them taking him. When he woke up early Sunday morning after a restless night thinking of Charlie in the next room,

George was sleeping so soundly that his heart began to thud with an awful temptation. He listened to George's heavy breathing punctuated with snorts and snores, and slipped cautiously out of bed, prepared to come right back if he stirred. He didn't. He tiptoed to the bathroom. He flushed the toilet and splashed unnecessarilly while he brushed his teeth, thinking that Charlie might hear him. His signals unanswered, he was drawn irresistibly to his door. He stood in front of it listening, his hand hovering over the knob. Did he dare risk it? The door opened. They stared at each other for a startled moment and then Charlie grabbed him and pulled him into the room. Their bodies silently rioted together in bed.

"My God, you're good, hon," Charlie whispered when he had entered him again. "We better be quick. He'll kill us if we don't look out."

"Yes, quickly. It's crazy but I couldn't help it. I want you. You and George. I want you both. Oh God. Your cock, Charlie."

He crept back to George and was so relieved to find him still sleeping that he was struck by a backlash of remorse. He had taken an unforgivable risk with everything he treasured most. It was bad enough to cheat, but he could at least take care not to do it under George's nose. He felt sick with guilt. If he'd had doubts about his homosexuality, he couldn't use that as an excuse again. He knew now and didn't have to encourage himself. George had made no secret of his having been promiscuous, so Phil couldn't pretend that he'd been shocked into getting back at him. If he went on wanting Charlie, he was going to have to learn how to fit it in without its touching his life with George.

He and Charlie had their secret weekend, and Phil agreed to more after the approaching Easter vacation. The bliss of being with George again for two weeks almost made him forget about Charlie, but when school parted them once more Phil accepted an invitation to another secret weekend. It led to a third and a fourth. Charlie was becoming a difficult habit to break.

Phil was careful not to be seen around town with him so that there would be no risk of word getting back to George. All Charlie's banter and gossip evoked a lively life where everybody's sexual preferences were known and accepted. It made him increasingly aware of his and George's secretive isolation. Some of George's friends were already engaged. As their educations were completed, marriage would carry all of them off leaving George a conspicuous bachelor with a suspiciously devoted buddy. The need for constant deception could become a strain. For the first time, Phil was conscious of the dangers that were bound to threaten them more and more in the next few years. They couldn't afford to be careless with each other or take anything for granted; they must always watch for new ways to make themselves complete in each other.

He thought at length about fidelity. He wished that George had taken a firm stand about it one way or another so that he would have something to go on. His attempts to draw him out on the subject had led to nothing. George apparently didn't recognize it as a problem. He was used to seeing life as a succession of triumphs. Always a star at everything he did, he didn't seem to consider the possibility that things might go wrong. Phil was his. They were together. He would see to it that they stayed together. That seemed to be the sum of his thoughts on the subject. Phil wasn't even sure if he would mind if he knew what was going on.

He began to feel that he *should* mind and if he didn't that he was going to have to mind for him. He knew what was happening to himself, even if George wasn't aware of it yet. He was creating a rift between them. Believing in their unguarded love and trust, Phil hadn't hesitated to deceive him. It would destroy everything if he discovered that George was doing the same thing. He was learning that nobody could give himself equally to two people. Every time he was with Charlie he was betraying the person he cared most about in the world. He was cheating George of something that belonged to him. It wasn't a question of divided loyalties. His loyalty to George was unswerving except that he acted as if he had the right to adjust his loyalty to the pleasure he found with somebody else. It didn't matter if George never found out. He was living a lie and was bound to suffer for it. He learned that there was a reason for fidelity.

Faced with the long summer vacation, he knew that he had to put an end to Charlie. He couldn't imagine telling him he didn't want to see him again, but he couldn't go through months with George with his shadow falling between them. With the fifth weekend coming up, he wrote Charlie calling it off and explaining that it wouldn't be fair to George to go on. He had misgivings about putting so many details about their affair on paper, but he was sure Charlie would never let anybody see the letter.

His decision lifted a great weight from his mind, and he resolved that no matter how tempted he was he would never be unfaithful again. He was almost twenty, old enough to know what he wanted and act accordingly.

He missed Charlie and looking forward to their weekends together much more than he'd expected. It was a constant ache that made him even more sure that he'd done the right thing. Once summer started and he was with George again, he saw more clearly how close he'd come to wrecking their life together. Some area of his mind or spirit or whatever he wanted to call it had been filled by

Charlie and, without him, now lay vacant, a vacuum in him. He had allowed an important part of himself to escape from George, and it required an effort to get it back where it belonged. He knew that if he'd delayed his decision much longer, he wouldn't have been able to make the effort. His body's infidelity was the least of it. It was his prolonging and enlarging their relationship that had done the damage; the first lucky time probably wouldn't have mattered except to the extent that sexual laxness undermined moral stamina.

He learned what it meant to make a sacrifice to love; it made love more precious. He found out what jealousy felt like. All that summer he watched for signs that George was reverting to his old ways, and Phil seethed with rage and wounded feelings if he showed a marked interest in other guys. He had denied himself his indulgences with Charlie. If he caught George in similar indulgences, he would kill him and himself. There would be nothing left to live for. George was all he wanted in life and all that he was going to allow himself to have.

When nothing happened to mar the perfect harmony between them, it slowly occurred to him that George might have felt the same way right from the start and hadn't seen any point in discussing fidelity. Why worry if they were made for each other?

The secret weekends had at least helped Phil to understand and finally accept the fact that his life was going to be shaped and dominated by his perversion. His vice? To Phil, vice implied weakness and self-indulgence, but there was nothing self-indulgent about his homosexuality. At times he hated himself for it, but it was built into him as inescapably as his sight and hearing. His only alternative was to abstain from sex entirely; he thought he might have remained a virgin if he had been confined to finding satisfaction with girls, but George had saved him from that. Accepting the basic fact about himself, he was able to think of the future in practical if unfamiliar terms.

The law didn't seem to be a profession for a homosexual. All the lawyers he knew had wives who were useful to their careers, whereas there was nothing unusual about bachelor professors. Most of his were. He talked at length with George about it that summer, and it made sense to both of them. George's future was fixed here with the dairy business. If Phil found a teaching job somewhere near, ideally Ann Arbor, they could have their weekends together and all the extensive vacations. He was interested in literature and the theater. He decided to be a teacher. His parents were surprised and probably disappointed, but they couldn't object. He wished he could tell them about his happiness; if George were a girl, they'd all be rejoicing over his having found the love of his life. Being gay didn't live up to its name.

When George graduated, his father, inspired by his mother, gave him a little house in town so that he could be independent, and they began to actually live the life they had imagined. Phil's school curriculum was concentrated on English and the arts. His marks were high and he was popular with his teachers. In his senior year he was offered a junior position on the faculty for the fall. He had been deferred from the draft as a student, and now it was likely that he would continue to be deferred as a teacher. George's father had wangled him a deferment as an essential farm worker. Something was going on in Vietnam that posed a distant threat, but they weren't worried. The one secret little convulsion Phil had undergone was well in the past. They led charmed lives. Phil had learned to struggle successfully against temptations, and he supposed George had too if he had any. The years of promiscuity may have helped him learn his priorities. Being made for each other, they were naturally monogamous.

George wrote him just before his graduation. The letter bewildered Phil rather than upset him. Now that Phil was about to start out in life, George said, it was time for him to think about marriage and children and other such adult concerns. George admitted that he'd been selfish in allowing Phil to miss the important experiences of life for the sake of what was basically a schoolboy romance.

When he came home for the summer, he didn't think they should live together like an established couple. People would begin to think it was peculiar now that they were both making their livings. Phil should start taking an interest in the normal social activities of their contemporaries. Nothing would really change between them, he said. It was just a matter of putting it in its proper perspective.

The letter was so at odds with everything they'd talked about that Phil couldn't take it seriously. George must have written it in an uncharacteristic fit of guilt. It was something that would be cleared up in a few minutes' talk and an hour in bed, but he had to see him immediately before George began to think that he was making a valid point.

He sold a few books and borrowed some money from a friend and took the first bus he could get to Newcorners. It turned out that George's scruples about depriving him of his heterosexual birthright were embodied in a strapping blond called Ron. Phil arrived quite late at night and let himself into the house with his own key. He found George and Ron in bed.

Phil's rage outweighed the fact that Ron looked as if he could take care of Phil with one hand tied behind his back. Ron fled, leaving the field to his outraged rival. Phil calmed down as soon as the big blond was out of sight. Waiting for Ron to scramble into his clothes gave him time to remember that a similar scene might have taken place three years ago on that foolhardy Sunday morning with George only a few yards away. Jealousy was a torment that anticipated the worst, so actually seeing George in bed with another guy didn't have the shock of the unimaginable. The pain it caused him did.

They stood more or less facing each other but not quite able to look at each other. George had managed to find a dressing gown in the excitement. The agonizing silence between them seemed interminable. George finally broke it.

"You shouldn't've done that." He sounded as calmly reasonable as ever. "I asked him to spend the night."

"So I gather."

"Did you get my letter?"

"Why do you think I'm here? I've never read such nonsense." Phil was surprised to discover that he could speak quite calmly too. "You've said from the start that we'd be together always. We live together. That's the way it is."

"Of course, sweetheart. But we're grown-ups now. We can't go on acting like kids. People notice things now that they didn't pay any attention to when we were still at school. I meant what I said. If you gave yourself a chance, you might find out that you want to get married."

"And what about you? Is having your boyfriends spend the night your idea of getting ready for marriage?"

"I told you about Ron."

"You did?" Phil realized that he had. Having got a grip on the first shock of pain, he was slowly remembering who Ron was. He'd noticed him around when he'd come home for Easter. He was a farm boy George was training to be his assistant manager now that his father was withdrawing increasingly from the business. He remembered

George telling him that he'd been a class behind Phil at school. "OK. You mentioned him. You didn't tell me you were fucking him."

"What makes you think I am? Guys can share a bed without anything like that."

"Oh for God's sake," Phil remonstrated, finally looking at him squarely. "Most guys can, maybe. We can't."

"Maybe you know more about that than I do."

"What's that supposed to mean?"

"You're talking as if you can't imagine being in bed with a guy without making love. I don't feel the same way."

"Now listen. This is serious." He supposed he shouldn't expect George to admit to ordinary mortal weakness. Looking at him, he had to screw up his courage to even hint that he might do anything so disreputable as jumping into the sack with a farmhand. He was so supremely masculine, such a model of decency and clean living. He was above sexual lapses. They were together. There was nothing to worry about. "Don't let's kid each other for God's sake," he pleaded. "I came home unexpectedly and found you in bed with Ron. You were both naked and all wrapped around each other, in case you hadn't noticed. I saw your cock when I pulled the covers off him. It can't do much without being noticeable. Facts are facts."

"So I got a hard on when I saw you were angry. I don't think I've ever seen you really angry before. It was exciting for some reason."

"Oh, shit." Phil wanted to scream. He wanted to smash his face in. He wanted to tear his dressing gown off and hold him in his arms and put his big goddamn cock in his mouth. He took a hesitant step closer to him and continued to try to reason with him. "I admit *I* don't always find it easy living the way we do, being apart all the time. I'm tempted sometimes. Once long ago, right at the beginning when I hardly knew what was happening to me, I got sort of involved with a guy. When I saw that it risked coming between us I cut it off. It might've been easier if I could've talked to you about it. Why can't you talk to me? If you'd just tell me that you got carried away but that he isn't important to you, I'd understand. We're in love with each other. You're everything in life to me. I can make allowances if you sometimes do things that hurt me. I've always counted on you to make the rules. That's normal with any couple—one being sort of the boss.''

"Then why don't you pay attention to what I wrote you? I'm thinking about you. After all, I knew what it was all about when we started, you didn't. I'm responsible. We're too tied up with each other. If we go on, you'll never find out if you can make it with a girl.''

"I know that already. So do you. Are you trying to tell me that you don't want us to be together any more?''

"Of course not. We can be together whenever we want. I just don't want you to take it for granted that we're always going to do everything together. It's not healthy. We can try it my way at least for this summer so that when you start teaching you'll be more used to being on your own. Going to school and having a job are entirely different. You'll see. You're going to want to concentrate on what you're doing, not wishing you were with me all the time.''

"I doubt it, but I'll soon find out. You still haven't told me about Ron.''

"What about him? He's a damn nice kid. I like him a lot. Like you, I get lonely sometimes. I told him he could stay. You know I never wear pajamas. He didn't have any. I guess maybe being naked and everything we started to fool around a bit. How do I know? You came roaring in and I didn't know what was going on. I may've thrown my arms around him the way anybody would, just sort of instinctive self-protection.''

''Jesus,'' Phil muttered. George's elusiveness made him want to curl up in a heap on the floor and cry helplessly. Everything in him was falling apart. He couldn't get a grip on anything. He was torn between anger and despair and hoped anger would win out. It would be easier to handle. Why wouldn't George say that he'd wanted to go to bed with the guy and let them put it behind them? Because it wasn't as simple as that? Because he didn't want to put it behind him? George approached and put a hand on his shoulder. All of Phil's body tensed. He longed for him to put his arms around him. If George wanted him he wouldn't resist. They would make love and everything would fall back into place. ''Since you're here, you better come to bed,'' George said.

It sounded grudging. Phil slipped away from his hand and drifted around the room. He had to do something but didn't know what. If he knew more he might find his way through it. George wouldn't help. Would Ron? As the idea took hold, it suddenly became urgent. He had to do it before anything diverted him. It was the only way out of the dead end they had reached. He went decisively to the bureau where George always left the car keys. They were there. ''I don't think much of the idea of taking Ron's place in bed. You obviously don't want to talk. Maybe you need some time to think it over. I'll take the car. I'll be back in the morning.'' He pocketed the keys. He was so used to thinking of George's car as theirs that it didn't occur to him to ask permission. He started for the door.

''Now wait. If—'' George said to his back.

Phil couldn't look at him. ''It's all right,'' he interrupted as he hurried out. ''I'll see you in the morning.'' He ran down the stairs and closed the door carefully behind him without letting it slam. It was an old-fashioned house with a separate garage. The car was in it where it belonged. He was in it and speeding along the familiar road to the farm without giving himself time for second thoughts. He'd remembered quite a lot about Ron. He remembered thinking at school that Ron would make a promising candidate for the basement, but he'd thought that about quite a lot of boys. He remembered that George had told him that he'd moved into the manager's quarters at the farm. He felt as if his life depended on his being there.

There were lights on in the main house, but he avoided it and took the drive that led to the dairy buildings. The manager's quarters were at the end of a one-story building that also housed offices, set apart from the barns. There were no lights showing, but he knew his way around as well as if he'd been born here. He parked the car and skirted some flower beds and stopped at an open window. The room within was dark. He rapped softly on the window frame. There was a beat of silence.

"What?" a startled voice said and simultaneously a light flashed on. The lamp was beside a bed. Ron's tousled head was lifted from the pillow, and he looked around, blinking dazedly.

Phil climbed in through the window. "It's me," he said.

Ron sat up abruptly, letting his covers slip from his naked torso to his waist. He lifted a hand as if to ward Phil off. "Now wait a minute, sir. Don't start anything. It's obvious I can handle you, but I don't want any trouble."

Phil found the "sir" disarming. He was a nice-looking guy, not notably handsome but attractive, with a broad, open face and appealing blue eyes. The thick golden hair was beautiful. His body was too solid and chunky for Phil's taste, but it was a good body of its kind. He might have been a weight lifter; he had those sorts of muscles. Phil took a long breath of relief at things having gone right for him so far, and the wild beating of his heart slowed and steadied. He advanced to the side of the bed and looked down at Ron with a reassuring smile. He saw that he was wearing pajama bottoms. "I'm not going to give you any trouble," he said.

"You're not mad at me?"

Phil knew that Ron must be at least twenty-one in view of his school history, but his manner was very young, more like a teenager. "Why should I be?" he asked.

Ron pushed a pillow up behind him and lay back, relaxing after his momentary fright. "Well, I know about you and George. I mean, well, I guess everybody does. He's talked a lot about you. He said he was going to work it out so that we can go on being together when you come back for the summer. Anything he wants is OK by me. With a guy like George I don't expect exclusive rights."

Phil swallowed with difficulty, trying to find out if he could still speak. This was what he'd come for. He preferred finding out this way than hearing it from George. He could let his anger boil in him without having to fight back a howl of despair. "How long have you been sleeping with him?" he managed after a moment.

"Ever since I started work here last fall. I thought you must know. We took one look at each other and pow—the next thing I knew I was being fucked in B barn alongside the milking machines. George doesn't waste any time. I guess you know about the others as well as I do, but he's still crazy for me. It's the greatest thing that's ever happened to me. I'm nuts about him, of course. He gives me everything. I'm almost certain there hasn't been anyone else since Christmas. Except you, naturally. I expect to share with you. It's only fair. You got there first."

Phil sank down to the edge of the bed, unsure that his legs would support him any longer. Even his anger had failed him. His life had ended. He had to pretend to go on living. One way to pretend was to take his obvious revenge. He pulled the cover off Ron for the second time.

"Hey," Ron exclaimed without making a move to stop him. Phil looked into his clear blue eyes while he opened Ron's pajamas. His cock stood upright in his hand. Ron smiled encouragingly. A gratifying glance at what he was holding confirmed Phil's impression that it wasn't as big as his own. He stood and began to undress, looking down at him. Ron doubled up his legs and peeled off his pajama bottoms and lay back, watching Phil expectantly. For the first time in his life, Phil wanted to fuck a guy. He had that to keep him going. He was going to have Ron the way George had him. His anger had turned to masculine aggression. Ron was going to be his before he threw him back to anybody who wanted him. When he was naked he stood for a moment, his cock soaring, feeling bigger and more powerful than it ever had in his life.

"Cripes, you guys are hung," Ron exclaimed, awe mingled with admiration as his eyes traveled over it. "George's is the biggest I've ever seen, but you're not too far behind. Big ones turn me on. You want to fuck me?"

"That's the idea."

"Right. I have some stuff." He rolled over, revealing fleshy muscular buttocks, and reached for a drawer in the bedside table. He dropped a tube onto the bed and rolled back. "Are you going to tell George?"

"I don't know."

"I guess you better not. He's funny that way. He's not giving anybody exclusive rights, but he expects exclusive rights with the guys he wants. Only a guy like George could get away with it."

Phil leaned over and got a grip on his beautiful hair and pulled him up to him. He came willingly. Phil held his face just out of reach of his rigid cock. He swung his hips slightly so that it brushed his cheeks and his parted lips. He was going to make this big hunk beg for it. The sense of power in him was stunning. "Do you suck his cock?" he demanded.

"Well, sure, but you know, it's too big for me to do much with it."

"I've never had any trouble. Do you want to try mine?"

"Hell, yes. Yours is perfect. I can really go to town with it."

"Go ahead." He dropped down onto his knees on the bed. Ron shifted around so that he could get at him easily and opened his mouth wide for Phil to thrust himself into it. Phil watched him working on him, his jaws stretched, his lips and tongue and hands entering enthusiastically into his effort. He knew how to go about it. George's private property. George's lover. Love and sex were a farce, good for a thrill or a laugh. Why had he thought that life would be a pure dedication to his passion? He thought of his struggles against temptation and wanted to shout with rage. Why hadn't he grabbed the Rons as they turned up? One look and pow. Ron was stirring up some very agreeable sensations in him. He was ready for him. His heart began to thud with excitement.

He put his hands on his heavy shoulders and pushed him back. "You've got me pretty close," he warned. "Use some of your stuff on us." Ron did so, his eyes held by Phil's cock. "Good. Just stay there," Phil ordered.

"On my back?"

"That's right."

Ron lifted husky, docile legs into the air and dropped them over Phil's shoulders. Phil drove hard into him. For a moment he thought he was going to come and then his orgasm was contained by his thrusting hips. He was taking a guy at last. He was in possession of the muscular body; it was his by right of conquest. It belonged to him for as long as he wanted to leave his cock there. His omnipotent cock. Why hadn't he ever wanted to use it the way it was meant to be used? It was a sublime instrument, capable of fucking everybody in sight. He thought of girls, girls pining for it, girls swooning under him. Maybe George was right. Maybe he didn't know himself. He was going to have time to find out.

"God, your cock's good," Ron gasped. "I love it. I always knew I would. Both of you. When I was a kid at school I'd've given anything for you to fuck me, both of you. God, Phil, it's you now. Go on. Fuck me blind."

Phil wasn't reluctant to exercise his newfound prowess. It was an extraordinary power in him that he hadn't known existed. He became a god, a source of divine retribution, a ruler instead of a subject. If he went on feeling like this, he wouldn't care if he never saw George again. Maybe George had done him a favor. Maybe he really had blocked his natural development. He drove into Ron like a conqueror, looking down into his victim's grateful blue eyes. Ron's quick orgasm seemed a tribute to his newfound power. His own followed, and Ron showed him where the shower was. When he'd washed, he let George's lover coax him back to bed.

"I'm in luck. How come you're not with George?" Ron asked.

"Well, I got a look at you and thought I'd like more." He felt his voice breaking and hastily turned away, his eyes closed. He offered his body freely to the explorations of Ron's mouth. Their mouths were joined in prolonged kisses, but these were only interludes in his cock's proud possession of him.

"You're fabulous," Ron told him. "The way your cock stays hard in me is unbelievable. If you're around this summer, I hope we can get together often."

Phil didn't know much, but he knew he wasn't going to be around this summer. He didn't want to dwell on the things Ron had told him, but he knew what they added up to. George had deceived him, probably from the start, certainly for the last year or two. Involvement could easily get out of hand and forgiveness was part of love, but he'd learned the hard way that love could also tell you when it was time to call a halt. For George to let Ron believe that they could work it out on a sort of sharing basis after he came home was too shocking to think about. He had almost convinced himself that he was glad it had all come out.

"You're going to spend the night, aren't you?" Ron asked.

"Sure." He had nowhere else to go. He didn't want to wake his family up in the middle of the night. His life was a shambles. He couldn't hope to put it together. He was pretty sure he knew what he was going to do in the morning, but he didn't know where he'd find the strength to do it. He went to sleep while his cock was getting hard again in Ron's mouth.

He left the keys to the house and the car on the table in the entrance hall shortly after dawn without seeing George, and he returned to Ann Arbor. He didn't think there was enough left of him to survive a confrontation. Being without George and the loving thoughts of him that had constituted his whole adult experience left him feeling maimed, as if he were blind or had lost a leg. One of his first positive acts was to inform the English department that he wasn't going to take the job in the fall. He knew that it would probably result in his being drafted as soon as he graduated but he didn't care. He didn't think he'd ever care about anything again.

George wrote. He said that Ron had told him what had happened and he understood and accepted it but that Phil had been wrong about Ron. Nothing had happened that justified destroying their life together. Of course they would go on living the way they had been if Phil was sure it didn't make sense for him to have a little more independence. He was waiting for him to come and take back his key to the house.

The letter didn't repair the damage Phil had suffered. If George had said he was sorry about Ron, that he'd ended their affair and wanted a chance to start over again, Phil would have gone to him like a shot. Saying that nothing had happened didn't get them anywhere. George and his exclusive rights. He was ashamed of relieving his anger with Ron and began to be ashamed of everything he'd done since the first momentous afternoon with George. He fed his shame, seeing in it the possibility of salvation, telling himself that queers were disgusting with their dirty pictures of sex with each other and calling each other "she." Ron had said that everybody knew about them, and George had warned that people would begin to wonder. Phil couldn't stand the idea that he was being publicly labeled a queer. It had been time for the break. He wouldn't have anything more to do with guys. It shouldn't be difficult if he didn't let himself look at them. Ron had revealed sexual elements in him he hadn't known existed. He'd make it with a girl or give it all up. That was what George wanted.

He made approaches to several girls he'd found attractive, but when it came to the point, he had no will to follow through. His aggressive masculinity had been a fleeting phenomenon. Ron apparently had exclusive rights to it. It had worked because he'd wanted to take a guy away from George.

Every day became a test of his self-discipline and self-control. He steeled himself against feeling. He was amazed that he managed so well. George and his parents came to his graduation. Phil realized that the elder Hudderstones had come to spare themselves the embarrassment of openly acknowledging that their son's love affair had gone sour. He was able to smile and be polite, but several times he caught George's candid eyes on him, pleading with him. He came appallingly close to breaking down, but he managed to get through that too.

It was the last bad moment with George. Phil's own family was of course there for his graduation, and he'd agreed to go with them for a visit to relatives on the way home. When he got to Newcomers a few days later, a notice from his draft board was waiting for him. Within a week he was in uniform and soon after that he was sent to officers' training camp. The rigid routine of army life was a blessed release. He didn't have to think about anything any more. Even when George's letters began to undermine his resistance, there wasn't much he could do about it. George wanted him back. Even if it meant being celibate for two years, he would wait for him. George finally admitted that he'd been careless in the past but swore that he wouldn't touch another guy if only Phil promised to come to him as soon as he was discharged and help him get things back the way they'd been before.

If Phil had had more privacy, he might not have been able to get through the first few repentant letters without collapsing, but the control it required to read them in public blunted their effect and extended to his answering them, which was also a fairly public act. He tried to be noncommittal while avoiding a definite break. The fact that he answered at all was enough to indicate that he was willing to preserve a tenuous link. He wrote that the future was too uncertain for vows of chastity to have much meaning. If they wanted each other and only each other, they didn't need vows to govern their acts. He was in an entirely new environment, he explained, and wanted to take advantage of the chance to put aside his schoolboy ways. Maybe George would turn out to be right after all and marriage was what he really needed. Time would tell.

After his first few letters, George slowly adopted a tone of simple camaraderie, with news of home and family and mutual friends, and Phil was convinced that he had conquered his feelings at last. A period of his life had ended. When his first assignment as a lieutenant took him to the West Coast, he felt even safer.

His cock had obligingly gone into hibernation. The atmosphere surrounding him was so coarsely male and without privacy that there was no room for the old temptations. No thoughts of romance crossed his mind. He had a boring job to do and he did it as well as anybody and hung around drab bars with his fellow officers on weekends. For his last months in uniform he was shipped back across the country to New Jersey, and he began to take weekend passes to New York. A few of the other officers were on home territory, and they amiably included him in mild mixed parties of drinks and flirtations.

He met Helen and they immediately hit it off. She was a junior executive in a publishing house and was interesting about her work. She was dark and brisk and bright, and he found her intelligent face very attractive. He supposed that what they were doing might be called flirting, but he thought of it more as making friends. She gave him her telephone number at the end of the evening, and he asked her to have dinner with him the next time he was in town.

He took her to a little restaurant he knew, and they were shown to a banquette in a dark corner where they sat beside each other. They had a few drinks and ordered food and talked some more about publishing, this time directed at the job possibilities he might find in the business. It involved telling her a lot about himself. The waiter brought their first course and withdrew. Starting to eat her shrimp cocktail, Helen put a hand on his crotch. Phil almost leaped out of his seat, but she imperturbably caressed him into a very uncomfortable erection.

"It's so sensible that nobody expects men to make all the passes any more. It *should* be up to women. We can find out so easily if they're apt to lead to anything. It's a bore wondering all evening, that is if you hope it's leading to something." She opened his fly and extricated his cock and let it stand upright under the table. She ran her hand along it appraisingly. "I like it enormously. I haven't done very extensive research, but it feels very big and determined. Are all men so handsomely equipped?"

"How would I know?" Phil said with a forced laugh that he hoped wouldn't sound guilty.

"Maybe not, but so many men are gay these days that I'm never surprised when they know much more about that sort of thing than I do." Her hand moved up and down on it, exerting almost unbearable pressures, and her fingers fluttered around the head in a way that nearly lifted him out of his seat again.

"We better be careful or there's going to be an unfortunate accident," he said huskily.

"Really? That's marvelous. I'd love to take care of it, but I don't want to attract attention. Is anybody watching?"

He darted a dazed glance around the room. "I don't think so."

"Are you really ready to come?"

"I'm doing my best not to."

"Quickly, I've dropped my napkin." She leaned over him and he felt her tongue touch him. His pelvis lurched and he released months of unexpended ejaculations into her mouth. She licked and sucked on him for a few more delectable seconds and then sat up with a satisfied smile. "That was delicious, much better than a shrimp cocktail." Her hand remained on him so that although his cock lowered slowly it remained considerably enlarged. "Did anybody notice?" she asked, stroking it as it settled in her hand.

"I wasn't exactly in any condition to pay attention." He was still trying to absorb the fact that he'd been sucked off by a girl.

She giggled. "Nobody notices anything in New York, but it was clever of you to have us put in this nice dark corner." Her hand closed firmly around him. "It's so lovely and soft this way, like satin. I think it must be bigger than most men. When my women friends describe them, they sound rather like the few I've seen. I've never felt one like yours. I was afraid for a second I wouldn't be able to put it in my mouth. I want to tell you that you're the most exciting man I've ever met so you won't think I behave like this with everybody. Aren't you just a little bit gay?"

"Yes. Maybe a lot. I'm not sure." As he spoke, Phil felt as if air were filling his lungs for the first time since he'd been a kid. He took an enormous breath. He could breathe. He was free. Helen wasn't a buddy he could say anything to; she was the public that he'd taught himself to hide from for years. His breath came as deep infusions of liberated energy and his cock gave an exultant leap as it began to harden again.

"I thought you must be," she said with her junior-executive manner. "Most of the men I like are. If I can make you come so quickly, I don't think you can be entirely gay."

"I was thinking the same thing." He was also thinking that he hadn't had any sex for over a year. He hoped that wasn't the only explanation. Her hand began to move caressingly on him again and he felt himself swelling under her touch. He wanted it to get big for her again. He wanted her to prove that he needn't be humiliated by the truth.

Her eyes studied him intently, almost as if she were listening for something, and then a light sprang up in them as her hand traveled along his growing length. "Am I imagining it or is it getting hard again?"

"If you do that a little more, you won't have to ask."

"Oh." She uttered a little gasp as she found the pressure that brought him surging up into full erection. Her lips parted and her breasts lifted with the acceleration of her breath. "It *is* big. It must be a thrilling sight. We've got to eat the lovely dinner you've ordered for us, but it seems a shame to miss a minute of this. Will you let me have a long look at it later?"

"I have a feeling it's going to be highly visible tonight."

It was the start of a new life. He assumed at first that it was going to be with Helen. Once his sexual starvation had been appeased, his desire for her was never intense, but she wanted him enough to make up for any apathy in him. The unadorned act of copulation was no problem for him, but further play in her genital area was a trial of self-discipline. He couldn't bring himself to do things that he knew guys were expected to want. He couldn't get used to not finding a cock where a cock should have been. There was a peculiar smell that he knew was supposed to turn guys on, but for him it was something else that took a lot of getting used to. Her breasts were lovely, a major discovery for him, and she seemed satisfied with his attentions to them.

She lived alone in a smart little midtown apartment, and it was understood from the beginning that he would spend all his free weekends with her. They were soon talking about marriage, but they agreed that they should live together for a while before making a decision. She knew that she was the first female that he'd been to bed with.

"If you've been mostly gay you may want men. We'll see how that works out." She sounded quite relaxed and tolerant about it, but she watched him like a hawk if he showed any particular interest in the guys they met together. "Did you want him?" she asked frequently. "If you ever do, you know, you can tell me. I ought to know how I'd feel if it actually happened. I don't think it would bother me in the least, but even if it did I think I can take it."

She was invaluable when, with her enthusiastic encouragement, he decided to look for a job in her field. His discharge was finally in sight, with only a couple of months to go. She guided him through the maze of the publishing world, arranged for him to meet the right people, taught him how to present himself to make the best impression. He managed to wangle a few Friday passes for job hunting and received an offer quite quickly as an underling at practically no salary. Helen assured him that it was a brilliant start and celebrated with champagne.

George still wrote as if he were expecting him home as soon as he was free, and he finally told him about Helen and the job. He explained that she knew all about his past and that for her sake they would have to reduce their contact to Christmas cards and an occasional note for special occasions so that she wouldn't suspect that something was still going on between them. He didn't send an address or telephone number but told him he could always reach him through his parents.

He moved into Helen's apartment and started his job early in the summer. If he wasn't married, everybody treated them like a married couple, so he thought of himself as a family man. It gave him a nice sense of stability, of having a recognized place in the social order. His work was too unimportant to be interesting, but he was keenly interested in the work he would be doing as soon as he'd been employed long enough for advancement. Thanks to the army and Helen, and even George by default, he was embarked on a reasonable, manageable life. He was meeting interesting people. New York was a fascinating unknown he had yet to explore. Learning to live with Helen on a permanent, daily basis was a challenge he welcomed as part of growing up.

The simple fact that she was female grated on him frequently; he missed the deep, close companionship he had known with his male lovers, even for an odd moment with Ron. She was mad about his cock, which pleased him, but they never seemed to drop their guard, to settle down *into* each other. The male–female relationship seemed to be a sparring match. She made much more money than he did, which he didn't think he'd notice with a guy but which made him uncomfortable whenever they went out together. There were a lot of things they couldn't do unless she paid.

As winter began, they quarreled about silly things like whether or not to take a taxi. He told her to do things without him when expenditure was involved, and little by little she did. Quite by accident at the office Christmas party (his first of many) he met a staggeringly beautiful young man called Danny Brazillan. He was a photographer who had done a job for Phil's publisher and reminded Phil of somebody. A chance reference to Newcorners established the connection; Danny had been George's partner and had taken the pictures that had so shocked Phil five or six years ago. Danny's face was as exquisitely beautiful as he remembered, so he could undress him in his mind and feel that he was in the presence of an erotic fantasy that had recurred from time to time over the years. They agreed that it was too embarrassingly obvious to mention but they'd fallen for each other.

Later that night, despite his determination to suppress his homosexuality, he discovered that Danny's willowy body was still the poem of delicacy and elegance that he'd sometimes dreamed about. His cock was as modest as it had looked in the photographs, but he had an ethereal quality that would have been shattered by emphatically masculine characteristics. The exquisite beauty of his features was unequivocally feminine. His hair was silvery-blond silk and his skin fine-textured and flawless. He was amazed that Danny was a couple of years older than George. The kisses of his angelic mouth took Phil's breath away.

By mutual, unspoken consent that night, they confined their lovemaking to oral play so that Phil didn't consider that he'd suffered a total relapse. He hadn't relinquished his newly acquired male status. They both knew how to make it a complete physical union without one surrendering to the other. Phil went home to Helen that night with excuses about too much drink and the party continuing at somebody's place, but he knew that he and Danny would be together again.

Helen's sometimes independent social life favored them. Without making any further demands on each other, Danny introduced embellishments—mirrors, lights, poses—that turned their encounters into full-scale productions. He took photographs. Phil had to admit that they were beautiful, if obscene. He was pleased that his cock looked so big and didn't even recognize his ass at first glance. He thought it was the sexiest looking thing he'd ever seen until he realized that it was his own. Danny showed him samples from his collection. The photographer wasn't in many of them, and Phil didn't think much of most of his models, but one most definitely took his fancy. Danny suggested asking him around, and he came within half an hour. He and Phil put on a show for Danny to photograph before they made it a threesome. Phil knew that his perversion was getting an inexorable grip on him again.

His break with Helen came over a trivial quarrel at the beginning of summer about their vacations. He pointed out that he couldn't afford to go away anywhere farther than Coney Island. Even though he'd received one small raise, he couldn't save any money. She insisted that he come to New England with her and let her pay the expenses he couldn't manage. They both remained adamant. He was aware of thinking that he wouldn't mind some uninterrupted time alone in the city, and he supposed that she realized that he'd been slipping away from her ever since Danny had entered the picture, even though he hadn't told her about it. As a matter of fact, Danny had offered to take him to London as a clothed model for a job he had coming up, but he was going to be gone a week or so too long for Phil to seriously consider it. Helen ended the quarrel by telling him that he'd probably better move out while she was gone. It wasn't a dramatic parting. There was no doubt that they were genuinely fond of each other. Wheth-

er or not she was fully conscious of it, it was obvious to
him that his attempt to become a suitably heterosexual
married man was a failure. The profound satisfaction he
had felt in being socially acceptable was losing its novelty.
He loved it and it was what he would want if he could
choose, but it wasn't worth trying to turn himself into
something he wasn't.

He found a clean, furnished room. He suspected that
now was when he was really going to miss George,
without the buffers of army routine and a fake married life
to help him believe that he could make it on his own. He
hadn't seen him for three years, about the same amount of
time that his life had been wholly dedicated to him. He
didn't regret his decision three years ago, but he regretted
his loss. He admitted to himself that he didn't really expect
to recover the sense of direction that George had given
him. He wrote him, this time including his address and
telephone number as well as the name of the publishing
house where he worked, more or less inviting him to
resume communications. To his relief, he had an affectionate letter in reply, without the reproaches or lamentations
that he had feared. George brought him up to date on local
news, an item of particular interest being that Ron had
gone away to another job. He was sorry about Helen but
felt sure that the experience had been necessary for Phil's
development. It somewhat vindicated his having written
the letter that had triggered so much heartbreak. He went
on hoping that they'd get together again someday but was
willing to wait until they saw how the future was shaping
up. They were still well short of thirty and had a lot of life
ahead of them. Reading between the lines, Phil suspected
that he was caught up with a replacement for Ron.

He took a few tentative steps into the city's gay life that
he'd heard of but knew nothing about—not the bars, which

didn't appeal to him, but the social life that went on behind closed doors. Danny was an experienced guide, and he slowly, reluctantly, settled into it. He found himself surrounded by a large proportion of the city's elite—stage and movie stars, famous writers and musicians, leaders in all the professions courted him as a striking new face. He kept a strict check on himself and gave himself to only a few. It was pretty thrilling to be taken by a cock that millions of women around the world dreamed about. It would be a frightful shock for them to know that one of their heroes had the hots for Philip Renfield.

He was given an important promotion and graduated from the small room to a tiny apartment that he slowly furnished with things he picked up around town. He began to dress with more conscious style, like George. He was no longer a hick from out of town but a familiar fixture of the city's undercover life. It wasn't much of an accomplishment but it gave him something to think about other than George. He couldn't help measuring everything that happened to him against what his life would have been like if they were still together.

All in all, he thought he was better off the way things were. They wrote fairly regularly and George called a couple of times. Phil asked him not to make a habit of it. Hearing his voice but not being able to talk satisfactorily left Phil feeling frustrated and out of sorts with the world. He was still steeling himself against feeling. Life proceeded on an even level, with no joyous highs and no crushing lows.

There was the winter when a casual little affair led to a discovery of Greece and Greek. He was fascinated by the history and literature, not least by the Greeks' attitude to homosexuality. It hadn't always everywhere been anathema. He added a trip to Greece to the list of things he wanted to do when he had some money.

There was the spring of George's trouble. It was serious trouble, involving a teenager he'd picked up at the lake where they used to go to swim. There were parental rumblings and hints of the police getting into it. George called in a panic. It was undoubtedly the first time he'd been treated as anything less than a god or a hero. He was counting on Phil to come immediately.

"How can I? I have a job. I live here."

"I mean just for the weekend. I'll pay for it. We've got to talk about everything. We can't let it go any longer. We've got to be together. Life doesn't make any sense without you."

Phil suggested his coming to New York, dreading the possibility. George quite correctly pointed out that this wasn't the moment to look as if he were running away. Anyway, he said, cows didn't take time off. He was tied to the farm.

Phil had so successfully steeled himself against feeling that he was able to turn him down with only a small stab of pain. The circumstances didn't exactly appeal to his sentiments. George thought he could get away with any-thing. The story as Phil pieced it together was that the kid had led George on and then through some careless accident had been found out and had blamed it all on him. It was a classic tale of its kind. Phil supposed he might have done the same thing if he'd been caught on the riverbank with Teddy. Teenagers were inclined to be trollops. As Phil had expected, the scandal blew over with a small loss to the Hudderstone pocketbook.

Later there came Phil's temporary insanity with Alex. As that stormy affair went through its ups and downs, he and George were frequently on the telephone. During the downs, he came closer to rushing to George's arms than he'd thought possible after all these years. George wanted him. They could figure something out about Phil's work. Newcomers needed a really good bookstore, for one thing. George could back him. It must be clear to both of them by now that they needed each other.

Danny was a helpful and restraining influence. He always seemed to be conveniently between affairs, hence available, and he could talk about both George and Alex with firsthand knowledge. He offered Phil worldly wisdom as well as sexual consolation; never let love affairs interfere with the serious business of living. They should be enjoyed as pleasant interludes. Two guys who attempted an imitation marriage were almost always doomed to failure. Men were by nature wanderers, especially George and Alex.

During the ups, Phil didn't want to spend a minute of his life with anybody but Alex, even though they never got the sex right. They both wanted to be taken and Alex was orally inhibited, claiming sulkily that Phil was too big for him. This was a tribute he could have done without. He did it Alex's way as in everything else, but he couldn't recapture the satisfaction he had found in taking George's lover. It didn't make him want Alex less. By the time he had conquered his madness, he was so emotionally drained that he didn't think he would be powerfully attracted to anybody ever again. He was all used up.

---

The dawn light was dim when Phil's eyes fluttered open. He emerged from a dream in which George wouldn't let him have his clothes (at least that was what a fragment of it was about) and discovered that his dream of Manoli was real. He was on Phil, in him, taking him slowly and with the assurance of a lover whose right to him had been acknowledged. His hard body fitted him everywhere, as if there wasn't a part of him that hadn't been made to fill a need in him. He soared with the peaceful physical well-being he hadn't known for years. He pretended to be more asleep than he was to remain passive and let Manoli take what he wanted and show him that they were as good together as Phil thought they were. Manoli shifted him so that he could handle his cock. He did it as if he liked it.

Phil muttered incoherently and grunted a few times, making a little show of being fully awake and their bodies began to move together, responding to a need that was in both of them. He wasn't sure the need had been in Manoli last night, but he couldn't be mistaken about it now. There was love in the way he used his body this morning. Manoli wanted him. He wanted him because he was a male, not in spite of it. His insistence that he was a man for women had been forgotten. Phil had made love with confirmed homosexuals whose desire had been more guarded. He and Manoli were sharing as Phil could share only with men, sharing their approaching orgasms, sharing their ecstasy as a joyful celebration of their masculinity.

The light was acquiring an edge when they crossed the room to the shower, highlighting the outlines of Manoli's swarthy body—the sleekly muscular balance of his shoulders, the lovely taper of his torso to narrow hips, the lean, sinewy power of his legs. They stood under the feeble stream of water while Phil studied the structure of his dark face, the setting of his fierce, gentle eyes, his straight nose, the hollows under his prominent cheekbones, his strong chin and jaw above the smooth young vulnerability of his throat. A Greek warrior-athlete. Was he still capable of falling in love? Why worry? He would succumb to his spell for a day or two and then rally his controls to take charge. He pulled him out from under the shower and put his mouth on Manoli's firmly modeled lips. He felt no resistance but he didn't push it. Their tongues touched and Phil drew back. Manoli's hands were on him again.

"You are mine, Philip," he said.

"Yes." Despite the caressing hands, he forced himself to add, "For now. Not when I go away."

"I will go with you. You will see. Your body feels good. It pleases me." His hands strayed over him, moving down. Phil held his breath and released it as they reached his cock. They looked into each other's eyes. "This pleases me too."

"I'm glad."

"We'll be together this evening on the yacht. Later we will have the night together again. Now I go."

"Is very early, I think."

"A good time. I don't want people to see me." He let go of Phil's cock, leaving it in an intermediate state of development.

Phil turned the water off, and they dried themselves while Manoli's eyes remained on his cock. Phil wondered if Manoli would go on claiming to be straight. Guys were peculiar about it. He'd been with one or two youngsters who swore that he was the only guy they'd even considered having it off with. Manoli's cock looked as if it needed only a touch to make it spring up into erection. Feeling that he had to go on trying to break down his resistance kept Phil in a high pitch of suspense. If Manoli ever let himself go, maybe Phil would lose interest in him.

Manoli led him to one of the rooms in the back where Phil saw his clothes neatly folded on a chair. He slipped them on, the expensive-looking American-style clothes of the night before, but kept Phil near him, having no difficulty in coaxing his cock into full erection. Manoli's hands were as eager for him as any Phil had ever felt.

"There," he said, stroking all its length and fondling his balls. "This is the way it was when I saw you first. It pleases me to see you like that. You are a fine man." He touched his cheek and turned away, looking outrageously sexy in his tight pants. Phil watched, puzzled, as he went to the tall French windows and opened them. There was a tiny balcony outside. He stepped out and threw a leg over the rail and dropped startlingly from sight. Phil leaped forward to see what had become of him but remembered his nakedness and veered aside to grab a pillow from one of the beds to cover himself. He approached the window cautiously and peered out. There was a flat tin roof only about six feet below. A few yards beyond it the rocky hillside rose steeply. Manoli was gone. He supposed that there might be helpful footholds here and there, but a pillow was inadequate attire for further examination. It was chilly. He took his erection back into the room and smiled down at it. He'd made it very happy. A glorious start to something, but God alone knew what. Even he couldn't get started on the game of "if" that had kept him going so often with Alex. If only—. What if—? If only Manoli were an American with a job and money everything would be different, but there was no point in the game if there weren't a few facts to sustain it. He was a hustler. He was a Greek who would have trouble enough just getting into the States as a tourist, let alone finding work. Phil could never accept the idea of keeping a guy. Where did he go from there?

He went to the front room to check the time and was momentarily surprised by the disarray he found. He'd forgotten that the night before Les had had him too. He made beds and tidied up to remove the evidence of his disreputable conduct, hearing activity below. He went out to the stairs and called down for breakfast. He would soon be with Johnny. Johnny and the boat were godsends. They would give him time to think clearly.

Johnny greeted him with a joke about his having ditched him for Lester. "I sort of expected us to meet up on the port. Harvey knew better."

"It was quite a night."

"You don't look any the worse for wear. Now that you mention it, you have rather an unearthly glow. Quite bewitching."

They set out for the port, Phil leading them on a slight detour to let the Shackletons know that the yacht's arrival would preempt his evening. They told him to look for them on the port if he got away early.

The morning light was clear and golden, giving everything a pure crystalline outline, an extra element that looked as if it could be touched, like water. The day was going to be warm. Phil noticed that the westerly breeze was moderate, which suited him. He wanted to learn how to handle the boat before they got into heavy weather. He felt a little tightening of anticipation in his muscles.

"I've been meaning to ask you," he said as they skirted the familiar cafes. "What are we supposed to tell people when we go off on our little mission?"

"Do we have to tell them anything? I should think we'd get on the boat one morning and sail away."

"Won't that make them wonder?"

"I don't think so, do you? Nobody notices if I disappear for a few days."

"I'm not sure it'll be the same for me. I might be expected to account for my movements."

"You've undoubtedly created quite a stir one way or another, but has it reached that point? Surely not Lester?"

Phil glanced at him. He was looking at him quizzically. "No."

"Blimey. Has it happened?"

"Yes."

"You can't say I didn't warn you."

"No, but it's not at all what I expected."

"Crashing chords and heavenly choirs?"

"Something like that. Not so much heavenly choirs maybe. Plenty of crashing chords."

"Well, blow me. You know you're quite mad, don't you?"

"Yes. He seems to think that he's taken me over."

"If that's his game, he undoubtedly will. Are you suggesting that you don't want to join me in my nefarious adventure?"

"Of course not. You're counting on me, aren't you?"

"As much as I count on anything in this uncertain world."

"He asked if I was planning to go away anywhere with you. I told him we might do a little cruise around the island later. He says he's done some sailing with you. He wants to come with us."

"That *would* be jolly, but I'm afraid it's not on for this particular caper. No Greeks, much as I hate to thwart young love."

"It's pretty silly, isn't it? Did he have some sort of trouble under the Colonels?"

"Let me think. There *was* something. Was I away? It couldn't have been political, I shouldn't think. That's not his style. I think he simply took to the hills when the Colonels were having one of the mobilizations they were so fond of."

"You can't blame him for that. He admits to a lot of things but insists that he isn't a whore."

"No? Well, strictly speaking, perhaps he isn't. All I know is that he's buggered quite a few chaps while pointing out that he's doing them an exceptional favor."

"Yes, that sounds like him," Phil agreed reluctantly. Johnny would help him come to his senses, but he didn't have to pretend to himself that he'd enjoy it. He was glad to see the boat riding at anchor like a swan among ugly ducklings. This was going to be good for what ailed him, a tonic of sea and wind and sparkling light, with the swift clean motion of a boat to soothe his soul.

He was as excited as a kid at a Christmas party while Johnny directed their preparations, removing sail covers, clearing lines, making sure that he knew how to work the anchor winch. When they were ready, Johnny showed him how to start the motor, which responded with a reassuring roar, and threw off the stern lines while Phil ran forward and began to crank them out on the winch. He got the anchor aboard without difficulty and the motor settled into a steady throb as they began to move forward slowly past the crowded working craft and headed for the entrance of the harbor. Phil made sure that the anchor was securely lashed to the deck and went back to the stern and dropped into the cockpit beside Johnny. He put an arm around him and gave him a hug.

"This is great, ol buddy," he crowed happily.

"Smashing, what? Here, you can take the wheel." He stepped aside and let Phil take his place. "We're clear now. We can speed her up a bit." He eased the throttle forward and they picked up speed. He pointed to a dial. "This is a good cruising speed. Just keep the needle there. We don't want to push her. About seven knots is comfortable. When we get out, you can head into the wind and we'll get the sails up.''

Phil gripped the wheel, trembling slightly with excitement, and found that the boat responded sensitively to his guidance. He held a steady course between the lights on the rocky arms of the harbor and slowly relaxed. He looked at Johnny and grinned. "How'm I doing, captain?"

"Brilliantly. That's about all there is to it on motor. Reversing is a bit tricky, but you can try that when we go in. We couldn't ask for a better day for a trial run."

The sun danced on the wavelets beyond the breakwater. In another few minutes they were out in them, feeling them slap against the hull. Phil beamed at Johnny as if he'd accomplished a major feat of navigation. "Now do we sail?" he asked. His eyes felt as if they were dancing too.

"Right-oh. I'll take over so you can see how the sails work. The main first."

Johnny moved in behind the wheel, and Phil ran forward again to the mast, teetering slightly with the unfamiliar motion. He checked the winches and looked up along the mast to make sure he had the right one and started cranking. Johnny swung up into the wind and cut the motor down to a subdued purr. The sail started up smoothly and unexpectedly quickly and then all hell broke loose. Canvas cracked and thundered. Lines snapped around his feet. The boom crashed from side to side as the boat heaved in a heavy swell Phil hadn't noticed before. He clung to the mast to keep from falling overboard. He secured the mainsail and got the jib up while it slapped his back. Johnny let the boat fall away from the wind. The sails filled. The bow lifted and burrowed cleanly into the sea. The boat steadied and heeled over and surged smoothly forward. The motor was off. They were enclosed in sudden peace, the peace of restored order, of the perfect balance of sail and wind and water.

He teetered aft and fell into the cockpit, laughing breathlessly. His mouth was dry from the brief excitement. "OK, captain?"

"You're a dab hand. I don't have to tell you about keeping the sails full but holding her as close to the wind as possible and all that rot, do I?"

"No, I know the basics."

"You should practice going about a few times so you know the form and then you can sail across the Atlantic. She's all yours." He stepped back from the wheel and Phil replaced him.

He stood, getting the feel of it, exhilarated by the sense of controlling the elements that it gave him. The boat was beautifully responsive to his touch as they headed out into open sea. "OK? Shall I come about?" he asked after a few minutes.

"Why not? I'll help the first time and then you can try it on your own."

It seemed at first like a dauntingly complicated operation— throwing a lever to release one stay, pulling down a lever on the opposite side to take up slack on the other, switching the jib sheet from one cleat to another—but after he'd done it a few times he learned that it was only a matter of quick footwork and precise timing. He noticed that Chania had already blended into the island landscape behind them. He came about once more and held to the starboard tack that headed them out to sea again.

"Jolly good show," Johnny said approvingly. "We can take it easy on this tack until we get out far enough to head back to Soudha Bay."

"Would it be indecent to suggest a beer?"

"I wouldn't allow you back on board if you didn't."

He went below. Phil threw off his clothes, retaining only his jockey shorts, which he rolled down around his hips so that his cock was barely contained. He didn't want to get a pale patch on his ass but wasn't sure Johnny would approve of stripping. The sun stung into him. He hadn't felt better in his life. Johnny returned with two glasses of beer. He dropped Phil's into a holder beside the helm. "My word. It gives me a delightful shock to think that I know your body rather well," he commented. "I daresay even Manoli must question his dedication to the opposite sex when he looks at you."

Phil realized that he hadn't thought about Manoli for at least half an hour. He laughed. "He's getting there."

"You can take that thing off it you want. I won't molest you."

"You can't, really, if we want the boat to go in the right direction. I'll tell myself that that's the only reason you can control yourself."

"You'd be right."

Phil pushed his shorts down and let them drop to the deck. He kicked them aside. Better and better. The sun and air on him everywhere and thoughts of Manoli made him feel that he was being caressed. Once the thoughts started, he couldn't make them stop. If he didn't goof seriously during the day, Johnny would probably let them take the boat out together. Manoli would like that. Manoli was obviously trying to work him, but whore or no, he couldn't fake the way he touched him. Whatever else he wanted, Manoli wanted his body. He wanted money too, but Phil wasn't so far gone that he couldn't think clearly about that. He'd learned his lesson with Alex. That bastard had laid waste his bank account as well as his emotions. No money. Never any money where sex was involved. He remembered too well the gnawing resentment of feeling that that was all Alex needed to make him happy.

He wondered what Manoli was doing. He'd gathered that he spent a lot of time with his family. Was he at the house somewhere along the beach, looking out and wishing that he was there? He couldn't bear not to be available if Manoli wanted him. Maybe he'd find another faggot tourist to amuse him. Why would he? He insisted that he didn't usually go in for guys. It was unlikely he'd find another a day later who attracted him equally. Maybe he'd spend the day with him tomorrow if they went out on the boat so that Don wouldn't know about it. The thoughts continued, around and around in circles, not nagging yet, full of wonder and promise. Johnny kept the beer flowing.

"We've got to keep track of this so I can pay you," Phil said.

"You can bring some more on board if you like," Johnny agreed. "I've had the water tanks topped up. We have plenty of tins and dry rations to keep us alive in case of shipwreck. I'll bring some fresh food on at the last minute."

"Do you have any idea when that will be?"

"I heard something last night. I should think it'll probably be the end of next week, not before. Does that suit you?"

It suited Phil perfectly. A week to get used to Manoli. A week possibly for his passion to cool. In a week he should be able to leave him for a few days without being tormented by wanting him. "How about my taking Manoli out one day?" he asked. "Tomorrow maybe?"

"Quite so. When we go in I'll show you how to moor. If you can handle that, I'll issue you your captain's certificate and you can help yourself. He's a good sailor."

"Marvelous."

Johnny looked at him with a sardonic lift of his brows. "You know, if you're going to go on with this I hope you won't attempt to be sane about it."

"How do you mean?"

"We talked a little bit about it before. You give the impression of being as tiresomely sane as I am, but I don't think it comes very naturally if you can fall for Manoli. Have you?"

"Like a ton of bricks, but I'm not fooling myself. I know I can't let it become important to me."

"A pity. It might be the best thing that could possibly happen to you. I'd dearly love it to happen to me. Throw caution to the winds. Give him all your money. Go mad. We only live once and all that sort of thing."

"God, Johnny. It's bad enough without your egging me on. If you're talking about sex, it's the most sensational thing that's happened to me since the first time."

"God knows how you managed to fit it in with all your other activities, considering that he didn't get back till yesterday. But I'm reasonably sure of one thing: If you aren't prepared to go mad, you'd better seriously consider not seeing him again. You might even think about leaving."

"That's what he wants. He wants me to go and take him with me."

"What a smashing idea. We'd all be able to draw a peaceful breath again. Where?"

"That's the interesting question. If you'd like to lend us the boat, we could sail away until we dropped off the edge of the world, but aside from that I haven't the slightest idea. There's no place where I can go mad except here, and I haven't the time."

"I don't generally ask indiscreet questions, but are you suggesting that he says he's in love with you?"

The question hit Phil's cock. He felt it stirring and its

dimensions altering. He turned slightly away from Johnny and edged in closer to the wheel. "He put it the other way around. He says I'm in love with him. I'm the first man he's really wanted, or words to that effect." His cock gave another little leap.

"There's a first time for everything. I told you it was inevitable. By this evening he'll be ready to make a declaration of love and demonstrate in bed with all the trimmings. What sport for you."

Phil's cock was acquiring weight. "I'm glad you think it's funny. How about telling me what to do about it from a practical point of view?"

"Do what I say. Give him all your money. It'll be easier in the long run. When we've done our little cruise, you'll have enough to get home. Just make sure he knows you've given him all you've got so he won't wear you out trying to get more."

"You really are a bastard when you want to be, Johnny," Phil laughed, although he knew the joke was undoubtedly on him.

Johnny looked at him with his wry, ironic smile. "I told you. I'm all on the side of young love." He took Phil's glass and went below.

Phil glanced down at his cock. He could see that it wasn't in perfect repose, but unless Johnny was keeping an eye on it he probably wouldn't notice. It didn't matter much except that he didn't want to be a tease. Why in the world did the impossible thought of Manoli being in love with him turn him on? Where did he think it would get him? It was amazing that their bodies felt so good together. If Manoli ever made him feel that he was in love with him, he'd be lost. So far, he was keeping himself in fighting trim. He was going to retain his sanity for once. If Manoli was able to turn himself into a perfect lover in one night, he could look forward to a few fabulous weeks. That was enough. His cock jutted out briefly and then began to settle down. It was behaving itself when Johnny returned with more beer.

They sailed for an hour or maybe two and slowly became aware of their vast isolation in the empty sea. Crete was a featureless mountainous hump behind them, and Phil began to pay more attention to the binnacle as he realized how easy it would be to get lost. They'd stayed more or less on the same compass reading from the start. If they followed the reverse reading on the way back, they should end up close to Chania. Self-taught navigation. He hadn't paid much attention to such things in the South of France because he'd been with guys who knew the landmarks and stayed in sight of them.

Eventually Johnny made them huge sandwiches of salami and tomatoes, and they switched to wine. Phil ate and drank ravenously. It was sinful to feel so good. They turned back as the sun started down the western sky. Johnny showed him where the mouth of Soudha Bay was. If they'd followed the course Phil had picked out for himself, they would have been close enough to it. His confidence grew that he could take care of himself in this unfamiliar world. When he pulled some clothes on and started the motor again outside the entrance to Chania harbor, he felt as if he'd been gone for days and had discovered a universe. The sails came down with a rush and a clatter. Chania was home.

He motored slowly into the narrow port, and Johnny directed him where to position the boat for dropping the anchor. Phil reversed, swinging about wildly on his first attempts.

"Don't rush it," Johnny said calmly. "Just be careful

not to run up on the anchor. We don't want to get chain tangled around the propeller.''

It sounded like a major catastrophe to Phil, but Johnny seemed unruffled by the possibility. His voice was a steadying influence. Phil tried again and brought the stern in at more of an angle than he intended but close enough to the quay for Johnny to jump ashore with a line. Phil tossed him another. By the time he'd made them fast, the boat had straightened itself. Phil switched the motor off, hoping he hadn't flunked his test. "That wasn't exactly brilliant," he said as Johnny leaped back on board.

"Not bad. You've got the hang of it. Nobody gets it right every time. I sometimes make a balls-up when the wind's tricky.''

"You're an understanding teacher, Johnny. Is your friend's yacht here?''

"No, but it will be. Harry runs it like a train. He said six o'clock. He has an hour to go. Drinks for six-thirty or seven. We have plenty of time to clean up.''

They left the boat as neat and tidy as it had been that morning and went to their respective rooms to prepare for the evening. Phil's heart was beginning to behave unpredictably at the prospect of being with Manoli again. He'd been through it all before. It raced. It slowed peacefully. It skipped a beat and thudded alarm, although he couldn't quite place what there was to be alarmed about. It wasn't like the times with Alex, never knowing if he was going to be stood up. There wasn't much doubt that Manoli would be there; a rich man with a yacht would be just his dish if he was as much of a whore as Johnny seemed to think.

At about six, keeping watch from his windows, he saw an impressive black yacht with two masts motoring into the harbor. The party was on. He took extra care with his appearance. It was the first proper social engagment he'd had with Manoli and he wanted to dazzle him. He put on the chunky gold chain that his movie star had given him. He always had George's platinum one with him but never wore it. He picked out his favorite sports shirt, a colorful affair of Indian silk, and buttoned only the bottom buttons, leaving his chest bare. He went to the only mirror in the place that was big enough to include his chest and shoulders and looked himself over. His tan was a marvel; it had turned several shades darker during the day. He wasn't bad for an aging editor.

When he and Johnny returned to the port, the black yacht was tied up at the other quay, a gangplank let down from the stern. They climbed it and stepped off onto a spacious afterdeck strewn with comfortable-looking outdoor furniture. Men stood up at their appearance. A slight youngish-looking man advanced to Johnny and embraced him on both cheeks. He turned to Phil.

"This is Phil Renfield," Johnny said. "Harry Whitelaw."

Phil shook hands and looked at him, but he had no face. He saw eyes, a nose, a mouth, but they didn't add up to anything. A blank. He was bald and his eyebrows were pale and sparse, which added to the impression of nullity.

"Pleased to see you," Harry said in a shy, muted voice with an American accent. Phil caught sight of Manoli over his shoulder and his heart gave a great bound of happiness. He wanted to run to him and throw his arms around him, but he was aware of Don standing nearby, eyeing him beadily, and he warned himself not to give Manoli away. He was looking irresistible in crisp white shirt and slacks. Their eyes didn't meet.

He moved forward with Johnny. Names were spoken and they made the rounds, shaking hands. Phil had trained himself professionally to remember names, but only first

names were given—Bob, Bill, Ed, Sam—so he didn't
have to make a great effort. There were four of them, all
well-preserved middle-aged men dressed in casual but
expensive-looking summer clothes with sweaters around
their shoulders. They brightened visibly when Phil spoke
to them. His care with his appearance had apparently been
a success. He made a point of greeting Don cheerfully and
finally faced Manoli.

"Hello," he said, keeping his voice low and directing it
at him, trying to fill the word with the intimacy of an
embrace.

"*Ya sou*," Manoli replied gruffly. It was the minimal
greeting of villagers who passed each other daily in the
streets. Their eyes met. Manoli's were wary and unloving.
Phil felt the pent-up violence in him that had been there
before. Manoli probably hated being here, on show as
Don's creature before a gathering of effete older men.

Phil didn't want him to think he represented an additional embarrassment. He promptly turned and spoke to the
first person he saw. It turned out to be Sam. A steward was
serving drinks from a table on the port side. (Phil practiced
to himself the nautical jargon.) They got drinks, Sam's a
refill, and exchanged the usual chat about where they were
from in the States and how long they were staying in
Greece and what they had seen. Sam was flirtatious but not
insistently so. Phil settled down for a familiarly uninteresting
evening. He was determined to show Manoli that he
wasn't going to make the situation difficult for him; he
wouldn't approach him again. They were together. He
could sneak a look at him from time to time. It saved the
evening from being a total loss. Manoli didn't look as if he
was having much fun either. He was seated beside Harry,
but appeared to have been rendered speechless by their
faceless host. All the sweet, youthful animation Phil had

seen in his face seemed to have been drained out of him; his expression was set and fierce.

In an hour Harry led them through a pleasantly decorated main saloon that might have been a living room on shore to a small dining saloon. In the slight pileup at the door while people were finding their seats, Phil allowed himself to slip in beside Manoli and put his arm around his waist and give him a quick hug. He stiffened and shook him off and Phil immediately dropped his arm. It was the sort of thing he'd promised himself he wouldn't do, but for a second he'd felt Manoli's body against him. Incredibly, he had won the right to hold him. He thought of them lying naked together in a little while, and the evening began to sparkle.

Harry sat at the head of the long, narrow table with Manoli on his right. Phil was placed between Sam and Ed. Eating the excellent food and drinking the excellent wine, flanked by harmless companions, he found it increasingly difficult to tear his eyes away from Manoli. It seemed to him so obvious that they were meant to be paired off together that he wondered why the others didn't recognize it. They were the same general type. They were built alike. They were a different breed from the others. Johnny caught his eye across the table and winked. He knew.

Phil slowly mastered his eyes and was so successful in his determination not to let his infatuation become a burden that they had finished coffee in the main saloon and were well into the brandy and liqueurs before he noticed that Manoli was missing. He was sure that he would've felt his absence if he'd been gone long. A visit to the head, he assumed nautically. He went on with what he was saying to one of his fellow guests, but in another few minutes he couldn't resist taking another look around the room. Don beamed fatuously at him. Manoli was still missing. It was only then that he realized that Harry was gone too. Fair enough. Their host couldn't go far. He was probably showing Manoli the yacht in place of his etchings. He wouldn't dare make much of a play for him with Don sitting here and considering Manoli's present mood, his life would probably be at risk if he attempted even so much as a suggestive glance.

Phil sat back with an effort to look as if he were enjoying himself, but there was an unpleasant constriction in his chest that he attempted to ease with brandy. He tried not to be aware of time passing. He wondered why Don was looking so pleased with himself if Manoli thought he had to watch his step with him. Of course nobody was apt to think of Harry as a sexual threat. He glanced at Johnny, but he looked as if nothing were amiss. All the same, it was a bit odd for all of them to be helping themselves to drinks and making themselves at home on a yacht whose owner was conspicuously absent with his most attractive guest. It embarrassed Phil and he didn't understand why he was the only one who seemed bothered by it. He had been to parties where it happened, but they had been frank sex parties with a steady flow in and out of bedrooms and a free exchange of partners. Maybe Harry had something wrong with him that obliged him to retire after eating, something they all knew about. Maybe Manoli had got fed up and had simply cleared out. He might be waiting for him at home. The possibility made him increasingly restless; he wanted to jump up and go look for him. He kept watching Johnny for some signal.

Eventually Don stood and made a portly exit. Phil tensed, preparing for fireworks. Don wasn't gone long and returned looking more pleased with himself than ever. Phil didn't think he could stand it much longer. He'd drunk all the brandy he could take. He looked at Johnny with a plea in his eyes. Johnny came and sat on the arm of his chair.

"Are you ready to go?" he asked quietly.

"Well, sure, but aren't we supposed to say good night to Harry?"

"I'll explain about that. We might as well go."

"But— Has Manoli gone?"

"Never mind now. I'll tell you about it on shore."

"What is—"

"Let's go," Johnny said decisively.

They said good night to the others while Phil tried to contain his mystified anxiety. Something was wrong. Johnny had acted as if Manoli might be in some sort of trouble.

As soon as they were outside, Phil grabbed his arm and hurried him down the gangplank. "Now. For God's sake, what's going on?" he exploded as they started along the quay.

Johnny looked at him with sympathy and affection. He sighed and shook his head. "Poor sod. You're the classic cuckold, always the last one to know. What did you think was going on?"

"Nothing. I don't know. *Is* something going on? Did Manoli manage to insult our host when I wasn't looking and get thrown out? Is Harry having a nervous breakdown?"

"Not bloody likely. It was a setup. It's apparently been planned for some time. The chap called Bob told me about it. He thought it was very funny."

"Funny? So what's the joke? I don't know what you're talking about."

"I would've thought it was obvious. You saw they weren't there. Don gave Manoli to Harry for the night."

"Gave Manoli . . . ." Phil repeated the words dazedly. He struggled to grasp what Johnny was saying. He felt a great sob gathering in him and he halted abruptly while he fought to control it. He took a difficult, shuddering breath. "Where are they?" he asked, as if that were a pertinent point.

"On board. Tucked up together in a bunk, I imagine. I daresay Don may have done the tucking."

"I don't believe it," Phil gasped as a picture filled his mind of the beautiful body in the arms of a faceless deformity.

Johnny gripped his shoulder and spoke to him frmly. "You jolly well have to believe it, dear boy. You must've seen that Don gets some sort of kinky pleasure out of treating him like one of his possessions. What more extravagant display of his control than to make a gift of Manoli's person? The ultimate exercise of ownership, wouldn't you say? From what Manoli has told me, I presume it's leading up to the big payoff he's been waiting for."

Phil stood swaying slightly as if he'd been clubbed. A gust of rage dissolved into a terrible pity. He wanted to comfort Manoli for the humiliation he was subjecting himself to and help restore his pride. He felt as if somebody he'd cared about had died. Manoli had revived in him the joy he had known during the good years with George, but it had been too brief for him to have built any great hopes on it. It had been a short-lived dream. No matter how convincing his denials, Manoli was a whore. His regret was more for him than for his own lost pleasure. He was shocked by himself for being involved in the squalid situation. "Somebody should put that shit out of his misery." His throat ached and his voice came out with a rasp.

"If you mean Don, I'm inclined to agree with you. I wasn't amused. I sometimes think we go too far in this fucking paradise. Come along, mate." He put both hands on Phil's shoulders and gave him a little shake. "Shall we drown our sorrows on the port?"

"Sure. There's no chance you're wrong? He was going to come home with me. Shouldn't I go see if he's there?"

"Let it go for tonight, love. You can go mad again tomorrow if you still feel like it."

Phil fell into step beside him. He didn't think it was going to be the torment it had been with Alex. He just felt dead, the way he'd felt for a long time now. When they rounded the corner into the main harbor, they saw that the cafes were still well populated. He remembered the Shackletons without any noticeable brightening of his spirits. He didn't want to see them, but he didn't not want to see them. He didn't want anything except to be lifted and dropped into bed asleep.

"If we see the Shackletons, I might leave you in their tender care," Johnny said. "You told them you might meet them, didn't you? I want to get a good day's work tomorrow."

"Right. Thanks for the sail. I love the boat. I hope our nefarious mission isn't delayed. I'm going to have to start thinking about getting back to New York soon."

"I understand." Johnny put an arm around his shoulders and gave him a hug. "Things have a way of looking better in the morning."

"People are peculiar that way." He saw Lester and Harvey sitting at a table. They all waved at each other. He saw the Shackletons. They gave him their straight-armed salute and motioned to an empty chair at their table. A sailor was sitting with them. Johnny and he looked into each other's eyes for a moment and nodded. Johnny gave his hand a quick squeeze and went on. Phil turned in to the Shackletons' table. The sailor lifted his arms and pulled him down beside him when he reached it. It was Pavlo, the guy who had tried to teach him how to dance the other night.

"We were hoping for you," Bryan said. "This is the one you mentioned, isn't it? We somehow managed to winkle him away from his buddes. Our charm knows no limits. We thought a quartet might be a nice change of pace. Are you on?"

"We'll see. I've been out on Johnny's boat all day. It was wonderful but work. I'm sort of plastered too."

Angela poured him a glass of retsina from their copper tankard. "Did you have a grand dinner on the yacht?"

"It was OK. I'm sure yours would've been better." He drained the glass and made a face while Angela refilled it. Pavlo kept his hands on him the way he had last time, feeling him here and there contentedly. He took Phil's hand and put it on his cock. It was hard. Holding it made Phil's harden. Phil remembered thinking he was attractive. He supposed he might want him if he got any drunker.

They chatted, including Pavlo with occasional words of Greek. Phil drank several more glasses of retsina and ordered another tankard for them. Pavlo busied himself making Phil very hard so that he had to shift in his chair and help with a hand in his pocket to work his cock into a standing position. He could still get a hard on. If Pavlo kept at it, he could probably make him come. He could do that for himself. What was the point of playing games with their bodies after what he'd had? Putting it in the past tense made him feel the huge emptiness in him. He was going to have to find something to make himself feel complete again. It wasn't going to be as easy as he'd thought. Why had he let Manoli beguile him into dropping all his guards? A day or two ago, going home with the Shackletons and a Greek sailor would have been sufficient diversion to give him the illusion of living. It wouldn't do anything for him now. He was faced with the death in himself. He would have to start the agonizing business all over again of shutting himself off within himself, arming himself against the torment of emotion, accepting the failure of love. He was weary to the bone of trying to find a life worth living with the flawed gifts his nature had deceived him into thinking were quality goods.

They worked their way slowly through the wine until Phil was sure nothing could keep him awake. "I'm absolutely zonked," he said, deliberately slurring his speech. "I better fold up."

"The wine seems to be gone. There's more at home with other things," Bryan seconded him. "Our jolly tar is going to start taking your clothes off if we stay much longer. What're we waiting for?"

The narrow streets on the way home kept them together for part of the way. Pavlo stayed beside Phil with an arm around him. When they reached the Shackletons' turn, Phil stopped. "I'm not going to be much fun for anybody tonight," he said, pushing Pavlo away. "I'll go to sleep if I even look at a bed. We'll make it another time." He didn't listen to their protests as he hurried away.

When he reached the top of the stairs, he saw that he must have left the lights on. His door was partly open. He entered and closed it behind him. He looked at the bed and wished he could get into it without moving a muscle. He felt as if his body had suddenly stopped functioning. Manoli stepped out of the bathroom and approached around the bed. Phil wanted to shout his joyful welcome, but the events of the evening immediately dropped like a wall between them and he composed his face into an expression of aloof neutrality. Manoli was naked to the waist, wearing only his pants. His eyes were steely. "Where have you been?" he demanded.

"You think you have the right to ask? Everybody knows what you do."

"I do what I have to do. Why weren't you here waiting for me? You were with Lester?"

"You have to guess. I don't. Nobody tonight has to guess what you are."

"I'm a man. Nobody questions me."

"And I am your *pousti* waiting to serve you?"

"That is true. I do what I do to be with you. I do not do it for pleasure. Don wished it. He stood in the cabin door and laughed at me while I took my clothes off. It's the end. If he doesn't give me the money now, I'll kill him."

A shiver ran down Phil's spine. Manoli looked as if he meant it. He felt as if he were being crushed in a vise of remorse and compassion. His disgust was for the men who had corrupted Manoli, not for their victim. He shook his head slowly, his mouth working to form words. He wanted to hold out his arms to him but couldn't lift them from his sides. "It is wrong," he mumbled.

"It's life. And you? You think only of your pleasure. You haven't told me where you were."

Phil struggled against his spell. Why couldn't he despise him? If he tried to save him, he would be powerless to protect himself from him. Manoli was the last person who had the right to call him to account. He lifted his head defiantly. "I was with the Shackletons. You know what that means. There was a Greek sailor with us. His cock was almost so big than yours." He had only a moment to deplore his grammar before Manoli's fist landed on his chin. He bounced on the wall and crumpled to the floor against it. His vision dimmed. Consciousness slipped and faded. It returned with a rush of pain.

Manoli was on him, crouched over him, his pants open and his cock raised in front of him. He yanked Phil's slacks down to his thighs and heaved him over onto his stomach. Phil tried to pull himself up. He saw Manoli spit into his hand and drop it to his cock. Phil's heart was pounding as he attempted to twist away from him. Manoli hit him hard with the flat of his hand on the side of his head. He lifted his other hand and swung it hard against the other side. His senses reeled. Manoli dug his nails into his hips and was in him, raping him, tearing him apart. Phil shouted with pain.

"You be quiet. You want the family to come see?" Manoli snarled.

Phil subsided, his breath coming in sobs, exulting in Manoli's unleashed fury. Manoli wanted him enough to take him by force. He wouldn't be denied what belonged to him. Phil was his. Phil's orgasm completed Manoli's savage conquest. He moaned and whimpered while Manoli used him brutally to find his satisfaction in him. When he was finished with him, he pulled out of him roughly and sprang up.

Phil heard the water go on in the next room. He lay still, hardly daring to move for fear of discovering that he was seriously injured. He was stupefied by the fury of the assault. He hadn't known what a man's passion could be like. Manoli was probably the only wholly masculine man he'd ever known. All the others, like himself, belonged to a different world, soft, gentle, neurotically sensitive to giving offense. Despite his throbbing head and the pains all through him, he felt revived and invigorated. Manoli's will to dominate him was the expression of a need for him. He was superb.

Phil stirred cautiously, testing his body, and slowly sat up. Not too bad. He was filthy. His sperm mingled with dust from the floor streaked his beautiful shirt. There were a couple of small tears where buttons had been torn off.

His slacks were around his knees and the zipper of the fly was ripped. One of his sandals lay at his side, the strap broken. He'd been raped and looked it.

He heard the water running and felt Manoli's presence near. He'd come to him straight from the completion of his sordid bargain. He had wanted to be with Phil. Phil couldn't understand Manoli's attitude to hustling, but could try. Being fucked as a kid by all the guys on a freighter would hardly leave him with fastidious ideas about sex. It might give him a kick to profit from his body for a change; he could probably get it up for anybody if he was touched in the right places. Manoli minded Don's laughter more than that faceless creep's hands and mouth on him. That was Don's stroke of genius.

He felt a stab of love for him—somewhere in the chest and groin, not necessarily in the heart. He loved him in spite of himself and felt it was saner than the wild infatuation of yesterday. At least, he could now accept the fact that it could mean nothing except on Manoli's terms, which weren't the same as his own. Manoli was a man. Whatever distinctions he made between himself and *poustis* might seem strained, but they were real. If the social or moral climate were favorable, he supposed straight guys could want each other without thinking of it as homosexual. That was what good red-blooded Americans couldn't understand. Even he and George might have made the distinctions if given a chance.

He heard the water stop and pulled himself painfully to his feet. He shook off his shirt and bundled it into a ball and wiped off his front. He threw it into a corner and kicked off his other sandal and stepped out of his slacks. He saw that his shorts had been torn almost in two. He'd been raped and he wanted to be with the rapist. It probably wasn't unusual.

He dragged himself into the bathroom, embarrassed for both of them, not quite knowing what was expected of him. Manoli stopped drying himself and looked at him levelly, appearing relaxed and comfortable with him. He held out a hand to him and Phil went to him. Manoli held his arms and leaned forward and initiated a long open-mouthed kiss. It hurt Phil's jaw, but Phil wanted his mouth. Manoli drew back, still holding him.

"I don't wish to hit you," he said. His eyes were gentle and loving. "I'm your man. If you don't do as I like, I must punish you."

"I understand."

"Tonight was bad. Don is a bad man. Harry wanted me to stay all night. He gave me, what you say, a tip, and said he might give me more if I stay. I came to you. I don't want you to tell me about sailors' cocks."

"It wasn't true. I say it with anger. I didn't go with them."

"That's good. I didn't have to hit you. I must get the money from Don and then we will go."

"You get it soon?"

"A few days maybe. He promised again when he told me what I had to do tonight."

"I promise Johnny something. I must help him on the boat when he meets his friends for two, three days. I told you."

Manoli smiled confidently. "If I go, you'll go too. You love me."

"Maybe." Phil had given up trying to figure out how his mind worked. Manoli took everything for granted, that he could knock him down and still make love with him, that he would go to New York with him even though he'd told him he couldn't. Johnny was right. He had to let himself go mad if he wanted to see him. "You not love me?'' he asked. Manoli said something he didn't understand. "What you mean?"

"I say, I love you but not the way I love a woman. Almost, I think. You will see. Go wash now."

"Will you go out on the boat with me tomorrow?"

"With Johnny?"

"No. You and me."

Manoli's smile lighted up his face in a way Phil hadn't seen before, radiant and carefree. "Yes. We'll do that. All day. I'll see Don tomorrow night. Go wash."

Under the shower, Phil felt another stab of love as he watched Manoli use his toothbrush. If it meant that he was in love with Manoli, then he was in love with him. His head hurt but the rest of him felt all right. He could be raped by the guy he loved and not suffer any ill effects. He could let himself go because restraint was valuable only to people planning a rational future. With Manoli, he could do nothing to affect the outcome, but the emptiness of death he had felt in himself an hour ago was gone.

Manoli stretched out on the bed and pulled the covers up to his chest and watched him while he dried. Phil took his turn with the toothbrush, loving the. intense intimacy of sharing it. When he approached the bed, Manoli reached for him and pulled him down and laid him out flat close against him. He propped himself over him and looked down at him while he lightly stroked his cheek.

"I'm tired. Very much tired," Phil sighed, glorying in the bliss of being at rest finally with Manoli once more beside him.

"I'm sorry I hit you," he said with heart-wrenching tenderness. "Are you all right?"

"Of course. I don't mind."

"No. It is a necessity sometimes." He turned his hips and let him feel his hard cock against him. "You see? You make me hard when I watch you, sometimes more than a woman. I won't fuck you now. You must sleep knowing that I think of you."

"You can fuck me if you want to."

"No. We'll be together tomorrow. We sleep together now. I like to sleep with you." He lowered his head and covered his face with soft, healing kisses, his eyes, his cheeks, his nose, his painful chin. He held his parted lips against Phil's with their tongues touching, and they breathed each other's breath. His hand wandered slowly and lovingly over him, not shying from any part of him. It moved along his rigid cock and remained with his fingers curled around his balls. "There. We want each other. It's very wonderful. You're mine, my Philip."

"Yes. I love you." He felt as if his chest were bursting with happiness while he was lulled into caverns of sleep.

"We forgot the light," Manoli whispered with his lips moving against his ear.

"Don't go." He was aware of Manoli carefully lifting himself, and he opened heavy lids to watch him cross the room. The beautiful body was his again. The light snapped off and Manoli was with him. They rolled in to each other and gathered each other into their arms. They stretched their bodies to feel all of them against each other, and Phil abandoned himself to his lover's care. He slept.

They were awake and dressed early, eager for their day at sea. Manoli gave him twenty minutes to meet him at the boat, and let himself out the window so as not to be seen by the people in the house. Phil had his quick breakfast and was on his way, determined to be a mindless optimist for as long as events permitted. Life looked pretty good for the moment, if he didn't let himself wonder how it was going to end.

He picked up beer and bread and went on to another

shop where he got some tomatoes and oranges and cheese. He bought a ridiculously expensive tin of imported ham. It was the first time since he'd been here that he'd paid any attention to how much anything cost. Life without thinking about money had an eerie and unreal quality.

The morning sun was bright and still etched the buildings with pristine light. Yesterday had given him a new awareness of nature. He looked up at the empty sky and checked the breeze. It was westerly again, light to moderate as they said in the weather reports. It looked like another perfect day.

When he turned in to the port, he saw that the black yacht was gone. Manoli was already there when he arrived with the provisions, efficiently removing the sail covers. He was wearing one of Phil's jerseys and looked very handsome and manly. Seeing him in something of his gave Phil a sense of belonging with him. They were together.

"This is one beautiful boat," Manoli sant out happily without interrupting his work as Phil jumped aboard. He obviously knew what he was doing. Phil dropped into the cockpit and went forward to the cabin housing and looked up at him across it.

"You're doing fine. I help in a minute."

"There's no need. It's almost done."

"You know how to work the sails and everything?"

"Sure. I went out with Johnny once. One beautiful boat."

"I love it." He unlocked the cabin and took the provisions below and stowed them in the galley. He took care not to leave anything that could fall around and cause trouble. Johnny had told him that no matter how good the weather looked it was wise to always keep the boat in good shape for rough seas. When he returned to the deck, Manoli had put the covers away and loosened the sails,

making them ready for hoisting. He was up in the bow
checking the anchor. He was in his element. Phil felt a
quick thrill of entering into his life, of sharing and partici-
pation. He'd be a hell of a guy if only he had a few
breaks. Careful with the "ifs" he warned himself. The
"if" game didn't help; pure fantasy was the answer: He
owned a yacht and was going to spend the rest of his life
here with Manoli and there was nothing to worry about.

Manoli came trotting back along the narrow, cluttered
deck, as surefooted and lightly balanced as a cat. The
impact of his physical grace and control made Phil catch
his breath, and his eyes roamed over him with hypnotized
fascination. He jumped down into the cockpit.

"Ready to throw off the ropes?" he asked.

"Right." Phil switched on the motor and adjusted it to a
steady purr. Manoli ran to the stern and pulled the boat in
and climbed up onto the quay. He released the lines and
gathered them up and made a breathtaking leap onto the
stern. He ran forward to the bow and began to crank them
out to the anchor. Phil provided little bursts of power on
the forward gear to make it easier. He was conscious of the
deep satisfaction of working with Manoli, of forging a
bond of teamwork between them. When the anchor was
up, Manoli signaled and Phil pushed the motor into gear
and they motored slowly out into the open harbor and
headed for the entrance. Manoli jumped back into the
cockpit and stood beside him with his arm around his
waist. His eyes glowed.

"We are good together, my Philip," he said.

"It is true," he agreed, helplessly under his spell once
more. "I must practice with the sails. Will you take the
wheel?"

"OK. Do you want to go to Soudha Bay? I know good

places to anchor. Very private.'' His smile promised irresistible possibilities.

Phil chuckled softly, looking into his eyes. "You know
me. It pleases me out in the sun."

They cleared the harbor and he moved aside to let
Manoli head them up into the wind. Phil touched his
shoulder and moved forward to the mast, more cautiously
than had Manoli. He got the sails up with a repetition of
chaos, the cracking canvas, the snapping lines, the crashing boom, until Manoli had everything under expert control and let the bow fall off toward the east. He switched
off the motor as Phil rejoined him.

They stripped to the waist. Phil was content to stop
there today, at the risk of getting an uneven tan. He wasn't
sure Manoli would appreciate his waving his cock around
in front of him, and the following wind permitted them to
stay in close to shore on an easy reach. They passed other
small craft coming and going. This wasn't the place for
nudity.

Phil went below and returned with beer. They drank
thirstily. Manoli looked at him over his glass and smiled
with a dazzling flash of white teeth. "You're such a man
on the boat," he said approvingly. "A fine man, my
Philip. You make me proud. You know what it means? I'm
proud that you're my friend. I love you."

Phil bowed his forehead briefly against the side of
Manoli's head. There was a very unmanly knot in his
throat. "It's good," he said after a moment, brushing his
lips against his ear. He straightened and they lifted their
glasses to each other and drained them. Phil went below
for more beer. He was serving his man. He felt giddy with
dangerous happiness.

They sailed into the wide expanse of Soudha Bay. Far
ahead of him, Phil could see clusters of buildings and

important installations of some kind, presumably part of the naval base. There were many turnings and openings in what appeared to be a complex inland waterway. Once within, the breeze dropped to a whisper, but the boat continued to respond with the delicacy of a racer. Manoli stayed close to the western shore, watching alertly as land acquired definition and dimensions in front of them.

"With the sail, I think," he said quietly as if he were speaking to himself. He began to take in the main sheet. "The little one," he ordered. Phil quickly brought in the jib and they headed straight in to the shore, close-hauled but still slipping smoothly through the water. "Get the anchor ready," Manoli said in competent command. "Bring the sails down quick when I say. I'll call the anchor after."

Phil went forward to the mast and prepared the winches for release, feeling again the exhilarating satisfaction of their close working collaboration. He watched with trepidation while it appeared that Manoli was about to beach the boat. Land was too close for comfort. It receded magically before them, and they sailed into a tiny cove whose arms stretched out on both sides of them as they entered. The sea hissed against the hull.

"OK for the sails," Manoli called coolly. Phil brought the sails down with a swift clatter. They continued to hiss through the water, getting in close to rocks that were surely stationary. "Now the anchor," Manoli called. Phil dropped it and the chain rattled away beneath them. He felt a little tug as the anchor held and their way was killed. In a moment they began to drift back away from the rocks. Manoli remained at the wheel, closely watching the land on both sides of them. His concentration kept Phil poised for further action in the bow. He saw the anchor line rise from the water at an angle and stretch taut. He stood watching Manoli, awaiting orders, and after another moment saw his concentration lifting. He was as impressed by him as he'd ever been by anybody; it seemed to him an incredible feat of seasmanship.

"That's it," he called.

Phil ran aft and dropped down to him. He greeted him with a satisfied smile. "Very good, my Philip," he said.

"*You* very good," he said.

"We do everything together."

They draped their arms around each other's shoulders and stood looking around them. They were held by a silence as immense as the universe. Above the rocks, an olive grove sloped up away from them. The water was so clear that it looked as if the boat were sitting on the bottom. "It's beautiful," Phil murmured, moving his hand over smooth brown skin.

"Very private." They looked at each other and Manoli smiled knowingly. "I think you like it. We will stay. We will eat and drink and make love. Life is good when we're together. Come." He broke away and began to lift the sail out of the way. Phil leaped to the task and together they tied up the carelessly furled canvas.

"Good enough that way," Manoli decided with a pro's authority. "Today is not for work. We enjoy ourselves. The water is good here. Naked is best."

They stripped, frankly eyeing each other. When they were naked, their eyes lingered for a moment on their handsome brown bodies. Phil saw with the sense of having won a major victory that Manoli's cock was headed as conspicuously toward erection as his own. Their eyes met and they laughed and then Manoli sprang up to the afterdeck and plunged in. Phil ran below and grabbed a couple of towels. He'd been taught that dripping saltwater on a boat was a major offense. He dropped them on the afterdeck and made a long dive for Manoli. The water was a cold, stimulating shock, and they swam vigorously out to the entrance to the little cove. The boat looked small and trim riding at anchor close in against the olive grove. Turning back, they slowed down and Manoli began to play around him like a dolphin, swimming under him and over him, letting his sleek body slide along him. It was a sensual bonanza, and Phil reacted accordingly despite the cold water. When they reached the boat, Manoli swam in behind him and circled him with his arms and closed his hands around his hard cock, prodding him with his. They chortled and began to sink. Manoli released him and they bounced themselves up out of the sea and grabbed for the gunwale. They heaved themselves up and landed on the narrow deck in a tangle of arms and legs. Manoli pushed Phil out flat on his back and slid down over him and drew Phil's cock into his mouth.

"Now almost," he gasped in case Manoli wanted to withdraw at the last minute. He felt Manoli's mouth working on his cock in a passion of hungry craving, and Phil's body was lifted by the intensity of its response. He shouted and his body was flung about by the paroxysms of an enormous deliverance. Manoli clung to him, still sucking on him greedily. He suddenly reared back on his knees and brought Phil up with him. Phil opened his mouth for him just in time to receive Manoli's ejaculation. The almost simultaneous orgasm was evidence of shared ecstasy; Manoli wanted Phil that way as much as he was wanted by his lover.

He fell forward and lay on him, letting Phil have all of his body. Phil stroked him and kissed his neck and licked salt off him. Manoli laughed and began to lick him. "Is all right?" Phil asked. "You like that way?"

"Yes. It's you. It pleases me." He lifted his head and looked at him with a puzzled little frown. "I think maybe I might fall in love with you if you remain very much in love with me. I like you to be in love with me. We'll see.''

Phil's heart skipped a beat, but he felt so wonderful that he didn't see how it could make much difference. In any case, Manoli would fall in love as a man with a surrogate woman, not as George and he had been in love—maybe still were—man to man. He put his arms around him and held him close, feeling their perfect fit. "You will be in love with me today. We don't think about tomorrow."

"I do. So do you. You want me with you. I think we should have more beer."

Phil laughed and they let each other up. Phil went below, happy for the opportunity to serve his man. He loved the balance that was developing between them. He looked up to Manoli for his decisiveness and thought of him as older, even though he knew he wasn't. Manoli had been born at the end of the war, Phil during it. There must be a couple of years' difference between them, but Manoli was tougher, more independent, more self-contained. They fitted. Manoli was the boss, but they were bound by the equality of shared desire. They had everything they needed for a future together except the possibility of its coming true. That was something Phil wouldn't let himself forget.

He returned with the beer and the suntan oil he'd left aboard yesterday. Manoli had laid out the long cushions from the seats on the afterdeck, and they stretched out facing each other, propped on elbows, and drank and talked and simply looked at each other for long, silent moments. Phil put suntan oil on Manoli's nose and forehead and cheeks.

"I don't need that," Manoli said.

"No. I too not any more, but it makes better color."
Phil put some on his face. He realized that Greek was becoming increasingly their language and that his Greek

was coming out more easily. His sentences were haphazard but his vocabulary was improving.

"We'll get plenty of sun and then we'll eat in the shade of an olive tree. That will be good," Manoli announced.

They finished the beer and Phil went below for more. When he returned with full glasses, Manoli was sitting up with his arms wrapped around his knees. Phil sat sideways to him with his legs dangling into the cockpit and handed him his glass. "You're a nice man, my Philip," Manoli said. "I've never had a friend like you." He pulled him back and kissed him. Phil lolled against his knees and opened his mouth passively to Manoli's thrusting tongue, still hesitating to demand too much of him. His cock began to swell between his thighs as the kiss lengthened and Manoli made Phil's mouth his own, plunging his tongue deep into it. There was no room for doubt. Manoli wanted it. Phil put down his glass blindly and lifted his arms and held his head, their tongues parrying each other and darting in and out of each other's mouths. Manoli's arms slid around him and held him close. He shifted his hips and moved his legs so that they were clamped to each other, their chests heaving while they filled their mouths with each other's tongues. They broke apart breathlessly. Phil caressed Manoli's chest and abdomen and held his rigid cock. Manoli's eyes were alight. Shaky laughter broke from him as he found Phil's erection.

"Your cock is bigger than mine," he said with unexpected satisfaction.

"No. Very little only." It was astonishing that he'd noticed the slight difference, and Phil didn't want to make anything of it. Alex had been so worried that his was smaller that it often wasn't good for anything. Phil wanted to build on the passion of the kiss.

"It's very fine. It makes me want to fuck you and show you that mine is very fine too," Manoli said.

"I want you show me many times." Phil reached for the oil and applied it to him.

"On your back?"

"Yes." Phil threw his legs up onto the deck and sprawled out in front of him. Manoli swung himself up onto his knees over him. His cock glistened in the sun. Phil lifted his legs for it, and Manoli held his hips and slid it slowly into him. He pulled Phil in to him when he had completed his entry and held himself motionless, allowing him time to surrender completely to their union.

"You like my cock even if it's small." Manoli smiled down at him, confident of his prowess.

"Yes. It's very small like mine but very beautiful in me. Fuck me for a long time. I love you there."

"Like this, you're my woman." Manoli drew back until only the head of his cock remained in him. He made quick movements with his hips and tantalized him with small entries and withdrawals. He goaded Phil into a frenzy of desire. Phil writhed and flung his arms out and gulped for air.

"Holy saints," he gasped. "Take me. I want all."

Manoli continued to goad him, smiling wickedly down at him until Phil was clawing the air, his head back, his mouth open, choking on laughter and moaning with ecstasy, his body jerking convulsively. He thought of the rape. This was more refined punishment, exquisite and maddeningly incomplete. Manoli was demonstrating how much Phil wanted him, holding him on the verge of orgasm.

Manoli laughed with his triumphant control and drove hard into him. The sudden fulfillment of his own longing made Phil shout his gratitude and his orgasm erupted. Manoli used his cock with proud mastery, offering him all the satisfaction he had so triumphantly denied him. He massaged Phil's sperm into his skin and didn't let his own orgasm become a solitary pleasure. He looked ecstatically into Phil's eyes while his body shook with its spasms.

They jumped into the sea again. When they clambered back on board, they went below. Phil gathered together the food and stole a bottle of wine from the ship's stores, making a mental note to replace it. Manoli went to the head. Phil thought of warning him to be careful with water but supposed he knew more about that than he did. He was the most immaculate guy Phil had ever known; even his toenails were groomed and gleaming. He stepped into the gallery behind Phil, smelling of cleanliness. Phil turned to him.

"We carry all this on our heads?" he asked.

"One moment. I'll get a blanket to sit on and make a package. We can touch bottom at the bow. You can hand it down to me and we'll walk to land."

Manoli decreed that they should wear their shorts and they put them on. They were as brief as swimming trunks but more revealing. Phil assumed that he wasn't expecting a welcoming committee. They carried out Manoli's operation in the bow and reached the shore without difficulty. They climbed up over the rocks and entered the olive grove, where Phil found the stubble of the rough terrain hard on his bare feet. Manoli strode along as if he were crossing a lawn. Seeing Phil's discomfort, he stopped in the inviting shade of one of the first trees they came to.

"There's no need to go farther," he said kindly. "I forget that city men always wear shoes." He unfolded the blanket and smoothed it out, and they sat side by side while Phil took charge of the catering. He lined up the tomatoes and oranges and the hunk of cheese. He opened the expensive tin of ham. The breeze whispered through the trees. The only other sound was the sawing of cicadas, a rhythmic creaking that rose in volume to a climax and then stopped abruptly for seconds at a time. The sea was a sparkling indigo below them. After their hours under the blazing sun, it was blessedly cool under the slivery green of the olive trees. Their brown bodies blended harmoniously into the landscape. Phil put the glasses and the uncorked bottle of wine between them.

"We eat," he announced.

"I'm hungry."

They tore the crusty bread apart with their hands and put chunks of soft, fatty ham on it. They ate the tomatoes whole like fruit. They tasted of all the good things on earth and reminded Phil of the ones he and Teddy had picked off the vines at the farm, sweet and warm with the sun. Juice spilled down their chins. They laughed at the mess they were making and licked it off each other's faces. The wine was local and coarsely robust and subdued the harsh tang of the cheese. By the time they'd drunk the bottle, the euphoria that had been mounting and spreading all through Phil seemed like an emanation from some other world. It was unnatural to feel so good on this earth. He supposed he was as close to heaven as he was likely to get.

Manoli leaned in to him and put an arm around him and dropped his head against Phil's. He ran the flat of his hand slowly over him, down across chest and abdomen, over his cock and along his thighs and laid it on his knees. "Your body pleases me very much, my Philip. You please me in every way."

"I not speak so good." Phil attempted to laugh as the spell Manoli cast over him seemed to close around him. Maybe Manoli was really falling in love with him. The idea filled him with a panic that was at the same time part of his euphoria. What would he do? It would be glorious and terrifying.

"You will learn," Manoli assured him tenderly. "I will want no other man. I will want women, but that is different." His hand moved back along his thigh and lifted Phil's hardening cock out of his shorts and watched it complete its transformation. His own cock had escaped its flimsy confinement and was angled up against his groin. They dropped back and lifted their legs in the air and peeled the shorts off. They rolled in to each other and grinned.

They extended their tongues and teased each other with the tips of them. Manoli lifted himself and Phil urged him up on him and their passionate mouths were once more joined. Their lips drew apart to seek other areas for exploration, and they swung themselves around with their feet pointed in opposite directions so that they could both get at each other. Their open mouths moved over each other, licking and nuzzling and sucking everything they encountered, their armpits, the swell of their breasts, their nipples, their navels. Manoli's mouth matched Phil's in passion. Manoli wanted all of Phil. He wanted his balls and his toes and his buttocks. Their hands massaged and kneaded firm flesh. They held their cocks and caressed their faces with them. They devoted their mouths finally to a long, slow adoration of their manhood. Phil was no longer his woman. Manoli was unabashedly making love to a man. They knew when they could no longer delay their orgasms and their mouths received them with equal eagerness.

They sat up and smiled at each other, their eyes soft with fulfilled desire. "Fucking isn't convenient in a place like this," Manoli said. "That way is better here."

"Yes. Somebody must've invented it for picnics," Phil said in English, unable to make his little joke in Greek.

Manoli laughed and ruffled his hair. "You're my *pousti,* but you are also a man. With you I'm a *pousti* too. We're the same. I've never wanted to make love with a man like I want to with you."

"It is very beautiful like you do it."

"We'll do it often that way, not only for picnics. Your cock in my mouth pleases me. What comes out tastes good. I'll let you fuck me later if you wish."

Phil put an arm around him and hugged him, feeling the sting of tears in his eyes. He didn't want him that way any more than he had with George, but he knew what the offer must mean to Manoli. It was a recognition of their belonging to each other. The suspense was over. Manoli offered him everything he could hope for from a lover. He took a deep breath. "No. I want you so much in me."

"I understand. You're a *pousti.*"

"Why do you always say that word?"

"*Pousti?* It's the word for what we do with the mouth."

"In English, is faggot. I'm a faggot, but my friends don't say it."

"I've heard the word. Faggot. We're faggots together. I don't mind with you."

"I maybe not too."

"I think about what we must do. We must leave soon even if Don doesn't give me the money. You don't like me to do things for money. Now that I have you, I don't want to. We'll be together. I'll have women when you make me angry. You'll help me. You'll give me a little money sometimes to send to my mother until I make plenty of my own."

If he was whoring, he wasn't being devious about it. His conditions were clear and simple. Phil forced himself to face the possibility that he'd been carried to the heights of ecstasy by a skilled whore's body. He congratulated himself for having enough sense left to wonder if Manoli really wanted some of the things he had done, but he refused to believe that anybody could simulate the passionate desire he'd felt in him. Whores fell in love like anybody else. He had only to keep it firmly fixed in his mind that he wasn't going to allow himself to fall in love with a whore. "Where can all this happen?" he asked.

"In New York. Don't fear. I'll be there with you. Promise me only that you'll do nothing that lets Don find out. I'm afraid of him."

"Where does he think you are now?"

"Before I came to the boat this morning, I asked Johnny to tell him that he wants me to show you how to sail. He's going to say that I spent the night with him."

"But doesn't he know you might leave if he gives you the money?"

"No. He thinks I do everything he tells me to do. I have. That's why he must pay me. He knows I want the money for my mother. He thinks I will stay always. Only you know that I'm going."

"What if I not come here?"

"I would go. I'm waiting only for the money, but I don't have to wait longer now. You *are* here. This is a bad place for us. You know that. What happened last night wouldn't happen somewhere else. Not with you. I have fifty dollars from Harry. You'll give me a hundred, maybe a hundred and a half. That's all I need. I might have to stay in Athens waiting for a boat if what you say is right. If I jump ship without getting paid, I'll need a little money before I get to you. I must leave a little for my mother. When I'm with you, you'll give me what I need until I can work. That is only if Don still makes excuses."

Phil listened, struggling with himself, rallying his resistance. Manoli's innocent faith in him was touching and absurd. He had chosen him. He trusted him. That was enough to make everything turn out right. Manoli looked at him with clear, candid, untroubled eyes. Alex knew how to make his eyes appealing too. What was the use of experience if you didn't let it guide you? "I don't buy you," he said with determination but making it sound less decisive than he'd intended.

"No. I want only what you want. To be with you. You're in love with me. I think I'm in love with you. There is no question of money between us. We use what we have for each other. That is true."

"That is true, but I have more than you. That is bad. It is very bad for a man who want women. He is used to giving the orders. If you take money, you are angry with yourself and then me. I don't want you to do everything I say. We must do what we can do both, not only one of us. If you can do what you plan, I take care of you; you live with me but I don't give you money."

"Don't worry. I know it's not always easy for you to explain what you mean, but I understand you don't want to try to make me your woman. That's good. I don't want money. I will take only what I need. I know you want to give me that." He leaned forward and kissed Phil's mouth. His lips were soft and tender. Phil clung to them, stabbed by love, his resistance ebbing. How could he resist anything that made him feel so wonderful? He supposed it was obvious that Manoli was working him shrewdly, making his demands and cutting off his objections with a kiss, but he hadn't got anything out of him yet. He wasn't going to let him twist him around his little finger the way he apparently had with Don. He'd thought of Don as the evil genius, but he wasn't sure; Manoli must have done plenty to extract a promise of ten thousand dollars from the plump Canadian. He let Manoli's mouth go with a sigh.

"We must sail against the wind going home. We'll go soon," Manoli said, ignoring Phil's slight withdrawal.

"I not know what time it is."

Manoli looked up at the sky through the trees. "Early still. Two o'clock maybe. We have time for a little more wine on board." He gathered up their bits of litter, the tin, the bottle, scraps of bread, and put them in the paper bag the tomatoes had been in. They stood and put on their shorts and used the blanket again to wrap up the glasses and the oranges they'd kept for the sail home.

The boat was placed with uncanny precision for Phil to transfer the bundle he carried on his head onto the deck without getting it wet. They hoisted themselves out onto the stern and dropped their wet shorts and used the towels they'd left on the cushions. Phil ran forward for the bundle, and they carried everything below, wearing the towels.

"We have more wine?" Manoli asked, standing beside Phil in the galley.

"Sure. It gives us strength."

Manoli looked at him and laughed. "We need it."

Phil stole another bottle and Manoli took it into the neat little saloon and drew the cork. They sat side by side on a bunk-settee and drank. "This is a good place to live," Manoli said happily. "Do you have a big place in New York?"

"No. Three rooms. Not bad for New York. Everything is very expensive there."

"Three rooms. That's good. We'll be fine."

His fantasy was solidly rooted. Phil supposed that if you were used to having nothing it was natural to think you could go anywhere without being any worse off. Why not

New York? The world belonged to anyone without baggage. Manoli had selected him as a necessary stepping-stone to whatever he saw in his future, most likely a rich wife. It probably made perfect sense if you could see life as simply as Manoli did. "You do not fear to be in New York without legality?"

"No. My friends say it's no problem."

Phil tried to think of things that required papers. Aside from the major area of work, there was nothing. New York was an easy place to get lost in. Maybe his Greek ex-boyfriend could use him in the family grocery store without worrying about his being an illegal alien. The States were full of them. He was becoming infected by Manoli's simple faith in the possibility. He looked at his strong, handsome profile. Why not give him some money? He could afford a family. Why shouldn't Manoli be it? He would think about it carefully later. He ran a hand over his dark, vigorous hair and felt the stab of love. Manoli turned and looked at him with gentle eyes. "We'll be together, my Philip. No fears."

His faith was unshakable. Phil was deeply moved by him. Phil wanted him. He wanted to hold him and tell him that he need never fear anything with him. It would be exciting to have Manoli with him if he could keep a foot on the brake. That shouldn't be difficult with a guy who didn't pretend to offer him anything more than physical satisfaction on his own terms. Today might never be repeated if the Greek got what he wanted. Whatever Manoli meant by falling in love wasn't what Phil meant. Phil stroked Manoli's hair. "I will help you be with me if I can," he said simply.

Manoli refilled their glasses and they drank. The boat lay almost motionless in their little cove. The hull creaked occasionally and Phil sometimes heard a thin singing in the rigging. Peace invaded him. Euphoria made his body feel oddly light and buoyant. His hand idly stroked Manoli's neck and shoulders while they exchanged labored sentences about the American embassy and tourist visas and how much it cost to fly to New York.

"I will go see Don this evening when we get in. Then I must go to my mother. We'll try to be together tomorrow. If I get the money, I'll stay with you all the time." He refilled their glasses again.

"It's much money. Does he say how you get it?"

"In the bank with my name. I know nothing about banks. You'll tell me what to do. I learn many things with you." He looked at Phil and their eyes met. Manoli's danced with teasing promise. "I think the wine has made you strong again," he said. "Me too. We must go or we'll make love all night. I must see Don. I'll get things ready." When he stood, his cock jutted out under the towel. Phil started to reach for it but controlled himself. Sex risked curdling his brain. He watched him swing himself up through the hatch, his own body moving with him, feeling him almost as a physical presence in him. Manoli was making them belong to each other, and it felt as right as it had with George, regardless of consequences. Nothing could ruffle Phil's heady euphoria, not even suspicions about Manoli's opportune enthusiasm for kissing him and taking him with his mouth. Manoli might have started with a cold-blooded decision to please a *pousti*; whores adapted themselves easily to their customers' tastes. But nobody could fake a hard cock.

The sail home was work. Manoli warned that if they went out too far the wind would become more westerly and it would take longer, so they made short tacks and learned together how the boat's rig worked most efficiently for them. Phil rejoiced every time they came about and their bodies sprang into action in a fine-tuned collaboration. They were good working together.

When they'd tied up and put the boat in order, they went below to dress properly. Manoli wore Phil's jersey. "I keep this until tomorrow?"

"Of course. Always, if you want it."

"We wear each other's clothes now. Wear my shirt tonight. It's clean. We're like that together. Don won't notice that mine is new, but I will know and laugh at him." His eyes clouded ominously. He drew Phil to him and kissed him lingeringly, tying him to him till their next meeting. "It's getting hard?" he asked.

"Yes."

"Remember. I'm your man. You mustn't be with anybody else tonight."

"I know. I not want another."

Phil locked the cabin and they jumped ashore. When Phil pulled himself to his feet on the quay, Manoli had vanished. He looked around and shrugged and headed for home. He didn't expect ceremony from Manoli. He was a man, not a sentimental *pousti*. Phil was glad to be alone for a while to sort out the thrills and discoveries and decisions of the passionate day.

He stripped again when he got home and groomed himself at length to match his immaculate man. He even trimmed back the pubic hair that obscured the base of his cock to make it look bigger, since reticence about it was no longer necessary with Manoli.

He was always sensitively alert to signs of moral spinelessness in himself, searching endlessly for something soft and rotten at the core of his perversion. Why wasn't everybody queer if it was as normal as it felt to him? Whatever his weaknesses, he had never allowed himself to pay for sex. Ego and pride had a lot to do with it.

Self-respect demanded that he think of himself as attractive enough to stand a chance of getting what he wanted, but it was more than that. Lending himself to the corruption of another human being was repugnant to him.

As Manoli knew, it was natural to want to help somebody you cared for, but after today he couldn't be sure that his impulse to give him money was strictly charitable. He wanted him. He wanted to keep him. He was getting awfully damn close to being ready to buy him. Experience and his greater knowledge of the world told him that Manoli's plans to get to New York were impossible, but a couple of hundred dollars might give him the impetus to try to carry them out. Giving him the money would be to play God and radically alter Manoli's life for the sake of his own physical satisfaction. Seeing Manoli on the boat strengthened Phil's conviction that he'd be better off here in the environment that was familiar to him.

Phil had sensed in him a sort of tough integrity, a strength and competence and authority that made him much more of a person than he'd expected. He thought of Manoli handling the sails, running along the deck, bringing them skillfully into a dangerous cove. In spite of Manoli's squalid deals with Don, Phil felt that he could trust and depend on him. This wasn't what he had expected to feel as he embarked on a holiday affair. He was being drawn into a commitment to a man who commanded his almost grudging respect, a commitment that could lead to nothing. .

If only— What if—? It didn't work. He'd told him that he'd help him if they were together. That was as far as he could go. He would stick to his promise even if city life and city clothes made Manoli less exotically exciting than he was here. He told himself that Manoli could easily become a nuisance if he was always asking for money. Money ended by spoiling everything—so why get started? That was final. No money.

In any case, money couldn't make an important difference except in quantities he didn't have. He thought of George. Phil had been good at steeling himself against his feelings for him; with Manoli, he had gone madder than he'd thought possible. Johnny was a bad influence. Thinking of having Manoli with him in New York gave him a sense of direction that he hadn't felt since George, a purpose, something that would make life exciting again. If he didn't buy him, they might even discover that they truly loved each other. He was ready for the next step, whatever that might be.

He dressed, wearing Manoli's shirt. It smelled clean, like its owner. His cock stirred as he felt it against his skin and thought of what Manoli had said about wearing each other's clothes. It was a pledge of sorts. He looked forward to a companionable evening at the club, but he wasn't in the market for adventure any more. It felt good to know that he could spend a solitary night thinking about being with Manoli tomorrow without its disturbing his peace. He was sure that Manoli's faith in him would hold him; he was essential to keeping the New York fantasy alive.

The cafes looked lively. He nodded to familiar faces and Hilda called to him. She was sitting with John Robert and his Oriental friend. He joined them. Hilda held his hand as he sat beside her, and kissed his cheek.

"You're getting better looking every day. Your tan, darling. It's perfect for the costume I've found for you. One of my Egyptian robes. You'll be a dashing sheik."

"We're really all going to get dressed up?"

"Of course. It's Mardi Gras, darling. We must keep the

locals amused." She played tricks with her voice and made it sound rather wicked fun.

"When is it?" Phil asked.

"Why, Tuesday, of course. Fat Tuesday, as Lester would have it."

"What day is today?"

They all agreed noncommittally that it was probably Sunday.

"Have you seen Manoli?" John Robert asked.

"He was teaching me how to sail today. I don't know where he is now."

"Probably with the monster, poor boy, unless they're here." John Robert craned his neck and looked around. Phil looked too. They weren't. "He's got to be fitted for his costume tomorrow. The girls will be there. Even Don can't object."

"Are you making something formidable?" Hilda asked, giving the last word its French pronunciation.

"*Tout à fait. Il va être sensationnel.* I thought it would be fun if he wore it in public. He says he will. We're planning a charming little spectacle around it. We need your help. I'll tell you a secret later."

Phil wondered if Don knew about it. He had a feeling he wouldn't like it. It would be a score for John Robert in their rivalry for Manoli's attention. It was time for Manoli to finish with the Canadian and eliminate a jarring note in the cheerful foolishness of the community.

"I must go and give Annie her dinner," Hilda announced. She kissed Phil's cheek again and gave him a maternal hug. "You must come have dinner with me soon, my baby. I'm the greatest cook in the world on my lucky days."

John Robert and Sim soon followed for their dinner. Phil drifted on to Lester and Harvey and the Shackletons and had a few merry ouzos with them. Johnny appeared and Phil left the others to join him for something to eat. He asked about the day's sail.

"A little bit of heaven," Phil assured him. "Manoli can certainly handle the boat. You didn't mind my going out, did you?"

"Of course not. I told you to. I gather it's very much on again."

Phil felt his face lighting up. "Yes."

"You managed to digest last night?"

"It almost led to bloodshed but he won out."

"He always does. Madness has struck. Good for you. Enjoy it."

"It's mad, but not entirely. I haven't given him all my money yet."

"You will. Why wait? Money isn't everything."

"It can get to be, but I'm not going to let it. I'm trying to be tough." He carefully refrained from saying anything more about New York. He looked into Johnny's affectionate eyes and laughed lightly. "What can you do when he's so straightforward? He told me you were right about last night. He's waiting for the big payoff."

"And then you're going off together?"

"Oh." Phil shrugged guardedly. "That's probably just talk. He likes the idea of getting away and having somebody who'll take care of him in New York, but when he finds out how impossible it is, he'll probably forget it. Don't say anything about it."

"Quite. I wouldn't mind being a fly on the ceiling one day. You two must be a stirring sight together."

"We're pretty outrageous." Phil grinned happily. "Does everybody say he's sensational in bed?"

"I've heard complaints from chaps about his limited

repertoire. Like most Greek men, where sex is concerned he has a one-track mind.''

"What about women? Does he have many?''

"Yes indeed. It's early days still, but when the season's on, they swarm. He never keeps one for more than a day or two. I don't know if he prefers it that way or the ladies get bored. You'll doubtless learn the answers to these burning questions for yourself.''

"No complaints so far.''

"I daresay he hasn't either. You're quite a catch.''

Johnny wandered off and Phil had a sensible conversation with Anne about art in the States before he too headed home. He left the back window open just in case and went to bed in the one he thought of as Manoli's. He was asleep before he lay down. A day at sea was the best soporific he knew.

He was awakened by Manoli sliding in beside him. Their arms reached for each other. "Holy saints,'' Phil whispered. "It's you.''

"Yes. I went to see my mother, but I had to be in bed with you, my Philip.''

"Is all good?''

"I think so. He says the money will be here in two or three days.''

"Turn the light on.''

"No.''

"Why not?''

"I think he has somebody watching me. I don't want them to see your light. Your body is good to feel in the dark.''

"Yours too. I hoped you to come.''

"I am here.''

They lay in motionless silence, their hearts beating peacefully against each other, their hard cocks stretched out together without urgency. They had had so much with each other that it took them a moment of small stirrings and light touches to find it all again. They were lulled by the rapture of reunion. It seemed to Phil that he was being carried back into a state of innocence in which everything was known and sure, in which there was no fear or evil, in which all hopes were fulfilled. He was with George again. It had been so long since he had had this sense of being cherished and protected, freed from threats and uncertainties, that his chest felt as if it would burst with gratitude and tears came to his eyes. This must be the madness Johnny talked about, this opening of himself to an unscrupulous hustler whose kindness made him want to deny reason. He wept quietly with the heart-shattering certainty that they would never knowingly do anything to injure each other.

"You are sad, my Philip?" Manoli asked, kissing his face tenderly.

"I'm happy," Phil said, his laughter broken by sobs.

"I know. I want to cry sometimes when you make me feel how much alone I am always. Now we're together. You want me very much."

"Yes. You will fuck me?"

"I want my cock in you where we both like it, and then we can sleep with me there. I'm sleepy too now that I can hold you. There. You're mine, my Philip. I love you."

They awoke early and made love with luxurious indolence. Another day was dedicated to each other. "Was John Robert finding you last night?" Phil asked while they were washing. "He say he want to see you."

"I'll see him later."

"You wear the clothes he makes?"

"For *Apokréas*? Yes." The Greek word meant literally

"from meat" to describe the Lenten fast. Phil's Greek family in New York had made a big thing of fasting.

"You're not afraid Don gets angry?"

Manoli's eyes glittered with satisfaction. "He is angry. He says I'll make myself look foolish. He doesn't like me to do anything with John Robert. I'll show him that I do what I like if he doesn't keep his promises. You must give me the money today, my Philip."

Phil stopped drying himself and looked at him, trying to collect his thoughts. *The* money? Presumably he meant the hundred and fifty dollars he might want if Don let him down, but he hadn't yet. He shouldn't be asking for money now. "No," he said, clinging to his decision. The effort it cost him to say the simple negative made it sound querulous and unfriendly. There might be something he hadn't understood. "Don't you wait still for Don to do what he promises?" he added.

"Yes, but I don't do more to get it. Harry was enough. You don't want me to do more. I won't. I want to be with you. You must give me the money so I can leave when I choose."

"We have time," he said reasonably, trying to make his objections sound only like a postponement. "We not know what you do. We go together maybe. I must wait to sail with Johnny."

Manoli turned from him and started to dress. Phil gave himself a few more swipes with the towel to finish drying, waiting to see how he would take his refusal. Maybe it would be better to give him the money just to see if that was all he'd ask for. "I don't want you to go on the boat with Johnny," Manoli said, putting on the shirt Phil had worn last night.

Phil dropped his arms slowly to his sides. This was more than he'd bargained for. He could make a firm stand about money, but going off without him suggested indifference when he couldn't explain its importance. He felt the shirt against his skin and wanted to feel as close to him as he had when he'd put it on. He wasn't prepared to oppose him on two fronts. "I must go with him," he said. "It's a promise. He needs my help."

"I need your help too. We must be together. We'll have things to decide together. I don't want you to go away."

"We don't decide now what you do. We can decide when you know about Don." Phil hung up the towel and put on his robe and went to him. He was dressed and they stood facing each other with their hands resting lightly on shoulders and hips. Phil sensed no resentment in him for his not giving in to him. He wasn't the unscrupulous hustler he sometimes tried to make himself believe he was. His gentleness was real. "You understand? Is a promise I make before I know you."

"Yes, but now everything is different. We must stay near each other. If I learn that Don has deceived me, I must go. If I stay I'll kill him. If you go with Johnny, you must give me the money for when I decide. I take it only so we can be together."

"I don't go until you know. We decide together."

"You must trust me, my Philip. We're friends. You're my brother. You must give me money when I say."

"No. When I know you need it. Is better for us like that."

Manoli smiled slying and slipped his hands under Phil's robe. He ran them over his chest down to his cock. Phil shivered with delight as it filled out. "You see? We make much love together, but you still get hard when I want. Go to the beach where I found you when you're ready. I'll try to be there." He gave Phil's burgeoning cock a loving squeeze and turned and strode into the back room. By the time Phil had followed him to the door, he was gone.

He glanced down at the partial erection he'd been left with. It was pretty amazing to have a straight lover who wanted him as much as he could hope to be wanted, and he congratulated himself for having been able to make a firm stand. He could always change his mind if anything developed that made him feel that he was being overstrict about it. He was as willing to give him all his money as Johnny said he should be but knew that he would regret it in the long run. If there was even a faint hope of this leading to something durable, it could work only if they were equal and independent partners.

When his cock had settled down, he called for breakfast. He took his time, but it was still early when he reached the remnants of the shed on his beach. He had it all to himself as usual. The few people he could see here and there in the distance didn't encroach on his privacy. He stripped and lay on his towel with his swimsuit tucked around his cock. Being naked out-of-doors was a new turn-on. He wished it could become a habit. He envied Johnny being able to stay here indefinitely. He thought of New York and cringed. The icy winds of March. Jesus. Why did anybody want to go to New York when there was this? If he could stay here with Manoli, they wouldn't have to haggle about money. He thought about him and dozed.

When he came to, he had a hard on and was streaming with sweat. The place was an aphrodisiac, and euphoria was in the air he breathed. Why live anywhere else? He held his swimsuit over himself and went down to the sea and submerged, wanting to shout with joy at the bracing shock of the cold water. All of his body tingled with it. He had never felt so alive. He returned to his towel, hoping that Manoli would turn up soon but feeling too wonderful to be lonely.

He guessed that he'd been there for almost two hours when it occurred to him that Manoli might not come. He hadn't said definitely that he would. Was he punishing him for his stubbornness? Phil stirred impatiently, annoyed with himself. Why spoil his perfect tranquility with a fuss about money? That settled it. He'd go change a couple of hundred dollars of traveler's checks and have it ready for the next time Manoli mentioned money. He had to buy some presents for friends and colleagues in New York before he left, so he wouldn't have any trouble getting rid of drachmas if it turned out that they weren't needed. What could be simpler? No wonder Manoli thought he was making difficulties about nothing.

He looked at the sky. Even he could tell that it was somewhere around noon. He waited a little longer and then stopped by his rooms before going to the bank on the port to take care of his business. He went on to the mail-call gathering of the club, wondering if Manoli's failure to join him would be followed by an overt display of coolness or displeasure. He couldn't believe it. He had left him this morning soothed by the radiant harmony of their desire for each other. He touched the money in his pocket and decided that he might as well turn it over right away without waiting to be asked again.

Manoli wasn't there, but Phil hadn't really expected him to be. He was beginning to know his man. Manoli counted on finding him in bed when he wanted him, but he wasn't prepared to devote his entire day to him. Manoli had interests and preoccupations that would remain his own. Equal and independent. That was the way Manoli would expect it to be between two guys, except for certain rights he reserved for himself such as his right to women. Oddly,

Phil didn't mind that too much. Other things were more important. With every additional night they spent together, they were opening out more and more to each other, recognizing and accepting the major connection they were establishing with each other, becoming people to each other rather than just bodies. Phil was even beginning to believe that they might be together in New York, although he hadn't lost sight of the enormous difficulties that had to be overcome. If he was in love, he was being more realistic about it than he'd expected.

Hilda was waiting at the long noontime table with a neat parcel for him. "Your costume, darling. The cap I put with it is more Jewish than Arab, but you have to put something on your head when you dress up. I don't have a fez or those funny dish towels they wear. You can be a Jewish sheik."

Don was there going through a little pile of letters. If Manoli was with his family out near the beach, he surely would have come down to join him. He was off somewhere on business of his own. Johnny appeared and pulled up a chair beside him.

"How goes it, sport?" he asked.

"Swimmingly."

"Shall we have a spot of lunch and go to the boat for half an hour, if you're not otherwise engaged? There're some things I'd like to show you about the motor in case you want to go out without me again. Manoli knows all about it, but I'm in favor of disseminating knowledge."

"That sounds good, Johnny. We'll have a spot of lunch and you can disseminate after."

After Phil had learned something about oil sumps and various pressure gauges, he left Johnny and headed back to the beach. Manoli might have thought he intended to stay there all day. He stripped and folded the money carefully into his slacks before fixing them on his fence. He'd brought the suntan oil from the boat, and he slathered himself with it. He was going to have the damnedest tan in history. He stretched out with his swimsuit lying on him, his cock feeling even more unruly than it had this morning. He wished Manoli would come find him. It was pretty pointless turning himself on, but if he went on lying around naked out-of-doors, he could always become a jerk-off artist.

For the first time since he'd been away, he was feeling his idleness. Getting a tan wasn't exactly a full-time occupation. He'd been gone less than two weeks, more or less planning on a month, but he supposed that for anybody who was used to working, a couple of weeks was a long time without getting restless. There was going to be a lot to take care of when he got back to the office. Johnny's impending mission gave him something exciting to look forward to, and he had to be here to help Manoli get started on whatever he was going to do, but after that his usefulness as a tourist would be over. It was going to be a momentous month, perhaps even another turning point in his life.

He dozed and woke up and adjusted his swimsuit to retain some semblance of modesty. He dozed and woke up and looked into the eyes of a boy kneeling a few feet from him. He sat up with a start and fumbled with his swimsuit in a belated attempt to cover himself.

"Ya sou," the boy said.

"*Ya sou.*" Phil didn't think he could be more than twelve. He was small and dark and had enormous eyes. Long lashes brushed his cheeks as he lowered his gaze to Phil's fumbling hands.

"You have a big prick," he said composedly in lightly accented English.

"Not particularly. You'll have one like it someday soon. You speak English?"

"My grandfather lived in Sarasota, Florida, in the U.S.A. He teaches me. I think it's the biggest one I've ever seen. Is it hard?"

"It was, sort of. I was dreaming. You know how it is. What's your name?"

"Dino. Usually when men get like that they want to do it with me. Do you?"

"I don't think so."

"Why not?"

"Well, you're pretty young."

"I'm fifteen. Almost, that is. I know how to do it. I started three years ago. I like it."

"I'm not at all surprised." Phil laughed. The kid was very matter-of-fact about what was apparently his favorite topic of conversation. It was hard to believe Phil himself had been so young when Teddy was teaching him his forbidden games. Dino was a pretty urchin in a frayed, short-sleeved shirt and baggy shorts. He scooted himself closer on his knees and dropped onto one haunch and propped himself on his arm with his legs doubled up under him. Phil felt no stirrings of a child molester in him.

"Will you let me look at it?" Dino asked politely.

"You're already seen it, haven't you?"

"It was a little covered by your swimsuit."

"I guess there's nothing much wrong with guys looking at each other." He let the swimsuit go and sat back on the support of his arms. He'd lost his erection, but his cock was still enlarged as it lay between his thighs. Dino's eyes were wide on it.

"I call that a big one. Are you Manoli's friend?"

"Yes," Phil said. Everybody knew everything here.

"I saw him a little while ago. He was going to

Heraklion—a place near there. I've done it with him. He has a big one too. I like to make it hard. May I feel yours?''

"No. Definitely not," Phil said, more amused than shocked. The Greeks made morality a joke.

"Why not?"

"Well, you couldn't make it hard, for one thing."

"I'll bet I can if you'll let me."

"If you can, you shouldn't want to."

"Why not, if we both like it? You mean it might make me a *pousti*? I don't want to be a *pousti*, but I don't think I will be. My friend says that I won't like doing it with men when I have a woman, but that won't be for a long time. That's the way it is usually, so I don't think I have to worry."

"You grandfather will tell you that it's not the same in the U.S. Men don't do it together openly for some reason. Maybe that's why I don't want to do it with you. You mustn't think it's anything personal."

"Why shouldn't you be open about it if everybody does it? I've watched lots of guys doing it together down here."

"Things are different in different countries. Don't worry about it." He didn't want to give the kid any complexes. Greece was a great country. You could be a faggot without anybody noticing, just the way Lester could be black without its being visible.

"Your prick is smaller than it was," Dino said reproachfully. "I guess you just don't feel like it now. Do you think Manoli will go away?"

"I don't know. Does he say he is?"

"He's been talking to Gramps about the States, about getting work and everything. Gramps says it's important to know an American who will—there's some special word for it but you know. You say you'll take care of somebody so they won't become a bum."

"You mean sort of being somebody's sponsor?"

"I guess that's the word. You're Philip, aren't you? Isn't that what you're going to do for Manoli?"

"We haven't talked about it, but I suppose I could." It made sense. Phil was surprised he hadn't thought of it himself instead of worrying about giving him money. Manoli was being unexpectedly practical. He'd get to New York yet.

"He says you have the best body he's ever seen," Dino said, reverting to his favorite subject. "Even if you don't want to do it with me, I'd like to see your prick really hard."

"Wishes don't give you a hard on."

"Oh, I'll do that for you."

"Do what?"

"Like this." Before Phil could stop him, Dino dropped over him and lifted his cock into his mouth. He went about it with practiced efficiency and quickly produced the desired result. Phil couldn't help enjoying it. Being naked in the sun made him a pushover. When his cock was as hard as it could get, Dino lifted his head and looked at it while he ran his hands over it. "It's big, all right. It looks wonderful when it's hard. Now do you want to do it? I mean fuck me, naturally. Manoli does; not often, but he has. Just a second." He jumped up and shed his clothes and hung them on the fence. He looked more of a man without his urchin's outfit. His brown body was slight but well built. He had pubic hair and an adequately manly erection. Phil still didn't want him, but the idea of taking him seemed less ridiculous than it had. He stood to forestall further developments.

They were close enough to each other for their cocks to

touch. "I don't think this is a very good place for fucking," Phil said.

"Well, you do get pretty sandy. I hoped you'd let me see you like this. I made you hard, didn't I? That's the way *poustis* do it together, only they do it all the way to the end. Did you know that? I've never done it." He began to move his hands on Phil's cock with long, rhythmic strokes. If that was enough for his young friend, Phil was happy to oblige. He lifted a hand and joined in touching Dino. The kid's cock felt about the same as a lot of guys he'd been with. He was back in the basement, a child at heart. It was better than masturbating.

"Now?" Dino asked after a moment.

"Any time." They shifted slightly so that their cocks weren't directed at each other and had their businesslike orgasms within a few seconds of each other. "Let's have a swim," Phil suggested.

They swam and lay on Phil's towel to dry. Phil directed their conversation and formed a picture of Manoli's nearby neighborhood. The fact that Phil's name was known there pleased him. Manoli had talked about him. It was an additional recognition of their being together. Dino gave him the impression that Manoli had let it be known that Philip was his American guarantor. Phil assumed that Manoli had just found out that he needed one and hadn't had time to tell him. Manoli didn't hesitate to ask for what he wanted.

Dino said nothing damaging about Manoli. On the contrary, Manoli was obviously the local star, admired and respected as a maverick who might accomplish great things, such as making a fortune in the States.

By the time Dino made his amiable departure, Phil was feeling much more optimistic about the future. The Greek community was impressed by Manoli. That meant a lot.

Phil wasn't the victim of an aberration. He'd found a guy who could amount to something and was worth helping. He regretted increasingly that he hadn't told him that he'd give him the money. It could affect whatever arrangements he was making. When Phil gave him what he had already changed into drachmas, he would tell him that if needed, he could have a few hundred more. Phil wanted Manoli with him. Whatever he could spare was Manoli's.

He prayed that he would get back from Heraklion tonight. Until he did, Phil had nothing to do except pick up Hilda's parcel that he'd left with the waiter at the cafe. Important events in the life of a *pousti*. He had to go home and wash and change for an evening at his club and pick up his parcel. And pray.

When he reached the port, Manoli was the first person he saw. He was sitting at the cafe in front of the hotel where none of the foreign colony ever went, and the only reason Phil saw him was that his eye had been caught by a man with a mustache coming out of the hotel. It wasn't the mustache he knew, but it was definitely Manoli sitting with a woman at a cafe table. His heart gave a leap of delight and he hurried toward him. The woman wasn't young but conspicuously smart and expensive looking. As Phil reached the table, Manoli glanced up. His eyes immediately warned him away.

"I see you later," he said brusquely in his atrociously accented English.

"Sure," Phil agreed, making the best of it. He nodded awkwardly at the woman and beat a hasty retreat. The woman bordered on middle age with light, touched-up hair and a good figure. He tried not to look forlorn as he headed for the other side of the port where he belonged. He knew Manoli was going to have women. To punish Phil? Damn the money. He couldn't compete with nature, even though nature was more flexible for a Greek than for anybody else.

When he reached home territory, he saw that the colony was out in force. He table-hopped, being offered ouzo and ordering it in return. There was a lot of talk about Mardi Gras and what everybody was going to wear. Somebody wanted to know if they were supposed to take part in the parade, and it was generally agreed that that was for the locals.

"For the children mostly," Hilda said, "and it's not exactly a parade. The Greeks don't organize themselves. The music plays and they frolic around the port. It's very gay and disorderly."

Phil couldn't work up much interest in it. He was careful not to face the hotel. He didn't want to give Manoli the impression that he was watching him, and it was too far to see clearly what he was up to anyway. He was probably deploying all his macho Greek charm, a sight Phil would gladly spare himself. In a community of gossips, it was remarkable that only Johnny knew about the little romantic drama that was taking place in front of them. He was glad not to be the focus of curious eyes watching to see how he was taking every move in the game. Ever since Johnny had got him out of Athens without leaving a forwarding address, he had felt almost invisible, an odd man out despite all the intimacies he'd shared. He was leading an intense private life in full public view. Tonight everybody would enjoy seeing him as the abandoned lover, a guy who had lost his guy to a girl. They would be waiting to see if he got him back. He would. He was sure of that, but it didn't make this evening much fun, knowing that he might be with Manoli now if he hadn't made a stand about money. He supposed that was it. It would help to have just a few minutes together to

make sure that everything was OK between them, but
Manoli was a man, accountable to no one, least of all to
his *pousti*.

He ate with Johnny and the Hollywood pair. When
Harvey and Lester went in to look at the bill of fare,
Johnny put an arm around his shoulders. "Did you see
him?" he asked quietly.

"Yes. I guess the season's started."

"Quite. At least you won't have any surprises."

"I guess I'm in love, Johnny. That's enough of a
surprise. I've just been wondering. When you told me not
to leave an address in Athens, did it have something to do
with our secret mission?"

"To a degree perhaps. I'm accustomed to not leaving
traces. I daresay I instinctively wanted to erase yours too. I
didn't really think it through. Mind you, I had the feeling
that you needed a complete break, and I wanted to see you
let yourself go. That first night you seemed to be holding a
great deal in. You'd locked yourself up and thrown away
the key as it were. You're really not the same person."

"Have I changed that much?"

"Good heavens. When you go home, they probably
won't let you in your office. They'll think you're an
impostor."

Phil laughed. "I'll probably feel like one if I ever get
back. God, how I wish I could stay."

"Be a con man like me. The way you look, you could
con anybody into anything. Being in love suits you, but
I saw the lights coming on earlier. On the boat, I should think.
That's when I almost became one of cupid's victims. I'll
never forget you in our luxury cabin. Your body is enough
to make strong men weep, and you *do* have a bit of a
mind, which one doesn't expect. Has he got all your
money yet?"

"He's getting there. I'm lost, Johnny. What am I doing with a guy who likes women? There's nothing on the subject in my textbooks. I'm ready to do anything for him except give him up. Whatever else he may want, he wants me. It doesn't matter how much of a whore he is, our bodies can't lie to each other. You can't imagine what it's like. We want each other. It's wild."

"I've never heard anybody else talk about him like that, so you may be what he's been waiting for. If so, your mind, such as it is, should prove useful. Wallow in him for the time being. That's my advice. Perhaps yon lady will shed some light on the situation."

"Are they still there?"

"Now that you mention it, no."

Harvey and Lester returned and they ordered. If he'd caused any friction between the Hollywood friends, there was no trace of it left. Lester treated him with the open, affectionate familiarity of a guy who'd had him. All three of them teased him about his movie-star good looks and his spectacular tan.

"He's just a honky who's trying to pass," Lester said. "You better frizz up your hair, man, if you expect it to work."

Johnny was probably aware of the effort he had to make to enjoy himself, but by the time they'd eaten and shared a couple of bottles of wine Phil was well on the way to recapturing his euphoria. A bouzouki band was playing in the next-door cafe. The sky was full of stars and the night air was almost balmy. He was ready to become a con man.

It was still quite early by local standards when he collected his parcel and headed for home. He climbed his stairs and saw light through his partly open door. He hurried forward, hoping to see Manoli step through the bathroom door, preferably naked. The room was empty.

The light was coming from somewhere in back. He stood uncertainly, waiting. He heard muffled voices, a man, a woman, fragmentary phrases, muted laughter, unmistakably amorous sounds. He put down the parcel and went into the bathroom, making no effort to tread lightly. He turned the water on as an additional announcement of his presence.

"Philip," Manoli called. "Here."

Phil went on to the room Manoli used as an entrance. They were lying in bed together, covered but obviously naked. The woman moved away from Manoli as he entered, but he could see her hand still on his crotch under the sheet.

"My Philip. You are here," Manoli greeted him exuberantly in English. "This here is Vera, one fine woman. Philip, my friend. Is one big faggot. Fine friend." His atrocious accent was slightly slurred with drink.

Phil couldn't think of anything to do except pretend that he was used to meeting naked women while they were making love. He approached the end of the bed and smiled and nodded at her. She returned his smile, looking understandably flustered. He didn't expect her to shake hands; she had something interesting to hold on to. Manoli flung the sheet back. Phil had a brief look at a slim well-preserved body with only slightly sagging breasts before Manoli put a hand behind her head and pushed it up and forward to his cock. She put it in her mouth. She shifted so that she could get both hands on it and lay doubled up against his thigh while her mouth played court to it. Manoli smiled down at her and then glanced up at Phil.

"See. She say it's plenty big. She·do·it good like you."

"Like you too," Phil said quietly.

"Sure. Me too sometimes." He chortled. "She one good woman. You want her after me? I bet she like that."

The woman interrupted her pleasure to lift her head and

look at him. Her eyes moved over him and met his with undisguised assent. Phil had an impulse to take his clothes off. Let her have another one to play with. Showing off with Manoli would be exciting. His hands lifted to his shirt, but he checked himself. The Shackletons had a nice amused, self-mocking approach to threesomes, but Manoli in his present mood could easily turn it ugly. He didn't want to be treated like his faggot sidekick. "I don't want to interrupt anything," he said apologetically to Vera. He looked at Manoli. "I'll come back later." He turned quickly before he could change his mind and hurried to the door. He longed to feel Manoli's arms around him, even under these dubious circumstances. In spite of himself, he hesitated at the door and turned back. Manoli had lifted himself to his knees and was straddling her. Their tongues were extended and they were teasing each other with their tips. She was holding his cock and directing it to herself. He could tell from the rapid little movements of his hips that he was darting it in and out of her. Phil knew it all well. She probably found it even more exciting than he had; she had things there that he lacked.

He flung himself down the stairs and turned again toward the port. Where could he go? This was a great place when you wanted company, but there were no dark little bars where you could nurse a drink and mope. Foreigners, sailors not necessarily on the make, waterfront strays, there was always somebody ready to strike up a conversation with a solitary American. They all seemed to be conspiring to keep loneliness at bay. He should have brought the keys to the boat. Nobody would bother him there.

He settled on a little cafe just beyond the hotel, well off the foreigners' beaten track, and ordered a bottle of wine. He'd already had more than enough to drink, but he could hardly ask for a glass of water. From where he sat, he would see Manoli bringing Vera back if she was staying at the hotel, unless he was planning to keep her all night. He did like Manoli's using the rooms as if they were theirs, and he forced himself not to regret the incident. Seeing it made it real and showed him what it felt lke. It hurt much more than he was ready to accept.

Was this the sort of life he wanted at home—wandering the streets waiting for his apartment to be free? As unlikely as it might be, if he wasn't thinking of a future with him, what was he thinking about? Holiday sex? It was great, but if Manoli could reproduce it with anyone, he couldn't think of himself as special. Just another body for Manoli to conquer. He had to think his way through it all over again.

At least he hadn't had a chance to give him the money. Because he was reasonably sure that the money would have kept Manoli away from Vera, he couldn't give it to him now. He'd promised himself that he wouldn't try to buy him. It was no good dressing it up in ambiguous phrases; he'd been ready to buy him ever since he'd been to the bank. Buying him away from Don might be excusable, but buying him away from his normal attraction to women was all wrong. Seeing him with the woman had made that clear to him. A step in the right direction.

He drank slowly, making the wine last as long as possible. His mind went around in circles. There was really nothing to think about. He was crazy about Manoli, so all Phil's decisions were reversible, subject to his lover's whims. He couldn't do anything about it except wait and see what happened to them. He hadn't the right to try to swing the balance one way or the other with money. He was too unsure of himself. He guessed that at least an hour had passed, maybe more, when he climbed his stairs again.

The door was closed and he entered to darkness. He switched on the light and listened. No voices. He went to the table where he'd left the money and hid it more carefully in the case where he kept his papers. He went on to the bathroom and stopped abruptly. Manoli was asleep in their bed with the covers over him. He crept a little closer to make sure that he was alone. He stood in the dim light and looked down at him while the knots of tension in him smoothed out, listening to his breathing. They were together again. He had everything he wanted for the moment.

He slipped off his sandals silently and crossed the room and began to undress. He heard Manoli stirring. "My Philip. You're here," he said drowsily. Phil loved him more when he spoke Greek.

"Yes."

"Turn on the light."

Phil did so, stripped to the waist and held up his slacks. Their eyes met. Manoli's blinked at the light and cleared. They were gentle and full of welcome. "Yes. Take your clothes off and come to me. I wanted you here."

Phil continued to undress. He realized that he was no longer translating everything he said word for word, but was finally hearing the language. He felt Manoli's spell-binding presence. Phil's cock was beginning to respond as he dropped his shorts. "You have enough sex for tonight?" he asked with an ungrudging smile.

"Not when you're here." Manoli rolled over onto his back and threw off the covers. His erection lay on his belly. "I want you very much." He wasn't drunk any more.

Phil's cock was erect by the time he reached him. Manoli gripped his arms as he dropped down onto the bed and held him on his knees in front of him. "You're a beautiful man, my Philip. I had to have a woman to know how much I want to be with you." Manoli sat up and leaned forward to kiss the full length of Phil's cock. He thrust his tongue out to his balls. Phil's breathing became labored. Manoli moved his mouth back along it, closing his teeth lightly on it. He held it with his fingertips and drew it into his mouth. Manoli wasn't humoring him or practicing an exotic skill. His passion for Phil's body was genuine.

Manoli released Phil's cock but held it motionless with one hand and kept his lips against it when he spoke. He used his tongue to punctuate his words. "It's very strong, your cock. I'm in love with you, my Philip. It's true. You're a man. You will be my man. You must fuck me now. I started to want you that way on the boat. I couldn't believe it." He dropped back, still holding his cock, and looked at him with a funny little naughty-boy smile. "I've never asked to be fucked before."

Phil stared down at him, swaying slightly on his knees, his heart pounding. He hadn't lost his grip on the language. He had heard the words. He tried to speak but couldn't find his voice. "You truly want it?" he managed finally.

"Truly. I think we want each other very much."

Their eyes held each other. Phil searched for a hint of guile in Manoli's. They were unflinching and soft with desire. Phil was too stunned to move. Had it been only yesterday or the day before that he had still been exercising caution so as not to offend Manoli's straight sensibilities? They were all gone now. Manoli had been disarmed. They could be together in the equality of their masculinity.

For a moment, he thought his cock was going to fail him, but it hardened into an ache of longing as he saw in

Manoli's eyes the confirmation of his offer of himself. Phil wanted to take him. He wanted to make him his own. He had to learn how to adapt to this momentous reversal of roles.

He leaned forward and lifted Manoli's shoulders and brought him up to prove to himself that he was in command and to prolong the wonder of being wanted in a new and unfamiliar way. Manoli held his cock and didn't shrink from its caress when Phil guided it over his parted lips. Manoli wanted it in him.

Phil held his head close against him for another moment, exulting in Manoli's unguarded acknowledgment of his passion for a man's hard flesh, encouraging him to commit himself unequivocally to it with his lips and tongue, and then pushed him back gently and dropped down and lay on his sublime body. Manoli lifted his arms to welcome him and their mouths found each other. They remained locked together, their teeth clashing, their bodies writhing until they were both struggling for breath. They broke apart, gasping.

"You have your oil?" Manoli asked when he could speak.

"Or the other."

"No. I want it the same as the first time I fucked you."

"I'll get it." Phil lifted himself from him and went to the front room. When he returned, Manoli was lying on his stomach. Phil brought him a towel and climbed onto the bed on his knees over him. He applied the oil to himself and ran his fingers between Manoli's buttocks. Manoli was his; he pulled his knees up under him, waiting for him. Phil looked down at his cock. It was going to join them to each other. He held Manoli's hips and thrust it into him, imitating the way Manoli took him.

"Oh, my Philip," he called, accepting his subjugation, surrendering to him.

Phil was staggered by the transformation that seemed to be taking place in him. It was his turn to become his lover's ruler. Manoli belonged to him as he had wanted to belong to Manoli. The power that drove them into each other's arms was his. The thought of having this with George flashed through his mind. It was inconceivable, but he wished it had happened. It changed everything. He could feel his domination of Manoli growing. Phil could no longer be treated like his *pousti,* subject to his high-handed demands. He had ceased to be his lover's slave and became a force capable of shaping love to his will. Manoli had given himself to him. He intended to keep him on his own terms. Manoli needed him. He would take care of him.

"My Manoli," he proclaimed victoriously. "My friend."

"Yes. You're my man. We are together now."

Phil began to move in him, experimentally at first, still not quite believing that Manoli was capable of acknowledging him as an equal. His confidence grew as he demonstrated his prowess and as he felt all of Manoli's body surrendering to his will, wanting him, offering him whatever pleasure he might find in it. Phil was staggered by the power he found in himself to absorb and to shape another's need. There was so much in him he didn't know; he felt as if he were expanding to make room for it all. He exulted in Manoli's orgasm but managed to withhold his own until Manoli was whimpering with need and his erection had been restored. Phil's possession of him became a shared triumph.

They didn't speak again until they were in the shower. The sense of being transformed persisted in Phil. He felt older and bigger than Manoli. He was in fact a fraction of an inch taller than he, a difference that hardly counted, but tonight it felt like more than that. He soaped him thoroughly everywhere and was struck by how young and vulnerable he seemed, almost like Dino. It made him feel wonderfully protective and possessive. He wished more than ever that he spoke better Greek. There was so much he wanted to tell him and explain to him.

"I loved your cock doing that," Manoli said, letting himself be soaped between the buttocks like a child. "It's very fine. You should have had Vera with me."

"I am able to have a boy called Dino on the beach this afternoon if I wanted," Phil said with a touch of defiance, assuming that he'd find out if he didn't know already. Dino liked to talk.

"You did?" He burst out laughing unexpectedly. "I didn't know you wanted it that way until now."

"Not usually. Not with you until now. He—I don't know how to say it—he talked to me to do it."

"He suggested it? Yes, he likes to be fucked very much. It's no matter, but I think now you must do it only with me. We'll have each other in all ways whenever we like."

"And you?"

"It will be the same. I'm speaking only of boys and men, of course. Women are different. We will have them together the way we could have had Vera if you'd stayed. You're a man. I think you will like women if I'm with you."

"Maybe."

"She gave me a present. I didn't ask, but I thought she would. She's rich. She has a big house in Atlanta, Georgia. Is that far from New York?"

"More far than here to Athens, but not far in the United States."

"She wants me to stay with her when I get there. She wants me very much after tonight. She likes my cock."

"No husband?"

Manoli smiled rakishly. "A widow. That's the best. She wants me to come see her in Heraklion in two days. She promised me another present. You don't want me to take your money. I must get what I can. I think she will soon want to marry me to keep my cock. She's thirty-eight. That's not very old."

Vera was a liar and Manoli a not very subtle blackmailer. If Phil didn't give him money, he would sell himself to Vera. He may have thought that offering himself to him would undermine what little resistence he had, but he'd miscalculated. Phil had never felt stronger or more sure of himself. If anybody was going to keep Manoli's cock, he was and he wasn't going to have to give him presents for it. Manoli had let himself get in deeper than he realized. Manoli belonged to him. Phil felt it all through his body in the way he stayed close enough for them to touch everywhere and in the soft, playful little kisses he gave him at every opportunity, on his chest and neck and ears. Manoli was in love with a man, whether he liked it or not.

"Did you go to Heraklion today?" he asked.

"Near there. I have a friend who has been to the United States. I wanted to find out what it will be like for me. He says there are ways of getting what he calls a Social Security card. It's very important for getting work. He says everything will be easier if I don't wait for papers but go and jump ship. I also went and put on John Robert's costume, and he touched my cock a lot when he was arranging it. Then I saw Vera sitting alone and looking at me the way foreign women do, very openly, and I spoke to her. I knew she also wanted to touch my cock."

"Don't we all," Phil said in English, smiling to himself. "What do you do with her now?"

"She's with a lady friend in the fine hotel in the new town. She's rich."

"Did you let her out the window?"

"No. I don't mind the family seeing me with a woman. I don't want people to start saying that I come here for you. Don would hear."

When they had rinsed, Phil turned off the water and held him, running his hands up and down over his delectably wet body and kissed him lightly on his mouth, strongly aware of the fractional difference in their heights that obliged him to lean down a bit, equally aware that his cock was definitely bigger than Manoli's. With encouragement, he'd soon be ready to take him once more and they'd have to wash all over again. Fucking his guy for the first time was enough for tonight. "Come. We will use our toothbrush and go to bed now."

"I look very foolish in John Robert's costume," Manoli said while they were drying themselves. "I don't want to wear it. It will make Don angry and I don't want more trouble with him. Because we are together, I don't want to see him again. I think the bank is closed tomorrow, but the next day I will go there and arrange for any money I get to be given to my mother. I think that is possible. The day after that I will meet Vera in Heraklion. I think she wants me to go to Athens with her. She will pay, of course. I will wait for you there."

"No," Phil said, testing his new authority. "I not wish you to go with her. You know I must wait to do the boat with Johnny. Then I will go with you."

"If you give me only one hundred dollars, I can wait. That's enough if Don is very bad and I have to go. I will stay with you and not see Vera unless you come with me. That's what I want too."

"Why do you go if Don is bad? This is your home."

"I told you. If we're together like this all the time, he'll find out about you. That frightens me. I don't want him to part us. He might say something untrue about me to the police. It's easy for a rich foreigner to make trouble for a poor man here. I might have to go quickly."

"If you go to Athens, how do I find you?"

"Did Johnny take you to Pano's bar?"

"In the Plaka? Yes."

"I thought so. They told me Johnny was there with a very handsome American. They will know where to find me."

"Good. Then we decide in Athens. I think of you today. I will give you money, maybe five hundred dollars, but only if we know you need it. Is not a promise. I tell you. I do not buy you." He paused, prepared to be threatened with Vera again, but saw no signs of displeasure. Should he be suspicious of such meek compliance with his decision? Was Manoli preparing a surprise for him? He added hastily, "In New York, if you're not in Atlanta, Georgia, I will give you all you need until you find work. That is a promise."

"Of course. We don't think of buying between us. We are in love and want each other very much. What we have is for both of us so we can be together and fuck each other very often. That is natural."

"If we truly love each other, it will make many differences, my Manoli. Is the first time you love, not so?"

"Yes. Not you?"

"No. Once before. And another time a little maybe. Not like you. The first time and you now. Do your teeth." Phil took their towels and hung them up. Offering small services was a pleasure but he no longer felt that he was trying to win favor. He stood beside him at the basin and stroked Manoli's lean bottom while he brushed his teeth. Phil's satisfaction at having stood his ground again was profound and strengthened his resolve. They were getting somewhere. If Manoli pulled off the miracle of reaching New York, they might make it work so long as he remained a strong-willed guide until Manoli found out what being in love was all about. He probably never would in a romantic or sentimental way. He was very much a man even though he did all the things that Phil had always thought were strictly for faggots. Manoli had been brought up to take many of them for granted, like everybody here. He wondered why the question of a sponsor hadn't been raised and realized that if he went without papers there would be no point.

"Can I leave the light on in the other room?" Phil asked when he'd taken his turn with the brush. "I like to be able to see you."

"Yes, I too. I like to look at your face and your beautiful body."

Phil flicked the switch and lay down beside him in the half light. He held Manoli's chin and kissed his eyelids. Manoli put his arms around him and moved in close against him. They lay face to face in each other's arms, accepting their need for each other in perfect peace— except for the small stirrings of their cocks against each other. The sweetness of it brought tears to Phil's eyes again and there was a constriction in his throat. They were more completely together than he had ever been with George. He couldn't imagine George wanting him in the way Manoli had. It had never before seemed a lack between them, but he couldn't help wondering now. Would they still be together if they'd had that extra nudge of

union? Everything was so neatly reversed in their triple
alignments that it seemed like a pattern fixed by fate. He
was the older one this time. He had the money, such as it
was. He was the confirmed homosexual, Manoli giving in
to him. He had become George. There was no escaping
him.

Sleep crept over him while he felt their cocks slowly
hardening against each other until they were both erect.
They acknowledged it together with a quick tightening of
their arms around each other.

"It's big and hard, my Philip," Manoli murmured
dreamily. "I want to hold it while I go to sleep. Whichever
wakes up first can take the other." Their hands moved to
each other. They slept.

Manoli woke up first. Phil was awakened by him
entering him. All of his body immediately opened to him
and gave him a blissful welcome. He was Manoli's. this
was the way a day should start.

When they had washed and Manoli was dressed, they
opened Hilda's parcel together and unfolded a long dark
blue garment of heavy cotton or possibly linen with silver
braiding around the flowing sleeves and deep V neck. Phil
dropped it over his head and pulled it down until it touched
the floor. It fitted snugly around his chest but was beautifully cut and from what he could see of himself, flattered
his figure. The skullcap was like a Jewish yarmulke but
had odd little wings. Phil thought it rather fetching.

"You will look very handsome and I very foolish,"
Manoli decided, looking him over with an approving
smile, as if he'd forgotten this morning that John Robert's
costume might provoke a clash with Don. "I must go now.
I must see my mother. If you go to the beach, I will look
for you if I'm there. I will be with you tonight after we
wear our costumes."

"Can we go out on the boat tomorrow?"

His face lighted up. "Yes. That will be very good." He could look like a happy-go-lucky kid when he was in the right mood. "You must come with me when I go to see Vera the next day. We will have her together. She will give me a big present for that."

"We will see." Phil didn't want to argue about it now. Tomorrow on the boat would be a good time to get a few more things straight. They had drifted into the back room, where the bed had been neatly made up. Manoli would be easy to share the apartment with, as meticulous about housekeeping as he was about his person. They went to the window together and Manoli dropped down and ran along the roof below and disappeared. Phil stood in the window in his robe and watched him go. He could see how easy it was for him to climb up to his little balcony. Romeo and Juliet. He hoped they'd have a happier ending.

When Kyria Vassiliki brought him his breakfast, she wished him "many years," the standard Greek greeting for special occasions. He lingered after his coffee-milk, going over the books he had brought with him to see if there was anything he really had to do. It could all wait. He wondered if there was any way of eliminating Don. Manoli's fear of him was a communicable disease. It probably *would* be easy to charge a penniless Greek, like Manoli, with theft or even an indecent proposition and have him locked up for a few weeks. Phil didn't dare intervene directly, but Johnny might have an idea. John Robert's costume seemed to be some sort of turning point. Phil hoped that he could help bring Don's shameful rule to an end.

By the time the sun was blazing, he was ready to test the temper of the day. Was it going to be festive, feverish, jolly, or simply routine? The beach would keep till the afternoon. Outside, he had the impression that it was going to be a family affair. He hadn't ever seen the port so crowded with locals. Women and children promenaded, men of all ages overflowed the cafes. It was early for the mail-call gathering, and anyway there probably wouldn't be any mail today. He wandered aimlessly, enjoying the passing scene. He found Greeks en masse surprisingly dignified and respectable looking for a people with such free-and-easy ways.

Johnny plucked him out of the crowd. "Come along," he said with a hand on his shoulder. "You must want a beer as much as I do." He led Phil out beyond the little humped chapel to a tiny cafe with only three tables outside and no customers. The beer was cold. They drank. "Happy Mardi Gras," Johnny said, lifting his glass to him. "Have you tried Hilda's costume yet?"

Phil smiled. "An admirer tells me that I look very handsome in it."

"I'm sure you do. Can't you persuade your admirer not to wear John Robert's?"

"Johnny, I don't know what it's all about," Phil complained, worried by Johnny's sober tone. "Who cares what Manoli wears?"

"They do. You don't know the background. They've been vying for Manoli's favor. Don's definitely been getting the upper hand. For Manoli to wear John Robert's costume will be a dreadful setback for him. It's ridiculous, but you have to live here awhile to understand how trivialities can become matters of life-and-death importance."

"All I know is that last night he sounded as if he was sorry he'd agreed to wear the blasted costume. This morning he seemed quite pleased with the idea."

"Does he spend the night with you?"

"It's a deep, dark secret. Yes."

"Crikey. I've never heard of that happening before. Females have complained that he'll never stay all night. I'm going to have to start taking you seriously."

"I wish you'd help me get rid of Don. We could tie a rock around his foot and push him off the boat."

"I'd rather enjoy it, 'specially his piteous cries for help as he sinks. I don't imagine we'll take the trouble, so he remains a menace. I don't much care what he does to John Robert, but I hope he doesn't misjudge your man. Don was pushing his luck with the Harry business the other night. These people often look quite phlegmatic and law-abiding, but there's a savage in all of them, particularly Cretans. I once watched Dimitri—you know, the chap who owns the cafe where we usually sit—walk up behind a naval officer who'd been rude to one of his children and bash him over the head with a chair. It laid the naval bloke out cold for fifteen minutes. Dimitri disappeared for a few days on the chance that he might've killed him. There's some law that sets a limit on how long the police have for catching the culprit in such petty criminal cases. It's something to keep in mind if you lose your temper with anybody. I daresay there may be more murderers at large on Crete than anywhere else in the world."

"I love your island lore, Johnny. If we all survive the night, is it all right if Manoli and I take the boat out again tomorrow?"

"Of course. You'll be careful about the water, won't you? In another couple of days I'm going to have to ask you to leave her tied up so that we'll be ready to take off on short notice."

"I hope we go soon. Manoli's threatening to leave. He's afraid of Don too. I've had to be tough with him about waiting till I've had my little cruise with you, but I'm a marshmallow at heart. As soon as we get back, I'll go to

Athens with him and stay as long as I can while he finds
out if there's any possibility of his getting to New York.
The whole idea is insane, but he takes it as a matter of
course so maybe he'll succeed. I won't be able to wait
with him for more than a week. My time will be running
out by then.''

"My word, you *have* made progress. Don's still in the
dark? What a lark. A proper love story. I do hope you'll let
me know how it ends.''

"Don't worry. I'll be in touch. I still want to try to get
you to do a book for us.''

"You'll leave your mark on all of us. Your passage will
go down in island history. I admire you for sticking to our
yachting plans, but don't overdo it. Love has its priorities.
I daresay I could manage. Bryan would probably jump at
the chance to go with me. I wouldn't be as comfortable
about it as I would be with you, but I think he's more
trustworthy than he looks.''

"Don't worry. I'm going with you. I've learned that the
marshmallow in me mustn't be indulged.''

After they had wandered ˋabout together and greeted
everybody and eaten, Phil set off alone for the beach. He
went through his usual routine of stripping and oiling
himself and stretching out on his towel, but he remained
on edge. All the talk about Don and the costume made him
nervous about the evening. He wished Manoli would find
him; he wouldn't mind reenacting their meeting with their
roles reversed. He felt as if he'd grown physically and
acquired an authority he wanted to exercise. Manoli must
have played Don very shrewdly and wouldn't risk letting
him off the hook at the end, so it was unlikely that the silly
costume would cause a serious breach between them.

In another few days everything would be settled and
they would go together. Phil wondered if anything could

make him consider taking advantage of the out Johnny had offered him and leave immediately. Definitely not. His commitment to Johnny was final. Manoli would have to accept it. That was what authority was for.

He was a prey to premonitions. Maybe he should have tried to persuade Manoli not to wear the costume. Maybe he should consider letting Johnny down and be guided by Manoli's instinct that it was time to go. They had reached such a peak of perfect, ecstatic union last night that it seemed like tempting fate to allow the faintest ripple of discord to throw them off balance now. He felt as if even breathing was taking a risk; he wanted them to be frozen and suspended in time.

He went into the water and stayed in longer than he ever had before, giving his body a thorough workout. In spite of the plentiful drinking of the last week or more, he felt in better shape than he had for years. He was raring to go. He couldn't complain about being sex starved, but he was ready for more. He wanted to be free of Don and spend his days as well as his nights with Manoli. They were together. He wanted them to start living together. He'd had enough waiting and wondering.

He would never kid himself again into thinking he was satisfied being alone. People needed each other. Marriage hadn't been invented just so babies could be born. Marriages existed because people wanted mates. Maybe two guys couldn't have a real marriage, but with care and determination they could come close. Knowing that he would soon be with Manoli, here or in bed, made him feel more sharply than ever how empty the last ten years had been. He was going to do everything he could to help him get to New York. He had a pretty clear idea of all the drawbacks, but it was worth taking his chances to be with him. They wanted each other enough to make it work one way or another.

When he still hadn't turned up after another hour, Phil decided that what he wanted almost as much as Manoli was a real siesta. He hadn't been getting much sleep. He went home and fell into bed and passed out.

When he woke up, the sky was filling with the pastel shades of sunset. His vague premonitions of disaster must have been brought on by lack of sleep. He sprang out of bed looking forward to joining the crowd. When he was arrayed in Hilda's robe and the perky little cap, he couldn't imagine why he'd let Johnny worry him. The evening would be a change of pace, if nothing more.

It was getting dark when he reached the port. It looked much as it had at noon, crowded with locals. If they'd been at the cafes all afternoon, he supposed they were well on their way to getting plastered. Music seemed to crowd the air. He could hear it coming from various sources, the poignant fiddle and flute of the wild mountain music and the beat of the bouzouki band. A handful of kids with painted faces and wearing what appeared to be their mothers' clothes rushed past. One of them paused as he ran to lift Phil's skirts. Phil continued toward foreigners' territory, feeling conspicuous as a Jewish sheik but beginning to catch the spirit of the occasion. It was going to be a free-for-all. A lot of outdoor cooking was taking place on the paving, sheep and pigs being turned on spits over primitive charcoal braziers. Tables were strewn with remnants of food and discarded bones. Faces glistened with grease. Everybody looked as if they were stocking up for forty lean days. The lights came on around the port.

When Phil reached home base, his first encounter was with a man wearing a bird cage over his head, with patches of steel wool stuck on his face for eyebrows and mustaches and beard. He was draped with what looked like a bit of torn sheet hastily daubed with Cubist designs. When he spoke, he turned out to be Johnny. Phil burst out laughing.

"You said you weren't going to dress up," he said.

"I didn't. This is my usual formal attire. We kept a chair for you."

They joined the familiars. Hilda was gorgeous in a multicolored sari and was loaded with massive fake jewelry, collars and chains, enormous pendant earrings, heavy bracelets. Some of it looked real.

"Most handsome," she said as Phil kissed her cheek.

"You're breathtaking," he told her. He was beginning to feel conspicuous for being so decorously conventional. Harvey and Lester had put on everything from what must have been a well-equipped kitchen, pots and pans and cooking utensils ingeniously arranged to resemble armor. They clattered when they moved. John Robert had turned himself into some sort of monster, mostly a rather terrifying cat. It wasn't a mask but an assemblage of different textured elements pasted to his face and attached to his head, startlingly beautiful in a grotesque way. Anne was hung with lengths of the thick succulent plant that trailed over all the walls on the island so that she looked like an ambulatory bush. The Shackletons had settled for swapping clothes. Since Angela's wardrobe wasn't emphatically feminine, the switch was scarcely noticeable except for the pert mustache she had painted on her upper lip. At a neighboring table, Don was above it all in his customary natty sports clothes.

Phil wondered when Manoli would make his appearance. He understood why he'd been uncomfortable about wearing John Robert's costume. It was too much of a serious artistic creation to be appropriate for this rowdy, haphazard celebration. Drink kept appearing in its usual mysterious fashion, and eventually platefuls of roughly carved chunks of roast lamb, crisp outside and tender within, were placed before them. It was the best thing Phil had ever eaten. When he caught the waiter's attention, he told him to keep the whole evening's bill for him. He knew that the lavish gesture might cost him as much as twenty dollars.

They were soon howling with laughter, caught up in the spirit of the occasion. Everything they said or saw made their sides split. A group of children came along in native dress, the girls in high bodices and full skirts, the boys in crisp white pleated kilts and short red vests, and performed a halting little formal dance accompanied by drum and fife. The children's solemnity was the funniest thing they'd ever seen.

More bottles of wine were put in front of them. They shouted at each other across the table. The strolling crowd on the quay grew denser. Phil decided that he would never leave Crete; Johnny would teach him how to become a con man. The crowd parted for a couple of men in comic bull's masks (Disney or the bull of Minos?) who circled each other with a rhythmic step accompanied by a lilting fiddle. One made a lightning leap at the other and gripped him around the waist with his legs. He lay back horizontally while his partner swung him around slowly to the rhythm of the music. It was an impressive feat, undoubtedly sexual in origin, but the atmosphere was too convivial for it to seem obscene. Everything appeared to be impromptu, as if anybody who felt like putting on a show could join in.

The horizontal bull released his partner's waist with a acrobatic somersault and landed on his feet. He charged through the crowd, his bull's head lowered, and seized Lester's hand. The tall dancer sprang up with a clatter of pots and pans and went tapping out onto the quay amid a din of kitchenware. The bulls pawed the ground and tossed their horns, charging and feinting while Lester performed a parody of a flamenco dance, his long body a comic arc of arrogance, his feet drumming a threat to the retreating bulls accompanied by clashing hardware. They went off around the port, the bulls in pitiable flight. Lester's abandoned companions cheered and rocked about in their chairs with laughter.

Platters of roast pork and heaps of fried potatoes were put on the table, and they all set to the feast with their fingers. Lester returned with a heaving chest and they welcomed him with shouts of congratulation. They were aware of some sort of commotion over near the hotel and they craned their necks. They heard shouting and applause and saw a confused swirl of bobbing figures headed in their direction.

The crowd parted again and formed an aisle along which a drummer pranced, beating out a syncopated rhythm. Following him was a bevy of cavorting youths in make-shift drag, some of them with pants under their dresses, some in high heels, others in rough sandals, all of them outlandishly made up. They darted in among the crowd and threw themselves on the people sitting at tables, kissing and fondling both men and women. Everybody was laughing and cheering. A homely youth dropped onto Phil's lap and threw his arms around his neck.

*"Orea. Poli orea afto,"* he shouted to his cohorts, stroking Phil's cheek with a rough hand.

"Look! Here comes Annie," Hilda cried at his side and uttered a peal of her lovely throaty laughter.

The very drunken transvestite on his lap blocked Phil's view, but Phil didn't want to spoil his fun by pushing him off. The youth leered gruesomely from behind his makeup and waggled his tongue at him before lurching to his feet to bestow his favors on another victim.

When Phil could see again, he caught a glimpse of Annie through the intervening crowd, wearing his hat with a garland of artificial flowers around his neck, flanked by John Robert's handmaidens in Botticelli draperies. Phil stretched himself taller in his chair. A slim naked demon with an extravagantly fanged monkey face preceded the donkey, darting at the crowd, stopping and staring, wobbling his head with mock menace. A scrap of a G-string was all that he wore to preserve public decency. Phil recognized Sim. The girls advanced on either side of Annie, strewing flowers from the baskets they carried. The crowd fell back, revealing the small garlanded cart that the donkey was pulling. Manoli was standing in it. Phil's heart gave a leap of startled delight.

John Robert was a magician. Manoli had stepped out of a make-believe world. The ambiguous cut of the costume robbed him of sex. He was a fairy-tale prince-princess threatened by contact with gross humanity. He wore an intricately contrived headdress like a turban, with a panel down the back. He stood steadying himself with a hand on a garlanded pole in the front of the cart. The gossamer costume seemed to float around his body. He looked naked under it, remote and untouchable.

The cart advanced slowly, the girls daintily tossing flowers, the demon darting forward erratically in an odd, crouching, hip-swinging Oriental glide, stopping abruptly, raking the crowd with a glare, wobbling his head. Manoli was borne superbly to some apotheosis of John Robert's whimsical imagination. The mobile tableau had a heart-piercing pastoral charm. Phil was aware of a hush falling around him as it neared, and heard a murmur of appreciation sweep through the onlookers. When it was almost abreast of the motley foreigners, Phil glanced back at Don. He had a preoccupied smile on his peevish lips. The monstrous cat opposite Phil bristled with gleeful malice. John Robert had won this round. Phil turned back and met Manoli's eyes and shot his arm up involuntarily to proclaim the secret that bound them.

"POUSTI," a voice shouted suddenly behind him.

"MALAKA," another voice shouted.

Something hurtled through the air like a pointing finger and an egg splattered against the cart. An outcry arose around them. Another egg flew over Phil and landed on Annie. The air was filled with shouts and cheers. An egg hit one of the women and another finally found its target on Manoli's shoulder. His face was transfigured by rage and his body seemed to stiffen into a tightly contained explosion of violence. He catapulted from the cart and plunged into the crowd. His turban was gone. His costume fluttered behind him as he was swallowed up by the milling throng.

Phil leaped to his feet. His heart was pounding. He had to get to him to prevent him from taking revenge on the whole town. He couldn't see where he'd gone. He caught Don beaming up at him with eyes that told him he knew everything. Phil dropped back to his chair and leaned across the table to John Robert.

"Did he change at your place?" he gasped.

"No. And not at yours?" His malicious voice made it a lewd suggestion. "At Don's perhaps?"

It had happened so quickly that it might not have happened at all. It had been an instant torn from a nightmare. Phil's emotions felt bruised and battered. The pounding of his heart made it difficult to breathe, but he had to do something. Manoli needed him. He could persuade him to go away now by promising to go with him, but he was terrified that he would get into serious trouble before he could find him. Manoli had probably seen the man who had taunted him.

He started up again. Johnny reached out and gripped his arm. "Let him go," he muttered close to his ear. "The fat's in the fire now. He'll hate us all tonight for having seen it."

Phil sank back, paralyzed by dread. He realized that he was pretty drunk. He couldn't think clearly. What should he do? Manoli had to get out of his costume somewhere. He knew that would be his first thought. If Manoli had any sense, he would go to their place and wait or borrow something of Phil's to wear, but Phil couldn't expect him to make any sense after what had happened. Only Phil knew fully what it must have done to him. He'd be gripped by rage. As long as Don stayed here he was safe. Phil could imagine Manoli smashing up the house, but that wouldn't do Don any great harm and he deserved it. He realized that he was assuming that Don had organized the brief nasty demonstration. He didn't know what had given him the idea, but he was sure of it. John Robert's little production had been inappropriate but not a provocation. Manoli must know it too.

He could still hear the venom in the shouting voices. *"Malaka"* was a word he had never quite grasped, but he knew it had something to do with masturbation and was as bad as the other one. He saw Hilda standing beside Annie, wiping egg off the beast and talking to the women. The crowd had resumed its promenade. The incident had caused only a small rupture in the evening's harmless festivities.

Hilda returned and resumed her seat beside him. "Poor Annie," she said dramatically. "He has never been so humiliated." They all laughed. Phil wanted to slap her.

They were so damned frivolous. They were laughing at a man's humiliation.

He turned to make sure Don was staying out of harm's way. He was no longer there. All of Phil's body tensed into a knot of foreboding. He wished he could convince himself that he was taking it too seriously, but he knew Manoli's pride and the violence that was in him. There was nothing he could do now except to be where Manoli could find him when he wanted him. He didn't think he would come looking for him on the port in front of everybody. He leaned to Johnny. "I've got to go," he said.

"Quite. Try not to get caught in the cross fire. It may be just as well for them to have a showdown. A proper bashing might teach Don a lesson, although I doubt it."

"You agree with me? Don arranged it, didn't he?"

"Without the slightest doubt."

Phil took a grip on himself and looked up with a smile. He nodded and waved to the others and forced himself to his feet and hurried away through the crowd. Did they all know? It was possible here, despite Manoli's precautions. Their day together on the boat could have set tongues wagging. It didn't matter any more. Manoli had surely had it as far as Don was concerned. He might make another try for money, but he wouldn't give in to him again to get it. They were free to do what they chose together.

He walked fast to ease the tension in him, praying that he would find him at home waiting. He didn't, nor did he find any trace of his having been there. He switched on lights and made a quick tour of the rooms to make sure he wasn't already asleep, alone or with a woman. Phil would have been glad if there had been a woman tonight; she would have kept him out of trouble. He judged that less than half an hour had passed since Manoli had been publicly jeered.

He returned to the front room and took off Hilda's robe and put on a dressing gown. He sat at the table with his head in his hands and tried not to let his imagination run wild. If Manoli was with Don, he couldn't imagine them spending more than an hour together—time to change, time to say whatever they had to say to each other. He'd probably be here fairly soon. Manoli must know he was waiting for him.

His heart raced and steadied. He thought of the time Don had treated Manoli like a servant. Manoli had been able to handle it without losing his control. Phil wasn't afraid of the savage in Manoli as much as Don's petulant and perverted egotism. Manoli knew Don well enough to be convincing when he insisted that Don would contrive to come between them if he knew about them. Don knew now. Phil was sure of that. If he was as vindictive as Manoli thought he was, whatever Phil and Manoli were finding together was as good as done for.

Time dragged while he tried to imagine what Manoli was doing. Would he fall back on seduction in a final attempt to get some money out of him? He quite simply might be in bed letting Don do whatever he wanted with his body. Obviously it wouldn't be the first time, although he couldn't imagine what form Don's sexual inclinations might take. For Manoli to have kept him on the hook for so long suggested that there could be more tease than performance in his dealings with him, but that might be wishful thinking. You never knew what people wanted.

He took another turn around the rooms, making sure that the back window was ajar. He wished he had a radio. The silence was a dead weight on his mind. He went through the small catch-all case where he kept his papers.

There were a couple of contracts he should have studied, but he couldn't concentrate on them now. His return ticket was still there. His passport. His traveler's checks. Manoli's money. Not much in the way of distraction.

He'd waited an hour when he decided he couldn't stand it any longer. He had to find out what was going on. If Manoli was going to spend the night with his tormentor, he'd figure out how he felt about it later. For the moment, he just wanted to know. He thought of what Johnny had said. At the time Phil had been sure that he wouldn't be included in Manoli's all-embracing hatred of the foreign colony, but he was beginning to wonder. Why shouldn't Manoli hate him too for not helping him to leave as he'd wanted to do? *You must go, and take me with you.* They had been among the first words Manoli must have spoken to him.

He tried to take his time getting dressed, hating to risk missing him, but when he was ready he wanted to rush out into the streets to find him. He forced himself to take another moment to leave a message. He couldn't write Greek and he didn't know if Manoli could read English so he scrawled WAIT in big block letters on a sheet of paper and left it on the table where he was bound to see it.

He kept to the back streets, avoiding the port. He was sure Manoli wouldn't make another appearance there tonight. He cut across to the road that connected the port with the new part of town and saw that his memory hadn't betrayed him. The walls of Don's garden were ahead of him, set slightly apart from the houses around it. It seemed like a long time ago that he'd been here. He slowed down. He didn't quite know how he intended to go about it, but he hoped to find out if Manoli were there without Don seeing him.

He passed through the open gate stealthily and stopped

just inside the garden, looking at the house through a filigree of olive trees. Light showed in a number of windows; it didn't look like a house where people were sleeping. He wasn't sure whether this suited him or not. He advanced with caution, careful not to stumble against anything.

He saw the shadowy shapes of garden furniture under a tree. He crept closer. Light showed through the partly open front door. As he remembered, the door gave directly into a living room. He didn't want to walk in on Don, and he altered his course. He saw now that his best bet was to have a look through the windows. He was close enough to hear music, the crackle of static indicating it was a radio. It was turned low, but it was loud enough to cover quietly conversational voices. For them to be chatting over a peaceful drink was the last thing he would have expected, but he supposed it was possible. Maybe Manoli's version of Don was an overdramatized fantasy invented to keep Phil from interfering. No, Johnny had corroborated most of it and added a few unsavory touches of his own.

He lingered near the window closest to the door for an indecisive moment. His heart was beating rapidly, but his senses seemed to be in good working order. He stepped boldly up to the window. He hadn't taken into account the fact that the light would fall directly on him. He felt as if a spotlight had been turned on him and backed hastily away, but he'd seen enough to be reasonably sure that the room was empty. He was ready to risk going in. After all, he'd maintained ostensibly friendly relations with Don. He couldn't go on skulking around his house. If he encountered him, he'd say he'd wanted to check with Manoli about sailing tomorrow.

He turned back and approached the door, taking less care. He gave the partly open door a single light rap with his knuckles to be able to say he'd knocked, and slipped inside. He remembered being impressed by the interior. Except for the subdued music, the silence was dense. In here, he could hear if anybody was talking in the neighboring rooms. The house felt deserted. He remembered that there were several small interconnecting rooms leading back to the kitchen. He crossed to an open door and looked in. It was a small study with shelves of books that he remembered wanting to look at. He crossed it, making no further attempt at stealth. He was almost sure there was nobody here, and he was already wondering where else Manoli might have gone. He knew very little about his habits. Greek men seemed to lead such outdoor, nomadic existences; the cafes were more home than their houses. He could go to the beach and from the fence strike inland and ask where Manoli lived, except that everybody was probably down on the port tonight.

He remembered that one of these rooms led unexpectedly into the kitchen. Going out the back way would save him from returning through the house again. Now that he'd seen what he'd wanted to see, he wanted to get away without being caught trespassing. He approached another lighted doorway and saw that it was the room where he and Bryan had misbehaved, with the collection of arms and the Oriental shrine. It was surely odd that so many lights had been left on.

He went in and came to an abrupt halt. Several of the weapons had fallen to the floor, two daggers and a couple of murderous looking battle-axes. They formed a still life of conflict. For some reason, they looked as if they had just fallen. He could almost hear the clatter as they hit the floor, as if his arrival had interrupted something. He whirled around, feeling that he was being watched. There was nobody there.

A few more steps brought the alcove and its idol into view. He hadn't realized that he and Bryan had been so well hidden. He looked in and was flung back on his heels. His veins turned to ice. His scalp crawled. He couldn't make his eyes see what they were looking at. The body on the floor was strangely twisted and contorted. There was a great deal of blood. Something was wrong with the head; it didn't seem to belong to the body. Phil's eyes suddenly focused with ghastly clarity: the neck was almost severed.

He whirled away and bent over, fighting back waves of nausea. A scream was caught in his throat. He couldn't breathe. He heard himself making odd animal grunts. He staggered to the door and supported himself against the frame, waiting for his stomach to settle. He dragged himself on in a trance of horror. For an instant Don's bulging eyes had stared into his.

He somehow found his way through the garden. Once in the street, he ran, fleeing the horror. His breath came in sobbing gasps. His sense of direction was dislocated. He heard the growing sounds of the festivities and veered off into the back streets to get away from the port. He felt safer there and slowed down.

It had happened. The brutality of it was hideous, but the shock hadn't been a shock of surprise. He'd been dreading it all day. He had dreaded it ever since the first night on the port when he'd seen the violence in him. Manoli had been taunted and tormented until he'd turned and fought back with the primitive instincts of the jungle. It had cost Don his life, but Don had succeeded in parting him from Manoli.

As Phil's head cleared, his own sense of guilt became unbearable. He could have prevented it. If he'd abandoned his well-disciplined controls, if he'd gone mad as Johnny had advised and given him all the money he asked for, it wouldn't have happened. It was difficult to spare any regrets for Don. Phil, too, was guilty of destroying Manoli's life.

Phil's chest was heaving when he reached the top of his stairs. He paused in front of his door, trying to catch his breath. He had to sit down and pull himself together before he could think about what he should do. Reporting it to the police was the obvious thing, but he knew he wouldn't. He went in and saw immediately that the sheet of paper was no longer on the table. He glanced around at the floor in case a draft had blown it off. He turned. Manoli was standing in the bathroom door. Phil recoiled from him, aware of danger. He was dressed like the sailors from Soudha Bay, in a thick dark crew-neck jersey and thick dark pants. They were too small for him. He looked spent and shrunken. Phil's heart was wrung by the sad defeat he saw in his body. There was no danger in him now.

"You do it?" His voice was little more than a whisper.

Manoli gave an almost imperceptible nod of his head. "You know?"

"Yes. Does anybody else?"

"They will," he said in a dull voice. He slowly crossed the room and stood beside Phil, looking at the floor. "It happened. He boasted about paying those men to insult me. He laughed at me. He said he would have half the money tomorrow. The other half—he wanted me to do things—I can't tell you. I was naked, trying to get dressed. I pushed him. He fell against that thing he has with weapons hanging on the wall. Some of them were knocked off. He reached for a knife. He looked crazy. I grabbed a thing like an ax and hit him. It just happened. I didn't know what I was doing. I couldn't stop. I'm frightened."

"What are you going to do?"

"I don't know. There will be fingerprints, won't there?"

"I'm not sure. Some things are not good for finger-prints. They must be smooth."

"The handle of the ax had rough sort of carvings on it. I remember how it felt in my hand."

"There may be no fingerprints."

"It's no matter. That woman who works for him knows I changed my clothes there. The man who lives next door saw me coming out after it happened. He knows me. The woman goes to work there at six-thirty in the morning. She will find him. The police will be looking for me soon after. There's no morning boat for Athens. They will watch the planes too."

Phil's brain was beginning to get into gear. How do you help a murderer escape? He couldn't provide him with an alibi if the family downstairs was prepared to swear that only he had been here during the day. "Where is the costume?" he asked.

"I left it inside John Robert's door. A friend lent me these things. He will keep my clothes for me. They won't be looking for a sailor."

"You were naked? There is no blood?"

"No. I washed carefully. It was— I should have gone away. I told you. I should have been with you."

"I know." He brushed his hand against Manoli's. It was caught in a desperate grip. "I think of later, to be right to you. It was wrong. We have the boat. Is there a place enough near where you can go to Athens easy?"

"You will do that for me?"

"Most surely." The grip of their hands tightened. Manoli suddenly went slack and he dropped down to a chair and buried his head in his arms on the table. His shoulders shook with silent sobs. Phil stood over him with a steady-ing hand on him, waiting for the spasms to subside. He was sick with regret and longing. The world had turned unreal again. He was in a room in Crete with a murderer. It couldn't be happening to him. He published textbooks in New York. Their brief, blasted passion was an unreal as the rest of it. He hoped only that he could arouse Manoli's native cunning; it was his only hope of saving himself.

"If there is no fingerprints, there is no proof," he said. Manoli lifted his head. His eyes were dry but haunted. He had gone away from him, locked into his awakening will to survive.

"They will take me anyway if they catch me," he said. "Who else could have done it? I'm very frightened."

"We must decide what we do."

"We can go to Andikythera. It's not far, less than fifty miles. We can get there in ten hours, maybe eight. There's little there. Nobody goes, but I can find a caïque to take me to Athens. It will be easy to hide in the city."

"Isn't there a law that says how long the police can take to catch you?"

"That's for small matters, not for this. They can take time."

"If we go quick by one o'clock, we can be there at twelve o'clock tomorrow?"

"Sooner. Ten or eleven maybe."

"That's good. Maybe the police start early, but it take time to think what to do. If this place is small, they maybe don't think to look there. You get a caïque quick you're OK." He reached for his case and took out the wad of folded bills and handed it to Manoli. "I have it from yesterday for you."

Manoli looked at the wad of money in his hand and tested its thickness with his thumb. "If I had known— You're a good friend, my Philip," he said with a ghost of an effort to reproduce his familiar jaunty affection.

"You have your papers, everything you need?"

"It's better without papers. I don't have to tell my name."

Kythera was on the chart Johnny had showed him; he thought he remembered seeing Andikythera on it too. "You know how to get to this island?" he asked, to be on the safe side.

"No worry. I used to go there often when I worked on a caïque."

"Then we go?" He wasn't sure Manoli had heard him. He sat slumped forward, staring at the table. Phil could see the effort he made to drag himself back to his immediate danger.

"I think we must," he said as he struggled to his feet. He looked as if he were drawing on his final reserves of strength.

"Is there a way to go to the boat without going around the port? I think is no good for people to see us together."

"I know a way, but it's difficult. It's better for me to do it alone. I'll meet you at the boat. If you stay away from the cafes and close to the water, your friends won't see you. There will still be many people out."

Phil's eyes clung to the sad shadow of a man in front of him, searching for the electrifying vitality of the guy he had loved. He had an impulse to put his arms around him in an effort to revive it and feel it again but remained motionless, paralyzed by guilt. He didn't dare distract him from the dangers that faced him. He had given him the money—too late. If he'd made the painless gesture yesterday, everything would be different. Manoli would have obeyed his instincts and left. For the sake of his sterile principles, he had refused him the means of escape even though he had sensed what was at stake. He was locked away once more in his loveless self-righteousness.

It was very strange to be with him and feel so alone.

Manoli had turned to him automatically for help and Phil felt no reservations in offering it, but there was no real contact left between them. He wondered if anything could break through the horror that isolated them from each other. For the moment, he had to do his best to get him to safety, if there could be any safety for him anywhere ever again. He watched him shove the money into his pocket. It was enough to take care of his immediate needs. Phil hoped he'd thought of everything. He gathered up the three sweaters he had with him. "OK?" he said.

"I will go the usual way. Nobody will know I've been here."

They nodded to each other. Manoli's stride was unfaltering but lacked its customary spring as he left. Phil picked up the case with his passport in it and tucked it under his arm with the sweaters and went out to the stairs.

The port was less crowded, but there were still plenty of people around. Staying out by the quay's edge, screened by strollers, Phil didn't think he would be noticed. Manoli was already on board taking off the sail covers when he reached the boat. He unlocked the cabin and threw his things down the hatch and joined him in silence. There was enough light from shore for them to get the boat ready without difficulty. When everything was in order, Manoli joined him at the wheel.

"Shall I throw off the lines?" he asked in an undertone.

"Sure." He switched on the motor and the running lights, wishing he didn't have to. It was necessary but dangerous, calling attention to their departure. When Manoli ran forward to get the anchor up, it was worse. The clatter of the chain coming aboard tore at his nerves. Everybody on the port was bound to come running to see what was going on. It seemed to go on forever. Did they always drop so much chain? There was a blessed silence finally, and in another moment Manoli signaled that they were clear. Phil put the engine into gear and they began to move at last. The throbbing purr of the engine was a soothing, reassuring sound. The danger was past.

It wasn't until they were out in the harbor, heading for the lights of the entrance, that Phil was struck by the outrageous liberty he was taking. He was going off in a boat that wasn't even Johnny's but had been entrusted to his care. The fact that Johnny knew that he was planning to take it out tomorrow made it a little less unforgivable. He would have it back in less than twenty-four hours, so there was no risk of his fucking up Johnny's mission. If he was lucky. Knowing that Johnny would approve of what he was doing eased his conscience. There were no ifs about it. He had to be lucky. Manoli stood beside him while they cleared the lights and were caught in the swell of the open sea. "The wind is good for us," he said dully. "We go to the northwest. The wind is from the west. I think it will stay the same all night. We will set the sails and not have to change our course."

The wind was brisk but steady. Phil headed into it and reduced speed while Manoli ran forward to the mast. The few minutes of chaos ensued, dark adding a special element of tense suspense while the sails went up. If there were any hitches, they wouldn't be able to see what was wrong. Phil was glad it had become a familiar routine. He got the sheets in, main and jib, and let the bow fall off to take the wind. The sails filled and he felt the hull cut into the water. Manoli ran back to him and he switched off the motor and stood aside to let him take the wheel. He adjusted their course so that they were sailing on a close reach.

"There. If it stays like this, we will be there in the middle of the morning, ten maybe."

"You know the place on the compass for where we go?" Phil asked

"No. I go by the stars. You see that bright star above the mast? If we go a little to the west of it like this, we will be there."

Phil checked the compass reading for his solitary return. He hadn't had time to think about that, and he didn't want to start worrying about it now. He would do it because he had to do it. "You must sleep," he said, thankful for his afternoon siesta. He was wide awake, keyed up and cold sober.

"I think I must," Manoli agreed. "If I feel like this when I arrive, I might do something stupid. I'm very tired."

"I get some sweaters. A blanket too I think. Is cold." He dropped down into the welcome warmth of the cabin and switched on a single light, mindful of the batteries. He wedged his case on the shelf with the charts and put on a sweater. He pulled a blanket out from under the bunk where they were stowed and took a generous swig from the bottle of whiskey that Johnny had told him comprised the boat's medical supplies. He draped the blanket over his shoulders like a cloak and returned to Manoli. "Now I sail," he said. "You sleep. Leave the light on if I want things from the cabin." It was a comfort to be able to look down into the cozy cabin; he was afraid of being alone in the dark with tonight's hideous spectacle still fresh in his memory.

"Thank you." Manoli touched Phil's arm hesitantly as he relinquished the wheel. "I think I will sleep. Call me if you need me, but there should be no trouble tonight."

Phil settled down at the wheel, warm in his blanket, fortified by the whiskey. It was only a few minutes after one. He checked the compass reading against Manoli's star. He discovered that on this course the boat more or less sailed itself; he had only to give the wheel a light adjustment from time to time to remain on course. Sailing at night under a bright canopy of stars was exhilarating, but whenever he began to get caught up in the challenge of achieving a perfect balance between the elements and the man-made craft, the realization of why he was here intervened. Perhaps someday he would look back on the night he helped a murderer thwart justice as an occasion of high adventure, but the gruesome event that had led up to it didn't make it easy to see it that way now. He couldn't erase from his memory the staring eyes in the near-severed head.

He wondered what Manoli's chances were. From their brief discussion, he assumed that police machinery would be set into motion by seven. He thought it was bound to take another hour for them to settle on Manoli as the most likely suspect and check his mother's house and other places he was known to frequent before deciding that their quarry had gone to ground. He figured that the police would have at least two or three hours to cast their net before Manoli set foot on Andikythera. If communications were adequate, the police would be already watching for him, but an out-of-the-way island might not be easy to contact quickly. That was undoubtedly what Manoli was counting on.

For the first time, he wondered if his involvement would lead to difficulties for him. If he had only himself to consider, he wouldn't mind being held for questioning, but he had to get the boat back. His barely formulated intention of staying with Manoli at least long enough to make sure that he had no further need of his help was out of the question. He wouldn't have a minute to waste. The trim little yacht would attract a lot of attention in an unfrequented port where such sights were a rarity.

Now that he had time to think, he could see that he had plenty to think about. If worse came to worse, if the police made the connection between the boat's nocturnal departure and Manoli's disappearance, their next logical step would be to concentrate their attention on the islands closest to Crete. He could imagine a grim uniformed welcoming committee waiting for them as they sailed into Andikythera.

He had to be prepared. He could say that he was performing a friendly service. Manoli had asked to be taken to Andikythera, and he had readily agreed because he liked to sail. Hadn't he thought it peculiar for Manoli to want to get away in the middle of the night? It was Mardi Gras and he'd been a little drunk and it seemed like good sport. Something of that sort. He mustn't let himself be cornered into becoming an accessory after the fact or whatever they called it, or they could hold him and the boat indefinitely. When Manoli had had some rest they could work out a story together. He couldn't imagine the inner torments Manoli must be undergoing, but he was tough. Manoli wouldn't let him down.

Phil had been letting the boat sail itself for long enough to know that he could safely leave the wheel for a moment. He slipped below to check on his passenger. He was sleeping deeply, his breathing slow and regular. The horrors of the night had been smoothed from his face. He was in the full bloom of vigorous manhood.

For an instant Phil was gripped by the illusion that there was still hope for them. It was all there, the curious fumbling love, the blazing desire. They would get through this together. Manoli would disappear. They would find each other later and begin to put together the life Manoli had imagined with such innocent single-minded faith.

Even as he thought it, he knew that whatever slight hopes they might have had for a future together were doomed. His throat tightened with the sadness of loss. Even if he got away, Manoli's life was finished. The poor bastard would be left with nothing but the wreckage of his harmless fantasies. Passion was dead. It had been powerful while it lasted and had built up a solid foundation of camaraderie between them. Phil knew that he would always want to help him if their paths crossed again.

He took another quick swig of whiskey and climbed back to the helm and made the small adjustment that his brief absence necessitated. The novelty of sailing the open sea at night kept him alert and his mind occupied. He scanned the empty horizon around him. They could be the last two men left on the face of the earth. The hiss of the sea against the hull, the rhythmic lift and dip of the bow, the top of the mast tracing a path through the stars, everything combined to offer him an intense experience of the natural world that enclosed him.

He watched dawn slowly dissipate the inky dark of the eastern sky. The sudden burst of gold on the rim of the sea made him want to sing a jubilant paean of praise to the sun god. They had got through the night. He threw off the blanket as the first bright rays hit him and watched the molten disk break from the sea and begin its climb up the sky. Manoli appeared in the hatch. They looked at each other cautiously, almost shyly.

"Is everything all right?" Manoli asked.

"I'm hungry. Are you?"

"Probably." He emerged from the hatch and stood beside Phil at the helm. He moved with his customary agility. Phil expelled a breath of relief. He had recovered his strength and was ready to face the day. He peered forward at the empty sea and glanced over his shoulder at the sun. "Soon we will see the island. We will be there at ten."

An hour less for the police to get themselves organized, Phil thought. He moved aside. "Here. I go see what we have to eat."

Manoli took the wheel and Phil went below. He found a can of corned beef and got out some beer. There was no ice on board so the beer wasn't cold, but that seemed like a trivial detail. He opened the can and carried their breakfast above. They speared the meat directly out of the can with forks and polished it off ravenously. The cool beer was filling.

"The port we are going to is called Potamos," Manoli said. "There is little there. The telephone works only part of the day. I think I will be all right, but if I'm stopped I will say you know nothing about why I wanted to leave. I will think of why later. If they ask you in Chania, you must say the same. You brought me here because I asked it. If we let them know we're lovers, they will believe it."

"All right. It's OK if I say we come here?"

"If they haven't stopped me by the time you get back, it will be unimportant. You mustn't tie up in Potamos. I will jump off and you must go out again right away. Don't turn back for anything. You will be gone before anybody can think."

"What will you do then?"

Manoli looked at him with a faint smile. "Come to New York, of course." Phil dropped his eyes, his heart wrenched by Manoli's gallant attempt to make fun of himself. He gave Phil's shoulder a pat. "You will get some sleep now?"

Phil shook his head and looked up. "No. If I sleep now,

I will sleep very much. Is better to wait until the boat is back. I feel good. You must sleep again. You look better.''

"I was very tired. A little more sleep maybe. I'm not frightened any more. It is done. He deserved it.''

"I know.''

"I'm sorry he has done what I knew he would try to do. We won't be together now.''

"No.'' They stood side by side in silence, searching the horizon ahead of them for their destination. Phil's vision was blurred. He stepped to the hatch. "One minute,'' he said. "I get the chart.'' He dropped below and found the chart that Johnny had shown him and climbed back to Manoli. "OK. You sleep now. I call if we get close.''

Their bodies stirred and shifted almost imperceptibly closer to each other. Their eyes met. Phil saw in Manoli's the touching bewilderment that had been in them when they first met and, beneath it, pain. Manoli lifted his hand and touched Phil's cheek with infinite gentleness. Neither dared risk more. The world threatened them. Manoli lowered his hand and nodded and dropped down the companionway.

Phil took a deep breath and shook his head. He spread the chart out in front of the wheel and forced himself to find the speck Johnny had marked to the north nearer Kythera. He was going to be an expert on this run. He took a rough compass reading from the chart and found that it corresponded to the course they had followed. The stars really worked. Potamos was at the northern tip of Andikythera and looked as if it would present no problems. He liked to see everything confirmed on paper.

As the sun rose higher, he suddenly saw the clear outlines of an island far ahead of them. They were headed straight for it; the plunging bow blocked it from view. It seemed to him nothing short of miraculous that they could find the small outcropping of land in the wide expanse of water. He wanted to shout the news to Manoli but knew that only their not finding it would surprise him. The sea was as easily navigable to him as a highway system.

He made another slight adjustment to bring them to the northern end of what looked more like a steep rock than a real island. As he watched, it faded into haze until it became little more than a smudge on the horizon. If Manoli was right about their arrival time, they had less than three hours to go. The wind had dropped a bit at dawn but was picking up again. He prayed for it not to get any stronger during the day.

He made another quick trip below to shed a sweater and get another beer. Manoli was sleeping. He wondered how much longer he would be able to do as he chose. He returned to the deck almost hoping that the smudge on the horizon would disappear. Had they made the right decision? Would he be better off hiding out on Crete, as he had under the Colonels? He thought of turning around and taking him back, but Manoli obviously had no doubts about what he was doing. He must know where his chances were best. Last night panic might have driven him to do almost anything, but this morning he seemed to be thinking clearly and calmly. Phil's nerves began to tighten.

The smudge remained obstinately a smudge. It seemed to take forever to acquire an outline again, but when at last it slowly began to emerge from the haze it looked much bigger, a high, rocky mass that appeared to have no low-lying cultivated areas. They were getting there, whether it was the right thing to do or not. He hated the idea of taking off without knowing how Manoli was making out, but there was no question that Manoli was right about that. Once he was ashore, Phil's only responsibility would be for the boat. He watched as the island acquired definition.

He began to make out gradations in height. The hills were in back of lower ground in the foreground. He still could see no cultivation. It looked like a bleak, inhospitable place.

Manoli emerged from the hatch and turned immediately to observe their progress. "Good," he said after a moment. "Head a little more north of that point."

"You take it."

They shifted positions and Manoli pointed. "The entrance to the port is there. We will go about when we're far enough beyond it to sail in. We'll have to take the sails down and use the motor to pull into the quay. Don't worry. It's easy to get them up. I've done it alone when Johnny was in the cabin."

Phil dreaded it. He would do it because he had to do it, but the less he thought about it the better. "I can do it, I think," he said.

"Truly. Think only of the mainsail. When it is ready, the little one is easy. Don't worry. You will have no trouble getting back. You will see Crete long before dark. You will see a high mountain. It is behind Soudha Bay. If you go a little to the west of it, you will be in Chania. The entrance to the port is marked by lights. They go on and off. You will see them."

"Thank you. I think I can do it. I must give the boat to Johnny."

"You're a fine man, my Philip. I'm glad you were my friend."

"I am your friend."

"Yes. Truly. We will always be friends."

They watched as details became visible. Phil saw a few houses scattered about on the lower ground. After another hour, they cleared the northernmost point of land and soon he could see a deep bay opening beyond it. It looked uninhabited. Manoli went on until Phil began to wonder if he had misunderstood him. His body was tense. He longed for activity after the long night's vigil on the wheel. Touching land, if only for a moment, would be a welcome respite.

Manoli kept an eye on the bay as it fell astern of them. After another endless moment, he nodded and Phil sprang into action. The bow swung around while he released the stay and threw off lines and reversed the procedure on the other side. They came about smartly and took off on the new tack with only momentary loss of headway.

"Very good," Manoli commented as he pointed them toward the mouth of the bay.

They entered it and buildings became visible at the head of it. Phil could see why they had to use the motor. The bay narrowed between high, rocky sides to the quay, leaving little room to maneuver under sail. A row of low, dilapidated buildings ran along the back of the quay, and a few caïques were tied up to it. Off to the left, a white building that looked like a fort stood on a low hill. He saw a few people wandering about and some tables in front of what was presumably a cafe. It all had a cheerless look. Not even the bright sun enlivened it. Its only advantage as far as Phil could see was that the telephone might not be working. It was hardly a place where a newcomer would pass unnoticed. Maybe if Manoli had come here often, he would be among friends. His heart sank with foreboding.

The wind lightened as they sailed deeper into the protection of the bay. Manoli swung the bow up into it. "I will let you get the sails down," he said, "so that you will be sure they're ready to go up again." He switched on the engine.

Phil ran forward and did as he was told. He made sure

the jib sheets were free, and moved aft along the boom, rolling the sail in on itself so that it would be clear and out of their way. When he jumped back into the cockpit, Manoli was gazing in toward shore.

"I have never seen a policeman here," he said thoughtfully.

Phil's heart skipped a beat. "You see some now?" he asked, following the direction of Manoli's gaze.

"One. He went that way. He's gone."

They were still quite a long way out; Phil didn't see how he could distinguish one uniform from another at this distance. "You are sure you want to go in here?"

"Yes. It's the best place. No matter. There are more policemen everywhere since the Colonels." He gave the wheel a turn but left the engine idling and the bow drifted around toward the quay. "Bring us in slowly near those caïques. When we're close enough, I will jump. Don't wait. Go." He paused and looked into Phil's eyes. "Be careful."

"Yes. You too."

Their arms lifted simultaneously. They flung them around one another and hugged each other in a close embrace. Phil felt a tremor in Manoli's body and tightened his hold on him. His eyes filled with tears again as their lips touched. Manoli broke away.

"I will be all right. Take us in. Gently, gently." He jumped up onto the deck and strode forward and crouched in the bow, leaving Phil an unobstructed view. He put the engine into gear and accelerated, anxious to get a better look at what was going on ashore. When they were within a couple of hundred yards, he reduced speed until they were making no wake. He saw some boys gathering and starting along the quay in the direction of the caïques where Phil was heading. His heart skipped a beat again as he caught sight of two policemen at the far end of the buildings, strolling lethargically in the same direction. Nothing to worry about so far, he assured himself. He had expected the boat to attract attention.

When they were less than a hundred yards off, he reduced speed further so that they caused hardly a ripple as they slipped through the water. The boys had gathered into a knot of motionless onlookers. The policemen had stopped quite far off along the quay and were talking to an old man. A few other men wandered here and there, paying no attention to their arrival. Phil gripped the wheel so tensely that his knuckles were white. His heart was hammering, as much from nerves at having to perform the delicate maneuver as for Manoli's safety. He thanked God for the sheltered port; he wouldn't want to attempt it in rough water. There was a troublesome swell, but he counted on Manoli's timing to save him from smashing the boat against the quay. He could see that it wasn't much higher than the deck, which would make it an easy jump.

Except for the caïques, it was free of hazards. He eased the boat in astern of them while his eyes made quick calculations. If he came in broadside, staying off about six feet, the swell would probably rock them in close enough for Manoli to leap ashore. If it didn't work out that way, he could try a different approach.

In another few minutes they were sliding in beside the caïques. He threw the engine into neutral and nudged the bow around so that they were lying broadside, still making some way. His hands ached with his grip on the wheel. He saw that he hadn't dared bring them in as close as he had intended. He held his breath, waiting to see what part the swell would play in his maneuver. It was stronger than he'd realized, pushing them in, rapidly narrowing the gap of water. He couldn't stay here for more than another few seconds. He reached for the gear lever, preparing to act.

Manoli shot to his feet in front of him and flew through the air and landed on his feet on the quay. Phil shoved the motor into gear and accelerated with infinite caution so that he could inch away from the quay without swinging the stern into it. He watched as the gap widened, and he was able to edge the bow out until he was facing the entrance to the harbor. The boat was safe for the moment. He shifted into neutral and looked back. Manoli was walking along the quay, the boys straggling after him. The policemen were making a lethargic approach from the opposite direction. Manoli made no attempt to avoid them. He continued on his way, paying no visible attention to them. Phil thought for a moment that they were going to pass each other, but the policemen stopped slightly to one side of Manoli and he turned to face them. The boys gathered around. Phil could see them talking. The policemen gestured toward the boat. Phil moved his hand quickly to the gear. The policemen stepped closer with a new air of menace. Manoli broke away and sprang forward. The boys scattered. Manoli took a few running steps. There were shouts and a big man moved forward and blocked his path. Manoli swung his fist and the man fell back, but the slight delay was all the policemen needed. They shed their lethargy and were on him. There was a brief scuffle and then Manoli was pinned between the two policemen and they began to march him back along the quay in the direction they had come from, followed by a growing procession of men and boys.

Phil forced himself to shift into gear and gun the engine. The boat surged forward. He had to get it back to Johnny. The little scene might not mean what he feared. The policemen might have been making a routine check. Why had Manoli provoked them? It had looked like an act of pointless bravado. Had he done it to divert attention from the boat?

The sense of oneness he had known at moments with Manoli was strong in him now. He could feel the policemen's hands on him, an affront to his pride, ending his freedom. He was overwhelmed by a vast desolation, a sense of life's cruelty. There wasn't much to be said to excuse Manoli's brutal act, but Manoli wasn't evil. Loss of control could lead to crime, but so could cold self-discipline. Phil's freedom wasn't threatened, but he shared his guilt. He could have averted disaster if he hadn't been so determined not to indulge his softer feelings. There was nothing left to do now except pray. He was glad the boat demanded all his attention.

The bay was widening out around him. He began to feel the wind again, the same brisk westerly they had had all night. He realized that the sooner he got the sails up the better, before he was exposed to the full force of wind and sea, and he was suddenly gripped by blind terror. How could he cope with the cracking sails and crashing boom all alone? The slightest error could wreck the boat. It made all the difference having somebody on the wheel.

He waited until he had plenty of sea room, all his muscles tense and his body beginning to tremble. When he could think of no further reason to delay, he swung up into the wind and cut back the engine. It was now or never, before he lost his nerve entirely. He watched to make sure the helm was holding steady and then took a deep breath and flung himself forward along the deck to the mast. Speed was all that mattered. His hands were trembling too much to act with precision, but this chore didn't require dexterity. He threw his shoulders into the winch and the canvas went up without a hitch. The sail began to take the wind while he secured the halyard, and he rushed back to the wheel to correct the course until he had engaged the starboard stay and taken up on the sheet to leeward. When he had everything under control, he sailed for a few minutes toward the mouth of the bay while his pounding heart slowed and his trembling subsided. So far so good. He was tempted to leave the jib alone but knew that the return would take much longer without it.

He steeled his nerves again but didn't trust himself to do without the motor. He left it idling and forced himself to repeat the operation, more terrified than ever because it seemed to be tempting fate to try it twice. The mainsail seemed to help this time, although he had a grisly moment when he almost lost the jib overboard after the first few turns of the winch. There was always a new danger to learn about.

He could hardly believe it when he was finally running under full sail, everything properly trimmed, the motor off, speeding toward the mouth of the bay. He risked taking a quick look astern. He couldn't see much of the port; the few buildings that were visible looked very far away. Had he really left Manoli there? He took a deep, difficult breath and prayed that the slight skirmish on the quay had been a false alarm.

He checked his progress against the land. In another five minutes or so, he would be out of the bay. He made a dash below and had a couple of swallows of whiskey to keep his courage up. When he returned to the wheel, he could feel the restless motion of the sea and the full force of the wind hitting him, still steady and no stronger than it had been all along. Something else to pray for. He prayed that he wouldn't run into a storm. It was utter insanity for a novice to set off alone across fifty miles of open sea, but there was nothing he could do about it now. He didn't understand why he had had no qualms about suggesting it, but of course he hadn't been thinking about getting back, only about getting Manoli away.

As he cleared the arms of the bay, everything he thought he knew about sailing suddenly deserted him. What was he supposed to do now? His mind was a blank. He was heading north and he wanted to be heading south. Why didn't he turn around and go where he wanted to go? He leaned on the wheel but stopped himself in time as he realized that he couldn't go around farther without jibing. The perils of jibing had been drummed into him in France. He let up on the helm and tried to think around the appalling block in his mind. Panic began to rise in him. It was perfectly simple, he assured himself. He just had to think it out step by step to see what he had to do.

If he came about now, he'd be forced back into the bay, but if he went out far enough to clear the northernmost tip of the island to the east, he could come about and run before the wind until he had the island to the west of him and then alter his course for the straight run home. What was he in a sweat about? There was no big problem. He pictured it in his mind. When he went about, the boom would be on the other side, where it would remain all the way to Crete so long as the wind didn't shift. He relaxed, satisfied that he'd recovered his wits.

When he'd gone through the paces he'd rehearsed in his mind and set the sails for the unobstructed run for home, he stripped to his shorts, trying to make the best of the sparkling day. He watched the island drop away astern. He looked at the vast expanse of empty sea ahead of him and thought of the hours it was going to take him to cross it. Alone. He told himself that there was nothing to it but sit here and steer in the right direction, but he was scared out of his wits. Even if he made good time, he was still going to have to find his way in the dark for the last hour or two.

He didn't think he'd ever let himself be coaxed onto a boat again.

He began to get hungry and guessed that it must be getting close to noon. He'd seen a can of frankfurters among the supplies and decided that they would be perfect for his purposes—they'd be easy to eat and the can looked big enough to keep him going for the rest of the day. The more he thought about them, the hungrier he got, but he discovered that it wasn't as safe to leave the wheel as it had been. With the wind more on the beam, the boat had a tendency to veer off in its own erratic direction. He headed up straight into the wind and waited for the boat to lose way. Except for the nerve-racking flapping of the sails and the crash of the boom, the boat seemed to be behaving itself. He switched on the motor to make sure he could recover control quickly no matter what happened, and ran below. He grabbed the can and an opener and a bottle of beer and clambered back up to the wheel. The boat was just beginning to gather way on the wrong tack. He threw the engine into gear to get back on course. He was out of breath and trembling again but only slightly. He knew how to do it now, but he was going to have to get awfully hungry or thirsty before he'd try it again. The tepid beer was no great temptation.

He munched the sausages, leaving half for later, and drank the beer. He could pee over the side without letting go of the wheel, but if he had to do the other, he'd be in a real mess. He guessed he was too tensed up for it to have become a problem yet. He sailed, keeping track of time by the passage of the sun. When Andikythera finally faded from sight behind him, the sea became a waste of loneliness. He remembered that he'd sighted it soon after dawn, at least halfway from Chania. With luck, he might have only an hour of darkness at the end. He began to feel confident that he was going to get back safely. He prayed for Manoli. Maybe his brush with the police hadn't led to anything and he had already found a caïque to take him to the mainland.

He was puzzled by his being able to face the likelihood of their never seeing each other again with something close to equanimity. He missed him, of course, especially the companionship he had offered during the night's sail even asleep, and he felt a sort of dead core of loss where there had been warmth and passion for a few days, but he felt strangely unhurt. He supposed that his ghastly discovery in the silent, brightly lighted house had been such a profound shock that all emotional ties between them had been broken in an instant. The pain might have been intense, but it had been submerged by horror.

Without any immediate crises threatening him and nothing but the physical world around him to occupy his attention, his mind wandered among the wreckage of the last few passionate days, wondering what it added up to. It might take time to discover all the ways the experience had altered him, but he knew that they were profound. He had learned how much damage his self-discipline could do. He still hadn't found a balance between reason and instinct, the life of the mind and the life of feeling, but he knew now that it wasn't an easy trick to pull off. According to Johnny, no balance was possible. You had to go all the way or not go anywhere. Johnny chose the latter while advocating the former. Phil had tried to play it safe both ways. The more he thought about it, the more appalled he was by what he had done to Manoli. He had toyed with him as shamefully and egotistically as Don.

Whether it was love or simple physical desire, Manoli had restored him to life, but he had refused to pay the price frankly demanded of him. He had expected an uneducated Greek to adopt overnight a middle-class American code of behavior. He was a self-righteous shit. Manoli should have fucked him like the *pousti* he was and knocked him down and left him where he lay if he made any trouble. He had wanted Manoli to be George.

Reason at least made it possible for him to judge himself clearly. He had the strength to go through the physical ordeal of this trip in an effort to make up for the part, however nebulous, he had played in the monstrous calamity, but that was the only virtue he could offer his self-esteem. He had once belonged to a guy who had made him feel that he had a reason for living. He hadn't had the guts to risk getting hurt in order to keep him, but he went on searching for a substitute. It was a pointless search that only led him into withdrawing into the closely guarded prison of self where Johnny had found him. He would never let himself do that again. Manoli had reminded him how glorious life could be.

He knew suddenly, incredulously, what he was going to do. It was fully formed in his mind, as if he had known and been planning it for months. It was folly but a folly he could embrace wholeheartedly, with no strings attached. Maybe folly led to reason if you let yourself go. It hadn't led to anything at all with Alex, but even folly required some substantial ingredients. Alex had been as elusive as smoke. If he was going to choose folly, the sooner he committed himself the better. He would find Johnny as soon as he got in, no matter what time it was. He knew he must be too exhausted to make sensible decisions, but he didn't feel it. He felt fine—clearheaded and alert. He wanted to go on feeling alive no matter what the price.

He risked a dash below for another beer without altering course, taking only the precaution of switching on the engine. He was back at the wheel in time to cope with impending chaos. He was beginning to know the boat without having to make a constant conscious effort to master it.

It was late afternoon when he noticed that the cloud bank ahead of him was acquiring the shape of land. It soon became a long mountainous ·mass stretching across the horizon. It wouldn't have been easy to miss it. He was headed for a high peak at the western end of it, as Manoli had promised. He was a navigator. He guessed that he had three hours or so to go. He should be in before ten. That would give him time for a good night's sleep before taking off for Athens first thing in the morning. In a plane. No more boats for a while. He hated to let Johnny down, but in view of what he'd said, Phil didn't think it would oblige him to change his plans. Wanting to know what was happening to Manoli was a persistent, nagging worry. Johnny should know how to find out without drawing attention to him.

Sunset was a long drowning in loneliness. He watched the day drawing to an inexorable end while he plowed on eternally through the darkening sea. He longed for the comfort of another human voice. It was against nature to feel so alone; it gave him a paranoiac impression that the world was against him. Even the sun was leaving him to his own devices in a waste of hostile sea. He had had enough of his stubborn insistence on some ill-defined ideal of the perfect relationship. It was time for him to make the most of what he could have.

Land looked tantalizingly close as dusk descended. He could make out details of heights and valleys, cultivated land and clusters of habitations. The darker stretch of water slightly to the east of the course he was following was presumably Soudha Bay, where he had spent one of the memorable days of his life. It all looked irresistibly inviting; he yearned for it. He couldn't bear to be robbed of it by the dark. He felt as if he'd been away for weeks.

When he could no longer hope that night was somehow going to be postponed for him, he turned on the running lights and reached down and snapped on a light in the cabin. He needed all the help he could get. His courage had never been so severely tested. Finding himself once more in the dark made him feel as if he were trapped in an unending nightmare. It was going to go on forever, night following day while he continued to wander the tossing sea. If it went on much longer, he thought he might easily lose his mind.

His eyes strained against the night, searching for lights ahead of him. He could see a few but they were too high, a road or houses. He began to wonder what he would do if he had gone astray. He wouldn't dare put in anywhere without the help of plenty of light. If he got in close enough to see the sea breaking against the shore, he would know that he had to stay off. He supposed he would have to head east and sail God knew how many more hours until he came to a big enough port, like Heraklion, where he couldn't get into serious trouble. He choked back sobs of helpless fear. He felt like a lost child crying for its mother. He wanted to scream.

He caught a blink of light just off the bow. He thought for a moment that something was going wrong with his straining eyes. It came again, no more than a wink in the dark. He saw another a little to the right—or was it the same one? A wink. Another. He could see that it was definitely to the right now that his eyes were trained on it. It happened again. Left. Right. It was too good to believe without cautious confirmation. The lights signaled again. His heart gave a great leap of gratitude.

"Holy God. I'm here," he shouted at the wind.

The rest passed in a daze of what had become routine, shot through with thanksgiving for his deliverance, while the coiled tensions of his nerves and muscles slowly unwound. Sailing into Chania harbor was a homecoming, as if he'd lived here all his life. He was surprised to find the cafes so brightly lighted and lively. He had supposed that after last night (was it really only last night?) everybody would be having a quiet evening. He brought the sails down, so stunned to be actually here that he managed it with careless efficiency. He motored slowly into the inner port. He would have taken bets that berthing the boat alone was an impossibility, but he set about it as an unavoidable necessity, part of the bargain he had made with himself to get the boat back safely.

He jockeyed the bow into position and dropped the anchor. Running back and forth between the bow and the wheel, he brought the stern in with painstaking care, letting out chain, gunning the motor and letting it idle, keeping an eye on the quay as he inched in closer. There was enough light for adequate visibility. As soon as he was close enough, he gathered up the stern lines and made a leap for the quay and scrambled to his feet. He lurched and almost fell. The quay swayed beneath him. He knelt to make one of the lines fast. He didn't remember putting on his clothes, but he was warmly dressed. He staggered with the other line to the next bollard and tied it off. He sat with his legs dangling over the side of the quay and pulled in on it with all his strength. The anchor held the stern a couple of yards out. Too close probably for bad weather, but he'd warn Johnny to check it in the morning.

He gathered himself together and jumped back on board. His legs were more dependable on the boat than they were on land. He stumbled down through the hatch and got out the bottle of whiskey and a glass. He poured himself a real drink and added a bit of water. The only water they'd used as far as he knew. The whiskey hit him at the same moment as his exhaustion. He slumped down onto a bunk-settee. He still had an hour's work tidying up and putting on the sail covers, but he wanted a moment to savor the inexpressible relief of sitting in the snug cabin of the motionless boat safely tied up in port, a moment to muster whatever strength he had left.

He drank, trying to reintegrate himself into time. Only a day. It had been over twenty-four hours since he'd had any sleep, over twenty of them without interruption at sea. No great feat, but he felt it. He had come to a momentous decision somewhere along the line, but that didn't have much meaning for him at the moment. His only immediate thoughts were for sleep and getting away in the morning. He poured himself another drink. No more. He had to get on with his chores.

The boat gave a little leap. He sat up, wondering if the anchor was dragging. "Ahoy there," Johnny's voice called. He appeared in the doorway with a quizzical little smile on his lips. "Hello, mate," he drawled. "Have you had a nice sail?"

Phil started to pull himself to his feet. Johnny pushed him back with a hand on his shoulder and sat beside him. "Jesus, Johnny. I'm sorry. It was Manoli. He—"

"Did he do it?"

"Yes."

Johnny grimaced. "Well, that's it. Another bit of island lore. Did you get him away safely?"

"I don't know. I doubt it." He told him where they'd gone and about the brief scene on the quay.

Johnny nodded. "I daresay they were waiting for him. The police got to me at eight this morning. They wanted to know where the boat had gone. I hadn't the foggiest idea. I told them I doubted it had been stolen. I said I'd given you permission to take it out whenever you liked. They finally told me they were looking for Manoli and why. You say you got him there at ten?"

"Something like that."

"Poor sod. If you'd been an hour earlier, he'd've probably made it."

"He hoped the telephone wouldn't be working."

"Hasn't he heard that the police have radio and wireless these days? It was a good try."

"Have a drink. I owe you a bottle of whiskey."

"Think nothing of it. It's part of normal running expenses." He reached for a glass and poured himself a shot. He sipped it neat. "You're quite extraordinary. All the way to Andikythera and back without a break? You're a sailor, mate."

"Retired, Johnny. I felt awful about taking the boat. I swore I'd get it back tonight even if it killed me. It almost did. I didn't have any trouble. I was just scared shitless. I've got to leave, Johnny."

"Quite so. Not to worry. In any event, our project has been postponed." Phil questioned him with his eyes. Johnny shrugged. "My chaps have been keeping an eye on us, as we know. Our friend with the mustache and so forth. I daresay they want to make sure the boat hasn't been compromised by this little affair. I shouldn't think it has been, but I doubt they'll want you with me now. You've made yourself rather too conspicuous for their tastes."

"I didn't think about that side of it. I'm sorry."

"No harm done. After all, I was hired to do a specific job. We haven't done anything to jeopardize our client. They'll undoubtedly want me to carry on in a week or so,

as soon as they're sure I'm clean. I'll miss you, but I'd be
sorry if you hadn't done what you did. We can't really
have murderers running around as free as birds, but still.
The victim was a foreigner of dubious habits. I don't think
they'll be very rough on him if he handles his case right. I
have a lawyer friend in Athens. I'm going to put him on to
it.''

"I wondered about the legal side. You're a good friend,
Johnny.''

"I feel we're all responsible, to a degree. Are you all
right?''

"I think so. No, not all right. I may never be all right
again, but that might not be a bad thing. I feel as if I'd
been torn to shreds, but I'm not sure how much is physical
exhaustion and how much is emotional stress and strain.
I've been too busy sailing to think much about it. It isn't
as if we were lovers parting in the usual way. It was a
shock that just seemed to stop everything dead in its
tracks. You see, I found him.''

"Don? Good lord.'' Johnny looked at him with conster-
nation growing in his eyes. "I see. I daresay you don't
want to go into it.''

"No. I mention it just so you'll know that I didn't think
running off with the boat was a lark.''

"I'd say you've lived Crete to the full. I hope you'll
forgive me for bringing you here.''

"On the contrary. I want to thank you, Johnny. I can't
say I wouldn't want to alter a single detail, but I needed it.
I think it's changed my life.''

"I've got to get you home to bed. I'll put the covers on
the sails and then we'll run along.''

Phil drained his glass and stood. "I'll help. I want to
leave the boat shipshape.''

"I don't see how you manage to stay on your feet. Come along, if you insist."

They took care of the sails and tidied up the galley and smoothed out the bunk where Manoli had slept. Phil remembered the case and his sweaters. He locked the cabin and handed Johnny the keys and they jumped ashore.

The quay rocked under Phil's feet. He held Johnny's arm for support. "How long is this going to go on?" he asked.

"After a sail like that, you'll probably still feel it in the morning. It'll pass. Getting around the port is going to be a bit dicey. You can imagine what a sensation it's been. If they get ahold of you, they'll never let you go. Keep looking out to sea. I'll steer."

They climbed up to Johnny's door without encountering anyone. "You're sure you don't want me to go up with you for a bit?" Johnny asked.

"Thanks, Johnny. All I can think about is a bed and sleep." They turned to each other and hugged.

"You're planning to leave first thing in the morning?" Johnny asked with their arms around each other.

"Yes. I can't see anybody. I can't gossip about it."

"Nor should you. You're doing the sensible thing. There's no need for you to be bothered by the police. If they have Manoli, let them get on with it."

"I'll be waiting to hear how it all turns out. I'm counting on you to keep in touch. I'll send you my address. I don't think I'll be staying in New York. Give my regards to the gang, especially Hilda and the Hollywood kids. And the Shackletons too. Well, everybody. You, Johnny." Their arms tightened around each other.

"My word. I *have* grown fond of you, mate. Take care." They gave each other a final hug and let each other go. Phil teetered on to his own door while the street rose and dipped beneath him.

———————

**H**e packed quickly while he had his breakfast. He paid Kyria Vassiliki what he owed, plus an extra week for not giving notice. With the help of a waiter at the cafe, he found a car to take him to Heraklion and by eight o'clock he was on his way. He didn't look back. It wasn't an experience he could feel sentimental about.

At the airport he saw the newspaper. The front page carried a villainous-looking picture of Manoli and a smudged, almost unrecognizable one of Don. He couldn't read Greek, but he knew the alphabet and thought he could probably puzzle out the gist of the story. He bought the paper. He made out some form of the word "murder" in the headline. He didn't have long to wait for the plane. He spent a large part of the short flight piecing together what seemed to be still a rather fragmentary report.

A rich American had been the victim of a foul crime in Chania. A suspect, Manoli Skangos, had been arrested in Andikythera. Phil couldn't find any explanation of why the suspect had been found so far from the scene of the crime but realized it might be in the parts he couldn't understand. Fingerprints had apparently been found, but he wasn't sure that they had been identified as the suspect's. There were large sums of money in the house so theft had been ruled out as a motive. The language grew far too murky for Phil to grasp, but he got the idea that sexual references were concealed in it. Skangos had denied everything but under questioning had charged that he had been attacked—

indecently?—and had acted in self-defense, so Phil guessed that the fingerprints were incriminating. It seemed to him that Manoli had chosen a solid line of defense. With a smart lawyer and a few witnesses to Don's depravity, he should get off with a light sentence. At least he would stand a good chance at home. Phil had no idea how such things worked here. That was that. He didn't have to go away wondering. He stuffed the paper down beside his seat. He wished he could be with him to offer support, but it wouldn't help Manoli's defense if he had a male lover hanging around.

He reached Athens and the hotel where he had left his other bag just before noon. He wasn't sure about time differences but thought it was five or six, maybe seven hours earlier in the States than here. He checked in and put in his call for two o'clock and was given several letters, one from his mother, the others from the office. They could wait. He went out to a travel agency, where he had himself put on a night flight that would get him into New York in the morning, if he lasted that long. He was tired. He didn't think he'd ever get enough rest.

It was chilly in Athens. He settled down in the sun at a cafe on Constitution Square and ordered beer for courage. He saw the picture of Manoli in several of the newspapers around him. He thought of the mail-call gathering and wondered if he and Manoli were sharing the spotlight as the major topic of conversation. He finished his beer and ordered another, keeping an eye on the time.

Something was missing. He realized that it didn't feel right not being able to see the sea. He had the impression that he couldn't really tell what kind of a day it was without it. He had acquired a new identification with the natural world. Another reason for getting out of New York where you couldn't even see the sky. Now that the moment was approaching, he realized he'd gotten caught up in the sort of fantasy that Manoli could work himself into with the greatest of ease. But he wasn't Manoli. His mind came up with one practical problem after another. He had an answer of sorts to most of them, but even if he hadn't he wouldn't let them stop him. Practical problems had no place in fantasies. He ordered a sandwich and another beer and was back at the hotel at one-thirty. He checked to make sure that his call was being put through on time and went up to his dull little room. It was a hell of a place to have his fate decided, but maybe in half an hour it would look like paradise.

He took off his jacket and sweater and sat in a straight-backed chair beside the telephone. He tried to organize his thoughts and decide what he was going to say, but he couldn't find appropriate words. Should he keep it light or lay it all on the line? He began to get the shakes almost as badly as on the boat. He wondered if he should see a doctor. Was there something wrong with his heart? There was probably plenty wrong with it, one way or another. He breathed deeply, waiting to calm down. He considered canceling the call; it could wait until he got back, except that it couldn't. He had to know now so that he would make sense on arrival. The phone was going to ring in ten or fifteen minutes. All he had to do was pick it up and say what was on his mind. It could come out any way he felt it.

He slowly began to relax. The phone rang. He almost fell out of his chair. He grabbed the phone and answered.

"We have your call to the United States, sir," an accented voice said. Phil heard clicks and whirring sounds and then the voice he'd been waiting for. His grip tightened on the phone.

"Hello. It's me," he said. He cleared his throat.

"Phil? For God's sake. Where are you?"

"Did I wake you up?"

"No. I'm up. You know me. Cowhands are early birds. What're you doing?"

"I'm in Athens. The real one. In Greece."

"Greece? Is Alex with you?" He heard George's voice turn cool.

"God, no. That's been over for months. You know that."

"I thought maybe you were having a second honeymoon. What're you doing in Greece?"

"Lots of things. I'll tell you. Listen, I'm going to have trouble saying what I want to say. Talk to me. It's my nickel. Ask me how the weather is."

"How is it?"

"Great. I'm as black as the ace of spades."

"You sound funny."

"Maybe it's because I'm a big boy now. How about you? Any involvements?"

"No such luck. I'm still dreaming."

"Do you really mean it?"

"I know it's silly. Listen, are you in some sort of trouble?"

"Yes, but not because of anything that's happened here. I'm in trouble with my life. If you are too, maybe we can work it out together."

"What're you talking about?"

Phil's heart was pounding wildly. If he survived the next minute, he was set for life. He had heard the happy incredulity in George's voice. He swallowed and hoped his voice was still working. "Don't you think ten years is long enough for a trial separation?" he said.

"Jesus Christ. What do you think I've been telling you for God knows how many years? Are you sure you know what you're saying?"

"I may be crazy but I know what I want. If you want it too, we'll goddamn well make it work this time. I'm leaving tonight. It's afternoon here now. Can you meet me in New York in the morning?"

"You bet your beautiful ass. I'll go this afternoon. I'll be at the Fairleigh waiting for you."

"That's perfect. There's no way for me to give you the key to my place. I'll stay with you until we get squared away. I think I'll get into the city by about noon. Just hang in there."

"Oh, God, honey. I'm going to bawl like a baby when I hang up. It's been so damn long."

He heard the break in George's voice and felt a lump gathering in his throat. "Listen, do you think—no, never mind. I want to be with you."

"What were you going to say?"

"Nothing really. There's nothing to say till we're together. It's just that it's so damn important to us. Do you think I'm expecting too much?"

"Living happily ever after isn't too much, is it?"

"Not for us, it isn't. It's just—"

"Listen. We're not half-wits. We're not going to know anything until we see each other."

"No. That's it. Let's both hang up while we're ahead. I love you. See you tomorrow."

Phil put the phone down hastily and sat back, taking long, calming breaths through his open mouth. He felt as if he'd run a race. George would be waiting for him. He sat up and looked at the telephone and laughed. It might be folly but it felt wonderful. He played their conversation over in his mind, listening for every inflection of George's voice. He'd sounded almost as if he'd been waiting for him. No hesitations. He'd grabbed him without any ifs or buts. Can you meet me in New York? You bet your beautiful ass. No time wasted asking why, as if the long ten years hadn't happened. He could rest now, really rest. His struggle was over.

Or maybe just beginning. This wasn't a fantasy any more, with a guaranteed happy ending. The practical problems had to be faced practically. The very practical question of their sex life came first. Would they still want to go to bed together? He didn't know what time had done to George. People got fat and lost their hair. Athletes often fell apart in their thirties, though he'd kept himself in pretty good shape. But perhaps George's taste for kids had developed. Phil couldn't satisfy anybody who wanted teenagers. The rest of it didn't worry him. Ever since George had mentioned opening a bookstore in Newcomers he'd kept it in the back of his mind as a possibility. With a bit of reorganization, he could do his job if he spent only a few days a month at the office. He'd been successful enough to be pretty sure that his boss would offer him some sort of retainer to keep him in overall charge. He could earn his living. George would always have more money than he, but he didn't think his experience with Helen need frighten him. He'd been making only a pittance then; even if you couldn't make a fortune with a bookstore, he'd still be able to afford an occasional trip to Greece. Everything depended on whether he and George still turned each other on. It was probably a lot to hope for. After ten years, most couples were bored with each other sexually. He and George had the odd advantage of not having seen each other for ten years. He could think of it as an advantage until he learned otherwise.

He took his clothes off and stretched out in the bed with an irrepressible smile on his lips. He hoped he wouldn't be in bed alone again for a long time. The phone call had made him forget how tired he was; he wasn't even sure he was going to be able to sleep. He wanted to be in New York more than he wanted rest. Thinking about George gave him a hard on the way it always had in the old days. Of course, he couldn't help thinking of him as twenty-five still. He tried adding wrinkles and a paunch, but the picture wasn't convincing. He laughed out loud. He was twenty-three again, with all of life safe and secure ahead of him. He was getting drowsy after all.

The telephone rang and he snatched it up wondering if George had managed to trace his call. It was the man on the desk downstairs asking if he was still planning to leave tonight. Phil assured him that he was.

"The hotel is full. There's somebody here asking for a room. We can't rent yours again without your permission."

"Go ahead," Phil said. "I'll be going out at about seven."

"There's the problem of how you both will arrange payment. Will you speak to him?"

"Sure," Phil said, expecting another voice to come on the line.

"I'll send him right up."

"No. Wait," Phil protested, but the connection had been cut. He hung up with a sigh and pulled himself out of bed and put on his pants as a concession to formality. The management was being very honest; he supposed they should be encouraged. There was a knock on the door, and he went to the small entry and opened it. A guy was standing outside holding a suitcase.

"Hi. I'm Jimmy," he said, leaving no doubt as to his nationality. "I'm sorry to bother you. I'm not sure I've got it straight, but they seem to want me to speak to you about sharing the bill."

"Don't bother about it. I'd've had to pay for the night anyway. I'm going at seven. Be my guest."

"That's not right." He stood uncertainly, looking down at his suitcase. Phil saw that he was very young, probably not much more than twenty. He had a nice wholesome countenance, with broad, flat cheekbones that gave him a slightly Slavic look. His blond-brown hair was quite long but looked too clean to fit the fading hippie stereotype. He looked up with wide-set, guilelessly appealing eyes. "They told me to bring my bag up. Would it be asking too much if I—"

"Well, sure. Come on in." Phil stood back and opened the door wider. Jimmy sidled around him in the narrow entry. He put a hand on Phil's arm as he passed.

"You've got a terrific tan. Where've you been?"

"Crete." Phil's interest was stirred. The hand had been frankly friendly, if not more. His guest wasn't exactly good-looking but youthfully personable with an easy manner that disarmed him.

"I wanted to go there, but I had this package deal to Mykonos," Jimmy explained. "The weather wasn't so hot."

"That's a shame. My name's Phil." They smiled and shook hands. They were about the same height. "We seem to be roommates. I was about to take a nap," he added to explain the rumpled bed and his state of undress.

"I hoped to have a nap myself. I've been up all night on the boat getting here."

"The bed doesn't look as if it was made for both of us."

"Oh, I didn't mean that. I'll clear out and leave you in peace. They say the room is ten dollars. How about splitting it? Is that enough?" He pulled a five-dollar bill out of his pocket and held it out. Phil looked at the shapely, long-fingered hand that offered the money, a hand that suggested a nice physique. He couldn't tell much from the jeans and windbreaker.

"Honestly. Don't bother about it," he said. "I'm older than you. I ought to be able to afford five bucks."

Jimmy put the bill on the bedside stand. "Age doesn't mean much as far as you're concerned, not with a body like that. You're very good-looking."

"Thanks. You're making me forget my nap." He sat on the edge of the bed.

Jimmy pulled his suitcase in between his feet and sat on it so that their knees were almost touching. "You tell me when you want me to go."

"There's no rush." Phil let his eyes linger on his unexpected roommate's. They were more green than blue and looked willing. Phil's cock began to feel willing too. Never having gone in much for making passes at strangers, he was surprised at himself when he made the small move that brought their knees into contact. It was an initiative he wouldn't have allowed himself to take a month ago, and he was momentarily apprehensive until he saw Jimmy's eyes register it without disapproval. Did he want a final Greek fling? It might not be a bad idea to let off a little steam; he didn't want it to go on building up in him until it risked throwing everything off with George. Cool and easy, as if they had never been apart—that was the way he wanted it. There were so many dangers to guard against to make sure that the crucial reunion went well. He feared haunting memories of Manoli most of all. Maybe an hour or two with this appealing kid would help him finally emerge from the shadows of the immediate past. "Aside from the weather, how did you like Mykonos?" he asked to give himself more time.

"It's pretty wild. There's a beach where all the gays go. I'm gay, in case you're wondering. What about you?"

Phil was still a bit startled by the way young guys came

right out with it these days. "Same here," he said, trying to sound as if he were used to declaring himself.

"I thought so, but I like to be sure. What's the gay scene like here?"

Phil looked into his wide green eyes and smiled. "It's looking pretty good at the moment."

Jimmy returned his smile, showing strong white teeth. "I was thinking the same thing. How about it?"

"Are you twenty-one?"

"You mean, am I jailbait?" He laughed. "I'm twenty-two and about to start medical school. Does that mean yes?" He lifted his hands and held Phil's nipples between thumb and forefinger, circling and teasing them. It gave Phil a hard on.

"I guess we've solved the bed problem. The management seems to want to get us together. Why fight it?"

Jimmy dropped off the suitcase onto his knees. He parted Phil's legs and opened his fly and worked his cock out and let it stand up against his belly. "Nice," he said. He got a grip on the top of his pants and tugged. Phil lifted his hips and let him strip him. "Beautiful. You're the same color all over. Shouldn't you call down and tell them we've fixed it up so they don't give the room to somebody else?"

Phil laughed. "Three would definitely be too much for the bed."

"Tell them I'm sucking your cock, if you think it'll make them happy." He moved in against him and held his cock and ran his tongue over it. He slid it into his mouth while Phil picked up the phone and explained that they'd made their arrangements. He hung up and ran his fingers through Jimmy's thick hair and held his head when his mouth began to threaten him with orgasm. Jimmy let him go and stood.

"You speak Greek."

"After a fashion."

"It sounded good to me." He took his clothes off, revealing a good American body, well-formed and healthy-looking, the youth in every line of it a delight to Phil's eyes—the wonderful concavity of his midriff, the loose-knit torso that hadn't quite set into maturity. The buoyantly erect cock looked slightly bigger than his own, which always pleased him. He lifted his hands for it when it was within reach, and Jimmy held it too and played with it while Phil welcomed it with his mouth. "I must admit I like my silly cock. You make me feel you like it too. You really suck."

Phil drew back and laughed up at him. "Silly is hardly the word for it. What a wonderful surprise this is turning out to be. I can recommend the management highly." He brought him down beside him and they lay back in each other's arms.

"I knew this bed would be fine for both of us if we didn't mind being close to each other," Jimmy said. "Your body must be just about perfect. I want you a lot, you know that? I mean, in a big way. I want you to fuck me. Is that OK with you?"

"Very much so. Just a second. I'll get something." He jumped up, eager to give him what he wanted. He was turning into a stud. It must have something to do with his tan. For years nobody had ever suggested his fucking them, and now it was getting to be a habit. He doubted if he would ever completely revert to his passive habits. Taking a guy really did add a new demanding confidence to the way he felt about himself.

He knew where his toilet case was. He pulled out the tube of lubricant and ducked into the tiny bathroom for a towel and returned to the bed. Jimmy was waiting for him on his back. He lifted his arms for him and pulled his head down and their mouths met. They kissed at length while their hands took possession of each other and their bodies moved against each other in voluptuous anticipation of being joined. Jimmy's felt as sweet and young as it looked. Phil recognized the surrender in it and was thrilled that he could provoke it. Without relinquishing his mouth, Jimmy edged over onto his side with his back to him. Phil prepared them both and their mouths parted as he entered him. It was beginning to come naturally. He wondered what George would make of this development. The sense of power it unleashed in him was intoxicating. Jimmy uttered a sharp ecstatic cry as he completed his slow penetration.

"It feels so damn good," he exclaimed while Phil savored his youthful surrender. "Don't move for a minute. Isn't it amazing? Fifteen minutes ago we didn't know each other and now this. You're inside me. Our bodies are part of each other. We may never see each other again, but now we belong to each other. Go ahead. Take me. I'm all yours."

P hil arrived in New York more dead than alive, but he was too excited to care much how he felt. He took a taxi into the city. It was raining and cold, just the kind of day that made you want to leave. He was leaving. With George. The Fairleigh was just off Park Avenue, only a few blocks from his own apartment; it was small and expensive, for people who wanted the best. Trust George. They were starting their new life in style. It didn't matter that he would never be able to afford it. If it was the sort of thing George wanted, he could pay without its causing any uneasiness between them. That was one of the wonderful things about being with somebody you'd more or less grown up with. They were used to George being the one to provide the luxuries.

With his heart in his mouth, he asked for George at the desk. Something could have gone wrong at the last minute. But Phil was expected. He was greeted by name and given a registration form to fill out. George was in a suite. The hotel porter took charge of his bags and escorted him to the elevator. Everything looked discreetly expensive. It was quite a change, like the weather, from yesterday. In another moment he was going to be with George. It was too much to take in. It seemed impossible that he was standing calmly in the elevator of a grand hotel, being carried to the most momentous reunion in the history of the world.

The elevator doors opened and he followed the porter along a corridor. The porter stopped in front of a door and pressed a button. The door opened. Phil had stopped breathing and gone blind. He was in a small mirrored entrance hall. A figure who was bound to be George was dealing expeditiously with the porter. A bill changed hands. The door closed. Suddenly, Phil and George were clinging to each other, laughing breathlessly. Yes, it was definitely George. Phil drummed on his back with his fists. They backed away, holding hands at the end of their extended arms. They were reflected from every angle by the floor-length mirrors around them. George gave him a tug.

"Come in here where we can be sure we're really looking at each other."

George's voice. Intelligent humor gleaming in George's eyes. He was dressed with his usual subdued elegance. He looked older but only in appropriate ways. He hadn't lost his hair or got fat. His body looked and felt as if it had thickened a bit. His face showed signs of wear and tear. He had a slightly battered look. After a moment of adjustment, Phil decided that he was more glamorous than ever, with a worldly and experienced air. He was only thirty-five, for God's sake. Why had he been prepared for him to look like an old man?

They went into a luxuriously furnished living room, more like somebody's house than a hotel. "You're right on time," George said. "I checked the flights from Athens. I've never seen you look so marvelous. I've always thought you were the handsomest guy I've ever seen, but you're more so now than ever. Aren't you dead?"

"I guess I must be but I don't feel it yet. How could I, being with you? Here we are again. Are we crazy?"

"I don't know what's going on yet, but if you meant what you said yesterday, it doesn't sound crazy to me." They sat in matching armchairs at a coffee table, facing each other, within reach but not in a position to get launched on physical intimacies. Phil suspected that George shared his reticence about lovemaking. He was probably wondering if the chemistry would still be right. Phil was already sure that it would be, as far as he was concerned, but he was willing for them to take their time. Any awkwardness right at the start was to be avoided at all costs. He was aware of the gulf that had to be bridged before they would be really together again. "Shall we have a drink or two and some lunch up here?" George suggested after they had taken a moment for their eyes to make sure that they were looking at each other at last. "After that, I'll put you to bed for the afternoon."

"That's probably where I belong. How long can you stay?"

"In New York? A couple of days. I could probably stretch it to include the weekend." A mischievous light sprang up in his eyes. "We have a good assistant manager. He's almost as old as my father and has a wife and five kids. It's all work and no play."

"I was an idiot about that, but all I knew about love was you. I thought if you could want anybody else, nothing meant what I'd believed it meant. The world really crashed around my ears."

"Poor baby. Mine too. I couldn't believe I'd lost you for that silly kid. I'd've thrown him out in a second if you'd given me the chance, but the next thing I knew you were in the army. We've talked and written enough about all that. You know how much I've wanted you back. Are you coming home with me?"

"Yes."

George dropped his head back and closed his eyes. When he opened them again and sat forward, the wear and tear had vanished from his face. It was shining with youth and barely contained joy. "It's pretty overwhelming to discover that you've finally got something you've wanted so much. I know lots of people who haven't fallen in love until they were thirty-five, so I don't guess we have to feel that we've lost the best years of our lives. We just got things a bit backwards, that's all—love first and the experience we needed after. Now that we've got it together, we should have quite an act. You won't walk out on me again if I make another mistake?"

"Never. I've been making some fairly serious mistakes myself. I guess if you want to live at all, you're sure to make mistakes. We'll be together and help each other through them."

"You better tell me all about everything. How about a drink first?"

"Something light. Make it a short whiskey and water with plenty of ice. I don't want to be knocked on my beautiful ass."

"No, we don't want to damage that." George rose and went to a door. When he opened it, light flashed on to reveal glass shelves bearing an array of crystal and bottles. There was a built-in refrigerator under them. George brought drinks to the coffee table and picked up the phone and dialed a couple of digits. He asked for the menu from room service and hung up and looked at Phil with radiant expectancy. They were getting closer minute by minute. The gulf had almost been bridged. "So what's the program?" he asked.

Phil outlined his plans as far as he had got with them. They talked about money. Phil told him about the few thousand dollars he'd put aside and made a guess at how much the publishing house might pay him as a sort of managing consultant. George had a salary of thirty thousand dollars a year, which was about what Phil had thought, but his father was slowly turning over shares in the business and other investments so he was accumulating capital too. As far as Phil was concerned, George was rich. Talking about money opened up a whole new area of intimacy between them. They were grown-ups discussing family affairs.

"A bookshop won't cost much," George said, more stirred up and exuberant than Phil had ever seen him. "I looked into it when I was hoping you'd come home. We can finance it any way that makes sense tax-wise, through the banks or as a personal loan from me. The main thing is that I don't want us to start out thinking of money as yours or mine. It's ours. We can have a joint account or you can take charge of the books. You're probably better at it than

I am. Aside from pocket money, I don't want to spend anything that we don't spend together. Is that OK?''

"It sounds as if I'm finally going to be kept." The doorbell rang and George stood. Phil put a hand on his knee and looked up at him, marveling at the deep contentment that already felt like a permanent element in their life. "I don't have to bother with the menu. I'll have eggs Benedict if they have them. Anything like that is enough for me.''

"Me too." George touched his hair and went out.

Phil heard him ordering. It sounded like a friendly exchange, punctuated by laughter. George seemed very much at home here. In a sense, their lives were still running on parallel lines. When they had brought each other up to date and caught up on everything, they would finally join. It was happening.

"I ordered a bottle of Burgundy," George said, returning. "Is that all right?"

"Perfect."

"Remember having milk with our first banquet together? We're getting decadent in our old age. Shall we have another drink before we eat?"

"Why not? I feel as if I'd been smoking opium. It's lovely and vague. I may be taking a lot for granted about this retainer business, but I think they'll go along with it. I'm sort of the whiz kid of textbooks. I dropped a few hints when Alex was driving me crazy and I was thinking of running home to you. They don't expect me back at the office for at least another week, but I'll try to see the boss tomorrow. The sooner we know what the powers that be think about it the better. I'll probably have to spend quite a lot of time here in New York at the beginning while I'm getting the arrangement set up. If you have a good assistant, you can stay at my place. We don't *have* to stay in a place like this.''

"This was strictly show-off. I thought you might love me for my money if all else failed. Anyway, I'm doing some business for Dad, so it's deductible. We can move into your place tomorrow if you want. I'd like to get an idea of how you were living these years you've been away.''

"Yes. That's important. We've got to fill in the gaps. I've got to tell you about Greece. That was pretty incredible." He took a swallow of the second drink and put it down. "I'll take a quick shower before lunch. I feel as if I've been wearing these clothes for a year." They both stood.

"Don't bother with your bags yet. I brought an extra dressing gown for you. That'll do for lunch. I'll slip into something more comfortable myself.'' George headed him for the entrance hall with a hand on his shoulder. Phil almost bumped into himself in a mirror before George showed him the bedroom door. They entered another luxuriously furnished room with two big inviting beds pushed together against one wall. There were several more floor-length mirrors around the beds. It looked like an exhibitionist's paradise.

"I'd better not get near those beds or I may never get up again," Phil said. They looked into each other's eyes and smiled, love tranquilly erasing the estrangement of the years.

"As soon as we've given you something to eat, that's where you'll be,'' George said. He took off his jacket and sat to remove his shoes.

Phil could still feel the reticence restraining them. They were working up to it slowly, like a honeymoon couple. When it finally happened, it was going to be better than ever. For life. He stripped to the waist, while George carried his things to a closet and disappeared into it. When he emerged, he was wearing a dressing gown and carrying another. Phil saw immediately that he was wearing his silver chain. A shiver of delight ran down his spine.

"My God, what a tan," George exclaimed. "Are you like that all over?"

"Every gorgeous inch of me. I can't wait to show it off."

"I'll give it a thorough inspection later." He brought Phil the dressing gown. "There. Have your shower. I'll let lunch in." He touched the chain. "I haven't taken it off for ten years. I knew it would bring you back to me."

"I always have mine with me. It's there in my bags." Their bodies stirred almost imperceptibly, closing the space between them. Phil knew that the slightest move would bring them into each other's arms, clamoring for union. Having waited this long, he wanted to wash away the stale film of travel that clung to him. He drew back and laid his fingertips lightly on his cheek. "I'll be right out."

When he returned to the living room, he found the lunch table being set up under George's supervision. The room-service waiter was a cute kid in a bobtailed white mess jacket. He had a funny, endearing, clownish face.

"Phil, this is Simon," George said. "He keeps the hotel going."

"Hi." Simon offered a casual hand as he passed. Phil shook it. The young waiter did a little double take. "My goodness, that's a beautiful tan. I hear you've been to Greece. I'll bet I know somebody who's glad to see you back. I would be."

"Thanks," Phil said, laughing at Simon's saucy flirtatiousness. It was a thrilling novelty to have their relationship so openly acknowledged. He and George sat opposite each other while the waiter showed George the wine and pulled the cork. He tilted a bit into George's glass and waited for George to taste it and nod. He placed dishes from a portable oven in front of them and whisked off the covers and took a step back.

"There we are," Simon announced. "Enjoy. I'll come get the table later, or you can call."

"Leave it till I call," George said. "We don't want to be disturbed."

"I'll bet you don't. Have a nice day." He flipped his neat behind as he left.

They looked at each other and laughed. "He's sort of cute," Phil said.

"How amazing. That's the first time I've heard you say you thought somebody was attractive. Aside from myself, of course."

"I've always been so damned uptight. You know that. When it happened with us, I thought I was going to roast in hell. I've never been able to be open about it the way the kids are now."

"That's one thing that's changed, thank God. We don't have to hide any more. Even my father's got used to the idea. Did you know there's a gay bar in Newcomers now? Everybody will know about us."

"Do you think my parents will?"

"How can they help it? People talk about everything. It's no great hush-hush secret these days. We'll be living together. Everybody will treat us like an old married couple."

"Good. I want to be able to talk to you about everything. We never used to. We didn't even talk about infidelity. I just thought it was something that didn't happen to decent people, even though it happened to me. I don't think I'll ever be uptight again. Not after Greece. I've got to tell you about Manoli.''

They ate and drank the excellent wine while Phil described his passion for a Greek hustler, trying to make him understand the part Manoli had played in making him realize at last how much he wanted to get back to the great love of his life. ''Thinking of you was the only thing that got me through that brutal sail the other day. When was it? Day before yesterday? Yes. Amazing.'' They looked at each other and their hands reached across the table and gripped each other. Phil knew that their reticence had been dispelled. They were flesh-and-blood people once more whose bodies wanted each other. The grip of George's hands gave him a hard on.

''Everything you say sounds so sexy,'' George said after a moment of silence. ''The guy climbing in through the window to get you. Sailing together. The day you spent naked in that deserted bay. I want us to have times like that together. I want you, baby. I want you all for myself. I hate having let you go so that other guys could have you. I'll try not to let that happen again.''

''When I called yesterday, were you afraid we might not still want each other?''

''Not really. I thought maybe the shock of being together again might make it difficult at first to pick up the pieces. It wasn't.''

''No. I guess there really weren't many pieces to pick up. It was all still there.''

George drained the bottle into their glasses. ''Let's finish that and go where we both want to be.''

''That won't take long.'' Phil tossed back the wine. George laughed and followed suit. They rose and they both burst out laughing. Their erections lifted to each other from the folds of their dressing gowns. ''I remember that first banquet. Our dressing gowns weren't much use then either. That's quite a cock to come home to.'' Phil went around the table looking at it. He didn't suppose it had grown, but it certainly hadn't shrunk. It was one of nature's masterpieces. He pushed silk out of the way and ran his hands along it. He didn't have to take George's word for it; George wanted him.

George displaced his hands by removing Phil's dressing gown and holding his brown body at arm's length. ''Fantastic. It's not fair to come back to me looking like an illustration from Body Beautiful. Haven't you heard that you're supposed to age with time? I have.'' He let go of Phil and threw off his robe and stood facing him, as if awaiting his verdict.

Phil managed to lift his eyes from his cock and look at all of him. His body had an unfamiliar solidity. His lean physical grace had been replaced by imposing power and strength. Coupled with the prodigious cock, it was a body that seemed to make a point of male supremacy. Phil was shaken by a blaze of excitement at the prospect of their coupling.

''I've got to lose ten pounds. I know that,'' George said. ''I've let myself go, but I won't now that I see the competition.''

''You notice how my cock is wilting at being faced with the ruins of age.''

George uttered a yelp of laughter and made a lunge for him. ''Come here, you blind fool. I'm going to have my way with you.'' They were both laughing helplessly as their mouths found each other. They sank to the floor, devouring each other. They shouted and gasped and erupted with laughter as they rolled about in a frenzy of rediscovery. They somehow struggled to their feet without relinquishing each other and staggered to the bedroom. George tore off the covers and they fell into bed. Phil sobbed his surrender while his big lover reclaimed him. He was back where he belonged. He was complete again, realizing that fitting with each other wasn't what it was about at all.

Love was contained in memory, in the touch of a hand, in the way hair curled around an ear, in a voice. He rediscovered all the precious secret places of George's beloved body that were waiting for him to fit himself into again. He didn't have to worry about their not still wanting each other; desire for each other had been built into them during the untroubled years when they had lived for each other. They gave each other the huge satisfaction that made all other physical pleasure seem trivial.

He was aware of George leaving him briefly, sponging him tenderly, holding him again when suddenly he must have plunged into oblivion. He woke up reaching for him in a panic, feeling the boat rocking under him, and saw him smiling down at him at the end of the bed. He was wearing his dressing gown again.

"Goodness gracious," Phil sighed. He stretched and yawned and wriggled down closer to him. "I don't think that quite made up for ten years, but it was a good start. What're you doing out there?"

"I've ordered some replenishments for the bar. We were running out of whiskey. Don't move. I'll bring us drinks in a minute and then we'll see. I'd forgotten it was possible to want somebody so much. Did we use to do it on the floor?"

Phil giggled and for a moment thought he was asleep again. "We were young and unimaginative," he murmured, not quite sure what he was talking about. The doorbell rang. He opened his eyes. "Sometimes on the floor, but we were very pampered children. We usually had a bed."

George laughed and leaned over and wobbled his foot. "I'll be right back. Sleep some more."

Phil drifted behind closed eyes. He heard a door slam and opened them, wondering where he was. His eyes wandered around the room and came to a halt on a mirror. George was framed in it, pressed against the back of a guy in a white mess jacket. It was Simon, the room service waiter. George's hands moved down over him and settled on his fly. He opened it and lifted out a very presentable cock, erect and ready to go in George's appreciative hands. Simon backed in closer against him and dropped his head on his shoulder. George nibbled his neck. Phil was fully awake now, his cock standing up. Simon turned in George's arms and put his hands under the dressing gown and pushed it back. Phil could see them speaking. It was like watching television with the sound turned off. The familiarity with which they handled each other made it obvious that they'd been to bed together. Fair enough. Both he and George had found company while they were waiting for each other. Such things happened, but they shouldn't happen when they were together. Phil had learned that long ago without even getting caught. If he walked out and confronted him now, he could expose George's weakness and shatter his self-esteem—but only at the risk of destroying once more what they had so triumphantly recaptured. He needed George. There were other ways to teach him to behave himself.

George had shrugged off his dressing gown and held it trailing at his side while Simon dropped down to George's erection and put it in his mouth. It had been in Phil's mouth a little while ago. Phil was going to have to throw one into George. It conferred authority and provided leverage for laying down the law. Nobody had ever laid down the law to George. No wonder he thought he could get away with anything.

Simon stood and George slipped on his dressing gown while Simon picked up something from the console table beside the door. George moved to the edge of the mirror as he opened the door and closed it. The show was over.

It was all pretty harmless, Phil thought, when you could see it. He might even find it sort of exciting to watch George giving a guy the works. It was the imagination that made it so shattering. Nothing was perfect, but they had an awful lot going for them. They would be all right if he didn't let distractions like Simon make Phil pull back and deny that his life depended on George. He mustn't try to reshape his feelings any more. He was going to have to fight for him no matter how much it hurt. Follies didn't have degrees. His attempt at restrained folly had been fatal.

Go mad, Johnny had advised. Let yourself go. Never trust a chap whose head rules his heart. Phil's heart had ruled him when he'd let George take him on the floor in front of a blazing fire. You had to plunge in over your head even if you drowned. He could go as mad as anybody. Thank you, Johnny.